The Lost Carousel of Provence

Also by Juliet Blackwell and available from Center Point Large Print:

The Paris Key
Letters from Paris

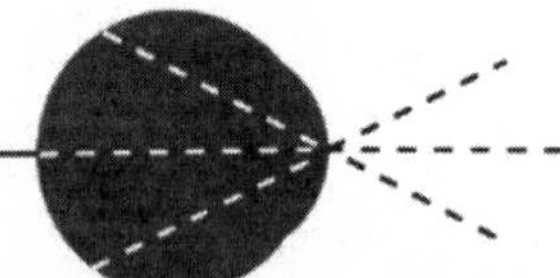

This Large Print Book carries the Seal of Approval of N.A.V.H.

The Lost Carousel of Provence

JULIET BLACKWELL

Center Point Large Print
Thorndike, Maine

This Center Point Large Print edition
is published in the year 2019 by arrangement with
Berkley, an imprint of Penguin Publishing Group,
a division of Penguin Random House LLC.

The text of this Large Print edition is unabridged.
In other aspects, this book may vary
from the original edition.
Printed in the United States of America
on permanent paper.
Set in 16-point Times New Roman type.

ISBN: 978-1-64358-042-5

Library of Congress Cataloging-in-Publication Data

Names: Blackwell, Juliet, author.
Title: The lost carousel of provence / Juliet Blackwell.
Description: Center Point Large Print edition. | Thorndike, Maine : Center Point Large Print, 2019.
Identifiers: LCCN 2018045109 | ISBN 9781643580425 (hardcover : alk. paper)
Subjects: LCSH: Women photographers—Fiction. | Merry-go-round art—Fiction. | Americans—France—Fiction. | Large type books.
Classification: LCC PS3602.L32578 L67 2019 | DDC 813/.6—dc23
LC record available at https://lccn.loc.gov/2018045109

To CJ

You held me up when I could not stand
Carried me when I could not walk

ACKNOWLEDGMENTS

Thanks are due, always, to my wonderful editor, Kerry Donovan. It's been quite the odyssey so far, and I can't wait to see what's in store for us next! And to my ever-supportive agent, Jim McCarthy: It's a wonder to have you in my corner, always.

Special thanks to the incomparable artist Lise Liepman for sharing her expertise in the art of carousel renovation—as well as her personal library on the history of the carousel. Thank you to Jessica H. and LaShawna J. for sharing their personal experiences in the foster care system. Thanks to Marc-Antoine and Corinne Stauffenegger for opening their home to me and showing me around Avignon, and introducing me to Fontaine-de-Vaucluse, to la Sorgue, and to the rest of Provence. Special thanks also to Sylviane Lacroix and the gang in Saint Pargoire, and in Paris.

This book required a great deal of research from too many sources to mention, but of particular use were Frederick Fried's *A Pictorial History of the Carousel* (Vestal Press, 1997) and

Anne Sebba's *Les Parisiennes: How the Women of Paris Lived, Loved and Died in the 1940s* (Weidenfeld & Nicolson, 2016).

A very special thank-you for writer friends who kept me sane this past year, especially Rachael Herron, Sophie Littlefield, Chris Logan, Faye Snowden, Nicole Peeler, and Muffy Srinivasan. And to Anna Cabrera, Mary Grae, Bee Green Enos, Pamela Groves, Jan Strout, Wanda Klor, Bruce Nikolai, Sharon Demetrius, Suzanne Chan, Susan Baker, Kendall Moalem, and Karen Thompson. To Hanna Toda for letting me call her "daughter." To new seaside friends Dan and Denise Skinner, and to the Mira Vista Social Club. And finally, to Steve McDonald: We miss you.

Thanks are due to my father, Robert Lawes, a proud veteran who has taught me so much and has never, ever left me feeling unloved. And to my sister, Susan, who shares the family love of reading and art, and who preorders all my books! And with much love to Eric Paul Stauffenegger, who corrects my French, shares his wine, makes France feel like my second home, and suffers life with a writer.

And to my beautiful son, Sergio. Always.

Mi alma es un carrusel vacío en el crepúsculo.
My soul is an empty carousel at sunset.

—Pablo Neruda, *Crepusculario*
(Ediciones Revista Claridad:
Santiago, Chile, 1923)

CHAPTER ONE

1901
PROVENCE, FRANCE
CHÂTEAU CLEMENT

Josephine Clement

No one has seen.

The château's usual ranks of gardeners and servants, grape pickers and kitchen staff, have been joined by Monsieur Bayol's crew of men hammering, sawing, sanding, and painting the newly arrived carousel. The cats, dogs, pigs, and rabbits were carved, painted, and gilded in Bayol's factory in Angers, but it has taken nine men to transport the pieces by rail, then by steam traction engine from the station to the château, and then to assemble the machine on-site. It will take another two weeks, perhaps a month, to complete the elaborately decorated salon that will house the carousel.

Josephine wishes it would take longer. She would be happy if they stayed forever. Especially the carver's apprentice.

She and the apprentice have placed confidence

in each other; they will keep each other's confidences.

Josephine knows her neighbors think of her as secretive and scheming because she was not born here. She comes from faraway Bretagne, and yet she stole the heart of their local favorite, the eligible Yves Paul Clement, heir to Château Clement. Bretagne and Provence were meant to be part of France now, but deep-seated regional stereotypes and allegiances do not respect random borders.

She understands. After all, before Yves brought her to Château Clement as a young bride, Josephine had always believed the Provençal people to be lazy, unfriendly, and afflicted with a harsh accent.

She has found the accent and unfriendliness to be apt, but though her husband is accustomed to taking a *sieste* every afternoon, he is anything but lazy. Yves rises early to capture the light of dawn on his camera; he works late into the night in his darkroom. He is an educated gentleman: He reads in his library, he composes poetry, he draws. Unlike most in the region, he does not hunt. Instead, he observes and makes note of the birds that perch on the limbs of the plane trees and olive orchards: the short-toed lark and tawny pipit in spring, the red-crested pochard and moustached warbler in fall.

Yves's keen eyes observe the forest creatures,

the turning of the leaves, the changing quality of the light throughout the day, throughout the seasons. By virtue of the incessant clicking of his cameras, he records the world around him.

And yet, he does not see.

CHAPTER TWO

PRESENT DAY
OAKLAND, CALIFORNIA

Cady Anne Drake

Cady had never realized how many empty platitudes people voiced when confronted with grief, how they felt compelled to say something, to say *anything,* in response to a situation that had no answer, no response. No solution.

In point of brutal fact, there was nothing to say. Maxine had died.

One moment she was there, Cady's ever-present rock in the shifting sands of life. And the next she had fallen to the floor behind the register, struck down by a sudden heart attack. Maxine had disappeared into the ether, just like that, along with her snarky comments and wise eyes and calm, slightly haughty demeanor that never failed to assuage Cady's inner demons. She was gone. No one else in this life would be lucky enough to know Maxine Caroline Clark.

All that remained of the old woman was her shop, called Maxine's Treasures, its junky (or artsy, depending on your perspective) inventory, and the back room, where Cady had set up her photography studio and darkroom. Even though Cady had no intention of taking over and managing Maxine's antiques store, she wasn't ready to give up her studio. Not to mention that she'd been living in the back room of the shop—which was not strictly legal—since she'd lost her relatively affordable apartment to a condo development several months ago.

What now? Where would she go? What would she do?

Maxine was family. She was all Cady had.

A desperate, breathless weariness reached out its icy fingers to grip Cady's bones. And it wasn't the strain of carrying her wooden carousel figure, Gus. She saw reproach in the rabbit's glass eyes as she maneuvered him into the shop; could this last shred of hope gone be her comeuppance for having tried to sell him?

Maxine had given Gus to her ten years ago, on Cady's wedding day. The marriage hadn't lasted long, and the only thing Cady took from it—besides bitter experience—was Gus-the-rabbit.

It was embarrassing to admit, but Gus had always made her feel . . . loved.

According to Maxine, Gus was a genuine piece of carousel history, hand-carved by the famous French sculptor Gustave Bayol. Which would have meant he was worth thousands—maybe *tens* of thousands. But this morning Cady's last-ditch financial dreams had been dashed by an earnest young man named Scott Ripley. Peering through a huge magnifying glass, the *Antique Forum*'s acknowledged expert in nineteenth- and twentieth-century European carvings had examined the rabbit's loosening joints, noting how the bands of basswood had pulled away from one another at the tops of the legs, and the gap where the neck section met the body. Carousel figures are hollow, built like boxes with slats of wood joined, laminated, then carved, and primed to conceal the joints. Not only were the sections falling apart—Gus's ears were now barely connected to his slightly tilted head—but the bright paint and gold gilding were flaking off, with gesso primer showing through in patches.

At long last Ripley had straightened, shrugged, and pronounced: "It's not a Bayol."

"You're wrong," Cady said. "Look again."

"Your rabbit is most probably European, and from Bayol's era, at the turn of the twentieth century. In some ways, it is very much in his style; Bayol carved farmyard animals with sweet expressions like this one, so that fits. But a hallmark of Bayol's carvings was their simplicity. His work almost never included flourishes like the lily of the valley here," he said, pointing to the offending flower. "And this rose carved in high relief, with the detailed thorns? I don't even know what to say about *that.*"

"But Bayol did custom work, right?" Cady replied. "Couldn't a client have asked for the flowers?"

He shook his head. "I know Bayol's work well; I'm also very familiar with the American carvers Dentzel, Looff, and Carmel. Like all artists, carousel carvers leave their imprints on their work, like signatures. Also, Bayol nearly always attached a small plaque to the saddles of his carved animals, and yours doesn't have one. Your rabbit might have been carved by one of Bayol's apprentices, or a competitor—if you could establish its provenance, it would be worth more."

Cady's impulse was to argue with Ripley, to rail at him and cast aspersions on his professional qualifications, not to mention his parentage.

But it wasn't his fault. Maxine had been wrong. It wasn't surprising: Maxine always had insisted upon seeing possibilities in the junk other people threw away.

So Cady had concentrated on reining in her emotions, fighting an almost overwhelming, and wholly uncharacteristic, urge to burst into tears.

Get it together, Drake, she had scolded herself. *We've been in worse situations than this one. Much, much worse. We'll just have to come up with another plan.*

As a child Cady had developed the quirk of using the royal “we” when talking to herself; otherwise the only “we” in her world was wishful thinking. Later, the “we” came to mean Cady and Maxine, and finally, now, Cady and Gus-the-rabbit. It was a silly, childish habit, but Cady had more important things to worry about these days, such as where she was going to get the money to escape the wildly expensive San Francisco Bay Area, to move to a town where normal people could work a regular job and afford a decent place to live, and where she could become a foster mom, or maybe even adopt a child. The thought of change terrified her, but she was desperate to create the sort of family that she’d always wanted for herself. True, being a photographer wasn’t the best career option in a small town, but she didn’t care what she did for a living. She wasn’t proud.

The important thing was to start over. To reinvent herself. Cady yearned for the anonymity of a second chance, a clean slate, a tabula rasa. To make a home someplace where no one knew where she came from, where no one knew she had nothing and no one.

No family connections, no Maxine, no . . . baby.

Without volition her hand went to her stomach. The only bump there now was from stress-eating her way through countless bags of potato chips and boxes of Petit Écolier cookies—scraping off the chocolate in an embarrassingly juvenile ritual—as she sat on the couch for weeks, watching endless reruns of *Hoarders*.

The nurse in the emergency room had smelled of antiseptic and was very nice in the impersonal way of a kindhearted person saddled with far too much to do. She had instructed Cady to finish the round of prophylactic antibiotics, to abstain from sex for six weeks (no problem there—Cady couldn't imagine being intimate, ever again, with anyone), to get plenty of rest, and to be prepared for sudden hormonal shifts as her body adjusted to what her medical chart referred to as an "SAB": spontaneous abortion.

The baby Cady had accidentally conceived in an exceedingly rare one-night stand, then after weeks of fear and trembling had decided to keep and come to love, had been lost in a gruesome rush of pain and cramps and blood, a gutting experience referred to simply as an SAB.

An SAB.

Cady's appalling, alien urge to cry must be due to shifting hormones. Nothing more. Surely.

First Maxine had died. Then Cady's own body had betrayed her. And now even her precious carousel rabbit had turned out not to be who she'd always thought he was.

Cady was on a merry-go-round, and no matter how fast she galloped, she kept winding up at the same place.

Her eyes stung, tears threatening. *So . . . okay.* Maybe she would allow herself a few quick minutes of weeping in the back of the shop, while cursing Mr. Scott Ripley of the *Antique Forum* and his so-called expertise.

Then she would come up with a new plan.

CHAPTER THREE

PRESENT DAY
OAKLAND

Cady

The banging on the door wouldn't stop. Cady had hung the Closed sign on the window of the shop door, alongside a note about Maxine's death. But some of Maxine's regular customers could be as persistent and annoying as a broken tooth.

"Go away!" she yelled from the back room.

The banging continued. She turned the television volume up.

"Cady?" A woman's voice. Olivia.

Cady often thought of Maxine as the only person in the world who loved her, but there was also Olivia Gray.

They had met years ago, right after Cady got divorced, in an adult education course on photography—genuine, old-fashioned photography and film development, taught by a cranky old man who didn't take to what he called "that modern digital crap."

Olivia was everything Cady wasn't but had always wanted to be: pretty, petite, quick to smile at others and to laugh at herself. It was the first time Cady had understood the concept of a girl crush; she was enamored, sneaking glances under her bangs during class, following Olivia out to the vending machines during break.

One night the machine ate Olivia's rumpled dollar. She banged on it ineffectually and yelled, *"Gol-darn it!"*

Cady had never heard anyone say something like that except on television.

"Early training," Olivia explained to Cady, with an embarrassed smile and a chagrined little shrug. "My mom's a stickler for polite language. If she gets really, really mad she might say, *'Dammit!'* But then she always follows it up with: 'Pardon my French!' "

Cady smiled, hitting the machine just so while reaching in the back, the way she had learned to do as a bad kid with no spending money. The mechanism started to hum and a PayDay bar banged down into the metal trough.

"There you go."

"Thanks! That's a neat trick. So, what's your name?"

Olivia didn't even know her name? It figured. *Stuck-up jerk.*

But nipping at the heels of anger was shame: Try as she might, Cady just didn't pick up on social cues like other people did. She wondered whether it was something integral to her—some mysterious bit of genetic code she had inherited from her unknown parents—or if it derived from her detached, frenetic childhood. Ultimately it didn't matter. She had always known she wasn't . . . *likable.*

She turned on her heel and stalked back to the classroom.

After class, as Cady was gathering her things, Olivia made a beeline across the room. "So, I'm an idiot in general. And I can never remember names."

Cady shrugged and zipped up the battered leather backpack she had scored at the flea market for five dollars.

"I'm a bit of a sleuth, though. Not to mention stubborn," Olivia said, holding out her hand. "It's nice to officially meet you, Cady Drake. I'm Olivia Gray. How do you do?"

Cady stared at her hand for a beat.

"Like I said, I know I'm clueless," Olivia continued. "But since we're the only two people in this class under the age of forty, I was wondering, do you want to go grab a drink?"

Maxine's voice whispered in her mind: *"Get over yourself, girl. Don't assume everyone's out to get you."*

So Cady nodded, and they stopped by George O's. It was a seedy dive bar, typical for this part of Oakland, but when they walked in, Olivia's eyes lit up like a child's on Christmas morning.

"This is great," she announced, taking in the dartboard, out-of-date Halloween decorations, and half a dozen men slouched over the bar. She ordered bourbon on the rocks, and Cady did the same.

"So," Olivia said as they took their drinks to a table. " 'Cady' is a pretty name. I saw on the roster that you don't spell it the traditional way, K-A-T-Y."

"Yeah," said Cady. "I mean, I came with it."

Olivia smiled. "I always hated my name."

"Why?"

"The kids used to taunt me at school, calling me Olive Oyl," she said in a low voice, as though confiding a shameful secret.

"Gee," said Cady after a beat, "that must have been very traumatic for you."

Olivia looked surprised, then started laughing. "You just made a joke! And here I thought you were serious all the time." She held up her glass. "Let's have a toast. To quote Humphrey Bogart in that movie: 'I think this is the beginning of a beautiful friendship.' "

And oddly enough, it was. After the photography class ended, they enrolled in French language courses, then Thai cooking, then botany. Olivia and her boyfriend, Sebastian, had Cady and Maxine over for dinner, and when they married, Cady stood up with them at City Hall. Olivia loved to tag along at antiques flea markets, asking questions, and furnishing her falling-down West Oakland Victorian one piece at a time. Eventually she landed a job at *Sunset* magazine, and steered the occasional freelance photography job Cady's way.

Through the years they joked about who had the upper hand in the "Trauma Olympics," and whenever she invoked her childhood, Cady was the hands-down winner. But Olivia had struggles of her own.

"Cady!" Olivia called again through the door of Maxine's Treasures. "Open up. I brought coffee, made with my very own hands."

With reluctance, Cady emerged from the back room and crossed the crowded shop floor.

"I don't want any," Cady said through the glass pane of the front door.

"Too bad. Open up."

Cady undid the dead bolt and crouched down to remove the rubber stopper she always shoved under the door. It made her feel secure.

"Here," Olivia said as soon as the door was open, holding out a commuter mug and pushing past Cady into the store. "It's French roast, your favorite. You're welcome."

"I was sleeping."

"No you weren't," Olivia said, raising one eyebrow as she looked over the jumble of inventory.

"And you obviously haven't been spending a lot of time cleaning."

"Not my strong suit."

"So, have you been working?"

"A little."

Olivia led the way into the back room, where they sat down at the little table by the kitchenette. Belatedly, Cady realized there was plentiful evidence of her recent dissolute lifestyle: crumpled Cheetos bags and cookie packages, old Chinese food take-out boxes, an empty vodka bottle.

"Liar," said Olivia, taking in the scene. "What have you *really* been doing?"

"Crying." Cady collapsed onto the sofa.

"But that's good, right?" Olivia said, sympathy shining in her big chocolate-colored eyes. "You never used to cry. I count that as personal growth."

Cady let out a humorless bark. "Only you could see crying as a positive."

"So, I was thinking," Olivia said, fiddling with her coffee mug, which boasted the garish orange-and-black logo of the San Francisco baseball team. "There are a lot of merry-go-rounds in Paris. Loads of them. I remember from when Sebastian and I went there on our honeymoon. A carousel in every public square, it seemed like."

"And?"

"You love photographing carousels. Have you ever thought of doing a *book* of photographs?"

"Of Parisian carousels?"

"Yes! Why have we been studying French all these years if you're not going to put the language to good use? And you never know what you might find. The food, the wine, the cobblestone streets . . ." She let out a sigh. "*C'est magique*!"

Cady managed a small smile. "You think everything is magical."

"And you think *nothing* is. But you're wrong." Olivia took another sip and let out a long, contented sigh. She had a way of savoring her coffee as though it were the elixir of life, the cure for maladies, the font of all contentment. And perhaps it was: Olivia was the sunniest person Cady had ever known. Before she met Olivia, Cady had believed sustained happiness was the stuff of fiction, found only in fairy tales.

"When did you become a San Francisco Giants fan?" Cady asked in a blatant bid to change the subject.

Olivia laughed, holding her mug out and inspecting the logo as though she'd never seen it before. "I have no idea where this came from. It just appeared, as things are wont to do around my house. But I like the way it feels in my hands."

Random items "appeared" at Olivia's place because people were forever passing through for dinners and parties, spending the night or staying for weeks at a time on the couch, leaving behind towels, a hairbrush, a coffee mug. But Olivia took the ever-shifting landscape of her home in stride, as though things appeared and disappeared by some enchanting sort of magic.

That would drive me crazy, Cady thought. She liked things organized, predictable. Even in the apparent muddle of Maxine's shop, Cady knew where each and every item was.

"Anyway, stop trying to change the subject, because I'm not falling for it," Olivia said as she set the mug down. "Maybe a change of scenery is exactly what you need. And you've photographed our local carousels enough."

"You're forgetting our road trip to see the world's largest carousel at House on the Rock."

"Not that I have anything against Wisconsin, but I was thinking Paris might be a slightly more dramatic change of scene."

Cady shrugged. "I'll think about it."

"Here's the thing, Cady: My mother always told me not to offer unsolicited advice. But I'm going to anyway, because I love my mama, but I love you, too, and you haven't had anyone besides Maxine to give you the advice you need."

"You do realize," Cady said, "that you are not required to fix my life. I'm—"

"*Excuse* me," interrupted Olivia. "When I was in the hospital, who brought me Thai noodles and Cherry Garcia Ice Cream?"

"You could have gotten as much from a delivery person."

"Is that right? And would this alleged delivery person have given me her absolute devotion and forced me to survive chemotherapy, not to mention surgery? Would said delivery person have read the entirety of *84, Charing Cross Road* to me when I was in the hospital, then popped the cork on a bottle of champagne when I finished my chemo? Would she also have watched endless rounds of basketball with Sebastian to keep him from going crazy from worry?"

"That was selfish on my part," said Cady. "You're my only friend."

With gut-wrenching clarity, Cady remembered the moment, three years ago, when Olivia divulged she had been diagnosed with breast cancer. In that instant Cady came to understand the true danger of loving someone: the absolute panic at the thought of her leaving this earth.

Olivia's only response was a gentle smile.

"And where would I even get the money to go?" Cady wondered aloud. She glared at her disappointing rabbit, propped in the corner.

Olivia perked up, sensing a potential victory. "Your landlord has been offering you cash to buy out the shop lease, right? And you can liquidate the inventory, which will add up to something. And *I'll* lend you enough for the plane ticket."

Cady snorted. "Like you and Sebastian have so much to spare?"

"We have some savings set aside for a rainy day; and in case you hadn't noticed, my friend, it's raining cats and dogs. Metaphorically speaking."

"It's *my* rainy day, not yours."

"Details." She waved off Cady's concern. "What good is money if I can't help a friend? And I believe in your art. What's that old saying? 'Anonymous was a woman'?"

"What does that have to do with anything?"

"Because you're bound to remain anonymous if you don't get your art out there for people to see. Taking student portraits might pay the bills, but you're an *artist.* And I can be your patron! Sort of. At least I can manage a plane ticket."

As photographers went, Cady did pretty well. She hauled her heavy camera bag all over the Bay Area, from Marin to Morgan Hill, from the beaches of the Pacific Ocean to the Tahoe ski slopes, and never turned down a job. She photographed weddings, bar and bat mitzvahs, first communions, anniversaries, birthdays, and family reunions. She had regular gigs taking yearbook portraits at local schools, including the Berkeley French American International School. And she did occasional shoots for *Sunset* magazine, and a few home design catalogs.

Still, paying her bills every month was one

thing, but putting aside a nest egg was something else altogether.

"Thanks, Olivia, but running away to Paris for a couple of weeks isn't going to solve anything."

"Think of it as running *to* something. Anyway, I have to get back to the office. But just promise me this," Olivia said, as she gathered her things to leave. "You won't close yourself off to possibility. If something exciting falls in your lap, you'll take it."

"Exciting? Like *what?*" Cady demanded, irked. She loved Olivia, but when was the last time something great had "fallen into her lap"? That was the kind of thing that happened to charmed, suburban-grown people like Olivia, not unwanted orphans like Cady. Cady had had to work and scheme—and occasionally steal—to get anything she had.

But Olivia lifted her eyebrows and flashed a cat-that-ate-the-canary smile. "One never knows what the future might bring."

Cady laughed in spite of herself, gave her friend a hug, and watched as Olivia ambled back to her car, turning her face up to the morning sun, taking time to wave at a passing bicyclist. Olivia saw the beauty in everything: the sunrise, the city lights twinkling off the bay, a stranger on a bike.

Whereas Cady, when faced with the same scene, saw the smog, the congestion of the freeway, a traffic hazard.

Cady leaned her head against the doorjamb for a moment, ignoring the dust collecting on the shop's inventory, trying not to look at the spot behind the register where Maxine had fallen. She wasn't doing right by Maxine—or even by her landlord, for that matter. She wasn't doing right by herself, or Olivia, or anyone.

She didn't think of herself as a true artist, as Olivia had suggested. But . . . surely Cady Anne Drake had *something* to offer this world?

If only she knew what it was.

CHAPTER FOUR

1915
PROVENCE, CHÂTEAU CLEMENT

Yves Clement

She's out there again, riding that cursed carousel machine.

It is a ghostly sight: a grown woman riding a children's toy, bathed in silver moonlight, her white dress floating out behind her, like a creature out of time. What does she think? What does she want? Josephine is a puzzle Yves has never solved, would never be able to solve. Perhaps she was too young when they married, or he was too old. Their age difference didn't seem to bother her, but it gave him pause. Increasingly so with the passage of time.

Yves thinks back to his father's pear orchard. Workers would fit bottles over budding branches in early spring, so that the fruit would grow to full size while captured inside the glass, as *poires prisonnières*, imprisoned pears. Once the pear matured, the bottle would be filled with brandy, called *eau de vie*, water of life. And at long last it would be set on a high shelf and brought out on special occasions, leaving everyone to wonder how the miracle had occurred, how the pear came to be within the bottle.

For the rest of his life, the sound of wind chimes would remind Yves of the glinting glass bottles hanging from those tree branches, clinking together in the famous winds that swept over the fields and orchards of Provence.

His Josephine is like a bud in a bottle, a prisoner of the glass, awaiting her *eau de vie.*

"What is she looking for?"

His thoughts, voiced by another. Marc-Antoine, their beloved son, joins Yves at the library window and gazes through the leaded glass at Josephine, as perplexed as his father.

Yves places his hand on his son's newly muscular shoulder, missing the sharp feeling of delicate little-boy wing bones under his palm. Marc-Antoine's dark hair and eyes favor his mother's secretive features, and unlike Yves, Marc-Antoine has always been large for his age, overtaking Yves in height two years ago, when he was but twelve years old. *Our boy is becoming a young man,* Yves thinks as fear pierces his heart. All too soon, Marc-Antoine will leave him alone here in this once-grand château, with only Josephine—a pale imitation of the woman he had married—as company.

"What is it she is looking for, riding that

ridiculous merry-go-round at night?" Marc-Antoine asks the question for the hundredth time.

Yves does not answer.

There is no answer, just the darkness of the night and the eerie song of the carousel.

CHAPTER FIVE

PRESENT DAY
OAKLAND

Cady

Cady was two drinks in when she bashed her toe, hard, on a leg of the couch. Whirling around in a fit of anger and frustration, she kicked Gus.

Harder than she'd intended.

The carved rabbit fell over onto its side, slamming against the granite edge of an end table. Several already loosened joints gave up, and chunks of carved wood scattered on the floor like so many Tinker Toys: the ears, two slats from one side, the front legs.

"I'm sorry, I'm sorry, I'm sorry. . . ."

Shame engulfed her. This was the sort of thing she would have done as a child. Cady had pursued counseling, attended mindfulness classes, and read dozens of self-help books to learn to stifle her violent impulses. She took a moment to close her eyes, take a breath for the count of four, hold it for seven, and release it for eight, as Maxine had taught her to do.

And then she grabbed her camera. She perceived more clearly when she peered through the lens. It allowed her to concentrate, to sink into herself and tune out the external world.

Like peering through a pair of corrective glasses, looking through the camera lens allowed her to *see* in a way she couldn't with the bare eye.

Now Cady realized: There was something hidden in the cavity of the rabbit's belly.

A bundle wrapped in pink fabric.

Crouching down, she tried to pull it out, but it was stuck tight. She would have to dislodge another of the laminated wood slats to get it out. After a moment's hesitation, Cady decided that poor, broken Gus was in for some heavy repair work in any case, so she carefully pried the torso apart.

The rosy silk material was incredibly soft to the touch and reflected the overhead lights with a slight sheen. Her heart hammering in anticipation, Cady pushed aside the fabric.

Inside was a carved wooden box.

A breathtaking box. A work of art. Made of pale ash wood, it had been carved with acanthus leaves, flowers, and swirls; it was lacquered, polished, and sealed with a brass lock.

Who would hide a box within a carousel rabbit? And why? If she broke the lock, would she be destroying a piece of history? Or . . . could there be something inside that was worth real money? Something that might finance a trip to Paris, or even allow her to move and reestablish herself, as she'd hoped selling Gus would do?

Could this be the little piece of magic Olivia insisted Cady would find someday?

No, she reminded herself. *Things like that don't happen to me.*

To hell with history. Cady grabbed a spackling knife, shoved it into the seam of the lock, and tapped the end of it with a hammer. She had to pry the box in several locations before the lock finally snapped.

She opened the lid.

A childish part of her hoped for a cache of jewels or gold, as though a pirate might have concealed his booty within this children's amusement. Instead, she found an ancient, sepia-toned photograph of a woman; a tightly braided plait of dark brown hair; an intricately carved wooden rose; and a note written in slanted letters. The ink had faded to a light brown and the script was hard to read, but she made out: *Je t'aime toujours, et encore. Souviens-toi de moi.*

"I love you forever, and still," Cady translated aloud. "Remember me."

She checked the box for a false bottom, just in case, but there was nothing else. Certainly no treasure. Disappointment washed over her.

"That was it? *That's* your big secret?" Cady

glared at the rabbit. "I gotta tell you, Gus, after all these years you're really letting me down."

Still, she snapped several more photos of the hidden cache.

Unless . . . the man at the antiques fair had told her establishing a provenance might increase Gus's value. Were there clues that could reveal where the rabbit figure had come from?

Stroking the silky plait of hair, Cady inspected the intricately carved wooden rose, complete with tiny thorns. It reminded her of the flower on Gus's side that had so offended Scott Ripley. There was no signature or marking of any kind, certainly no brass plaque indicating provenance.

She picked up the photograph. The woman stood stiffly in front of a carousel, unsmiling, looking directly into the camera. She appeared to be young, probably in her early twenties. Her hair was piled on her head, with several strands escaping to frame a heart-shaped face. She wore a dark, high-necked dress that fell to her ankles, topped by a work apron. No visible lace or other embellishment. Cady was hardly a fashion expert, but she guessed it was from around the turn of the twentieth century, certainly before World War I.

The photograph was slightly fuzzy and crooked, as though taken by an amateur. But a professional-looking photographic stamp on the right lower corner read: *Château Clement*.

Cady opened her computer and searched, but she found no results for that name. She read that only a few dozen historic châteaux still existed in good repair; most had been too expensive to renovate after being abandoned during the French Revolution and then further damaged over the course of the two World Wars. The great majority had fallen into ruin.

The woman didn't appear to be the lady of the manor—surely she would have donned her finest gown for a photo session? In fact, with the apron and the messy hair, she looked like a servant. Which led to the next obvious question: Who would have taken a servant's photograph and then tucked it away in a box along with a love note? And why?

Cady brought out her photographer's loupe to study the fuzzy details of the carousel in the background. She made out two carved horses, a carriage, and a rabbit that looked a little like Gus.

Gus. She gazed at her poor gutted rabbit.

"I'm sorry, little guy. Let's see what we can do about fixing you up."

She lifted him onto the big project table and turned on some Edith Piaf to get in the mood.

When Cady first started working for Maxine to repay her for items she had pilfered from the shop, she had simply cleaned and straightened and organized. But over time Maxine taught Cady how to do some basic repairs on antiques and how to make new things look old with crackle paint and sandpaper, using the contents of the vacuum bag to rub into crevices and voids. She learned how to apply gold and silver gilt, how to execute a proper French polish, and how to use glazes to suggest antiquity and increase value. At the flea market on weekends, Maxine pointed out what was valuable, what was a cheap imitation, and how to tell the difference.

Still, Cady wasn't a trained conservator, so she had always hesitated to work on the rabbit, afraid her efforts at repairing him would decrease, rather than add to, his value. But now, since Gus wasn't who she'd thought he was anyway, she figured she could at least piece him back together. Cady enjoyed using her hands and getting back to basics: sanding and scraping and laminating. The process was calming, healing.

As Piaf crooned her love for Paris, Cady's mind cast about, pondering the woman in the photograph. Was the note written *for* her, or *by* her? And how could Cady track down Château Clement? Might it be the name of an old photography studio, rather than a true "château" per se?

The phone rang. Lately Cady had been ignoring phone calls, but this was from Olivia. If she ignored *her* calls, Olivia would show up in person.

"Hey," Cady answered. "What's up?"

"Remember a couple of days ago, how I was saying you should hold out for a little magic in your life?"

"Yeah . . . why?" Had Olivia somehow intuited what Cady had found in Gus's belly?

"Addison Avenue Books wants to offer you a contract for a photo book of Parisian carousels."

"What are you talking about?"

"Which part didn't you understand?"

"They're offering me a *book* contract? Who are these people?"

"They're a small press based in San Francisco, but they've been around for a long time. They publish big, glossy coffee-table books. It's a niche market, but a profitable one. One of the senior editors plays golf with Sebastian, and he pitched her the idea. I sent her a link to your website, and she checked out your online portfolio. I told her the magazine *loves* working with you, you're *so* professional and exclusive and *very* much in demand, blah blah blah."

"Basically, you lied."

"I did *not* lie. I enhanced. Anyway, since you don't have an agent, I told her to send me the contract so I could look it over for you. Legalese and all that."

"I don't . . . I mean . . . I really don't know . . ."

"Cady, the universe is handing you a huge gift. Accept your landlord's offer to take over the lease, sell off Maxine's inventory, store your stuff in my garage, and go to Paris."

"Speaking of gifts from the universe, listen to this: Gus fell over—to be honest, I kicked him—and broke open, and—"

"You *kicked* him? Poor Gus."

"Yes, but listen: There was a box hidden inside."

"What was in it? Gold coins? Diamonds? Scads of old-fashioned currency?"

"No, unfortunately. Just a photograph and a lock of hair. And a love note, and a wooden rose."

"How cool! Are there any clues about where Gus came from?"

"Not right off the bat, but I did find the name of a château. I have no idea where it is, though. It doesn't come up on the Internet."

"Well, the book offer specifies photos of Parisian carousels, but there's no reason you can't wander a little farther afield once you're in the country," said Olivia. "You could track down that château. You and I both know you're going to become obsessed with your mystery box, anyway. It's what you do."

It was true: Cady was already reading and rereading the note, gazing at the photo, stroking the plait of hair, wondering about the significance of the rose. Maxine used to say that once something had caught Cady's interest, she was like a dog with a bone. On the one hand, her single-mindedness had helped her in her photography; on the other, her obsessions sometimes drove a further wedge between her and others.

"Seriously, Cady," Olivia continued. "Take the leap. You know what they say: The world's your oyster."

"I don't like oysters."

"Have you ever *tried* oysters?"

"No." Cady liked things to be predictable. Running off to Paris for a photography assignment felt . . . reckless. Just the prospect gave her a dizzying sensation, like the first time she had seen the ocean, standing on the edge of a very steep cliff.

"The pay's not great, but you're not a big spender, so it'll be enough. Honestly, Cady, what do you have to lose?"

Cady gripped the telephone so tightly that her knuckles hurt. Even she had to admit: It felt like the universe was giving her a big old shove in the direction of La Belle France.

"You don't have any room in your garage," Cady said. "Everyone else's stuff is jammed in there already."

"I'll *make* room," Olivia answered, a triumphant tone to her voice. "So, is that a yes?"

"*Mais oui*," Cady said, surprising them both.

CHAPTER SIX

1900
ANGERS, FRANCE
THE CAROUSEL FACTORY OF
GUSTAVE BAYOL

Maëlle Tanguy

A scrap of paper, crumpled and damp from being clutched in her hand for hours, holds the precious address of the factory: 215 bis, rue de Paris, in Angers. Maëlle Tanguy is weary from the train ride, and her muscles ache from carrying her bag all the way from the station . . . but still, the moment she walks in she knows the master's atelier is where she belongs.

She knows from the scents of the freshly sawn wood, the sharp tang of turpentine, and the mellow aroma of linseed oil. Orange afternoon light streams in through huge windows, hazy with caked-on sawdust. Half-built animals pepper the work platforms like so many carcasses, but rather than being butchered they are waiting for their final straps of wood to be cut and laminated, joined and carved. They lack wood filler and putty, sanding and priming with gesso. Most of all, they are in need of the bright paints of brown and yellow, turquoise and scarlet; the gold and silver and copper gilt; the carved tassels, bells, jewels, and rosettes that will transform them into miraculous carousel figures.

Maëlle knows.

"*Bonjour*, mademoiselle. May I help you?"

Maëlle's reverie is broken by the most beautiful man she has ever seen. His face reminds her of an angel painted by an old master. His brawny, muscular arms are like those of the butcher's son, who could carry an entire boar carcass over his shoulder without breathing hard; but the intelligence gleaming in his gray-green, sea-colored eyes is something else entirely. The sheen of sweat on his broad brow—and on the intriguing triangle of skin revealed by his open collar—only serves to make him more attractive.

"*Bonjour*, monsieur," Maëlle responds, suddenly breathless. The man looks far too young to be the famous Monsieur Bayol, but Maëlle can't be sure.

His eyes linger on her face for a moment before brazenly running down the length of her body. "What do you want, little girl?"

"You are . . . are you the master?"

The man's laugh is a deep, resonant sound that gives her a confusing, unwelcome thrill somewhere down deep in her belly. Maëlle is not entirely naive about men; she had briefly entertained—and then turned down—two rather lackluster offers of marriage: one from the butcher's son and another from a middle-aged widower with a small farm outside of town. But the men from her fishing village pale in comparison to the man standing in front of her now.

"No, I am not the master—yet. I am Léon Morice," he says. "It is lovely to meet you."

"I am Maëlle Tanguy. *Enchantée.*"

"You are from Bretagne?"

She nods. Her accent and her name give her away. She knows the rest of France looks down its Gallic nose at the Bretons, but she doesn't understand why; the rocky coast is wild and alluring, the fishing villages charming, the houses tall and straight. But it is true that her village does not compare to the majesty of the architecture of Angers; on her way from the train station she had passed an old stone castle and walked along the remnants of medieval city walls. There were half-timbered houses with leaded glass and window boxes full of flowers, and vast white-domed buildings studded with balconies, and ubiquitous dark-slate roofs that had given the town its nickname, the "Black City."

Maëlle had made the mistake of gazing up at the rooftops as she walked, narrowly escaping being run over by a carriage in the road.

"You see the man with the mustache, carving

the chicken?" Léon leans in close to her, his long arm pointing to the other side of the studio. "He is the master you seek: Monsieur Gustave Bayol."

"I . . . Thank you." Maëlle reminds herself of her mission. She buttons the high neck of her blouse, tucks an unruly lock of dark hair back under her hat, smooths her traveling coat, squares her shoulders, and makes her way across the crowded atelier to stand beside the small man wearing a wide-brimmed hat. The waxed ends of his mustache curl upward to form two sideways question marks, one on each cheek.

"*Bonjour*, Monsieur Bayol. I am Maëlle Tanguy." The words she had practiced on her train journey have flown as surely and swiftly as the marsh birds flushed out by her father's hunting dog. In place of the eloquent lines she means to recite, she blurts out: "I wish to apprentice with you."

Gustave Bayol laughs, his mustache vibrating.

The master's hands never stop moving over the giant chicken: each feather is individually detailed, curls of wood rising as he applies the planer and knife. *Scritch, scritch, scritch.* His hands are calloused and strong, scarred from countless nicks by blades and chisels. A sculptor's hands.

"Please." Maëlle's heart flutters, but her voice is strong. "I carry a letter of introduction from a talented sculptor, with whom I have trained for many years."

"Tell me, mademoiselle," Monsieur Bayol replies. "This sculptor, he allowed a young woman to apprentice with him? What is his name?"

"Emile Tanguy." Maëlle feels the heat rise in her cheeks. "The sculptor is my father, it is true, but he is very talented, and he has taught me everything he knows."

"Mademoiselle—" Bayol shakes his head, his humor giving way to annoyance.

"I am prepared to work for free for six weeks, monsieur. If you are not happy with my work, you may send me away." Maëlle has to raise her voice to be heard over *tinks* and *clanks* and the occasional chatting of the small army of men who swarm like ants over the carousel factory. "I will sweep sawdust and brew coffee; I can wash your windows for you, so you'll have more light by which to work. I am very practiced at honing tools and sharpening knives. But much more than this: I can carve. I am an artist, monsieur."

All she wants is to be part of this world, to work, to create, to feel the wood under her hands, to transform a plain stump into something new and magical. It is the only time she feels fully alive. What will be her future otherwise?

Her father, poor man, had sired four girls and only one boy, Erwann, who is sickly and lacking in talent for anything but poetry. Maëlle is the child who picked up her father's blade at the age of four, caressing it, fascinated by its heft and shine, and over time learned how to sharpen it with the strap, grinding the edge on the whetstone at night by the fire. Maëlle is the one who watched, rapt, as her father set his chisel to the wood and tapped it with the hammer, sending tiny bits flying as he uncovered the form that dwelt within what had once been a tree.

Maëlle's father is more cabinetmaker than sculptor, but this is by necessity rather than the limits of his talent. He is a frustrated artist, as is she. Her father had carved a gnome for each of his children; hers was soft and slick with the rubbing of her hands as she felt the crevices and hollows, following the curves and lines.

Her brother, Erwann, was Maëlle's closest friend and confidant as they grew up; he is the one who encouraged her to come to Angers. To learn to carve, to fight for what she wanted, no matter how absurd it might seem. Erwann had written her a sonnet titled "The Aspiring Apprentice of Angers." She keeps it in her bag, rereading it on the train, drawing strength from the memory of whispering at night in their shared cot, confessing their dreams, their aspirations. Until they got too old to share a bed and she was sent to sleep with her sisters. Still, Erwann is her best friend; he is the one who understands.

Her father's gnome is the only sentimental item, besides Erwann's poem, that Maëlle has brought with her to Angers. Besides those treasures, her bag holds only a single change of clothes, a work apron, a roll of her sketches, and one exquisitely carved rose wrapped in a scrap of pink silk. She sculpted it from a single piece of chestnut wood she had hauled, by herself, from the hill outside of town, near the cemetery where her mother was buried. Maëlle had worked on the rose for months, listening to Erwann cough at night, sometimes so hard that he spit up blood.

Maëlle is sick, too. Sick to her soul of paying for the sin of being born a girl and growing into a woman. It makes her angry, and the anger gives her strength.

"These are some of my projects," Maëlle says as she displays her designs, smoothing the papers out as best she can on the dusty worktable. "But please believe me: I am far more talented in carving than in drawing."

Bayol glances at them, nods distractedly.

Then she unwraps her pièce de résistance. Her rose—the petals delicate, the leaves complete with intricate veins, and all perfectly proportioned, down to the thorns.

Monsieur Bayol sets down his hammer and chisel, extends his hand, and she places the rose on his open palm. He studies the workmanship, turning the flower to view it from all angles. He exchanges a glance with his apprentice, Léon, who has approached to see what Maëlle has brought.

Léon's only response is a shrug.

"Please, messieurs, I beg you," Maëlle says, looking from one man to the other. "I spent everything I have on the train ticket. I have nowhere else to go."

"You come to a strange city without resources?" Bayol frowns. "You have no family in the city of Angers?"

She shakes her head. Maëlle had run away from home with nothing more than what she had tucked into her satchel. She had been so sure.

"Then already you have proven you are a foolish girl," says Bayol, handing the rose back to her and running his fingers over the section of feathers he had just been carving, examining the depth of the grooves.

"I beg to differ," Maëlle responds, desperate. "Would you say that if I were a man?"

She jumps at a loud bark of laughter. Behind her, several other workers have gathered to listen in on their conversation.

"But you are *not* a man, my child," Monsieur Bayol says, sounding distracted. He picks up his gouging knife and cuts another tiny section of wood, blowing the debris away. "You are a girl. Surely I don't have to explain the essential differences to you."

"Men are not accustomed to bravery in a woman," Maëlle says, pleased with how calm her voice sounds, despite the pounding of her heart. Indignation fuels her confidence. "You mistake it for foolishness. We are entering a new century; are we not ready to embrace a new way of life?"

Bayol straightens, placing a hand on his chicken and glancing behind her at Léon and the others. When he looks back at Maëlle, one side of his mustache lifts as he gives her a smile.

Maëlle feels a sweet, liquid triumph flow through her veins.

CHAPTER SEVEN

PRESENT DAY
PARIS

Cady

The alienating, dehumanizing experience of international air travel, which most people complained about, was par for the course for Cady. She had been trained as a child to stand in line and wait, to shuffle silently through from one checkpoint to the next, losing herself in her thoughts.

Paris, on the other hand, was terrifying. The foreign language, the unfamiliar streets—even the charming but minuscule Left Bank apartment she had rented, three stories up a winding stone staircase—knocked her off-balance and left her feeling even more out of place than she usually did.

So she focused on the carousels.

A month ago, and what seemed like a world away—when she was still in Oakland and planning this trip had been a theoretical exercise—Cady had researched Parisian carousels and composed her “must include” list. While Sebastian cooked dinner, Cady and Olivia had spread the map of Paris out on the kitchen table and pinpointed the locations of the historic machines, noting the nearest Métro stations. There were so many carousels to visit, in places with enticing, exotic-sounding names: Trocadéro, Montmartre, Jardin du Luxembourg, Forum des Halles, Bois de Vincennes, Jardin du Ranelagh, Musée des Arts Forains, Square des Batignolles.

Now, as the days passed, Cady took immense pleasure in checking each carousel off her list, jotting down meticulous notes about date, time of day, weather, and the names and e-mail addresses of the parents of any children included in her photographs.

The morning after she arrived Cady dragged herself out of bed before dawn to photograph the Trocadéro carousel. Styled in traditional wood and illustrated with Parisian scenes, with the orange and pink light of dawn reflected in the great water mirror of the Warsaw Fountain, it was the perfect place to photograph the Parisian sunrise.

It seemed clichéd to include the Tour Eiffel carousel in a book of Parisian carousels, and yet how could she not? Cady headed to the corner of the Pont d’Iéna and Quai Branly, situated right below the twinkling lights of the Eiffel Tower. With its prancing white horses, the two-story carousel provided the ideal opportunity to take a classic shot of the Eiffel Tower—with a carousel in the foreground. She angled the camera to include some nearby palm trees, their fronds waving lackadaisically in the breeze.

Next, she moved on to the carousel at the Hôtel de Ville, Paris's town hall. The light in the evening created harsh shadows against the pretty tones of the panels painted with classical scenes. The ornate double-decker merry-go-round was similar to the one located at Trocadéro, so she made sure to catch the iconic hotel in the background.

The small green-roofed carousel in the Jardin du Luxembourg claimed to be the oldest in Paris, dating back to 1879. The rather run-down, weathered animals, ridden by thousands of children for more than a century, were designed by the architect of the Paris Opera house, Charles Garnier. Its main attraction, Cady learned as she watched the machine go round, was the *jeu de bagues*, or game of rings: Children sitting on the outside horses used sticks to attempt to spear tin rings as they rode past. A wrinkled elderly man rapidly loaded rings into old wooden shanks in an intricate, practiced motion.

Every day when Cady stopped for lunch at a bistro or brasserie near wherever she was shooting, she would try to engage the waiter in a discussion of carousels, but to a person they seemed hopelessly bored and uninterested in this American tourist and her quest.

Far from being put off, Cady enjoyed their surliness. It seemed . . . *authentic.* It had always embarrassed her to go to her local grocery store in Oakland, where the poor cashier was forced to read her name on the receipt and say, "Thank you, Ms. Drake." Even when it was delivered in a warm tone, the endearment wasn't genuine; Cady found she preferred the Parisians' slightly standoffish attitude.

So Cady kept to herself, exploring the disconcertingly cobbled streets, figuring out how to buy groceries, hunting down carousels, exchanging as few words as possible with parents when she asked their permission to photograph their children on the rides.

But even as she watched the carousels whirl round and round, each one more charming than the last, Cady felt something shifting within her. Bit by bit, she was easing into the sense of anonymity she felt as she walked the streets of Paris. With each new stranger she met, stumbling through conversations in her clumsy French, she felt increasingly free to present a new face, a different aspect of herself.

About a week after she arrived Cady had been sitting at an outdoor café, savoring an extravagant meal served by an efficient but unfriendly waiter, looking out at the bustling plaza in front of the

Panthéon, when it dawned on her that Olivia had been right. Cady was starting to feel . . . if not happy, at least sort of comfortable. Somehow her usual manner, which people in friendly California described as overly forward and abrupt, seemed to fit in here. Or maybe it was simply that since she was someplace foreign and didn't understand all the language or customs, she allowed them to flow over her instead of trying to fathom every little thing.

And every night when she retreated to her tiny apartment, Cady opened the mystery box she had found inside Gus. She reread the handwritten note, stroking the silky braid of hair, studying the wooden rose and the photograph of the woman who had loved, or who had been loved. Or both.

Souviens-toi de moi.

Somehow it seemed like an answer to a question she had never known quite how to ask.

CHAPTER EIGHT

2001
OAKLAND

Cady, Age 13

Her childhood wasn't all bad. Cady had vague, watercolor memories of being held in the lap of a woman who smelled like talcum powder and almond-scented hand lotion, overlaid with the slight sourness of old milk. She could still recall the warmth of the woman's skin and the reassuring thudding of her heart. Strong, plump arms encircling her like a loving shackle that would never let her go.

Or there was Ms. Greta, who had a deep, kind voice and an easy laugh, who kept a canister of red-hot candies that she would dole out like vitamins, making the kids giggle when she'd say, "Line up for your vitamins, now, kids, and eat 'em all up."

But every time Cady started to relax, to learn how things worked, to develop a fondness for someone, she'd be yanked out and placed in another situation. That's what the social workers called the succession of houses and apartments she was assigned to: "situations." A series of foster homes, then a string of group homes, moved from one to the next for reasons that made no sense to her; all she understood was that according to the Powers That Be, she was hard to fit.

Cady learned not to get too attached to anything or anyone, to carry anything that mattered to her on her person at all times, and to keep two big black Hefty garbage bags—her "foster kid suitcases"—ready to go.

As she grew, Cady would note the changes in her body when she looked in the mirror, searching her features for a hint of where she'd come from. She imagined her father's eyes in her own straightforward espresso brown gaze; she wondered if she might have inherited her mother's strong jawline, her stubborn chin. *Did she look like anyone in this world?* What would it be like to share a family resemblance with parents and siblings, grandparents, cousins?

What would it be like to belong?

Once Cady hit adolescence, she graduated to a group home, to the roster of yet another over-worked social worker, this one more focused on keeping her wards out of prison than on finding them permanent homes and families.

The other kids taunted Cady with possible origin stories: claiming she had been abandoned at a fire station, or that her father had died in prison after denying paternity, or that she had been taken away from a drug-addled mother. All Cady knew for sure was that there had been a legal issue regarding paternity when she was very young, which was why she hadn't been adoptable as an infant. There were no immediate relatives and no way to trace family.

The file is sealed, the subject is closed.

A kind librarian once helped her to look up her last name: Drake. It turned out to be a relatively common surname, so it didn't provide any clues as to her people. But the librarian read that it might have derived from the word *dragon.*

Cady liked that. When the anger arose inside her, she imagined it as her inner dragon, a scaly, ugly thing that surged up from her gut, swelling with rage at the unfairness of it all. She would watch with vicious envy as harried parents picked their kids up from school, imagining her classmates going home to mothers and fathers and nannies, their bedrooms decorated with pink flowers and soft white coverlets, rooms fit for the princesses their parents believed them to be.

Cady's only friend at the group home was a girl named Jonquilla, after the jonquil, a kind of tiny daffodil. She went by Jon—some of the kids tried to call her Daffy behind her back, but she beat up the biggest boy and that was that.

Cady recognized in Jonquilla a kindred soul: a fiery, discontented creature. She was drawn to Jon's fury, her confident righteousness. Soon they were a pair; Cady stopped hanging out with the younger kids, instead choosing to skip school and pilfer candy from Abdella's Liquor Store on the corner.

One day Cady and Jonquilla walked past a shop Cady had never seen before. Metallic gold letters spelled out its name in a bold arc on the glass.

A carousel horse painted in bright red, blue, and yellow stood in the display window, its prancing legs positioned as though it had just alit. It had gold gilding on its saddle, and its silver mane glittered in the afternoon sun.

"Hey, check this out," Cady said to Jon. "Do you remember the Tilden Park merry-go-round? Did you ever do Prospective Parents Day there as a kid?"

"Coupla times," said Jon. "It was lame."

"I like this horse, though. Do you remember the sea creature at Tilden?"

Jon rolled her eyes. "I dunno. I guess. I thought merry-go-rounds were cool when I was, like, five. Wanna go down to the park, see if we can score something?"

"Maybe . . . but want to check this place out first?" asked Cady. "What's it called?"

"Maxine's Treasures. Can't you read?"

Beyond the carousel horse Cady spotted a mishmash of oil paintings and wooden furniture, gold-framed mirrors and strange dolls and an old-fashioned record player. She longed to go in, but hesitated. Shop owners had a way of knowing that kids her age who were out and about during school hours were up to no good. Still . . .

Cady's gaze lingered on the fascinating jumble of items crowding the store.

"C'mon, Drake," Jon urged.

Cady followed her friend, but couldn't stop wondering: Where had all those things come from? Who had they belonged to? What were their stories?

A week later, the clerk at Abdella's Liquor Store caught Jon red-handed with a family-sized bag of M&M's down her pants.

Cady ran.

Two blocks away, she dashed down an alley and rounded the corner, only to realize she was in front of Maxine's Treasures.

Fearing that someone from the liquor store might be on her tail, Cady ducked into the store. A bell tinkled over the door.

Sitting behind the register was an old woman who nodded to Cady as she walked in. Her head was capped by a stiff-looking helmet of salt-and-pepper hair. *Probably a wig,* Cady thought meanly, wondering what the woman would look like if Cady snatched it off her ugly head.

Cady smiled to herself, thinking she would make Jon laugh with that story.

Her stomach clenched. She hoped Jon didn't land in juvie—what would Cady do without her only friend? Also, Jon was going to be mad at her for running—she'd probably get beaten when she went back. But Cady had *told* her the family-sized bag was too big not to be noticed.

Cady tried to act casual as she looked around Maxine's Treasures, as though it was typical for her to stroll through narrow aisles crowded with bureaus and side tables, rusty tools and chess sets and carved painted panels. Her gaze fell upon an old magician's chest, complete with magic wand and a deck of tarot cards.

Where did these things come from? Everything seemed to vibrate with secret stories, with hidden histories.

"All these things belonged to someone once?" Cady asked the old woman from the other side of the store.

No answer.

"Hey, lady?" Cady tried again, raising her voice. "Didn't you hear me?"

"Of course I heard you." The woman flipped a page of her magazine and, still not looking up, added, "But when addressing your elders, you preface your statement with, 'Excuse me, ma'am.' "

Cady stared at her for a long moment, enraged on the one hand, intrigued on the other. With an internal eye roll, she channeled a phrase she'd overheard when the group home social worker insisted on watching the entire season of some stupid BBC program from England:

"Excuse me, *ma'am.* I wonder if you could be so kind as to inform me whether these items are all hand-me-downs?"

Maxine smiled and met her eyes. "What's your name, child?"

"Cady. Cady Drake."

"Nice to meet you, Cady. I'm Maxine. In answer to your question: Yes, these items once belonged to someone, or to several someones over the years."

"Where'd you get them?"

"You'd be amazed at what people throw away. Perfectly good things," Maxine said. Without changing her tone, she asked, "What you running from, Cady?"

"Nothing," Cady said. Why did people always assume she was a crook? Did she have "No one wants me but the police" stamped on her forehead? "A while ago you had a carved horse in your window, like from a merry-go-round."

Maxine nodded.

"I didn't know you could buy things like that."

"You can't, at least not very often," Maxine said. "That was a nice piece. It wasn't from a real carousel, just an imitation. Still, I made a pretty penny on that one. You're in the market for a carousel figure, are you?"

"No," Cady snapped. It's not like she had any money, or anyplace to put such a thing, for that matter. She had a sudden, humiliating vision of trying to stuff a carved carousel horse into one of her Hefty bags. Anger surged within her, hot and fierce, stomach-churning.

She had to get out. She rushed toward the door.

"Good-bye, Cady," said Maxine. "Thanks for stopping by."

"Go to hell."

CHAPTER NINE

1900
ANGERS
FACTORY OF GUSTAVE BAYOL

Maëlle

Monsieur Bayol offers Maëlle a position not as an apprentice but as a domestic servant.

Maëlle is brutally disappointed, but since she is homeless and without resources, she is in no position to refuse.

"My wife could use some help," Bayol says as he leads her to his house, which adjoins the carousel factory. The brick structure is not fancy; it is merely a series of small rooms crowded with furniture and books.

Madame Bayol is a broad-faced, unsmiling woman. She sighs when Bayol introduces the "new girl" to her. Maëlle smooths her skirts again, hoping she is presentable; she hasn't seen herself in the mirror since she left her home, more than twenty-four hours earlier.

"Don't mind her," says Monsieur Bayol to Maëlle. "My wife thinks I work too hard. Perhaps one day I will close my famous carousel factory and make small toys for children," he teases. "I shall sell my concern to Monsieur Coquereau, or Monsieur Chailloux. Or perhaps Monsieur Maréchal will take it off my hands."

"You say that as a joke," replies Madame Bayol, "but it is what you should do."

He laughs and leaves the two women standing alone in the parlor, each disappointed for her own reasons.

"He is a foolish man," mutters Madame Bayol. "As most men are. Come."

Madame Bayol shows Maëlle to a small room off the kitchen. It is furnished with a narrow cot, a coiled-rag rug, and a low chest of drawers topped by a pitcher and a chamber pot.

"You may leave your things here," Madame Bayol says. "Wash up, and then you will help me to prepare lunch. The married workers go home to eat with their wives and families, but the others eat together here."

A pot of soup simmers on the stove, and a cast-iron dish, still hot from the oven, holds a piece of beef surrounded by haricots verts, cabbage, and potatoes. Madame Bayol instructs Maëlle to place a chunk of meat in each wide bowl, then cover it with broth. Maëlle's stomach growls as the aromas waft up, teasing her nose. She hasn't eaten since her picnic of baguette and ham on the train.

Madame Bayol places a board with bread and

cheese on the table, and tells Maëlle to bring up two bottles of wine from the cellar.

The men file in, donning their jackets to appear presentable before sitting down to the midday meal. Maëlle pours wine; though the men have washed the sawdust and grease off their hands and faces, the scent of masculine sweat fills the air.

After the eight men are served, Madame Bayol invites Maëlle to sit beside her at one end of the table. A few of the workers look even younger than Maëlle; they sneak occasional glances at her, but no one addresses her directly. The younger men eat in silence, ceding lunch conversation to their elders. Maëlle catches the names of a few of them. It does not take long to learn that Monsieur Coquereau, the head joiner, is a joker; he laughs and teases throughout the meal. Monsieur Chailloux is quiet, his mind elsewhere, presumably on his designs for future carousels. Monsieur Maréchal, the factory foreman, is stern and unsmiling and sits hunched over the table, focused on his food.

But Maëlle's gaze finds its way, repeatedly, to Léon Morice. He sits to the right of his master, and throughout the meal Bayol seeks his apprentice's advice regarding several aspects of their work: whether they will be able to meet the expedited schedule for the delivery of a carousel to the city of Nice and whether it is possible to add extra space inside the figure of a cow to place a bellows, so the animal will make a lowing sound as it moves.

After the men have finished the soup, Maëlle and Madame Bayol whisk the plates away and make coffee. Appreciative murmurs arise when Madame Bayol serves the men narrow slices of cherry tart topped with a drizzle of sweet cream.

"I would like to announce a new commission," says Monsieur Bayol, addressing his staff. He extracts a cream-colored piece of stationery from his jacket's breast pocket and holds it up, waving it in a theatrical gesture. "I have received a letter of instruction from a Monsieur Yves Clement, proprietor of a country home not far from Avignon." Fitting half-lens glasses upon the bridge of his nose, Bayol reads: *"I wish to commission a carousel, with pigs, dogs, cats, horses, and rabbits, for my beloved wife, Josephine, on our fifth anniversary. We are dearly waiting for our family to come, and hope to fill the halls of Château Clement with the laughter of children. A carousel from the famous house of Bayol will be the perfect addition to our historic château."*

Nods and murmurs are shared up and down the table.

"I have instructed my advocate to make inquiries into the affairs of the family," Bayol adds. "But I believe the Clement carousel will be a grand opportunity indeed."

The men grunt their agreement, their chairs screeching as they push away from the table. Talking excitedly, they thank Madame Bayol for lunch, hang up their jackets, and file out of the kitchen to return to work.

Maëlle watches as they leave, longing to join them in the atelier. Instead, she turns her attention to washing the dishes. When the women are alone in the kitchen, she asks Madame Bayol, "Is this 'Clement carousel' a private commission, then?"

"Yes. It is rare but not unknown."

"It is hard to imagine a family ordering a carousel. They must be wealthy indeed."

"Perhaps not wealthy enough," Madame Bayol answers, scraping flour from her baking board. Pride tinges her voice as she adds, "My husband is a true master. His talents demand the highest fees in all of France. Perhaps this family does not have enough money. This is why he asked his advocate to make inquiries; a commission such as this is not to be taken lightly."

"But they own a château."

"Many châteaux are owned by families of dwindling fortunes," Madame Bayol says, shaking her head as she stores the leftover flour in a canister. "After the wars, and with the economy of our Third Republic . . . things have changed. The families are merchants and farmers, not the aristocracy of old; in fact, many bought their châteaux recently from the displaced aristocracy, not realizing how much they cost to maintain."

Maëlle had never thought about this sort of thing. There was a château outside her hometown of Concarneau; it was said a *vicomtesse* lived there, a solitary old woman whose royal title had survived the Revolution. Maëlle used to walk by, noting the faded curtains in the windows and the weeds in the drive, but she had always assumed these were genteel flaws, indications of a kind of discreet wealth that someone in her position would never fully understand.

Needless to say, the cabinetmaker's daughter had never been invited in.

As the week goes on, Maëlle learns about the carousel business by listening in on the discussions over lunch and paying attention to the men's chatter while she washes the atelier windows and sweeps piles of wood dust off the floor. It is fascinating, and she has enough food and a warm place to sleep, but she itches to be allowed to work and create as she knows she can, alongside the carvers and painters.

She is thrilled when Monsieur Maréchal teaches her to make gesso, the thick white primer used to seal the wood of the carousel figures before pigment and metal leaf are applied. In a double boiler, she adds amber flakes of dried rabbit skin glue, chalk whiting, and garlic cloves, stirring constantly to be sure it doesn't burn.

Madame Bayol exclaims and throws open the windows as the stench fills the kitchen, yet to Maëlle it smells like progress.

Whenever she is cleaning the factory, she watches the process and learns.

First, Monsieur Chailloux's drawing is approved by the master. Then a life-size cartoon of the figure—a donkey, a horse, a cat—is sketched onto paper tacked up on the wall. The design is then transferred onto large pieces of wood only about an inch thick. After they are cut to the specifications, these are laminated together and held in a vise until the glue has dried. Only then does the sculpting begin: Léon and the other apprentices do the bulk of the preliminary work, carving away great chunks of unnecessary wood, and leaving the crudely modeled body for the master's artistry.

It is magical, watching Monsieur Bayol conjure his sweet figures, cutting and nicking and smoothing for hours, days, weeks.

Afterward, all joints are filled with putty and carefully sanded, and the master applies his final touches. Finally the figure is completely covered in several coats of gesso, each application smoothed and polished with increasingly fine sandpaper, pumice, and rottenstone.

The gleaming, pure white creatures are as lovely as any sculpture made of stone; they remind Maëlle of grand statues she has seen in Angers' public squares. It seems almost a shame to apply paint.

But the creatures are brought to whimsical life through bright pigments and shiny gilt, rosettes and jewels and brass details.

Maëlle watches the younger workers with envy. Not one is as skilled as she. Soon she makes a decision: She did not come all this way to remain in the kitchen. Maëlle starts slipping into the factory late at night, after the master and his wife have gone to bed. She retrieves chunks of wood from the discard pile to carve her creations: roses and tiny cows and pigs. She spends hours chipping and shaving, sanding and oiling. Then she leaves them atop Monsieur Bayol's desk for him to discover in the morning.

But it is not until she begins to apply paint to the animals that Monsieur Bayol takes her aside after lunch, to say: "These little toys you have been making are atrocious, but they do show promise." He toys with his mustache, seeming to ponder something for a long moment, then finally adds: "I am afraid young Theodore is not working out; he does not have the delicacy necessary for the finished painting. In addition to helping my wife, you will learn to properly use the paints. Perhaps a woman's touch would be useful, after all. Have you ever gilded?"

"I . . . No, I am sorry, monsieur," Maëlle said. "I have not gilded. But I am eager to learn."

He chuckled. "Yes, mademoiselle. This much is clear."

CHAPTER TEN

PRESENT DAY
PARIS

Cady

As Cady checked off the carousels she photographed, one after another, she began to wonder just how many there *were* in the City of Light, but neither an Internet search nor questioning of the carousel workers offered up a clear number. The man at the corner grocery near her apartment suggested she pay a visit to the Musée Carnavalet, a museum dedicated to Parisian history.

She found the museum on the other side of the Seine in the charming Marais neighborhood, where it occupied two neighboring mansions: the Hôtel Carnavalet and the former Hôtel Le Peletier de Saint-Fargeau.

A museum worker directed Cady to the office of a fifty-something woman named Madame Martin.

"*Bonjour*, *madame*," Cady said, placing her business card on the desk. "I'm photographing

Parisian carousels for a publisher based in San Francisco."

The woman looked unimpressed. Madame Martin's hair was cut in a neat bob, not chic exactly—at least not by Parisian standards—and was a shiny steel color, too uniform to be natural. She wore chunky, handmade jewelry: big earrings and a large necklace that seemed to make a statement—"I am here."

Her air of irritated impatience did not deter Cady; she was used to being the annoying kid. When she was thirteen she had snuck a peek at her file and noted that several caseworkers had described her as "socially awkward/possible disorder." Far from feeling insulted, Cady had been relieved to know there really was something about her that put people off. The awkwardness lessened as she matured and became better socialized, though it had never fully gone away.

But Cady imagined that many Americans felt awkward around the urbane Parisians. It was comforting to know that in this way, if in no other, she belonged.

"Yes, yes. What is your question?" urged Madame Martin.

"I have several."

"*Asseyez-vous*," she said, and Cady took a seat. Madame Martin folded her hands atop her desk and gazed at Cady attentively, reminding her of Ms. Ulmer, a social worker from years ago. Unsmiling, but not unkind.

“How many carousels are there in Paris?”

Madame Martin raised her eyebrows. “There is no one who knows this. Not all are permanent; sometimes they are brought in for festivals or holidays. The famous ones are well known: the Trocadéro, the Eiffel Tower, the Hôtel de Ville . . .”

“Yes, I’ve photographed those,” said Cady. “They’re beautiful. I’m especially interested in the carousel carver named Gustave Bayol. Are you familiar with his work?”

“But of course! Gustave Bayol is the most famous carousel carver of France. There are at least two of his carousels in Paris; I believe one is in Jardin du Ranelagh, and another in Bois de Vincennes.”

“I haven’t visited them yet, but they’re on my list.” In fact, Cady had been avoiding them. The sense of betrayal she felt from her carved rabbit was still fresh. It was ridiculous, she knew. And yet . . . “I have an animal figure that I always thought was a Bayol.”

“Is that so?” Madame Martin said, sounding curious.

Cady took out her portfolio, set it on the desk in front of the other woman, and splayed it open.

The photos of Gus-the-rabbit were eight-by-ten glossies. Some were in color, others black-and-white; a few were close-ups, and some had been taken from afar to give a sense of perspective. Gus had been one of Cady's first, and favorite, models. She had experimented, using different cameras to yield different effects: in some photos Gus was mildly distorted, while others contained streaks of light or orbs that seemed to dance along the edges of the figure.

"I am no expert," murmured Madame Martin as she examined one photograph after another, "but it looks to me like this is from the same era, as though someone were carving in the style of Bayol."

Cady nodded. "I've been told that. I was hoping he was wrong."

"The delicate lilies of the valley there, you see?" Madame Martin said, pointing to the photos and warming to the subject. "Those are not what we expect to see in the work of Bayol. He was not a fancy man. Of course, Bayol had many apprentices. Léon Morice was the most famous—he went on to become an important sculptor."

"Is it possible this rabbit could have been carved by Morice?"

She shook her head. "Like most masters, Bayol may have had his apprentices work on the structure of the animals, or sculpt the rough form, perhaps complete some of the painting and gilding. But he would have finished the raised details himself. They were his signature."

"Maybe one of his apprentices went on to sculpt elsewhere?"

"After Bayol semiretired and went on to carve wooden toys for children, Morice and two others, the head joiner and the factory foreman, took over his factory in Angers. They continued to create carousels, but theirs were much fancier. More in the style of the Baroque carousels, like the double-decker at the Hôtel de Ville. For them, your rabbit would not have been fancy enough."

"Oh."

"Besides, I don't see a plaque or a crest anywhere. Everything from the Bayol factory carries an identifying plaque, whether it was made under Bayol or by those who later bought his factory."

Cady nodded. "I have another question. My rabbit . . . fell and split open, and I found this inside."

Cady handed her the antique photograph, which she had placed in a protective plastic sleeve. Madame Martin arched one eyebrow.

"This was *inside* the rabbit?"

"Yes. There was a box, like a . . . 'time capsule.' " Cady couldn't think of the term in French, so she said it in English.

Madame Martin nodded. "A secret from a different age. How exciting."

Cady watched as the woman studied the photograph. "It appears to have been taken around the turn of the twentieth century, right?"

"It does," said Madame Martin. "And this was the only photo in the box?"

Cady nodded. "Along with a note that said: '*Je t'aime toujours, et encore. Souviens-toi de moi.*' "

"How sweet. Perhaps an amateur carver fell in love with the servant in the photograph and made the creature for her."

"Maybe," Cady said. "But see? She's standing in front of a carousel."

Madame Martin brought out a magnifying glass and studied the photo, including the stamp. "Château Clement . . . ? That's odd."

"You know it?"

"I do," she said with a nod. "My husband's family is from that area. It is in Provence, not far from Avignon."

"I tried to look it up but couldn't find any information on the Internet."

"I'm not surprised. The château is in private hands still, and derelict."

"So you think the photo might have been from a studio in that area?"

"That's what strikes me as odd: From the stamp I would assume this photo was taken by the owner of the château, a Monsieur Yves Clement, who lived and worked around the turn of the twentieth century."

"Clement ran a photography studio?"

"Oh no, of course not. He was a gentleman; he did not work for a living. But he was a passionate amateur photographer, and even included his stamp when he developed his photos, as you see here. Normally his work is quite refined, however. This one does not seem typical."

"Are his photographs well known?"

Madame Martin's pounded copper earrings reflected the overhead lights as she shook her head. "As I mentioned, I know of him through my husband. A distant cousin actually pulled together several of Yves Clement's photos and approached the museum about the possibility of an exhibition, but since our focus is on the city of Paris I suggested he take them elsewhere."

"Is it possible . . . I mean, if Yves Clement was the one who took this photograph . . . and it was placed in the rabbit with a love note . . . ?"

Madame Martin arched her eyebrow again. "Are you suggesting that the lord of the manor was in love with this young woman?"

"I suppose that would be pretty far-fetched. But . . . how do you suppose he was connected to my rabbit in particular?"

"I cannot help you resolve that mystery," Madame Martin said as she picked up her phone and started scrolling through numbers. "But I know someone who might be able to assist you. His name is Jean-Paul Mirassou."

"John Paul? Isn't that the name of a pope?"

"It is," Madame Martin said, as she started

dialing. "But it is also the name of many Frenchmen."

She began speaking in a rapid-fire French, sounding almost angry. Cady did not even try to follow. Madame Martin nodded, then hung up the phone. "This afternoon, at three o'clock. He will meet you."

"Jean-Paul? He will? Why?"

Madame Martin shrugged. "I asked him to share his knowledge of the château with you. He owes me a favor."

"I . . . Well, thank you again. Everyone says Parisians are rude." Cady cringed as soon as the words slipped out; she wasn't supposed to say things like that.

But Madame Martin just smiled. "We are not rude. We are discriminating. Anyway, I can't speak for all Parisians, obviously. I am from Nantes myself, and Jean-Paul is from Provence. But in my experience, the Provençal people do love a good mystery. Jean-Paul says he will meet you at the Café des Musées. It is not far from here."

The Café des Musées was classic Paris: the glossy red-paneled façade featured awnings and arched windows, and little chalkboards advertised the menu of the day, written in a fancy and distinctly French script. Though it was a chilly April afternoon, the small outdoor tables were occupied by smokers huddling under large patio heaters.

Approaching the door, Cady realized she had no idea what Jean-Paul Mirassou looked like, how old he was, or anything about him, really. Inside the restaurant, half the tables were filled with women and men of all ages, many of whom sat alone.

As she scanned the crowd, a man met her eyes, then stood. He appeared to be in his thirties, handsome, with shaggy light brown hair, sherry-colored eyes, and a heavy five o'clock shadow.

"You are the American that Madame Martin told me about?" he asked in English. "Cady?"

"Yes. Jean-Paul? Thank you so much for meeting me. This is very kind of you."

He leaned toward her and kissed her on one cheek, then the other. Jean-Paul smelled like fresh laundry with just a tiny whiff of tobacco, and his whiskers tickled her cheek. Having spent many hours working at the French-American school, Cady was familiar with the traditional French greeting, but still found it uncomfortably intimate.

"How did you know I was Cady?" she asked in French as she sat down.

"You are very . . . American."

"Is it the jeans?"

"Not at all. Many Parisians also wear blue jeans, have you not noticed?"

She hadn't. "What, then?"

"It is the way you walk," he said in English, gesturing to the waiter.

"*Nous pouvons parler en Français, si vous preferez*," Cady offered.

"If you don't mind, I would rather speak in English," he said. "It is good for me to practice. Otherwise, my English becomes, how you say it, roosty."

"Rusty. Are you saying I walk weird?"

He looked rather alarmed at her response. "No, just in a very American way. It is hard to describe. It is . . . rather like a man."

"Huh."

"But of course, I meant this in the best possible way."

Cady wasn't the only one upholding cultural stereotypes. Jean-Paul was wearing a scarf and what appeared to be a cashmere jacket. He had been writing in a notebook with a fountain pen, and a beat-up leather courier bag lay at his feet. He was simultaneously scruffy and very well put together, exhibiting what Cady decided must be an innate—and unique—French talent. The only thing missing from the tableau was a cigarette.

The waiter appeared. Cady, unsure of what to order, asked for whatever Jean-Paul was having. In his glass was a pretty, bright orangey-pink liquid.

"It is Campari. Do you know it? It is an

aperitif," Jean-Paul said, holding his glass out to her. "Would you like to taste it?"

"Oh, no," she declined. "It's fine."

"*Les deux*," Jean-Paul said, and the waiter left.

"So, Madame Martin tells me you are an expert in early photography," Cady said. Privately, she couldn't help thinking that, like Mr. Scott Ripley, the expert who had destroyed her dreams of cashing in on Gus, Jean-Paul did not look the part. She had always imagined appraisers as one might see them in a Hollywood movie: old men with great shocks of white hair, beetled brows, and thick spectacles, harboring a lifetime of accumulated knowledge.

Instead, Jean-Paul looked more like a poet—a *European* poet—who spent his days drinking coffee, chain-smoking, and writing in his journal until the sun went down and it was time to move onto drinking absinthe.

"I am no expert."

"But Madame Martin said—"

He waved it off and gave her a half-smile. "Madame Martin likes to play—what is the word? *Matchmaker*."

The waiter arrived and set a glass of Campari garnished with a wedge of lime in front of her. Cady feared her cheeks were as pink as the aperitif.

"Um . . . then why did you agree to meet with me?"

Jean-Paul grinned. "Perhaps I was looking for a date."

"That's . . . that makes no sense." As an adult, Cady had come to peace with her features. She had pronounced cheekbones, demanding dark brown eyes, and straight nearly black hair. Though she had always yearned to be lithe and delicate like the heroines in the books she devoured, she was anything but; she had wide shoulders and broad, capable hands. Olivia had once described her as having a "strong" look, "more Meryl Streep than ingénue." All Cady knew was that she was not the type to bowl men over.

"Anyway," Jean-Paul continued, his gaze not leaving hers, "Madame Martin is like my mother. And one must do as one's mother asks, yes? Do you like the Campari?"

Cady took a sip, holding the liquid in her mouth for a moment. It was surprising: from its color she had expected the drink to be sweet, but it was bitter at the same time. She looked up to find Jean-Paul watching her carefully.

"What?" she asked, running a finger across her lips in case she had something on her mouth.

"Nothing," he said with a slight smile, his gaze not moving from her face. "You like it?"

She nodded.

"So," said Jean-Paul, "Madame Martin mentioned you are interested in my great-uncle's photographs."

"Wait—Yves Clement was your great-uncle?"

"He was the brother of my grandfather's grandfather—I am not a genealogist, so I'm not sure of the exact term. Does it matter?"

"No. I just didn't realize you were a relative. Madame Martin said only that you come from a village located near Château Clement."

"It is a small village, you see, so many of us are all related in one fashion or another. The family has been in that area a very long time, and my great-grandfather had ten children with two different wives, so there are many descendants."

"The village is near Avignon, right?"

"Yes. It is called Saint-Véran, for the man who is said to have slayed a dragon from a nearby well."

"When was this?"

"Long enough ago for there to have been dragons."

Cady took another sip, and felt herself relaxing. She wondered if it was the Campari or if Jean-Paul had a way of making her feel at ease. It was . . . nice.

"I can't get over you French," she said, "what with your bread and your aperitifs and your . . . *history*."

Jean-Paul chuckled. "Your people have no history?"

"Oh sure. Just not as much of it, and definitely no dragons. I'm from California, and a lot of our history centers on people stealing other people's land, and searching for gold or building semi-conductors. Whereas here, someone changes a road name four hundred years ago, and it's still worthy of note."

"Well, trust me," Jean-Paul said, "a long memory isn't always a good thing. I admire the innovation of the Americans."

"That counts me out. I'm an old-style photographer. The basic technology of cameras and photo development hasn't changed much over the last century."

"Ah, yes, back to Yves Clement. What can I tell you about him?"

Cady brought out the sepia photograph of the woman and laid it in front of him. He raised an eyebrow, then leaned forward and picked it up.

"That is Yves Clement's stamp, certainly," he said. "Where did you find this?"

"Inside my rabbit."

"Pardon?"

"My rabbit. Not a real one, of course. A carousel figure. There was a box hidden inside it."

"A carousel figure? In the United States?"

She nodded. His gaze remained on her for a long moment, puzzled, before turning back to the woman in the photograph.

"This would be an unusual photo for Yves Clement to have taken."

"Why?"

"It looks rather amateurish, slightly crooked. Also, he rarely took posed portraits—the only ones I've seen were of his wife, Josephine, and their son when he was a baby. This is why he is so interesting from a sociological point of view: His photographs focus on nature and architecture, and candid shots of people at work."

"What kind of work?"

"Châteaux were not just fancy houses. The owners were landholders, with vast orchards and farms. Clement took photographs of people tending the olive orchards, pruning the pear trees, gathering lavender; men with huge baskets on their backs, bringing in the harvest. He also took a series of photographs of the artisans who assembled the carousel for Château Clement. He—"

"Wait, there's a *carousel* at Château Clement?"

"Yes. I assumed you knew that."

"How would I know that?"

"Because you just told me you had a carousel figure, and you have a photo of a woman standing in front of a carousel, and because you spoke to Madame Martin about carousels."

She blinked.

"In any case," continued Jean-Paul, dropping the photograph onto the table as though he had lost interest in it, "I assume this photo was one of his series of carousel construction photos."

Cady slipped the picture back into its protective plastic sleeve, beside the love note. She pondered sharing the note with Jean-Paul but decided against it; it was her obsession, not his.

"So what can you tell me about the Château Clement carousel?" Cady asked.

"Yves and Josephine Clement commissioned the machine around the turn of the century. They had hopes for many children, but had only a single son, Marc-Antoine."

"Who made the carousel, do you know?"

"Gustave Bayol. He had a factory in Angers."

Cady sat back and blew out a frustrated breath. "I know who Bayol is. In fact, my whole life, I was told my rabbit had been carved by Bayol. That was what fostered my interest in French carousels in the first place. But Madame Martin, and another carving expert, assure me that he isn't a true Bayol."

"I would take their word for it."

"Yes, but then why would this photo by Yves Clement end up inside a carousel figure that was *not* carved by Bayol when there was a Bayol carousel on the property? Just how many carousel carvers were at the château?"

He shrugged and glanced around the room.

Cady persisted, asking,"Could I see the photos you have from Yves Clement?"

"I donated them to the Archives Nationales." He scribbled something on a piece of paper and passed it across the table to her. "This was the department I dealt with. You would have to apply to see them, and I should warn you: We French invented bureaucracy. They're not online yet. My mother has copies, but she's in Provence."

"I just wish I could find out where my rabbit came from. One of my goals for this trip was to reunite him with his carousel." Cady took a thick folder out of her bag and held it up. "This is Gus, my rabbit."

Jean-Paul looked amused. "Not a fan of digital photos? Aren't all you Californians high-tech?"

"I told you, I'm old-school."

"So I see." Once again, his eyes lingered on her just a beat too long. It made her uncomfortable, and yet . . . connected to him, in some strange way. Whatever it was, she did not look away.

"I mean" —Cady felt compelled to clarify—"I take plenty of snapshots on my phone, but those are mostly for reference. True photographic beauty, to me, is captured by a genuine camera lens."

Jean-Paul held up his hand in a subtle wave, motioning to the waiter to clear the café table and bring a fresh tablecloth.

"May I see the photographs, please?"

Cady handed him the folder.

He studied the prints—one after the other—for so long that Cady started to get nervous. She reminded herself to relish this moment: sitting in a Parisian café, sipping an aperitif just like she belonged. With a handsome Frenchman sitting across the table, no less.

But when he looked back up at her, something seemed to have shifted. It was subtle, but his formerly open—and occasionally bored—expression now seemed guarded.

"Anyway," Cady said, "I'm searching for the provenance of my rabbit. If it's not a Bayol, perhaps it was carved by one of his apprentices. If I could find a paper trail of some kind . . ."

"Then what? How would it change the figure to know who carved it?"

Cady wondered how to respond. She wanted to know Gus's background, where he came from, whose hands had carved the figure she had cherished for so long. But would she sound ridiculous if she uttered those feelings aloud? Finally she simply said, "There's always been something so . . . sweet about Gus. It's hard to describe—I have tried, and failed, for years to capture that quality in photographs. I would like to know more about him."

"I will buy it from you, as is."

"Why would you do that? You can see he's in bad shape." Cady had wondered why Madame Martin, and now Jean-Paul Mirassou, would go out of their way for a total stranger. Did they suspect something about Gus that she wasn't aware of?

Jean-Paul stuck out his chin and shrugged again, in what Cady was coming to learn was a classic French gesture. She was fairly sure it was meant as a non-response response.

"Madame Martin mentioned that Château Clement is run-down," Cady continued. "I was thinking maybe I could get in touch with the owner, see if there are other figures, or more information—"

Jean-Paul interrupted her. "The owner will not speak with you. He is a recluse. He doesn't like interlopers—or Americans, for that matter."

"You know him?"

"He is Fabrice Clement, the grandson of Yves Clement."

"So he's a cousin of yours."

"A distant one, yes. It's a moot point, in any case. Fabrice is—how do you say?—*dédaigneux*? Ah, 'disdainful' of family history. The only reason I had access to the photos was because they were in a package of effects left with my grandfather."

"And Fabrice Clement still lives at the château? Madame Martin made it sound like the place was a ruin."

"It's pretty close to that. Fabrice was once a well-known novelist. He retreated there decades ago, supposedly to write his next great novel. I believe he's still working on it."

"Have you seen the carousel?"

He shook his head. “It was said to be destroyed in a fire. Would you like another drink? Or perhaps you are hungry?”

“No, thank you. The carousel burned down?”

“It was powered by a steam engine, which used a type of kerosene. If the pressure wasn’t carefully monitored . . .”

“It would blow up.” She sat back in her chair with a sigh.

“You look disappointed.”

“I am, of course.”

“There are a couple of Bayol carousels here in Paris. Have you seen them?”

“Not yet.”

“You must. After all, that is why you are here, no? To photograph the famous carousels of Paris?” He gestured to the waiter for the check. “Come, I will show you.”

“Why would you want to do that?”

“Show a lovely American tourist the highlights of Paris? Why would I not?”

The waiter brought the check, and Cady earned a disdainful—*dédaigneux*, she recalled—glance from the waiter when she dove for it.

“The drinks are on me,” she said to Jean-Paul. “You’re a business expense.”

CHAPTER ELEVEN

PRESENT DAY
PARIS

Cady

Jean-Paul was a charming—and knowledgeable—tour guide. He had insisted on carrying her heavy camera bag as he led her into the Métro, along the avenues, and through the woods that housed the carousel. As they strolled through the Bois de Vincennes, he explained that the vast green space was a former hunting preserve. At the turn of the twentieth century an experimental tropical garden had been established at the far eastern end of the park, where rubber trees, coffee trees, banana trees, and other tropical plants were grown and studied.

"And during the First World War, the Dutch spy Mata Hari was imprisoned here in the fortress of Vincennes before being executed by firing squad. According to legend, she blew a kiss at the firing squad."

"That's some weighty history for a children's carousel."

Jean-Paul smiled. "With history comes drama, and tragedy."

After so many days of navigating the city by herself, it was fun to explore with a handsome, courteous escort. Still, Cady couldn't figure out what Jean-Paul was doing here, much less what he wanted from her. Was he after Gus? Could the rabbit be valuable after all?

Or was she just being paranoid? Cady was painfully aware she often perceived threats where there were none, while—in the next moment—trusting the wrong people. Maxine had called it her "curse."

"I don't know much about history," Cady said. "Even the World Wars. My education was sort of . . . unorthodox, I guess you could say. Was your family involved in the war?"

"Of course. Many of my uncles and cousins fought. The son of Yves Clement, Marc-Antoine, went to combat in World War I at the age of sixteen; and his son, Fabrice, was only fifteen in World War II."

"He fought at the age of fifteen?"

"Not as a soldier. But he was involved. I've never been clear in exactly what capacity; as I've said, he's a recluse and doesn't like to talk about himself. And here we are: the Bayol carousel."

The carousel was very simple, especially compared to some of the others Cady had been photographing, with their wedding cake frothiness, gold-gilt curlicues, and double-decker platforms.

But what it lacked in extravagance it made up in charm. The sweet faces of the child-sized figures—cats, dogs, rabbits, pigs, and horses—tilted up toward the audience expectantly, not smiling but still inviting. The tails and manes were intricately sculpted from wood, not made of real animal hair as in some carousels. Graceful, curved necks tapered to toy-like heads with bright, open eyes and upright ears.

Studying the precious faces of these genuine Bayol-carved animals, and knowing Gus as well as she did, Cady realized that the appraiser at the antiques show, and then Madame Martin, had been correct: Gus-the-rabbit had not been crafted by the same hand.

Cady fought self-consciousness as she unpacked her cameras and tripods, speaking with the young woman running the merry-go-round, and approaching parents for permission to take photographs of their children. Though these were all the usual things she did when shooting a locale, it felt different under Jean-Paul's watchful gaze. She walked around the apparatus several times, searching for the best light, the most interesting angles.

Finally, picking up her Leica camera, Cady focused on framing the world through the lens—and felt herself relax. She lost track of time, then was startled by a loud, delighted squeal.

She looked up to see a little girl hooting in victory after having speared a ring.

"We don't see that very often in the States," Cady said to Jean-Paul.

"You mean the rings? Catching the ring is the best part of riding. I was very good at it."

"It's probably an insurance issue. Kids leaning out could fall off and get hurt."

Jean-Paul gave a subtle shrug. "Falling off and getting hurt is part of childhood."

"Tell that to the insurance companies. Not to mention the parents of the kid with the broken arm. There are a few around, still—there's a Looff carousel in Santa Cruz with the original ring machine."

"That's near you, in California?"

She nodded. "Our local merry-go-rounds inspired me to start photographing carousels in the first place." She thought back to the carousel at Tilden Park, in Berkeley; Cady had returned to it again and again over the years, trying to capture its elusive magic. "There's a quote about human nature being revealed in the way children on a carousel wave at their parents as they go past, every time, even though they're just going round and round—and the parents always wave back."

"Of course they wave; they are children."

"Yes, but they do it every time, and then the parents do it back. Every time."

"What else would the parents do?"

Cady gave a humorless laugh. "I think it's a comment on faith, or the ridiculousness of the relationship, or . . . something."

"I suppose the children need to check in with their family and know that they'll always be there, even if they seem to disappear momentarily."

"I'm guessing you had the kind of parents who took you to carousels."

"Didn't you?"

Cady tried for that Parisian non-response shrug at which Jean-Paul excelled. She doubted she'd pulled it off, but he didn't ask again. Instead, his eyes settled on her, searching.

"Do you ever ride?" he asked after a moment.

"Pardon?"

"You photograph the carousels, but do you ever go for a ride yourself?"

She laughed, again feeling self-conscious. She hadn't actually climbed aboard a carousel since the Tilden Park merry-go-round, when she was a kid, still cute and adoptable.

Still hoping for a family.

CHAPTER TWELVE

1993
BERKELEY, CALIFORNIA

Cady, Age 5

The forest was no place for a city girl.

Cady's world was made up of gray concrete walls, rough to the touch; sidewalks smelling faintly of urine and uncollected garbage; alleys promising escape routes; chain-link fences topped with barbed wire to keep her in—or out.

Dread vied with excitement as she gazed out the bus window at the strange, alienating landscape of tall trees and thick underbrush. The social workers had described the redwood groves as beautiful, but to Cady they inspired a vague, unnamed terror. Surely the twisty road snaking its way through the mountains would eventually deliver the busload of children to a dark forest that sheltered the stuff of nightmares: bears and mountain lions, the bogeyman or Bigfoot.

The gruesome possibility that no one would want her.

But she wouldn't—*couldn't*—let herself think about that.

A mean boy sitting across the aisle made a face, hoping to pick a fight, but Cady looked away, refusing to engage. The rules were very clear, the stakes unimaginably high: No one wanted a bad girl.

She smoothed the name tag sticker—C-A-D-Y, with a daisy drawn next to it—on the chest of her favorite orange T-shirt, shut her eyes, and sang to herself: *The ants go marching one by one. . . .*

Cady's eyes flew open at a sudden squawk of air brakes as the bus pulled to a stop. Ms. Ulmer stood at the head of the aisle and repeated the instructions she had already drilled into the fidgety children: Do *not* leave the area, do *not* go into the woods, no pushing, no shoving, no bad words. Don't be shy. Talk to the grown-ups. Remember to let your inner light shine. Be your authentic self. Be good.

But what if her "authentic self" wasn't good? Cady didn't mean to be bad, but she often was. People told her so.

Tinny, raucous music greeted the twenty or so children as they climbed down, one by one, and went to line up beside the bus, where Ms. Ulmer directed them. Heat radiated from the parking lot blacktop, where every space was taken up by big Suburbans and sleek compacts, shiny and new-looking. A light breeze carried the scent of the park's golden grasses and eucalyptus trees, so much nicer than the cloying pine-scented air freshener in the social worker's office bathroom.

Cady took the deepest breath she could, hoping to make the aroma a part of her, replacing the institutional smell that seemed to cling to everything. The forest might be scary, but it sure smelled good.

And in front of them: the Tilden Park carousel.

It was colorful and raucous, whirling round and round, the music blaring, light and color seeming to reach out for her. If she stared, everything seemed a blur: the painted murals on top, the Baroque mirrors, the menagerie of animals, the children's laughing faces. Cady spied a rooster, a frog, a bunch of brightly painted horses, and also some kind of sea creature. Some figures went up and down, others remained with their hooves planted firmly on the circling platform. A round seat shaped like a giant teacup spun around. A sleigh with room for four tipped back and forth but never quite pitched over. She spotted a goat, and a zebra, and a pig. Her mind raced. Which did she like best? Could she ride any one she chose?

Cady fixated on the sea monster. She would have to beat out the others if she wanted to claim it. She was a fast runner. She could do it.

But then she glanced over at the long tables and booths set with food and displays for the fair.

Milling about the offerings were the smiley, eager grown-ups. Cady's heart flipped, it felt hard to breathe, and she had a sudden need to pee.

"Prospective parents" is how Ms. Ulmer and the other social workers referred to the grown-ups. Every child alighting from the bus, every orphan, every discarded girl and boy—even a bad one—dreamed of finding a match. Of being chosen.

Of becoming part of a family.

Prospective parents. For weeks, Cady had rolled the phrase around in her mind, whispering it in bed at night like a prayer. She liked the feel of the words on her tongue: *mother, father, mommy, daddy, mom, dad* . . . She imagined walking into school and telling the teacher she had a note from her *parents.* Every day after school she would enter the same house and sit down to dinner with her *mother* and *father.* They would be in the audience on Back-to-School Night; Cady would use her best manners when she introduced them to her teacher: "Ms. Mendez, this is my mom and dad."

Mom and *Dad.*

It made her too nervous to look at the grown-ups. Instead, Cady joined the jostling throng of kids waiting for their turn to ride the merry-go-round. It slowed, then finally stopped, and the riders got off. Cady shoved her way to the front of the crowd and raced to claim the sea monster. The mean boy from the bus noticed her interest and yelled, "I call dibs!" But Cady was determined. The sea monster was *hers*. She got there first and quickly threw one leg over the saddle, grasping the center pole and hoisting herself up, flashing a triumphant grin at the mean boy.

A man in a stained T-shirt came by and buckled a leather strap—a humiliating leash—around her waist. "No belt, no ride," he responded to her protest before moving on to the next child.

It took an eternity for the carousel to start up again, lurching forward with a jerk. Old-fashioned organ music filled the air, the world just beyond the carousel whirled by faster and faster, and Cady sat up as straight as she could. The faces in the crowd became a blur as the carousel reached full speed.

Cady was a princess on her steed, a mermaid astride her sea creature. The tinny music was her theme song. She was beautiful and free, going up and down, round and round, the eyes of the prospective parents on her.

One day she would have someone to wave at as she flew by on the carousel.

Cady felt a thrill, so deep, so fundamental, so visceral that years later she would still recall the sensation, would liken it to the breathless excitement and furtive anticipation of falling, headlong and desperate, in love.

Round and round she went.

Round and round.

CHAPTER THIRTEEN

PRESENT DAY
PARIS

Cady

I . . . No," Cady stammered, starting to pack up her cameras. "I photograph carousels; I don't ride them."

"Why not?" Jean-Paul asked as he came over to help.

"Thanks," Cady said, putting her hand out to stop him. "But I have a very particular way of doing it."

He nodded and backed off, his gaze still on her. She busied herself with her packing—each camera had its own case, its own place within the larger bag—and to her relief he let the subject go.

Afterward, they headed back across the city. The Jardin du Ranelagh's carousel was another simple design, this time with diminutive horses on a green structure that enthralled small children.

Cady once again went through her rituals: unpacking her cameras, framing her shots, and finally snapping a series of photos with one apparatus after another.

"It's a lot of work," Jean-Paul said when, at long last, Cady packed up her equipment again.

"It is. But I like it. It keeps me grounded."

"Do you see things differently through the lens?"

"I do," she said, wondering if he was implying that she kept herself distant from the world by standing apart, breaking it down into scenes and angles, and recording life for the future. It was a common theme among those who didn't understand the art of photography, who had never been swept away by the shifting images of the world as seen through different frames and lenses.

Normally she would have let the subject drop, but his eyes were still on her, and for some reason she felt compelled to explain.

"It's hard to describe, but when I look through the lens, it's like I can be a different person. I can enter a world that is calm, and knowable, and sort of . . . magical, but safe at the same time. Even though I'm seeing the same thing others do with the naked eye, it makes more sense, somehow. There's no noise, no unnamed desires, no strife. It's just . . . beautiful."

"Such beauty came across in the photographs you showed me of your rabbit."

"Oh, I wish!" She scoffed. "My goal, always, is to convey those feelings by way of my photographs, but I rarely succeed. Why are you looking at me like that?"

He smiled. "I enjoy hearing you talk about your work. There's passion in your words; your eyes flash."

Cady could feel herself blushing, and was glad for the distraction when a bell rang loudly and children started to laugh and run.

"What's going on?" she asked.

"The marionette show will start in a few minutes."

"A *marionette* show?"

"You are surprised?"

"I am. Paris is so cosmopolitan on the one hand, but so old-fashioned on the other."

"Perhaps that is why everyone falls in love when they are here," said Jean-Paul.

Cady slung her heavy bag over her shoulder, declining Jean-Paul's offer to carry it for her.

"This *marionettiste* is very good," he said. "If you have never seen the show, we really must go to it. But this time I insist upon paying."

"But—"

He held up his hand to stop her protest. "Not only is it my duty as a *Parisien*, but it is also very, very inexpensive."

CHAPTER FOURTEEN

1944
PARIS

Fabrice Clement

When Fabrice was a young child, he liked nothing more than to watch his father, Marc-Antoine, carve. His heart would fill with admiration and wonder, and a fervent desire to be just like him: to bring forth a figure where once there was none.

Now, Fabrice felt frustration. Embarrassment. Even disdain.

His father's chisel never stopped as he whittled a small piece of butternut wood to repair the chunk blown out of the crown of the four-foot-tall Madonna on the workbench in front of him. Once that was complete, he would turn to re-creating her missing left hand.

"After all, how can she pray for us with only one hand?" Marc-Antoine had said when she first arrived in the shop. "We need all the help she can give us."

The Madonna had been an innocent bystander,

caught in a skirmish between Nazi soldiers and a small Résistance cell outside of Dijon. Somehow a local farmer knew to bring her here for help, to Marc-Antoine Clement's workshop in the *cinquieme arrondissement*. An aroma of onions lingered about her; she was covered in the bulbs while being smuggled to Paris in the back of a delivery truck. Fabrice's mother, Germaine, was busy laundering and patching the Madonna's singed royal blue velvet robes; though the sculpture had carved wooden skirts, she seemed almost naked without her luxurious textiles.

Fabrice watched his father's skilled hands hover above the gap in the crown, hitting rhythmically in a *tink tink tink,* bits of wood flying like tiny paper airplanes with each tap.

"Papa, I want to contribute to the war effort," said Fabrice.

"You are too young. We've gone over this."

"But *you* were only sixteen when you left your family to join the fight in the First World War," Fabrice said, struggling against the humiliating sensation of tears burning the backs of his eyes. "That's only a year older than I am now."

"An important year; a *crucial* year. I was a young man; you are still a boy," said Marc-Antoine. He picked up a piece of fine-grit sandpaper, carefully ran it along the rough-hewn edge he had just chiseled, lifted the piece into the light, and blew. Wood dust flew through a shaft of orangey late-afternoon light, the particles looking like specks of gold, a miniature fireworks display like those they used to set off over the Champs-Élysées on Bastille Day, before the Nazis marched into Paris and the bans went into effect. Fabrice had read that the Free French Forces still marched every Bastille Day in London; the image of brave, exiled soldiers celebrating the beloved national holiday abroad filled his chest with a disorienting mix of pride and rage.

"God forbid, if this war goes on for another year," Marc-Antoine continued, "we can talk about it then."

"I can't *wait* another year," said Fabrice, mimicking what his friend Claude had said to him earlier when talking Fabrice into attending the clandestine meeting. "And neither can France."

"Have you forgotten that I was shot for my trouble? *Two* years," Marc-Antoine said, holding up two calloused fingers. Small nicks and splinters covered his fingers: the by-product of his craft. "For two years of my life I languished in a German hospital. No one expected me to survive. *No one.* By the time I was released, my parents were dead, my family home in shambles."

Fabrice used to crawl into his father's lap and beg to be shown the scar, fascinated by the puckered skin, shiny and raised in some parts, sunken in others, a stark red against the white skin of his chest. How could a German bullet find your gut, and yet not leave you dead? Fabrice would plead to be told the story, over and over: the confusing cacaphony of the battlefield, the heroic actions of the medics, waking up days later in a German hospital . . .

Now, though, Fabrice wondered about the nice things his father had to say about his time in the German medical center: the pretty nurses, the caring doctors, the officer who declared his survival a miracle.

The Germans were the invaders; there was no room for kind thoughts.

"I'm not a child," Fabrice insisted. "I can contribute. It doesn't have to be combat. There are other ways—"

"What your country needs from you now is your carpentry skills," his father reiterated. "Not your blood. Besides, this family does enough for the war effort right here in this atelier. Now, use that rottenstone to polish the filler on the John the Baptist from Tarcenay. I finally finished him last night."

Marc-Antoine's workshop had become a secret repository of sculpted artworks from rural churches and museums, châteaux and fine homes. Fabrice found the work insignificant, too *small* compared to the crucial struggles playing out on the streets of Paris outside these walls; still, he acknowledged that his father was taking a risk. Though these rustic saints and cupids, angels and saviors were nothing akin to the valuable artworks the Nazis had looted from the Louvre, they had an intrinsic cultural value reflected in their artistry and tradition.

Simply helping to maintain the histories of small-town chapels could be sufficient grounds for a death warrant, depending on the mood and character of the soldier who stumbled across their stash, or the dictates of the officer in charge, or the judgment of the dreaded Gestapo.

Fabrice barely remembered France's humiliating defeat after the six-week blitzkrieg in 1940. He had been only eleven at the time, and was convinced along with everyone else that France's fighting forces were up to the job. But the Nazis were a different breed.

In World War I, the Great War, the bloodshed had been based on a struggle over territory. This time the Nazis seemed to want to appropriate the very cultural life of France, to win Paris over by flattery as much as through repression. German officers mingled with Parisians in cafés and cabarets and nightclubs, acquired cases of fine wine and great art, and wolfed down foie gras and champagne. Their German-language newspapers glorified French singers, playwrights, and actors. The occupying forces even took it upon themselves to resuscitate the film industry in an attempt to show that French cultural life was flourishing under occupation. The Nazis declared that France was destined to become the holiday resort of the *Herrenvolk*, the master race.

Many Parisians found themselves collaborating out of sheer necessity. Fabrice had never blamed them; with Nazis living amongst them, and the threat of starvation looming, who could cast stones? Still, Fabrice felt compelled to act.

"Instead of volunteering to get yourself shot, you should thank the heavens we are in Paris instead of in my hometown. As hard as things are here, they are worse in Provence under the Vichy government." Marc-Antoine put down his tools and turned toward his son. His tone softened. "Don't you understand, my boy? Listen to me: Just getting enough to eat, merely *surviving,* is an act of rebellion."

The Madonna gazed back at Fabrice, her beatific expression never changing. Her mien of placid acceptance angered Fabrice.

The statues his parents spent so many hours on were relics of another time, a different way of life. Fabrice disdained his father's business: making cabinets by day, saving saints at night.

Fabrice's passion was for words: finding graceful ways to string them together himself, and reading the prose and poetry, literature and sonnets, written by others. Surely words were what would lead France into the modern world, not an ancient craft like carving.

Words were what transported Fabrice.

And those words had brought him to Paulette.

CHAPTER FIFTEEN

PRESENT DAY
PARIS

Cady

Despite her misgivings that Jean-Paul might want something from her, he simply bade Cady a polite "good evening" when they arrived at her Métro stop, thanked her for the lovely day, and kissed her on each cheek.

His rapid departure felt rather anticlimactic after the day they had spent together—not to mention the many questions that had nagged at her—but Cady was also glad to retreat, alone, to her small apartment, dining in silence on simple falafel takeout at her postage-stamp-sized kitchen table, gazing at the woman in the photo, and wondering who had carved Gus and why.

She spent the next day photographing the Montmartre carousel, situated at the very foot of the steps to the Basilica de Sacré-Coeur. Afterward she meandered up the hill to the cathedral, trying to ignore the way her photography bag dug into her shoulder as she explored the winding cobblestone alleys that had hosted so many well-known artists: Picasso and van Gogh, Degas and Toulouse-Lautrec.

Twice Cady stopped at cafés: first for coffee, then for a Campari. She liked to think it was proof that she was falling into the rhythm of the City of Light. When she asked a waiter if he knew of an English-language bookstore, he suggested she try the Abbey.

According to her phone, it was located not far from her apartment. She took the Métro back to the Quartier Latin, walked down Boulevard Saint-Jacques, then took a left onto rue de la Parcheminerie.

Cady spied a Gothic façade, carved arched doors, a Canadian flag waving in the breeze, and several book-crammed carts crowding the sidewalk. Inside was a warren of book-lined paths.

A slightly musty smell hung in the air, reminding Cady of Maxine's Treasures.

Grief, sodden and heavy, weighed upon her chest. If Maxine was looking down upon her now, Cady knew, she would be proud. But that didn't keep Cady from wishing, desperately, viscerally, hopelessly, that things were different. That she and Maxine were huddled over the counter in the shop, debating names for the baby, looking forward to adding to their unorthodox little family unit.

"*Bonjour*, may I help you?" asked a young man behind the register, in unaccented English.

He was thin and wore wire-rimmed glasses and a cardigan, as though sent from central casting to work in a bookstore.

"Have you ever heard of the novelist Fabrice Clement?" Cady asked.

"Oh, sure. Clement was one of the new wave of French authors that emerged after the Second World War. This area was a hotbed of creativity and radical thinking back then. Sartre and de Beauvoir, Albert Camus, they all hung out in cafés and jazz clubs in this neighborhood. Americans, too: James Baldwin and Richard Wright."

"Would you have any of Clement's novels? Preferably in English?"

"Let's see . . . we should have a copy of *Le Château* around here somewhere. That was Clement's biggest success by far, though he went on to write several other novels." He led the way along one narrow hall of books and down a steep staircase. Finally he stooped, scanned a couple of shelves, sneezed, and said, "Aha. Here it is."

He handed her a slightly battered copy of a book with a red-and-black dust jacket, titled *The Château*. A photo of the author on the rear cover showed a brooding, hawk-eyed man, good-looking but severe.

"It's a classic from that time," the bookseller said as he straightened and headed back to the register.

"Is he still writing?"

"I doubt he's still alive, to be honest. I haven't heard anything about him for years. People still read the book in university, sometimes, in courses about the Nouveau Roman or anti-novel movement."

"Oh." Cady had no idea what he was referring to.

"What I always thought was interesting about it is that it's a roman à clef."

"What does that mean?"

The young man looked surprised.

"Sorry," Cady said, trying to ignore her flaming cheeks. "I wasn't what you would call a literature person in school." She hadn't been *any* sort of person in school.

He smiled. "No worries. Really, I was just surprised because most people *pretend* to know stuff like that. Especially in here. A roman à clef is a book based on reality, and real people, but with all the names changed."

"To protect the innocent?"

"And to avoid scandal, or to maintain a certain plausible deniability, I suppose. But it's believed to have been written about his family, the family Clement."

"Great, that's perfect. I'm doing some research on Château Clement."

"Then you must have this! I must warn you, though: the Nouveaux Romans are notoriously—

and purposely—difficult to read, sort of like James Joyce's *Ulysses*."

"Why would an author write a book that's intentionally hard to read?"

"It was an experimental thing, to wake people up to romanticism and our implied assumptions about narrative structure. Or so my literature professor at uni told me."

Cady flipped *The Château* open to the first page. Slowly, painstakingly, she made out:

> Picture a château, symbol of power and privilege, lain to ruin by avarice and jealousy. Echoes of longing reverberate along its halls, their vibrations seeping into the grout, the mortar, the very stone of the walls.
>
> Mr. Petra appears, descending the steps in a handsome brocade jacket, holding a hammered copper bowl atop which sits a strap and a shaving blade. Steam rises, an unfurling question mark looming, threatening, over his morning chocolate.

It didn't seem *too* bad.

And whether it was traditional or "Nouveau Roman," Cady would struggle to make out the words, much less the meaning.

CHAPTER SIXTEEN

2001
OAKLAND

Cady, Age 13

One day, after Cady had been working at Maxine's Treasures after school and on weekends for more than a month to pay her back for the things she had stolen, Maxine handed Cady a set of instructions for assembling an old mantel clock.

Dread washed over her. She knew what was coming.

"Read these to me, will you?" Maxine said. "I don't have my glasses."

Cady slung her backpack over her shoulder. "Sorry, I really have to get going. I have a . . . dentist appointment."

"I thought you just told me you wanted to help with this. You said you didn't have anywhere to be."

"Today's Tuesday, right? I just remembered."

Maxine's eyes settled on Cady. They were near black, and so deep yet reflective that Cady sometimes wondered if they were full of sorcery, if Maxine was some sort of witch, sitting here in her enchanted store, making Cady believe life was beautiful and full of possibility when in fact every day was just the same pile of garbage and disappointment and heartbreak. Cady felt tears stinging the backs of her eyes.

Pain and humiliation fed her anger, her dragon surging up to destroy everything in a fiery burst.

She swiped her arm across the table, sending the dismantled clock to the floor with a satisfying crash. The glass face shattered, metal parts skittering along the plank floor and disappearing under a nearby bureau.

"I don't have time to spend with you every day!" Cady shrieked. "You're just a lonely old woman who wants me to do what she wants! You're just like everybody else!"

Cady stormed toward the door. She didn't know what she expected: maybe that Maxine would shout back, tell her to leave and never come back. But a tiny part of her hoped Maxine would race after her, hold her in her arms, smooth her hair and tell her everything was all right, that she was all right.

Instead, nothing but silence followed her. Cady made it to the front door, willing herself not to turn around. Still, she slowed her pace. Surely the old woman wouldn't let her just leave, without saying a word, would she?

Her hand reached out for the brass doorknob. Turned it. Opened the door.

"Cady." Maxine didn't shout or cajole. Her voice was calm, firm but gentle.

Cady halted, her hand still on the doorknob. She did not look back.

"Cady, do you know how to read?"

The tears finally came. "Of course I know how to read, you stupid old *bitch!*"

She slammed the door behind her and ran.

Cady didn't return to Maxine's Treasures the next day, or the day after that.

Three days later, she was called into the office of the group home. Maxine was sitting with the director of the home, Ms. Lee.

"You made a commitment to Ms. Clark," Ms. Lee said to Cady. "She expects you to work at her store tomorrow after school."

"I'm not gonna apologize," Cady insisted.

"Cady—," Ms. Lee began.

But Maxine cut her off. "I won't ask you to apologize, Cady. But you do need to clean up the mess you made, as best you can. First, though, we have an appointment at the library."

"What kind of appointment?" Cady loved the library—the hushed tones, the way she could sit for hours with nobody bothering her. Some of the librarians were intimidating, but others were kind and helped her look things up, or suggested books for her to read. She loved to sit and flip through the pages, looking for pictures.

Neither woman answered her question, but Ms. Lee turned to Cady and, using her I'm-not-fooling-around voice, said: "Go with Ms. Clark, Cady. Understood?"

Cady followed Maxine out to her car.

"What *kind* of appointment?" she repeated.

"We're going to see a literacy tutor."

"A *what?*"

"Is there something wrong with your hearing, too?"

"No."

"Nobody's good at everything, Cady. The only shame is in not asking for help when you need it."

"I don't need any stupid tutor." Cady's words came out as a sullen mumble.

"Well, *I* do," said Maxine.

"No, you don't. You know how to read."

"True, but knowing how to read doesn't qualify me to teach you. So we're going to meet with the tutor, and she's going to teach me to teach you."

Cady stared at her in disbelief. Anger surged, tears threatened, and she felt like throwing up. What was the old lady *talking* about?

Peering over the top of the car, Maxine fixed Cady with a look. "Here's the deal, Cady. I'm every bit as stubborn as you are, and because I'm a lot older I'm a lot more experienced at it. So don't even *try* to out-obstinate me."

Cady gaped at her. No one had ever spoken to her like this.

"We've known each other a couple of months now," Maxine continued, noting Cady's reaction. "Answer one question, and take your time to think about it before you answer. Will you do that for me?"

Cady shrugged.

"Here it is: Do you think I would take the time and energy to try to do you harm?"

When Cady didn't answer, Maxine added: "Or do you think, perhaps, that you can trust me this once? Trust me just this one time, and see if my years of experience might be helpful in making your life better."

Cady avoided her too-knowing eyes.

"You're not stupid, Cady," Maxine said, a weary note in her voice. "I've met lots of stupid people in my life, and you're not one of them. Not by a long shot. You've just had a very tough road. I don't generally like children, but for some reason I like you. You're moody and stubborn and a pain in my patootie, but I like you."

"*Patootie?* Who *says* that?"

Maxine gave a slight smile. Cady's heart soared at the sight of it.

Still, she hesitated, staring at the spot where the blue paint was chipping away from Maxine's junky old Ford sedan. Cady wanted so very badly to believe what the old woman was saying. To trust her. To know that someone understood what was going on, could (and would) give her advice and help her. She wanted it so badly, and yet it scared the hell out of her, took her breath away just to imagine such a thing, because what if she was wrong?

Cady reached a hand out to the chipping paint, digging her nail into it, feeling the sharp poke of a flake in the tender flesh under her fingernail.

"You ruin one more thing of mine, Ms. Cady Anne Drake, and we'll have more than words."

Maxine had come around the car and was standing right behind her.

Cady met Maxine's eyes. She could feel her lower lip tremble. She breathed in Maxine's scent: a mixture of some kind of cooking spices and the oil she used in the shop, paint, and old-lady perfume. Cady had come to associate the aroma with someone who was happy to see her every day, with being in a safe place. For the first time in her life.

Cady couldn't hold back anymore. She hiccupped, tears spilling down her cheeks. Maxine's stout arms wrapped around her, and Cady sobbed into the bodice of her ugly flowered polyester tunic.

After a few moments, Maxine held Cady at

arm's length, wiped the tears from her face with an old-fashioned cotton handkerchief, and said:

"Now that that's taken care of, let's you and I go learn to read."

CHAPTER SEVENTEEN

1900
ANGERS

Maëlle

Monsieur Maréchal, the foreman, barks his orders to the men. At first he had scared Maëlle, but now she appreciates his focused demeanor, his habit of remaining silent when not issuing demands or rebukes. Sometimes, over their morning tea, they speak of the smell of the ocean in the morning, of her hometown by the sea, and of the promise of the new century. He has two grown daughters, and he enjoys arguing with Maëlle about her views on a new future for women.

And she realizes how much she has to learn. Not only concerning the craft, but about the history of carousels. Monsieur Maréchal insists she can never be a gifted carver if she doesn't understand the origin of the art of the carousel.

"The word comes from the Italian *garosello*, which means 'little battle.' It was a training method used in Turkey and the Middle East, brought back to Spain and Italy during the Crusades," he tells her as he watches her sand the fourth coat of gesso on a prancing horse. "They became common in France after a jousting accident killed King Henry II, Catherine de' Medici's husband. Knights started practicing spearing suspended rings with their lances, rather than risking hurting each other."

Monsieur Maréchal pauses to point out a few spots Maëlle has missed; the primer must be absolutely smooth for the paint and gilt to adhere properly.

"Then in 1662, for the birth of the dauphin, Louis XVI held a huge, glorious festival in front of the Tuileries in Paris. Fifteen thousand guests watched as knights competed in extravagant *jeux de bagues*. The location of the grand affair is known today as the Place du Carrousel."

"I hope to visit Paris one day, to see it," Maëlle says, breathless at the thought.

"There is much more than that to see in Paris," says Monsieur Maréchal, with a nod. "And I have no doubt you will get there one day, Maëlle. You are ambitious, and smart. Just"—he glanced toward Léon, who labored over a small pig, the sinuous movements of his biceps clear under his muslin shirt—"remember what you are working toward, and you will achieve your dreams."

One day Monsieur Bayol tells Maëlle she will be working with Léon to learn the art of gilding.

“So, you have worked yourself into the position you wanted, I see,” Léon says, looking down at her with a slight smile on his lips.

Maëlle is so pleased she cannot keep the grin from her face.

“As in most aspects of life, gilding is primarily about proper preparation,” Léon says, his voice suddenly businesslike. “First, the bare wood must be perfectly smooth, the holes and nicks and joints filled and sanded, then cleaned of all dust. Afterward we seal the wood with rabbit-skin glue.”

The amber liquid reeks, but Maëlle does not shrink from the stench. With every stroke she is closer to her dream.

“Afterward, several coats of gesso are applied. The gesso is left in the double boiler—don’t forget to stir it—and is always applied warm.” There is a tiny gas burner in one corner of the studio. “Then the coat of gesso is left to dry overnight. And then there is recarving, which is a painstaking process where all the sculpted details that got lost with layers of gesso are recarved to achieve the desired profile.” He gestures to the dizzying array of chisels, veiners, gouges, planers, and bobs that are laid out on the primary worktable. Part of Maëlle’s job is to keep the precious tools cleaned and oiled and sharpened.

“In a big factory such as this one, if a worker is good at carving, that may be his only job, as it requires a lot of skill. Or, of course, if Monsieur Bayol is available, he likes to add his special flourishes at this point. The outside, or 'romance' side, of the animal is always the most ornately decorated."

Maëlle listens with care, but more than this, she watches Léon. The way his jaw moves as he speaks, the dark whiskers that shadow his cheeks. The way he impatiently pushes his white shirtsleeves up to his elbows, displaying hard, muscular forearms, the bones and sinew undulating as he applies the tools to the wood.

She leans in to catch a whiff of his scent: paint and fresh-sawn wood, but also something entirely his. He smells like the fennel that used to grow wild in the fields outside her hometown.

Maëlle has spent much of her life around men, dreaming with her brother, working with her father, interacting with her neighbors. But this is different. When she was young, Maëlle often wished she were a boy. She longed to run and fish and hunt, to carve and create like her father. She had never cared for cooking and sewing—much less cleaning—like her sisters and mother. But when Maëlle declared she would never marry, her mother told her she would change her tune when she fell in love. Maëlle had disagreed at the time, but now she wonders: Is this that feeling? The elusive sensations never roused by the butcher's son, or the widower farmer, or any of the other boys from town in their striped sweaters who stank of fish guts and brine from their time at sea?

All Maëlle knows is that for the first time in her life she finds it hard to concentrate on learning a new skill. Her heated gaze skips over Léon's hands, his arms . . . his mouth. She loses track of what he is saying, imagining the feel of those lips touching hers.

After the recarving, Léon and Maëlle stand back as Monsieur Bayol comes to inspect the piece. He picks up a sharp veiner—a tool like an ice pick—to add a few details, making *hmmm* sounds as he studies the depth and detail of the carving. Then he nods and moves on.

Léon glances at Maëlle and smiles. In a conspiratorial whisper, he murmurs: "When I first started working here, I would have given my right arm for a nod like that. Monsieur Bayol is a great man, a great artist."

Maëlle understands. It is like striving to please her father, but . . . more so.

"Now, the final coat of gesso must be sanded again."

"Again?"

"There is never enough sanding," he says with a smile, taking her hand in his. He guides her palm to the figure, brushing her fingertips over the swoops and swirls of the horse's mane.

"You feel how smooth it is? Like velvet."

She is speechless; her skin burns where he touches her.

"Now, we apply three or four coats of a soft clay—in this case, we will use yellow bole. Do you see the consistency?"

The bole looks more like a creamy mud than paint. Léon applies it with a long-handled, soft-haired brush that reaches into the deepest indentations of the crevices, the nooks, the cavities.

"Then more sanding and we apply one coat of red bole on the areas of highest relief. A final sanding and only then are we ready for the gold."

They wait until most of the heavy work has finished and the workers are heading home for the day; then Léon tells Maëlle to shut all the windows.

"The gold leaf is tissue-thin, you see? The slightest breeze will blow it. We always cut it on a special cushion."

The precious gilt gleams in the late afternoon light, wafting in air currents no one else feels.

"The glue, called size, is made of water and melted gelatin. It is applied with this special brush, made of goat hair." Léon shows her the flat, broad brush, wrapped with a copper ferrule, and sets the horse on an incline to keep the glue from puddling. "We work in small sections so the size doesn't dry."

He places the loose leaf on the cushion and cuts it into sections with a sharp knife.

"Never, ever, touch the gold. The slightest oil from your fingers will mar it. To lift it, use the gilder's tip, like this." He shows her the "tip," a short-handled brush made of fine, long strands of sable. "But you can run the hairs along your cheek for a tiny bit of adhesion. You see?"

He lifts the soft bristles to her face, runs them along the apple of her cheek. It feels like he is rubbing a newborn kitten along her skin. The breath leaves her body in a *whoosh.*

"Feel how soft?"

Maëlle can only nod.

The gold leaf is so delicate that it clings to the brush, and Léon brings the gilt to the carved surface, glistening with glue.

"You must be very precise; overlapped areas will not burnish the same as a single layer, and we must not waste the precious metal. Afterward, we use a small dry mop, which has a soft, domed tip, made of squirrel hair. The round shape reaches the deepest profiles. Tamp the leaf down on the surface to be sure the metal leaf adheres fully. The goal is for it never to 'sink' into the glue, but for the metal to sit on top so it can gleam properly."

"What of the spots you've missed?"

"For touch-ups, we use a pointed gilder's brush. And now, this will be your job: to burnish the gold to a high sheen with an agate burnisher."

He hands her a polished rock with a metal

handle and leads her to an already complete figure of a cow with small areas of gold gilding on its harness and saddle blanket.

She dons a pair of white cotton gloves. Though they are too big for her, and stained from use, they make her feel elegant, like a lady. Léon shows her how to run the smooth, cool stone along the gilt to bring out a high sheen.

"And now," he announces, pulling off his own gloves with a flourish, "*c'est l'heure vert.*"

"It's the 'green hour'?"

"*Exactament*. Time to meet my friends for an absinthe."

Maëlle looks up at him expectantly.

At that moment, Monsieur Maréchal walks in, making his last rounds of the factory for the evening. His sharp eyes flicker back and forth between the two of them; he does not seem pleased to see them standing so close to each other.

"Keep your mind on your work, little girl," Maréchal says. "You must burnish this cow tonight before you are done with your workday. And remember: Gold gilt is delicate, and precious. It can be ruined far too easily."

"*Oui*, *monsieur*," says Maëlle. "I understand."

Maréchal casts a severe look at Léon, who merely smiles and wishes him a good night. Then the foreman takes his hat and jacket from the peg near the door and walks out.

“One last thing to know about gold gilt,” says Léon in a quiet voice, his gaze returning to linger on Maëlle’s face. “It should never be left without its proper ending; only burnishing will bring out its true luster. See you tomorrow, little girl.”

CHAPTER EIGHTEEN

PRESENT DAY
PARIS

Cady

Late in the afternoon on the following day, Cady returned to the Musée Carnavalet carrying a pink box tied with rough twine and sealed with a gold foil sticker from the Pâtisserie des Rêves. She had spent a good fifteen minutes perusing the displays in the gloriously pink, sweet-smelling shop. Each pastry was more beautiful and enticing than the last, but she finally settled on a pastel rainbow of *macarons*, an elegant *fraisier*—a tiny white cake topped with crème brûlée—and a slice of Black Forest cake with shaved dark chocolate and sprinkled with powdered sugar.

"Just a little thank-you for setting up the meeting with Jean-Paul Mirassou," Cady said to Madame Martin. "He was very nice."

"He is single," Madame Martin said knowingly.

Cady's mouth open and closed, guppy-like.

Madame Martin laughed. She held the pink box

to her nose, closed her eyes, and inhaled deeply. Setting it to the side, she patted it as though it were a cherished pet.

"I apologize for being so forward. I am very fond of Jean-Paul. He was engaged to be married, but they broke up on the eve of the wedding. The poor man needs someone to take care of, and I have always thought he would make a very good husband. I have known him since he was a child. He acts very serene, but in reality . . ." She trailed off with a shake of her head.

"Jean-Paul mentioned that the current owner of Château Clement is a novelist," Cady said, to change the subject. "Have you read his work? I bought a translation of *The Château*, but even in English it's a little . . ."

"Difficult to understand?" Madame Martin scoffed. "To say the least. I never cared for that sort of experimental fiction. Give me a good romance any day."

"I was hoping it would give me some insight into the history of the château. Jean-Paul said that around the turn of the twentieth century Yves and his wife commissioned a carousel from the Bayol factory. An entire carousel for just one family. Hard to imagine."

"Today's wealthy families might own a private jet, or an island retreat. Different times, different indulgences."

"True."

"Of course, most of the châteaux owners lost everything over the course of the World Wars. Not only were many buildings damaged and looted, but afterward economic changes and increased taxes meant huge landholdings were no longer profitable. Unless, of course, the owners could produce wine, or turn their homes into hotels or resorts."

"Is that why so many were left to fall into ruin?"

She nodded. "The word *château* means *castle,* though it is applied to everything from a massive medieval stone fortress to a delicately detailed, slightly large house. The government stepped in to salvage some of the more noteworthy or historic châteaux, but can't afford to restore them all, much less maintain them. It is a great shame."

"You said your husband is from Provence. Has he been to Château Clement?"

"Oh no, I don't think so. Not inside, anyway. Apparently, the owner doesn't much like people."

"I just can't figure out why my rabbit, which apparently wasn't carved by the Bayol atelier, would contain a photo of a woman standing in front of a carousel that Bayol *did* make for a private residence."

"Have you considered that perhaps your rabbit was carved at a later time? Perhaps someone tried to copy a Bayol rabbit from the carousel, for the woman he loved—the woman in the photo! You said there was a love note. . . ."

"Now I see why you like romance novels," Cady said with a smile. "You're right—a man could have written the note for his love, but what would explain the lock of hair?"

"Perhaps she gave it to him, and he put it all together in the rabbit as a memento. As an engagement gift, perhaps."

"That is a nice version of events," Cady said, though she wasn't convinced. "How do you suppose it got to the United States?"

"Historical objects often end up going overseas," Madame Martin said. "As I mentioned, the château might have been looted at some point. Many artifacts were sold after the war as well, when France was struggling to get back on her feet. Americans had more money, and tourists love to bring home souvenirs."

Madame Martin's phone rang and she picked it up.

While she waited, Cady studied a large framed map of Paris that hung over a crammed bookcase, pleased that she was quickly able to pick out where she was now, at the Musée Carnavalet in the Marais, and the general location of her apartment in the Latin Quarter, and even the Abbey Bookstore. Having a sense of where she was in relation to the Seine, Cady realized, was a huge help in staying oriented in Paris.

Madame Martin hung up the phone and raised her eyebrows at Cady. "Guess who's here?"

"Who?"

"Jean-Paul," Madame Martin said in a loud whisper, like a schoolgirl.

Cady couldn't help but smile. Just yesterday she had pegged Madame Martin as a stern historian. But then, Cady reminded herself, she had never been a good judge of character.

Jean-Paul strode into the office but stopped in his tracks when he saw Cady. "Cady, *bonjour*, what a lovely surprise."

She stood and they traded kisses; then Jean-Paul greeted Madame Martin, calling her *tante*, or aunt.

"I just came by to thank Madame Martin for introducing us," Cady said.

Jean-Paul's eyes lit on the pink bakery box.

"But I realize now I should have brought you some treats as well," Cady added. "To thank you for escorting me all over Paris yesterday."

"Just a small slice of the city, really," he said, his voice dropping slightly. "And it was my pleasure."

"Or maybe you would prefer American bourbon? I was told they don't have much of it here, so my friend sent a bottle with me."

He smiled. "I do like whiskey, but honestly, no thanks are necessary."

"Jean-Paul, can you imagine?" Madame Martin said. "Cady is reading *Le Château*, by Fabrice Clement. She is hoping to find out more about the carousel they had at Château Clement."

The shift in his mood was subtle, but this time Cady was sure of it: The subject bothered Jean-Paul. He appeared relaxed and easygoing, but something told her there were secrets tucked within that handsome frame. Then again, Cady kept her own cards close to her chest as well. She certainly wasn't going to call anyone else on the carpet for such a sin.

"I believe I am done for the day," announced Madame Martin. "Let's go have *apéro*."

"What's *apéro*?" Cady asked.

"A little drink, and perhaps a snack. I know a lovely little café around the corner."

"Actually, *Tante*, I have dinner plans," began Jean-Paul, checking his watch.

"Nonsense," replied Madame Martin. "You have time for a quick drink."

He ducked his head. "I suppose I do."

As they left the office and passed through the museum lobby, Jean-Paul excused himself to make a phone call.

Cady said to Madame Martin: "You seem to have great influence over Jean-Paul."

"He owes me a favor," she replied.

"Must have been quite the favor."

Jean-Paul joined them, and he and Madame Martin traded glances but said nothing. Cady had been teasing, but realized—too late—that it sounded like she was snooping into something that was clearly none of her business. These two had gone out of their way to help her. That was more than enough.

As they walked toward the rue de Rivoli, Cady noticed an engraved stone on the side of a building and to break the silence, she said: "I've seen several of those around the city. What are they about?"

The plaque read:

GEORGES BAILLY
ETUDIANT EN PHARMACIE
ÂGE DE 24 ANS
EST MORT HEROÏQUEMENT POUR LA FRANCE
LE 25 AOÙT 1944 lA LIBERATION DE PARIS

"Some of the fighters in the Résistance took to the streets in a sort of guerrilla warfare, as the Nazis were starting to lose control," Madame Martin answered. "Many of them were killed in the battle to liberate Paris. Their families put bouquets of flowers where they fell, and left little handwritten signs. After the war, many were given official recognition."

"Poor Georges Bailly," Cady said. "Only twenty-four and going up against Nazis."

"Many of the soldiers were much younger than that," said Jean-Paul. "Just teenagers. And there were children as young as twelve and thirteen working with the Résistance."

"It's a sobering thought, isn't it?" said Cady. She often felt as though she had survived a war as a child, but Parisian children had survived an actual war. More than once.

As soon as they sat down at a table in the café, Madame Martin popped back up, exclaiming: "Oh! I forgot I need to make a phone call. I'll be back."

Cady watched as the woman left the restaurant. With a sense of relief, she switched back to English. "I think you're right; your *tante* is trying to get us together. I just can't imagine why."

The waiter arrived, and they placed their orders. Then Jean-Paul leaned back in his chair and folded his hands over his stomach. He tilted his head, as though assessing her.

"You do not seem typical."

"In what way?"

"You have no guiles."

"I'm sorry?"

"Is that not the right word? When you are without . . . guiles?"

"You mean guileless."

"Yes, that's what I said."

"Are Americans typically full of guile?"

"I'm not speaking of Americans. I am speaking of women. You are not a typical woman."

She let out a bark of laughter. "I didn't realize there *was* such thing as a 'typical' woman."

He frowned, as though confused.

"Jean-Paul, I am very grateful for everything you've done for me. You have gone out of your way to help a stranger, but I really don't need a French treatise on who I am, or who I should be, because I'm a woman."

"I meant no offense, I promise you. In fact, the opposite."

"I get that. I think."

"I meant only that you are . . . delightful."

She laughed again. "Okay, now I *know* you have an ulterior motive. I may be a lot of things, but I have never been accused of being delightful."

Jean-Paul held her gaze for another long moment.

"So," Cady said, clearing her throat. "I've found a few references to a carousel in the book, but it seems to become a metaphor for life. The book was written in the 1950s, so maybe the carousel was still there at that time? When was it destroyed?"

"Sometime during the First World War. I believe the remains of the carousel are still there on the grounds of the château, but the current owner has never allowed anyone to access it. Fabrice Clement is a . . . special sort."

"Your elderly cousin lives in a château right outside of town and you've never gone to visit?"

"Of course I've gone to visit," he replied with a shake of his head. "But he's never allowed me in past the kitchen. It's very complicated."

The waiter brought three tall flutes of champagne, a small bowl of olives, and another of walnuts. He arranged them on the table with paper napkins, then hurried away.

"Fabrice's father, Marc-Antoine, was my great-grandfather Pierre's first cousin," Jean-Paul continued. "Many in the family—including, very loudly, Pierre's son, Gerald, who is my grandfather—believed Marc-Antoine should not have inherited the château."

"Why is that?"

He waved it off. "It's a moot point, as far as I'm concerned—especially since I now stand to inherit the château, via my mother, after all—but it has caused a . . . *problem* within the family."

"A rift?"

"Exactly. Four generations of rift, to be precise."

"That's a lot of rift. But . . . why didn't you tell me before that you were going to inherit the château?"

"It did not seem pertinent. As I said, it's a complicated situation. Do you like the champagne? Try it."

He watched as Cady took a sip; the bubbles tickled her nose, but the wine was dry and crisp with subtle hints of apple and apricot, unlike any sparkling wine she had ever tasted. It had nothing in common with the cheap, sweet bubbly she'd served at her own wedding.

"Good?" he asked.

"Very. Thank you. But back to your family: You aren't involved in this rift?"

"I think it's ridiculous to fight over rumors and accusations based on something that may or may not have happened a century ago."

"Sounds like you're the family peacemaker."

Jean-Paul gave her a slight crooked smile. "I suppose I am. Though I'm not particularly effective in that role, I should add."

"Is that why you chose to live in Paris?"

"In part. I came here for university, began working, and never left. I enjoy visiting Saint-Véran, and have considered moving back there one day. As much as I love Paris, I would prefer to raise my children in my native village. With the TGV it's a quick trip."

"The TGV is the high-speed train?"

He nodded.

"I didn't realize you have children."

"I don't, not yet. But I hope to, someday. And you?"

Cady's hand went to her stomach, and it dawned on her that she now went for hours at a time without thinking about the miscarriage. Still . . . she did the math in her head. If she hadn't lost the baby, she would have been in her second trimester. If Maxine hadn't died, the old woman would have knitted ten baby blankets by now, and the two of them would have been gathering castoffs from Maxine's relatives: a top-of-the-line car seat, teensy onesies, a wooden crib. If things had been different, she would have been a mother in a few short months, and Maxine a grandmother.

But if things had been different, Cady never would have come to Paris.

Madame Martin breezed back into the restaurant and sat down with a plop, taking a great gulp of champagne.

"*Je suis désolée*," she excused herself. "So, what are we talking about?"

"Having children," Jean-Paul responded without hesitation.

Madame Martin straightened, her eyes wide, looking at one, then the other. Jean-Paul chuckled.

"Oh, *you,*" Madame Martin said, slapping him playfully on the arm. "You like to tease."

"We are talking about Château Clement and its surrounding drama," Jean-Paul said. "As usual."

"Did Jean-Paul mention to you that he is traveling to the village of Saint-Véran at the end of next week?" Madame Martin asked. "Perhaps you could go with him and see it for yourself."

"Oh, thank you. I'm heading back to California next week," Cady said.

"Paris is a world-class city, but there is more to France than Paris. There are many fascinating regions with their own histories and ways of doing things," Madame Martin continued. "You should see more of the country before you return to the United States. Provence is a different world."

"Oh, I couldn't—," Cady started to say.

"Jean-Paul, tell her she would be welcome."

"You would be welcome," said Jean-Paul dutifully.

"That's very nice of you, but no, thank you."

"You don't trust me," Jean-Paul said. It was more a statement than a question.

"Not really, no," Cady said.

Madame Martin looked taken aback.

"It's not him, it's me," Cady assured her. "I've never been particularly good with people."

Jean-Paul gave Cady a slow, searching smile.

"What?" she demanded.

He responded in English: "You see? Lack of guiles."

CHAPTER NINETEEN

1944
PARIS

Fabrice

Defiance of the invading Germans, and of his own parents, was what first led Fabrice to the meeting of the Résistance. But Paulette was his motivation to return. She was the true reason for the depth of his anti-German fervor, for his willingness to give his life for the Résistance.

Paulette. She was all he could think about.

He would not admit this to anyone, least of all to Paulette.

Fabrice knew he should hate the Nazis for occupying Paris, and he did; he avoided them on the street, refusing to meet their eyes or speak to them unless compelled. In silent protest he carried in his satchel a book, *Le Silence de la Mer—The Silence of the Sea—*by Jean Bruller; in it, an old man and his niece refuse to speak to the German officer occupying their house. At first Fabrice couldn't believe such a story had been published during the war, but later he learned it was put out by one of the underground publishing houses set up to circumvent Vichy and German censorship.

He found the book in the abandoned apartment of their neighbor Monsieur Schreyer, an ancient widower who used to feed stray cats and play his mournful violin late into the night. Monsieur Schreyer had disappeared one day, like so many others Fabrice had grown up with in the neighborhood: the owners of the jewelry shop that was set afire, or the kind woman who used to sneak Fabrice sweets out her window when he was a child. More than twenty students from his school, who simply stopped coming to class.

German officials claimed these people had been relocated to temporary work camps, but as far as anyone knew, none had ever been allowed to so much as pack a bag before they left, much less return to their homes.

It was when Fabrice—feeling like a revolutionary—dared to show the book to his school friend Claude that Claude began to speak to him about working against the Nazi occupation. After a few days, Claude took Fabrice to meet an old man below the Arc de Triomphe, who interviewed him extensively about his background, his feelings for the Germans, his talents.

"You must be very sure, and never mention anything, to *anyone*. Not even in your own family. It is risky," the man told him. "There is a constant danger of betrayal. The cells aren't in contact for fear that if one is brought down, the others will be revealed through torture. We meet in small groups, and we use false names. That way if someone is picked up, they can't betray the rest, even if they tried to."

"I want to help," Fabrice insisted. "I won't tell a soul."

The meeting took place in the apartment of a doctor named Duhamel, on the rue Paul Valéry, off the Avenue Victor Hugo.

"A doctor's office is a useful cover," Claude explained when they approached, "because so many different kinds of people can come in and out without arousing suspicion."

Fabrice learned that the wealthy Dr. Duhamel dutifully cared for wounded German soldiers in public, while secretly treating wounded British and American airmen, then facilitating their escapes across the border to Spain. This required finding extra food for the wounded at a time when some Parisians were forced to eat cats or "bread" made of chestnuts and sawdust. The doctor's office became a hub of information and smuggling; messages with ideas for bombing targets were hidden in stinky cheeses from Vichy, then transferred to those who had a radio and could broadcast the messages to London. Rural cells, called *maquis*, sent information on

German troop movements through notes sewn into farmers' underwear.

In the meeting were a handful of people of different ages and backgrounds: a student, a communist, a trade unionist, a Polish immigrant. And Paulette. Though Fabrice listened intently to the frightening, thrilling things people were saying during the meeting, he couldn't keep his eyes off her.

She was the doctor's secretary. She perched on the edge of a desk, a red beret on her head, her clothes old but neat, a thin belt defining her waist. But it was her blue eyes that captured his attention, flashing as she spoke with fiery conviction, determination radiating from her. Later Fabrice would come to realize that others did not find her anything special, and it amazed him; to Fabrice, Paulette was the embodiment of everything he could ever want, ever aspire to. The turn of her wrist, the flash of pale chest where her blouse gapped, the way she tucked a wayward lock of honey-gold hair behind one ear as though slightly annoyed, but continued undaunted with her impassioned speech.

Fabrice was enthralled.

Paulette was to be his official contact. She was brave, fierce, unafraid. She had been working with the Résistance since the very beginning of the occupation; as a young woman, she could bicycle through the streets without arousing suspicion.

"We of the Résistance come together with different visions, and different aims," said the doctor. "But we are united by love for country, and hatred for an occupying force which seeks to overwhelm and co-opt us. The Allies are working from without; we must help them from within. But bear in mind: You are entering a world of shadows."

While they spoke a plump, middle-aged woman sat by the window, peering outside, as though not listening. At first Fabrice thought she was rude; later he came to realize that someone was assigned to keep watch at the large windows overlooking the street. Usually it was this same woman, who turned out to be the family maid, named Carine. The fine furniture, carpets, and oil paintings in the office—and the fact that they still had a full-time maid—were evidence of the Duhamel family's privilege, and Fabrice's father used to speak of wealth as the font of evil. But at least with this family, Fabrice decided, their privilege was the basis for educated defiance of the enemy.

It was a little like being invited to play a part in a theater performance, Fabrice thought, as talk swirled around him: how to obtain false papers, adopting a false name. Paulette showed them all the back ways out of the building, in case they were found out. Even the doctor and his wife didn't speak to each other about what they were doing, for fear of being captured and tortured for information about each other. Those going undercover had to sever ties with family and friends to achieve *clandestinité*.

It was a shadowland fraught with danger. Fabrice had never felt more alive.

Fabrice was useful to the cause because he was young, and had inherited his mother's blond hair. There were very few young men left in Paris—most were in work camps or exiled with the military—but his papers declared him to be too young for obligatory work service, so Fabrice was able to move more or less freely through the streets.

Also, he had a gift with words.

The war was being fought not only on the battlefields but in the minds and hearts of the citizenry. Information was key.

"The Nazis keep control of the media, the *Pariser Zeitung*," Paulette told him. He tried to concentrate on what she was saying, and not simply the shape of her cupid-bow lips as they moved. "It is published in German with the occasional single-sheet supplement in French summarizing the news. As the only official source of information for the French people and the German army of occupation in northern France, it has its own correspondent in Vichy."

Fabrice was familiar with the paper. The

Pariser Zeitung was vehemently anti-British, anti-communist, and anti-Semitic. In a quiet act of resistance, citizens would go out of their way to use this paper to sop up the oil when they cooked or to line the bottoms of birdcages.

The newspaper flattered the French people and attempted to demonstrate that the two cultures were not only harmonious but complementary. Editorials heaped praise upon the French banking system and the businesses represented at the Leipzig fair and the France Européenne de la Photographie exhibition. Glowing articles raved about Paris, its monuments, museums, cafés, nightlife, gourmet cuisine . . . and the beautiful Parisian women.

"According to the Nazi line," explained a man known to Fabrice only as the Belgian, "Paris is to become the playground for the German overlords; this is the role France is expected to play in the New Order."

"Pigs," said Paulette, pretending to spit.

The Belgian grunted his agreement, then told Fabrice about the resistance efforts in print. An underground newspaper called *Le Médecin Français* encouraged doctors to approve collaborators for *service de travail obligatoire*, while medically disqualifying the others. *La Terre* told farmers how best to smuggle their produce to feed Résistance members, and *Bulletin des chemins de fer* urged railroad workers to sabotage

German trains and other transport. *Libération-Nord* and *Défense de la France*, both begun by student groups, had mass circulations in the tens of thousands.

Fabrice's favorite example was *Unter uns*, a newspaper published in German specifically for the occupiers; it printed stories of humiliating German defeats on the eastern front.

Fabrice started by writing tracts that were churned out on old mimeograph machines. Then a friendly printshop in the Marais allowed them to print their flyers in the middle of the night, running the risk that an astute German might notice the typeface was the same as officially sanctioned documents. They crowded the words together on a single sheet because printing materials—paper, ink, stencils—were scarce and precious, as their sale was prohibited to anyone but the occupiers.

Fabrice began to wear mittens, even out of season, to hide the telltale ink stains on his fingers. Working for hours in the printshop most nights, he barely slept. In the mornings he and Claude would shove thick sheafs of freshly minted pamphlets into the fronts of their jackets, then leave small piles on busy street corners and church steps, secured with a rock so they wouldn't blow away. When possible they might slip them directly into mailboxes, or hand them over to Paulette or other unnamed contacts in the dark.

While he had been warned of the tension of living with the constant fear of exposure and betrayal, Fabrice relished his new role. He made up lie after lie to his parents to explain his whereabouts, and hardly spared a thought for his little sister, Capucine. Eventually he went home less and less, preferring to sleep on a small pallet at the back of the printshop, or on one of the doctor's extra cots.

He was playing a role in a drama, and Paulette was his heroine.

Fabrice had lied about his age to his colleagues in the Résistance, claiming he was almost seventeen, but even so his nom de guerre was Garçon, or "the boy." Paulette's false name was Michelle. At nineteen, she was four years his senior. And those years were frustratingly significant to those around them. Worst of all, to her.

But he dared to believe that they shared . . . something.

Late one night, sitting on the floor in the printshop, shrouded in the darkness and silence of the citywide curfew, Fabrice and Paulette confided their true names to each other.

CHAPTER TWENTY

PRESENT DAY
PARIS

Cady

Cady made herself a simple supper of baguette, ripe pear, and an eye-wateringly stinky cheese called Époisses de Bourgogne that the owner of the *fromagerie* down the block had insisted she try. She poured a glass of garnet red Bordeaux and perched at her diminutive kitchen table, determined to slog through the literary quagmire that was *The Château.*

Everyone said *The Château* was difficult to understand, so at least she wasn't the only one. This time. Cady sometimes wondered if she had missed a critical developmental moment for learning to read, the way people who didn't learn to speak early in their lives never really made up for it.

She understood the meaning of the words once she sounded them out, so a dictionary wasn't helpful; her vocabulary had been honed over the years by *listening,* intently, intensely. That was how she had managed all those years when she couldn't read, but pretended she could.

The first books Cady had read voluntarily were how-to photography books. Her fascination had been sparked when she found a small stash of antique cameras in Maxine's cluttered back room. Noting Cady's interest, Maxine made her a deal: for every book Cady could prove she had read, Maxine would give her one of the cameras. Cady borrowed books from the library and plowed through one after another as best she could, reciting her book reports to Maxine as they puttered around the shop. She learned about the process of photography and studied the principles of the camera obscura, making her own pinhole camera. She pored over the majestic nature photography of Ansel Adams, Jacob Riis's gritty photos of urban life at the turn of the twentieth century, the Depression-era work of Dorothea Lange, as well as the photos Henryk Ross had taken in secret of the Jewish ghetto of Lodz, Poland.

When Cady discovered *audio*books, she thought she had gone to heaven, and eagerly devoured one after another. Short stories, essays, epic novels—it didn't matter. Audiobooks introduced her to worlds she hadn't known existed.

She used to listen while working in the darkroom, finding solace in an otherworldly solitude, an aloneness that felt anything but lonely. Even the sharp scent of the chemicals contributed to a sense of peace, of stillness. Everything was orderly: her pans were laid out in precise fashion, the jars and bottles and cans of supplies on the shelf lined up just so. There, in the dark, it was just Cady, the story she was listening to, and the magic of images appearing where once there was nothing.

Thinking of it now, Cady felt that old familiar itch to develop the photographs she had been taking, to see how the carousel shots were turning out. She always took reference photos with her digital camera, but as she had told Jean-Paul, it wasn't the same.

She blew out a breath and flipped a page. The erratic storyline of *The Château* was not holding her interest. She took another bite of the Époisses on a crusty hunk of baguette and let her mind wander.

Jean-Paul. What was his story?

After their champagne *apéro* earlier in the evening, Cady had bid farewell to Jean-Paul Mirassou and Madame Martin. Jean-Paul was headed to Provence next week, and she was going back to the United States, so it was unlikely they would ever see each other again. Which was totally fine, of course. It was not as though she was interested in a fling—just look what had happened last time.

He was attractive, she admitted to herself—*très*

beau—but what would be the point? Setting aside the fact that Jean-Paul lived in France and Cady lived in California, she was just plain no good at human relationships. Maxine and Olivia were total flukes, crumbs tossed her way by the fates to keep her from snapping one day and throwing herself off the Golden Gate Bridge.

Still, she would always remember Jean-Paul, Cady thought, sipping her wine. A man she had known all of two days. This wasn't like her. Could she blame it on the heightened senses, the strange openness, that came along with travel?

All she knew was that he smelled good. *Really* good. She liked the way his eyes crinkled when he laughed, the way they tilted down slightly at the corners, giving him a sad, romantic air. He had thick wrists and wore an old-fashioned dial watch with a brown leather strap. She thought back on the way his whiskers tickled her cheeks when they greeted each other, the electric feeling that ran along her skin when their hands had brushed together when he passed the bowl of olives at the table.

She should have asked to photograph him.

Still, as attractive and charming as Jean-Paul was, there was something simmering just below the surface that put her on edge. What it was she couldn't imagine, but this she did know: She was broken enough for the both of them. She could be friends with Olivia because Olivia was so healthy and even-keeled. And Maxine had been a rock, unflappable in the face of Cady's many challenges. Nothing could bring Maxine down.

The last thing I need is another broken person in my life, Cady admonished herself as she got up from the table. She wrapped up the leftover cheese and baguette, corked the wine, and took her dishes to the sink.

After washing up, she leaned against the counter and paged through *The Château* some more. She used Post-its to flag things that interested her, such as a few recipes that might be fun to try as well as a couple of references to a carousel.

Now she spied another:

> Round and round on the carousel. Will I
>   ever catch up?
> The apprentice Anon
> Round and round, chasing
> like a fairy tale
> The horses run and run but never arrive
> The carousel carver bows down
> And within the healed wound,
> the figure keeps the secret
> Anon

What in the world was *that* supposed to mean? Was this a reference to the apprentice carver she had been seeking? And what was the secret?

Cady scoured the next few pages, but the story careened off into a confusing mélange of musings about postwar taxes, the revolutionary notes of jazz music, and the generally decadent state of French society.

She had taken to using the mystery note as a bookmark. Gazing at it now, she drummed her fingers on the counter.

Souviens-toi de moi.

According to her plan, Cady was meant to stay in Paris for another week, continuing to photograph carousels and other related spectacles, such as carnivals and fairs, or vintage attractions like yesterday's marionette show. Out of hundreds, or even thousands, of clicks, only a handful of final images would warrant being published in a book, so she needed to be able to show the publisher plenty of options.

But what she really wanted to do was to find out if Gus truly had come from Château Clement in Provence. And if so, why he hadn't been carved by the famous French carver Bayol, and who had hidden the box in his belly, and how had a hundred-year-old carved carousel figure made its way into her hands in California? And who was the woman in the photograph, and who was begging whom to remember . . . whom?

You're obsessing, Drake, she told herself.

It was a stupid idea. Of course it was. But . . . Cady opened her laptop and located Saint-Véran on a map, not far from Avignon. Two rooms were available for rent in private homes in the village, both inexpensive. Giving in to impulse, she booked one, along with a ticket on the TGV from Paris to Avignon, and a rental car to drive from Avignon to Château Clement.

After hitting the last Send button, Cady sat back and blew out a shaky breath. She poured herself another glass of wine, feeling impulsive, reckless.

Round and round on the carousel.

She couldn't stop thinking about a derelict château in the Provençal countryside, inhabited by an elderly, reclusive novelist, hiding the remnants of a lost carousel.

It was probably a recipe for disaster.

But . . . it sounded a little like a fairy tale.

CHAPTER TWENTY-ONE

1900
ANGERS

Maëlle

The factory is in full swing, with half the workers finishing a carousel for the city of Nantes while the other half start on the carousel for Château Clement. Bayol spends many evenings with his designer, poring over concept drawings, developing the sweet barnyard faces for which he is so famous.

Maëlle has learned that carousel designs depend on tricks of perspective to increase the sense of movement and size. For instance, the figures on the outside of the platform are larger in scale than those on the inside, creating a heightened sense of perspective. Often the top section of the carousel turns slowly clockwise while the main mechanism turns counterclockwise, increasing the dizzying sensations of spinning.

The animal figures are the focus, but they are not the only artistic feature. There is also a richly decorated fixed ceiling over the top of the moving carousel ceiling. The movement of the prancing animals, spinning tubs, and tilting gondolas is achieved through gearing under the platform. The mechanism is built by the engineer Charles Detay.

Bayol's *atelier de mécanique* employs joiners, carpenters, and painters in the workshop, but the master calls on the famous landscape painter and professor of Paris's École de Beaux-Arts, Fernand Lutscher, to paint scenery panels and the decorative canvas ceilings that cover the wooden swifts and overhead cranks.

Eventually, Maëlle is allowed to carve some of the interior sides of the animals, the master closely watching her every chip and shave as she sculpts. She primes and gessoes and sands until her fingers are raw. Maëlle yearns to fully carve her own figure, but when she speaks up she is chastised.

"Do you know how long Léon Morice has worked for the master?" responds Monsieur Maréchal. "And still he does not carve his own figures. Monsieur Bayol is the artist here; he is the one who gains the commissions. Do you understand? An apprentice might work here for ten *years* before carving his own animal. You are too ambitious by far, little girl."

She hates it when he calls her "little girl." Her cheeks burn.

Lifting her eyes, she finds Léon's gaze on her from across the studio.

• • •

The workers in Bayol's atelier labor for many months over the Clement carousel. There are twenty-four animals—four pigs, four horses, four rabbits, four chickens, four cats, four dogs—plus a gondola rocked by gearing under the floor and two spinning tubs. But these pieces are just the beginning: There is also the construction of the mechanism, the engineering of the bellows, the installation of the steam engine, and the building and decorating of the salon room that will house it all. It is forty feet wide with sixteen-foot-high walls, all of which are decorated and covered in gilt-framed mirrors and exquisite murals painted by artists brought in from Paris. Monsieur Bayol sent plans to workers at Château Clement to prepare the foundation, but the true magic must wait until the carousel arrives.

The salon itself will not be fully assembled until arrival, and any problems will be worked out on-site. But the carousel must be tested in the factory before it is shipped across the country.

Madame Bayol has prepared a special lunch for the trial day.

"If all goes well, it will be a celebration," she says, a worried look in her eyes. "If not, we will need the extra sustenance to keep our spirits up. My husband does not deal well with failure."

Nine men have been chosen to put the carousel together. That is the greatest number of workers that Bayol can spare from the factory; they will accompany the apparatus on its journey by train. After arriving at Château Clement, they must be able to assemble all the pieces, including the engine and the gears, over the course of two or three weeks, a month at most.

Maëlle watches their progress as she works on her carving, priming, and painting. She has excelled at all of these crafts over the last several months, and is now allowed to recarve some of the inside halves of the horses destined for the next carousel—this one for the city of Nîmes.

Still, Maëlle is jealous that she will not be accompanying the Clement carousel to its final home. To travel by train across all of France, through Paris, sounds like the most exciting adventure she can imagine. Besides, there is Léon.

Léon will be going with the carousel. He will be gone for weeks, perhaps a month. She is bereft at the thought.

She looks forward to seeing him every day, to interacting with him. What will work be without him? She is already finding the tasks rote, sometimes even boring.

"You are too anxious. You want things to move too quickly," says Monsieur Maréchal. "Apprentices work with the master for years, not months, before they work on their own."

"But I am a better carver than half the

apprentices here," Maëlle declares. "And yet I am still not called an apprentice. Simply an 'assistant.' It isn't fair."

Monsieur Maréchal smiles. Though his manner is often gruff, his soft brown eyes are kind. "I admire your ambition, Maëlle. Truly. It is a rare thing in a woman, and I have no doubt that you will be well known one day."

"I have no desire to be well known," Maëlle replies. "Simply to carve."

"Your painting skills are very fine as well," he says.

"I don't mind painting," she says, drawing herself up to her full height and lifting her chin. "But I am a *carver.* It is a part of me, as surely as my hair is brown."

Maëlle has written to her brother, Erwann, every week since she arrived, telling him of her progress. He assures her that his poem for her, "The Aspiring Apprentice of Angers," was prescient, that one day she will surely sculpt her own creations. She carries the letter in her pocket, folded up tight, and rubs it like a talisman whenever her ambitions are frustrated.

One day Maëlle walks into the factory to find Monsieur Maréchal talking with Monsieur Bayol at his desk, their graying heads bent low.

Maëlle keeps her eyes averted and gets to work, but she feels a thrill go through her. One of the apprentices, a teenager named Philippe Boisson, has begun coughing, a terrible hack reminiscent of her brother's ailment. The other day she saw spots of blood on his handkerchief before he tucked it away.

He is one of the men scheduled to accompany the Clement carousel to Provence.

If Philippe is not able to go, Monsieur Bayol will have no choice but to send Maëlle in his place. She is the only one with the appropriate skills who can be spared from the factory. They have begun their contract with the city of Nîmes; Monsieur Maréchal is needed here, as are all the others.

Maëlle is ashamed to be glad of anyone's misfortune, but she can barely contain her excitement when the master approaches, his mustache twitching.

"Maëlle, I would like you to accompany this *manège* to Avignon. Léon Morice will act as master of the project, as you know." He hesitates, as though searching for the right words. "I don't need to tell you that I will expect you to comport yourself as a lady."

"I understand," Maëlle says, chafing at the implication. Madame Bayol has discovered Maëlle arriving late from an errand, flushed and disheveled, on more than one occasion. She has confided her suspicions to her husband. Maëlle wonders whether anyone asks the young men she works with—Luc or Romain or Philippe—

why they arrive five minutes late to the factory. If a clandestine kiss, or more, means they are bad men, worthy of disdain.

She wonders why being “a lady” seems to be such a heavy burden.

“There are always minor nicks and scrapes that need to be repaired, and the façade of the salon housing the carousel will need extensive gilding and decorative painting once it is set up,” Monsieur Bayol continues. “The family must be kept happy, so whatever Monsieur and Madame Clement ask for, you are to give them. Are you willing to remain as long as necessary to finish any details?”

“Of course, monsieur,” Maëlle replies. “It will be my honor.”

CHAPTER TWENTY-TWO

PRESENT DAY
PROVENCE

Cady

The TGV, or Train à Grande Vitesse, lived up to its name: The trip from Paris to Avignon took only three hours, which, to a Californian like Cady, was stunning. She had traveled across much of France in less time than it would have taken her to drive from San Francisco to Reno, Nevada.

But the true shock was how easy it was to rent a car. All she needed was her California driver's license and a credit card.

Why would a French car rental company allow an American, with no knowledge of the road signs or regulations, to take off in a shiny new Renault? At least the French drove on the same side of the road as the Americans; otherwise she'd have been toast. Once she got the knack of zooming through the roundabouts, however, she started to relax.

As she traversed France, first on the train and

then by car, Cady took note of the changing landscape: Outside Paris, thick forests gave way to grassy fields, where cows and lambs grazed, which in turn yielded to softly rolling hills hosting acres of vineyards, and lavender fields backed by jagged cliffs. As she drew closer to the town of Saint-Véran, olive orchards, ancient sycamore trees, and twisty Italian cypresses lined the country highways.

Luckily Cady had written down the address and directions to the room she was renting in Saint-Véran, because the last few miles her cell phone worked only sporadically. "Another perk of country life," she muttered to herself. "Bad cell reception." But before going into the village, she wanted to drive past Château Clement, which she had located on a map before leaving Paris. She couldn't wait to catch a glimpse of the place that had started to take shape in her imagination.

It was only seven thirty, but as it was early April, the sun had set. There were no streetlamps, but the nearly full moon cast silvery light over the landscape. Tall trees and bushes were inky shapes against the deep purple sky.

Cady pulled off the road and parked along a stone wall where a set of lopsided metal gates hung slightly open. Straight ahead, beyond the gates, a long gravel drive lined with overgrown Italian cypress trees led to the château. The drive was pockmarked with ruts and dotted with patches of healthy-looking weeds. The entrance to Château Clement was not just run-down—it looked abandoned.

She climbed out of the car and stretched.

From what she could make out at this distance, Château Clement was a strange amalgam of styles. The main façade was flat and symmetrical, at least three stories, made of a pale stone. Chalky shutters flanked the many windows. A pair of symmetrical curved staircases led up to a main door on the second level. Massive chimneys and pipes of unknown utility rose high above the red-tiled roof.

Cady hesitated, then stepped inside the gates. Gravel crunched under the heels of her boots. The air was chill and damp, and the wind began to pick up, tugging at her hair. She hardly noticed.

There were no lights visible in the building. What if she just walked right up to the house and knocked on the door? Would that be okay, or too pushy? This was the sort of thing she wasn't good at predicting.

To the right of the château was a pond, encircled with reeds and studded with what looked like statuary and lily pads, just like in a storybook. Several outbuildings formed a large U around what might have been a courtyard. Thick stone walls to the other side of the house appeared to be cruder, perhaps remnants from a different century.

Maybe the château really had been abandoned. Fabrice Clement had been writing in the 1950s, which would make him pretty old by now. Perhaps advanced age or declining health had led him to give up his reclusive ways, and he was being cared for somewhere else.

Crash!

Cady jumped at the sound of glass breaking. She saw a wavering light, like the beam of a flashlight, over by the clutch of outbuildings. She thought she heard a man's voice calling out.

"*Allo?*" she replied in a loud voice. "Is everything all right? Monsieur Clement?"

Spooked, she turned to leave.

But stopped. What if the old man had gone outside to gather firewood or something and tripped in the dark? What if he were lying prone, injured? She couldn't shake the memory of Maxine collapsing in front of her. She hadn't been able to help Maxine, but if Fabrice Clement was a frail, elderly man . . .

Finally, she opened the gates, jumped back into her car, and drove down the driveway, stopping near the outbuildings, where she thought the sound had originated.

"*Allo?*" she called out again, standing next to the open car door in case she needed to make a quick getaway. "Is everything all right?"

Silence. Slowly, Cady walked toward the closest building. It was an old stone structure, with grimy multipaned windows on the door. She tried to peek inside, but the interior was pitch-black. But . . . for a moment she thought she heard music, and in her mind's eye she saw a carousel turning majestically, with a woman dressed in white perched atop an ornate, whimsically carved horse.

She heard a footstep behind her and without thinking whirled around, crouched, and held her fists up, ready to punch or kick someone, as she had been trained to do in the self-defense class she had taken with Olivia.

"Cady? *C'est toi*?"

"*Jean-Paul!* You scared me!" Cady said, straightening.

"You didn't hear my car pull up?" Jean-Paul Mirassou asked.

"I guess I was a little focused. I thought I saw . . . Never mind. What in the world are you doing here?"

"I told you I was coming to see my family in Saint-Véran."

"You said you were coming next week."

"My cousin hurt his ankle, so I moved my trip up."

"But you said you weren't welcome at the château."

"I believe I also said *you* weren't welcome here, either. Didn't you tell me you were going to spend your last week in Paris?"

Cady recalled the advice Jonquilla had given her, so many years ago: *"If you're caught red-handed, deny it. Deny everything."*

"I was, uh, looking for my bed-and-breakfast."

"Uh-huh." He cast a significant glance around the dark courtyard and vacant buildings. "And you thought this was it?"

"I got lost."

Before Jean-Paul could respond, a gravelly voice shouted: "*Stop,* right where you are!"

A man limped toward them, a wooden crutch under one arm, a shotgun under the other.

"*Cousin Fabrice, salut*! *C'est moi, Jean-Paul,*" said Jean-Paul, holding up his hands in surrender.

Cady did the same.

The old man squinted at them, as though having difficulty seeing in the dark.

Cady tried speaking in her best French: "Please pardon me, monsieur. This is my fault. I couldn't tell if anyone was home. I thought I heard the sound of glass breaking and was afraid someone might need help . . . of some kind. . . ."

She trailed off as he lifted the shotgun and trained it in their general direction, holding it surprisingly steady.

"Fabrice, please—," Jean-Paul began again, but Cady cut him off.

"I have whiskey," she blurted. "American bourbon, the good stuff. Jean-Paul tells me you don't like Americans, but would you make an exception for an American with a bottle of good Kentucky whiskey?"

Jean-Paul and Fabrice stared at Cady for a long moment. Something rustled in the bushes, and they heard the soft hooting of an owl. Cady hoped it wasn't a bad omen. She felt a few drops of rain on her head, and the wind picked up.

"What do I have against Americans?" Fabrice asked finally.

"I'm, uh," stammered Cady. "I'm told we can be a little obnoxious. You know, like . . . coming onto private property without an invitation."

"American soldiers liberated this valley from the Nazis," he said and spat into the bushes. "That was in 1945. I was in Paris when the Yanks arrived, marched right down the Champs-Élysées. Suppose I should return the favor by inviting you inside."

"I can't take credit for that," said Cady. "That was before my time."

The old man snorted, but stepped out of the shadows. He no longer had much in common with the romantic young man pictured on the jacket of his book, *The Château*. Cady could make out a set of heavy-lidded hawk eyes, shaggy eyebrows, and thin white hair, long and scraggly. His wool sweater was frayed, and he looked generally disheveled.

"I certainly don't have anything against

whiskey," Fabrice said. "I don't like people, that's all."

"Ah, well, on that we agree. People are awful," said Cady. "Why don't I get the bottle from my car and we'll share a drink?"

There was another long pause as Fabrice studied her. He then turned to Jean-Paul.

"What are *you* doing here?"

"I heard you hurt your ankle. I wanted to see if you needed any help."

"Fell down the damned steps. What about that fancy job of yours in Paris?"

"The staff can carry on without me for a while."

Fabrice snorted. "I don't need your 'help.' What are you trying to do, hurry things up so you can inherit this place? Well, good luck to you. I'll go when I'm damned good and ready, and not one minute before."

Even in the dim light Cady could see a muscle working in Jean-Paul's jaw. "Don't be ridiculous," Jean-Paul said. "I wanted to see you."

"I don't like visitors."

"You just told Cady she could come in."

"She has whiskey. And she's an American. Why should I let you in?"

"Because I'm your cousin?"

"Your great-grandfather was my father's cousin. You're several times removed, or something like that." He waved a hand in annoyance. "Doesn't count once it's that far removed. Blood's too thin."

"According to whom? Seems to me the Clement family tree is pretty intricate and carefully kept. Also," Jean-Paul said, holding his hand out palm up to catch the beginnings of raindrops, "it's starting to rain."

"Why don't we all go inside and warm up over a glass of whiskey?" Cady tried again.

The old man sighed and gave them a barely-there nod, a gesture that reminded Cady of Maxine. He lowered the long barrel of his gun, turned, and limped toward the back of the château.

Cady and Jean-Paul exchanged glances, then followed.

"You were not frightened by the gun?" Jean-Paul murmured.

"I'm from Oakland. I don't scare easy."

He chuckled softly and waited while Cady hurried to her car and retrieved the bourbon from her suitcase. Jean-Paul led the way around the château to a rear entrance, where Fabrice had left a door ajar.

A single shaft of light spilled from a doorway down the hall. They proceeded toward it through an unadorned passageway that had clearly been a servants' entrance. With the hallway's low ceiling and damp stone walls it seemed colder inside than out. Here and there were scattered stacks of newspapers, books, and maps, and piles of discarded tools and dusty rags. *It's been a very long time since servants—or anyone—cleaned this place,* Cady thought.

At the end of the hallway a low doorway opened onto an enormous kitchen. Walls were lined with shiny, deep-ochre tiles, and the huge six-burner stove and honed Carrara marble island made it clear that this kitchen had been remodeled at some point. Open wooden shelves held heavy white crockery: cups and saucers, plates and bowls of varying sizes. Dirty dishes filled the ceramic sink and lay scattered across the long counters, but by and large it was a welcoming space. A huge grandfather clock, missing its hands, ticked loudly. On the opposite wall was a massive stone fireplace, large enough to roast an entire boar on a spit, where a small fire was flickering, the flames casting warmth and light across the room.

"Nice kitchen," Cady said.

Fabrice took a seat at a small wooden table next to the fireplace, grunting as he settled in. "Grab some glasses off that shelf there."

Jean-Paul found three clean juice jars and set them on the table.

Cady took a seat in one of the scarred wooden chairs, only half believing she was actually here, in the kitchen of Château Clement, speaking to the man who had written *Le Château*, who might know the origin of her carved rabbit figure—and perhaps something about the secret box it contained. There were a hundred questions she wanted to ask, but told herself to breathe, to relax. Given his character, Fabrice was likely to clam up if not handled with care. A shot or two of bourbon should help.

She held out the bottle for Fabrice to examine.

He eyed it and nodded, and Cady poured some into each of the three glasses.

"*Salut*," Jean-Paul said.

"*À votre santé*," Cady replied.

" 'Ere's mud in ze eyes," Fabrice said in heavily accented English, drained his glass, and poured himself another shot. Then he switched back to French. "I learned that from the American soldiers."

"I'm impressed," said Cady.

Fabrice waved his glass at Jean-Paul. "I heard you were getting married."

"Plans change," Jean-Paul replied, his voice subdued. He gazed into the amber liquid in his glass.

"I heard she left you at the altar," said Fabrice. "Ran off with your business partner. No surprise there. Typical Parisians."

Cady wondered if she was following their conversation correctly. Her French had improved dramatically since she had arrived in France, though she still stumbled at times. Judging by

Jean-Paul's bleak expression, she had indeed understood, but she pretended she wasn't listening, hoping they would keep talking. Family dynamics—even strained ones—fascinated her.

But she knew enough to gaze into the fire and keep silent.

After a long pause, Jean-Paul said: "For a hermit who hates people, you are remarkably well informed. And all the way from Paris. Very impressive communications system."

Fabrice let out a rusty laugh and downed the rest of his bourbon. Cady's glass was still largely untouched, as was Jean-Paul's. She took a sip. Smooth and smoky and ever so slightly caramel, sliding across her palate. *Thank you, Olivia.*

The three sat silently for several minutes, the only sound the subtle hiss and pop of the fire, and an occasional *plop* as embers tumbled.

"So, you live here all alone?" Cady ventured.

"See anybody else here?" demanded Fabrice.

"Not in this room, I don't. But it seems big enough for a dozen people to live here without seeing one another."

"Huh," was his only reply.

"Monsieur Clement—," she said, trying again.

He cut her off. "*Tutoie-moi*," which meant to call him the informal *tu* rather than *vous*. "My name is Fabrice; I don't like that formal *merde*."

"Okay, thank you, Fabrice," she said. "I wanted

to explain why I was trespassing. I . . . it's sort of a long story, but I have this rabbit—"

"You mean you two aren't together?"

She shook her head. "No."

"What, you met out there, in my courtyard? Both of you, trespassing in the same place, on the same night?"

Cady opened her mouth to reply, but wasn't sure what to say.

Jean-Paul intervened. "We met in Paris. Marie-Claude Martin introduced us. She is a director of a museum in Paris. She's the wife of Loïc Clement. Remember him?"

Fabrice frowned and poured himself more bourbon. He appeared frail and not in the best of health; Cady hoped the whiskey wouldn't do him any harm.

"I can't keep you all straight," he groused. "Too many Clements in this world. Which one told you I hurt my ankle?"

"My mother heard it from the cashier at the village grocery. Told her you've had Andres's son, Johnny, running errands for you."

"He was, but he ripped me off. *C'est un sale type*."

Cady wasn't sure of the precise meaning of that last phrase, but assumed it was not a favorable assessment of young Johnny's character.

"Have you seen the doctor?" Jean-Paul asked.

"It's not broken. I just need to stay off it for a

while, which would be easier if I didn't have to go out in the rain to confront trespassers in the middle of the night."

"Now that, I'll grant you," said Jean-Paul. "Still, it wouldn't hurt to have it looked at. Why don't I call Dr. Miller?"

"This whiskey helps more than anything the doctor could do," Fabrice said as he stood, placing his crutch under his arm. "But for now, I'm tired. See yourselves out."

"Monsieur Clement," Cady said quickly. "I was hoping to ask—"

Fabrice continued shuffling toward an interior door, closing it behind him without so much as a *bonne nuit*.

"Darn it." Deflated, Cady sat back and downed the rest of her bourbon.

Jean-Paul chuckled at her reaction. "I warned you he was a difficult sort. Tell you the truth, this is the longest conversation I've had with him in years. You okay to drive after the drink?"

"Yes. I didn't pour myself much. I don't suppose we could snoop a little before we go . . . ?"

"What is 'snoop'?"

"Um . . . look at things that are none of our business. Like trespassing."

Jean-Paul gave her a look from the corner of his eye.

"I just meant, since you're family, and you're going to inherit . . ."

"Yes, but that is in the future," Jean-Paul said, spreading the embers in the hearth to be sure the fire was safe to leave. "I think we've trespassed enough for one night, don't you?"

"Of course. Sorry. I was a bad seed as a kid."

"Pardon?"

"I mean, I have boundary issues. As in it's hard for me to recognize the proper ones."

"We can try again in a day or two, if you're still in town," he said as he put the iron poker back in its stand. "For now, we should go."

As they made their way back down the narrow stone corridor, Jean-Paul asked, "Do you have a place to stay?"

"Yes, I rented a room in a house on rue des Frênes. I'll be there for a few days."

"That's not far. You know how to get there? I could lead you there."

"No need. Honestly. I have the directions in the car. Go on, I'll be right behind you."

Jean-Paul opened the door, but lingered in the threshold. The rain had turned into a downpour, fat drops falling from a slate gray sky.

"You don't know the area," Jean-Paul pointed out.

"I'm a grown-up, Jean-Paul. I made it all the way to Paris by myself, and now here," she said, feeling suddenly tired, her lids growing heavy. "I'll be fine."

"All right, then, if you're sure." He hesitated

another moment, then said, "I imagine our paths will cross again. This is a very small town, and there's only one *boulangerie*."

"Good night. Thanks for everything."

"I didn't do anything. Thank you for the drink."

He dashed through the rain to his car and drove off.

Cady ran to her rental. Only when she got closer did she realize the tires had been slashed.

All four of them.

CHAPTER TWENTY-THREE

PRESENT DAY
CHÂTEAU CLEMENT

Cady

Now, that's *Oakland,* Cady thought. *Dammit.* Now what?

Jean-Paul's taillights had long since disappeared down the drive. Climbing behind the wheel to escape the rain for a moment, Cady checked her cell phone, but it had spent so much time diligently searching for a signal that the battery had died. She hadn't expected to be driving in France and didn't have a car charger with her.

There wasn't much of a choice. Cady climbed out of her car, ran back through the rain, and banged on the door. Could Fabrice even hear her, wherever he had disappeared to in this huge mansion? The only sound was the far-off noise of a dog barking.

She waited a couple of minutes. No one came.

Finally, remembering they hadn't locked the door, she eased it open. And yelled: "*Fabrice*?"

More barking. At long last, Fabrice yelled back: "*Casse-toi*!"

Cady wasn't sure what that meant, but Fabrice's tone didn't sound like "Come on in and make yourself comfortable."

She glanced at her Renault, sitting sad and deflated like a fallen soufflé. The storm was building, the sheets of rain blown sideways by a howling wind.

"I can't! There's . . ." Cady didn't know how to say "slashed tires" in French. "There's a problem with my car."

At last she heard a clanking and a shuffling, and Fabrice emerged from the kitchen down the hall.

"Please excuse me, Monsieur Clement," she said, still in the doorway.

"I told you to call me Fabrice."

"Fabrice, then." Cold water was dripping from her hair and running down her collar. "May I please come in and use your phone?"

He grunted and started walking down a different hallway as Cady closed the door and followed him. Another pause. The stone corridor was no warmer than outside, but at least there was no wind. Still, she yearned for the warmth of the kitchen.

"I don't have a phone," he said when she caught up with him. He opened a door that led into a sitting room. It wasn't as cozy as the kitchen, but at least it wasn't as chilly as the hallway. It smelled of cigar smoke and must, and contained more piles of newspapers and books, an ancient television, a worn swayback couch, and a plaid recliner.

"Oh . . . really? No phone?" Cady could not remember the last time she had met someone who didn't have a phone. But then again, Fabrice was a recluse. "Could I . . . if I could plug in my cell phone, I could make a call."

"Who are you going to call?"

"A, um . . . a service station?"

"Closed."

"What time do they open?"

"Normally early in the morning."

"Well, that's good. I'll call first thing in the morning."

"Can't. Arthur takes his saint's week off every year for vacation. Won't be open for a week."

"Oh. Then what—maybe . . . I'll call Jean-Paul and ask for his help."

He cast a jaundiced eye over her.

"What's *he* going to do about it at this hour? He's probably sitting down to dinner with his mama and a whole pack of relatives. And before you ask, no stations will be open in Avignon, either. This isn't New York."

"I realize that." Her teeth were chattering, and she crossed her arms over her chest for warmth. "Maybe I could call a taxi, or an Uber, get a ride to where I'm staying, and figure things out in the morning."

"Taxi," he snorted. "Out here?"

Cady felt a flash of annoyance and counted to ten. "I'm not familiar with how things work around here, in your lovely Provençal countryside. What would you suggest I do?"

She heard a dog barking again. Closer this time: not a yap, but a deep *woof.*

Fabrice studied her for a moment, and she felt herself standing tall, failing to breathe, feeling like a little kid at the adoption fair, hoping prospective parents would find her acceptable. What was that intangible quality everyone was looking for, which no one found in Cady? Was it her appearance, her posture, the color of her eyes?

"A trade."

"Excuse me?"

"I need someone for my dog."

"Okay . . ." Cady wasn't sure she had understood him. The French word for "dog" was *chien*, which she occasionally confused with *chêne*, oak tree. Could Fabrice be asking her to trim an oak tree?

"As you can see it's a little hard for me to walk him lately," Fabrice snapped. "If you take him out, you can stay here for the night."

"Oh. You want me to walk your dog? Yes, sure, I can do that," she said. As loath as she was to go back out into the wind and rain, she didn't see that she had any other option. Besides, a man of his age, with an injury no less, shouldn't be walking a dog at all, much less in this weather.

"Are you good with horses?" Fabrice asked.

"You have horses, too?"

He opened a wide oak door. Standing there was the biggest dog Cady had ever seen. Espresso brown with patches of white on her chest and the tips of her paws, she looked like she weighed more than Cady did.

"Her name's Lucy." Fabrice's sharp eyes watched Cady as he handed her the thick leather strap that served as a leash. "She's Great Dane and Irish wolfhound, maybe a little greyhound mixed in there."

"Um, great. Hi there, Lucy."

"Don't let her run. The estate isn't fenced. Usually she sticks around, but sometimes she goes too far afield, chasing rabbits. If she gets into the neighbor's vineyard they'll complain. I don't need the headache. You can go out this way."

Cady took the leash. The dog sniffed at her hand and wagged her tail, but Cady was still on edge.

Next to the door was a coatrack. "You can wear this," Fabrice said, handing her a bright yellow raincoat with a hood, the kind crossing guards wear. "And here are some boots."

She wasn't really a dog person, but to Cady's wary eyes Lucy seemed nice enough. She wasn't snarling or anything. Cady pulled on the rubber boots, which were much too large, and slipped on the old raincoat. *At least it'll keep me warm,* she thought.

"Ready?" Fabrice held the door, which opened onto the rear courtyard.

"Okay, let's go, pup," Cady said as she headed back out into the forbidding night. "*Allons-y*, Lucy."

Seemingly oblivious to the storm, the dog pulled Cady this way and that, stopping and sniffing here and there for no apparent reason, pawing at who knew what. The raincoat and boots protected Cady from a further soaking, but by the time Lucy did her business and Cady managed to maneuver the large canine back to the château, she was beyond exhausted. She grabbed her suitcase from the car and hurried inside.

Fabrice was waiting for them in the sitting room. He greeted Lucy like a long-lost daughter, cooing to her and drying her with a fluffy yellow towel.

Cady shrugged out of the raincoat and pulled off the muddy boots, fascinated by this glimpse at the softer side of Fabrice Clement. She was also hoping he might hand *her* a towel.

Instead, Fabrice pointed to a set of narrow

stairs in the corner. “Go up the servants’ stairs, down the main paneled hallway, down the green stairs, through the room with all the books, then up the other stairs and down the red hallway.”

He handed her a flashlight.

Cady repeated the directions to herself, then asked: “Is the electricity off?”

“No. But no use lighting up the whole house, assuming you could even find the switches. Take any room you want off the red hallway; they’re all about equally dusty. Sheets and towels are in the trunk at the end of the hall. You look cold; you should take a hot bath, warm up, or you’ll catch your death.”

He turned and walked out of the room, Lucy trotting behind him.

Exhausted almost to the point of weepiness, Cady hauled her bag up the narrow stairwell and pulled it down a wide, impressively paneled hallway. The bag’s wheels squeaked softly, and she feared she might be dripping on the inlaid-wood floor.

She shone her flashlight beam this way and that, illuminating a strange mix of elegance and decay: old oil paintings in elaborate gold frames hung on cracked plaster with peeling wallpaper. Intricate wood moldings on doorways and passageways led to half-remodeled rooms with dust-covered paint cans and dropcloths scattered about. Cozy built-in benches sat below boarded-up windows.

One beautifully paneled room was furnished with nothing but a grand piano and a bucket that caught a drip from the ceiling. Folding TV tables mixed with beautiful carved armoires; bare bulbs vied with crystal chandeliers. Piles of books, magazines, and newspapers were everywhere: atop side chairs and tables, and filling corners.

It was like making her way, at night, through a poorly tended museum.

Cady found the green staircase, which consisted of six short steps down into a room crammed with laden bookcases and a hodgepodge of furniture, then went up another set of stairs to a red hallway.

Still soaking wet, she shivered.

She reached out to open the first door.

CHAPTER TWENTY-FOUR

1900
EN ROUTE TO AVIGNON

Maëlle

Other than the trip from her coastal village to Angers, Maëlle has never ridden the train, and she has certainly never crossed all of France. Though she is excited, the jocular teasing of the workmen, released from the civilizing influences of the master and Monsieur Maréchal, puts Maëlle on edge. Her nerves make her queasy; or perhaps it is the persistent rocking of the too-hot train. She did not have this reaction when she first left home. She prays she is not coming down with ague, or whatever has afflicted young Philippe.

Léon reaches out one long leg and nudges her ankle from across the aisle. She glances up at him, and he winks. A thrill runs through her. She feels a tingly sense of anticipation, like the bubbles in the glass of champagne he had once bought for her.

Maëlle thinks back to that day, several weeks

ago, when she was walking listlessly through the intricate gardens in Angers's former castle moat. It was Sunday, and the factory was closed. She had attended church in the morning, but the rest of the long day yawned out in front of her; all she wanted to do was to carve, but Monsieur Bayol forbade his crew to work on the Sabbath.

"*Bonjour, mademoiselle*," said a familiar voice. "Isn't it a beautiful day?"

She turned and saw Léon. Her heart pounded, her cheeks flushed. She glanced around to see whether anyone else accompanied him. He was alone.

"But . . . what are you doing here?"

"I am appreciating the Renaissance gardens, same as you," he said with a smile. Then he dropped his voice to a conspiratorial whisper: "And this way that old cow, Madame Bayol, won't have an opinion."

Maëlle pretended to laugh, but although Madame Bayol is stern, she had taken Maëlle in, allowed her to live in her home. Maëlle felt uneasy about anyone speaking ill of her only female friend.

But this was Léon.

Léon. And the two of them were alone, for once, without the eyes of all upon them.

They walked silently through the carefully laid-out gardens, with topiary shaped like cones and balls, and box hedges cut into curlicues, framing bright plantings of geraniums and pansies. Maëlle tried her best to act casual, but though they weren't touching she could almost feel the warmth of his skin; he is a flame, and she the moth, drawn to his heat and light.

When they stopped to admire the tinkling of a fountain—a cherub pouring a never-ending stream of water from an ewer—Léon leaned toward her.

"Mademoiselle—or may I call you Maëlle?"

"Of course," she replied, breathless.

"Maëlle," he repeated, as though he liked the feeling of the letters on his lips and tongue. His sea-colored eyes studied her for a very long time, seeming to drink in every aspect of her face, every detail. Maëlle wished fervently that she had taken more time that morning with her toilette; she wondered whether her hair was smooth, whether he liked what he saw.

"Sweet, talented Maëlle. You are . . . unique, so very special. Do you know that? I have never met a woman like you. I have asked you many times, and you have always said no. But now, with no witnesses except God, I ask you again: Won't you please ease my heart, and join me for a drink?"

He held out his hand. It was long-fingered and scarred, like the hands of every sculptor she knew. When she clasped it, it was as fresh and warm and welcome as the first day of spring.

Later, he drank absinthe and ordered a glass of champagne for Maëlle. It was her first.

The trip is an odyssey. Everything must be transferred in Paris. As much as Maëlle likes to think herself the equal of men, she is glad she does not have to negotiate the crowds on the platform in order to move the shipping containers onto the train bound for Avignon.

She had thought Angers was big, but it is nothing compared to Paris. There are more people than she has ever seen in one place. Maëlle tries to take in all she can, but she cannot glimpse the Eiffel Tower from her position on the train, or on the platform. There is no time to leave the station in search of it, though Léon disappears for half an hour while the others are working. Maëlle is in charge of the paperwork, making sure that each carefully numbered box gets shifted from one train car to the next.

She smells absinthe on Léon's breath when he returns. She feels like pouting, annoyed that she can't see the Tour Eiffel, irritated at Léon's frequent disappearances, and mostly irked at the thought that as a man Léon can go where he wants while she is forced to stay with the carousel. Léon teases her and whispers that on the return trip, perhaps they will disappear in Paris for a few days, losing themselves in the famous cafés and cabarets and alleyways of the City of Light.

The possibility takes her breath away. She knows it is impossible, and wrong . . . but it takes her breath away.

For the rest of the ride, he makes eyes at her, trying to make her blush in front of the others. She finds it annoying and yet irresistible; all she can think about is the feeling of his lips on hers. The first time they shared a kiss it was . . . transformative. Surely she was not the same person after a kiss like that; it felt as if her soul had met its mate and surged up through their lips. She felt whole. She felt wild and passionate and daring, able to take on the world.

It was akin to the sensation she felt right after her brother had helped her onto the train to Angers: reckless and free and so very, completely, *alive.*

So now the merest glance, the brush of a hand as they pass, simply being close enough to him to breathe in his scent, sends her into paroxysms of joy and desire, a sensation of being thoroughly, and finally, a woman.

When, at long last, they arrive at the Avignon station, Maëlle hates to admit that she is so tired she could sleep for days. Monsieur Bayol has arranged for a steam traction engine to haul the pieces of the salon and the carousel on the final leg of the journey.

While the men are packing the engine, Léon slips into a café.

“*C’est la fée verte*,” says the apprentice named Romain, noticing Maëlle’s eyes following Léon as he disappears behind the façade of the restaurant.

“What do you mean by ‘the green fairy’?” Maëlle asks.

“Absinthe,” answers Guy, another of the men, with a knowing smile. “The military used to issue it to the troops in Africa, to prevent malaria. But it has a way of grabbing a man and not letting go.”

Maëlle watches the doors of the café until it is time to go over the paperwork, checking off each box as it is unloaded from the train and transported to the steam engine.

The train trip has been one long, grueling disappointment. But surely Château Clement, she tells herself, will make up for everything. There, she and Léon will work side by side with no one to disapprove.

At the château everything will be different.

CHAPTER TWENTY-FIVE

PRESENT DAY
CHÂTEAU CLEMENT

Cady

Cady wasn't sure what she thought might be behind the red hallway's door number one, and was relieved to discover an innocuous bedroom with a dramatic slanted roof. It seemed almost Spanish in style, with dark wood beams across the white stucco ceiling and walls and an earth red tile floor. A bare mattress sat on a heavy, dark wood frame so tall that there was a small stepstool placed beside it. There were two nightstands, a slipper bathtub in one corner, and what looked like a down comforter hanging over a quilt stand. There were no decorations or paintings, not even curtains or shades on the dormer window that opened out onto the courtyard and the outbuildings.

As in the rest of the house, the doorframes appeared to have been carved by hand, each unique in its design. They featured delicate flowers and flitting birds, unfurling leaves and plump berries. She ran her hand along their contours, promising herself she would inspect them further tomorrow, in the daylight.

Curious, she continued down the hall. The next room had twin beds, a fireplace, and a desk, and the stucco walls were painted a robin's-egg blue. A shaggy cream-colored rug covered the tiles before a fireplace, which was black with soot, though there were no ashes or signs of a recent fire.

Cady shivered again. As was true in the rest of the house, a deep chill emanated from the stone walls. A fire would be lovely right about now. Or a shower. Fabrice had suggested she take a bath, so presumably there was hot water available.

The next door revealed a bedroom with two rough stone walls and two stucco walls painted a pale yellow that contrasted cheerfully with the beamed ceiling. A queen-sized bed stood near a large leaded casement window. Cady felt compelled to look at the rest of the rooms on the floor. All were variations on the same themes: beamed or stucco ceilings, stone or stucco walls, a few with fireplaces that hadn't seen flames for many years. They carried a scent of dust, stone, and emptiness, and several had water stains on the ceilings and walls.

Near the end of the hall she found a bathroom that looked as though it harked back to the thirties: White subway tiles, a few cracked, ran along the walls, and the toilet had a tank fixed high up on the wall. She did a test flush, praying it worked. It seemed to.

She was tempted by the big claw-foot tub, but wasn't brave enough to fill it with hot water and sit back and relax. Not in this silent stone house with a man she barely knew—Fabrice appeared to be old and frail, but Cady had read more than her share of horror stories. Back in the day, Jonquilla had made it her mission to expose all the younger kids to horror stories featuring old homes and mysterious recluses.

A huge steamer trunk with brass fittings sat at the end of the hall, its black sides sporting tags from countries like Morocco, Italy, and Wales—the sort of trunk travelers used to take to visit unknown countries. Very Indiana Jones.

As Fabrice had promised, inside it she found clean towels and sheets.

Cady decided on a room with stone walls and a large bed, with an armoire and desk and a window that looked out over the outbuildings. She selected two flat cotton sheets, old and in need of an airing but incredibly soft. For some reason she couldn't stop thinking about the first night she had spent with Maxine, bundled up on her lumpy couch.

Maxine had tucked her in and said, "I'll say one thing for you, Cady: You're not picky."

She closed the oak door to the hallway, and

as she shook out the sheets a delicate sachet of lavender flew up in the air. Storing the sheets with lavender sachet seemed out of character for a man like Fabrice, but she shouldn't make assumptions. The sheets were a little musty but smelled vaguely of the flowers, and she made the bed as best she could. She remembered reading an old book that mentioned "hospital corners," but she had no idea what those were as she'd always had fitted sheets. No doubt there was some arcane trick to it, but she didn't know what it was.

On top of the sheets went the down comforter, and for good measure she grabbed the one she had spotted in the other room.

Cady went to the bathroom, locked the door, gratefully stripped off her wet clothes and hung them over the sides of the tub, then stood before the sink to bathe as best she could with a washcloth. Shivering, she pulled on her pajamas and topped them with an "Oaklandish" fleece sweatshirt zipped all the way up to her neck.

She sank onto the side of the claw-foot tub to dry her rain-wet hair with a towel, feeling more comfortable in this small, utilitarian room than in the grand bedroom.

"What in the world are we doing here, Drake?" she asked aloud.

Cady had spooked herself, thinking of scary stories and the scenario of a lone woman out in the middle of nowhere with a mean old man and his very large dog. In the movies the dog would be trained to do horrible things, and the apparently frail Fabrice would turn out to be faking it . . . or would have evil minions lurking in the cellar, or a crazy woman in the attic.

Or Jean-Paul would return in the dead of night, revealing his true self as a homicidal maniac.

“We’re fine.” She tried to reassure herself, brushing her teeth. “We’ll deal.”

But there was no “we” anymore. Just a few months ago she had sat with Maxine at the little table in the room behind the shop, a baby in her belly, sharing corn bread and talking about what the future might bring. Never in a million years would they have anticipated what had actually happened.

Sadness washed over her, and she stifled a sob. She wished she could see this as a grand adventure, as she had described it in her head to Olivia, but at the moment she just felt exhausted, inexplicably afraid, and unbearably alone.

She returned to the bedroom, where rain was beating a frantic tattoo on the windowpanes. She found the little rubber stopper she carried in her suitcase and shoved it under the bedroom door, hesitated for a moment, then scooted a heavy wooden bureau a few inches in front of it as well. She had to unplug the side lamp to plug in her phone, as there was no other outlet. Her phone came on and started to charge, but still wasn't receiving any service.

Nonetheless, she felt the urge to text Olivia. She would send it when she could.

> **Well, we've really done it now. I am sitting in a mysterious, dilapidated château, awaiting my fate. Seriously. I'm pretty sure there are murderers lurking behind these stone walls. How could there not be? This is a classic setup for a slasher film—not the cheap, blood-spurting Hollywood kind but the artistic European type—except that I am not a nubile teen. And in the movie version the cranky old man who owns the place would have a mysterious cat, rather than a goofy dog. But still.**

Cady thought she heard something besides the rain, and paused for a moment to listen; a faint sound was coming through a vent. It sounded like . . . singing. A man's voice, rough and aged, but surprisingly melodious. She tried to follow the notes, which reminded her of a French version of Sinatra's classic "My Way."

Cady continued her text: **I can't BELIEVE I let you talk me into this trip. I will NEVER forgive you.**

The windowpanes rattled as the wind began to howl.

She curled up under the covers, seeking warmth. In the faint light provided by her phone, she gazed at the old photo of the mystery woman and once again reread the love note, trying to focus on her goal in coming to *le château* in the first place.

But she couldn't help but wonder: Who in the world had slashed her tires? And why?

One thing was sure: This was not the fairy tale she had been looking for.

When Cady awoke late the next morning, it took her a moment to remember where she was. Sunshine filtered in through the dust-caked windows, filling the old bedroom with a cheerful brightness and dispelling the gloom from the previous night.

The stone walls still emanated a chill, but she was surrounded by historic beauty, and last night's ghosts had vanished.

She got out of bed and pushed open the leaded casement windows, feeling very European as she leaned out. The storm had passed, and the sun-warmed garden filled the air with the mingled scents of lavender, rosemary, and thyme. Cady breathed deeply.

Petrichor. She remembered finding the word in a book and asking Maxine what it meant. Maxine had told her, "*Petrichor* is an ugly word for a beautiful thing: the smell after the rain."

Looking out over the courtyard, Cady noticed details she hadn't seen in the dark of last night: garish graffiti tags on some of the buildings; an old car that probably hadn't run for decades covered by a bright blue tarp that rippled in the breeze; leaves and branches blown about by the wind. She smelled something else, too, something enticing coming from inside the building.

Was that coffee?

Her stomach growled. Her last meal had been a large lunch—Parisians, she had learned, liked to eat large lunches—a *salade composée* with duck and pâté. Plenty of bread and cheese as well as chocolate mousse and a tiny cup of strong espresso for dessert. At the time she thought she'd never eat again, but that had been a very long time ago. She'd snacked on some almonds while driving from Avignon, but that was it.

The hallway and stairs looked different in the day, not so ghostly but much sadder. Where there had been a bit of romance to last night's impression of a haunted mansion, the morning sunshine revealed dust motes hanging in the air and piles of yellowing newspapers. Her nose twitched at a hint of something that might well have been rodent in nature, and she skirted several small puddles where rain appeared to have dripped through holes in the roof.

She made her way through the book-lined room, along the broad paneled corridor, and down the next set of stairs to the kitchen.

The ochre tiles seemed to gleam in the daylight, the room untidy but charming with the sun streaming in through multipaned windows.

Lucy let out a loud woof and wagged her tail as she greeted Cady at the door.

"*Bonjour*," Cady said, scratching Lucy under her chin.

"*Bonjour*," said Fabrice. "*Tu fais la grasse matinée, n'est-ce pas*?"

Cady was familiar with this expression from her days at the French-American school; it would be invoked when students arrived late. Literally it meant "you are making a fat morning," and referred to sleeping in.

"I guess so," she said, feeling vaguely guilty as she stifled a yawn. It wasn't that late, was it? Fabrice was probably one of those old people who got up before dawn. "It took me a while to fall asleep."

He grunted. On the table sat half a baguette, a dish of butter, and a jar of jam.

"I know you Americans eat big meals for break-fast, but this is how we do it here."

"This is perfect, thank you."

"You want chocolate?"

"Pardon?"

"Chocolate or coffee?"

"Both."

"Both?"

She smiled. "Just kidding. I hate saying no to chocolate, on principle."

He looked confused, and she wondered whether her French was adequate to the task. Making a joke in a foreign language could be tricky. Or maybe Fabrice had no sense of humor.

"Coffee would be wonderful, thank you," she said, chastened.

He grunted again, then started spinning dials and moving levers on an intricate Italian espresso machine, the kind one saw in Parisian cafés. Steam filled the air and the copper hardware gleamed in the morning light.

"Nice machine," Cady said, for want of anything else to say.

"Bought it when I moved here. Damned idiotic. Don't know what I was thinking."

"So you didn't grow up here in the château?"

He shook his head. "I grew up in Paris. First time I saw this place, I was a teenager, right after the war. It was a ruin back then."

"Is that right?" Cady said, wondering how much worse it could have been.

He shrugged. "Parts of it were okay, but it had been empty for a long while, and then with the war . . ."

"Was that the Second World War?"

He nodded. "Nazis never stayed here, thank

goodness, but the Italians came through and took anything of value. Not sure it made any difference; place had been looted long before, anyway."

"When did you move here?"

"I stayed here for a little while after the war, but came back for good in 1973, with my father. I thought . . ." He looked around, as though seeing the surroundings in his mind's eye as they had once been. "I thought I had enough resources to restore it at that time, and we made some efforts, but no matter how much time and money you think you have, it's never enough for a place like this."

"It must be very inspirational for your writing. I'm reading *Le Château* right now."

He did not reply, seemingly preoccupied with the spitting espresso machine.

"I was wondering, in the book, you mention—"

"Don't talk to me about that book."

"But—"

"I'm serious. I do not wish to discuss this. If you persist, I must ask you to leave. *Dégage*."

"Okay, no book talk. Got it. I apologize. If I don't talk about the book, could I stay? I'll take Lucy out after breakfast."

He snorted but didn't answer.

"I noticed some improvements in the house," Cady continued, hoping architecture might be a safer topic. "The bathrooms, that sort of thing—"

"My grandparents were the last full-time residents, before me. They made some improvements, many of which are still working. Put in electricity, obviously."

"The woodwork is incredible. The intricate carvings on the door frames . . . Is that original?"

"Some of it. Here's your coffee. I don't have time to wait on you hand and foot, you know. Or to sit around all day talking."

He limped toward the kitchen door.

Cady was left in a quandary: How was she going to fix her car? Her phone still wasn't getting reception. And now that she was here, had actually spent the night under the roof of Château Clement, she hated to leave before getting some answers. How could she get Fabrice to talk to her about the carousel and the possible origins of her rabbit? If he was that touchy about a successful book he had written . . .

"Monsieur," she said to his back.

"*Tutoie-moi*," he growled. "I've told you before. I don't believe in the arbitrary usage of formality. *Je m'appelle* Fabrice. *Fabrice*."

"Thank you. Fabrice, then." Lucy woofed, looking at her expectantly. "I was thinking: What if I stayed here for a little while? I could take care of Lucy."

He fixed her with his hawk eyes. "What are you talking about?"

What *was* Cady talking about? Somewhere

between worrying that Fabrice might be a reclusive homicidal maniac with an attack dog, and her morning coffee, Cady had decided she wasn't ready to leave the château. She felt like she was channeling Olivia: How often did an opportunity like this come along? She wanted to learn Gus-the-rabbit's origin story and to see for herself whatever remnants there might be of the Clement carousel. She wanted to learn about the woman in the photograph. Given Fabrice's nature, she knew she couldn't come right out and ask him; she had to earn his trust.

And for some reason, she liked the grumpy recluse. Which was a little worrisome. She was a terrible judge of character.

"Looks to me like you could use some help with housekeeping and taking care of the dog, at least until your ankle is better," Cady said. "I could stay for a few days, lend a hand."

"I told you—I don't like people."

"And I told *you*—neither do I. This place is so big we wouldn't have to see each other unless we wanted to."

Fabrice narrowed his eyes. "Why would you want to stay here?"

Once again she tried for the Gallic shrug. "Get to know the place. You know how tourists are. We don't have châteaux where I'm from. Also, I can cook."

"Americans don't know how to cook."

"Try me."

His gaze settled on the dog: Lucy had her thick leather leash in her mouth and was pacing the kitchen, her toenails clicking on the tile floor. She clearly needed to go out, *now.*

"*Bof*! All right, I suppose if you walk this damned dog for me and cook a decent dinner, you can stay here for a while. Until I change my mind. You are sure you know how to cook?"

"Just you wait and see."

CHAPTER TWENTY-SIX

2001
OAKLAND

Cady, Age 13

"You've got to learn to cook," Maxine had said the first time she invited Cady to dinner, about a month after she had started working at the shop. "Either that or make a lot of money."

"What do you mean?"

"If you have money to spare you can afford to take people out to restaurants, or hire a personal chef. Hardworking schmucks like you and me, though, need to learn how to cook."

"Why?"

"Because it's the best and least expensive way to make someone feel cared for." Maxine slipped her hand into a heavy denim oven mitt and pulled a pan of homemade macaroni and cheese out of the oven. "Doesn't that smell like home?"

Cady didn't know what a home smelled like, but she nodded anyway because the heavenly aroma made her mouth water.

"Here's the secret, Cady: You don't have to

know how to make a lot of dishes, just one or two 'go-to' dishes that you make well. Mac-n-cheese is one of mine."

Maxine set the hot pan on the table, where Cady had already arranged plates and silverware. Cady stared at the dish for a long moment, remembering a dinner at the group home when Jonquilla got into a fistfight with an older boy because she insisted that she had once eaten homemade mac-n-cheese that hadn't come from a box. No one, not even Cady, had believed her.

"What is it, Cady?" Maxine asked, sitting across from her.

"I didn't . . . I didn't really know anyone made mac-n-cheese except from the box. The bright orange kind, with powder."

"Well, now you know," Maxine said, scooping a steaming spoonful onto Cady's plate. "My mama made it for us all the time. Sometimes she'd put a little bacon or chicken in there, or add peas and carrots to get us to eat vegetables. Whatever she felt like—that's the beauty of a go-to recipe. Try it."

Cady could barely eat for the lump in her throat. She put down her fork, willing herself not to cry, but it didn't work. A little hiccup escaped, and then she put her head in her hands and sniffled.

Maxine said nothing. When Cady looked up, Maxine had a bemused look on her face and the whisper of a smile.

"It's nothing special, child. I just mix macaroni with a couple of different cheeses and a little cream. Would you like me to teach you how?"

After that, they spent many hours together in the kitchen, trying new recipes and perfecting Cady's "go-to" dishes. They shucked corn, fried chicken, made cornmeal pizza and fresh-tossed salads from whatever was in season at the farmers market. Maxine encouraged Cady to try foods she'd never eaten before, like eggplant—which was not related in any way to eggs, she discovered to her surprise—and persimmons, figs, and fish that wasn't tuna and didn't come from a can.

The first dinner Cady made for Maxine all by herself was a simple vegetable stir-fry. Maxine couldn't stop exclaiming about how delicious it was. Cady, her eyes on her plate, was embarrassed but pleased to the tips of her toes.

When they finished, Maxine put down her fork with a sigh and said, "Cady, if I can get through all the paperwork and the bureaucratic nonsense, would you like to come and live with me?"

And once again, Cady burst into tears.

CHAPTER TWENTY-SEVEN

1944
PARIS

Fabrice

Paris was nearly emptied of young, healthy men. Almost two million were prisoners of war; others fled with General de Gaulle and the Free French to London; thousands more were missing or hiding. Fabrice was often stopped and questioned, his papers demanded. But he was young enough to escape suspicion, and he had blond hair, which the Nazis idolized.

Still, women and girls could more easily move through the city, so they were the primary couriers, carrying weapons and incriminating documents.

Members of the Résistance were not the only ones who showed bravery. A young music student named Vivou Chevrillon played her violin outside the wall of a Compiègne concentration camp, hoping her friend inside would recognize the song. A gallery owner named Jeanne Bucher defiantly showed the work of Kandinsky and other despised abstract artists, many of whom were Jewish.

But most citizens resisted in more prosaic ways. By managing to get enough to eat, Parisians demonstrated they would not be starved into submission. At the theater or in the movies whenever a banquet scene came on, the audience would cheer. Also, since no one knew who could be trusted, food became the constant—and only truly safe—topic of conversation: What can you find to eat? Where can you find it? How can you make dubious ingredients appetizing?

Fabrice's new friends would taunt and tease one another with descriptions of their favorite meals and menus. Paulette loved to recite recipes from her hometown: *truite Provençal*, daube—a kind of traditional stew—tapenade, *pan bagnat*.

Fabrice didn't care what she spoke about; he cherished the lilt of her voice. He listened, rapt, as she talked about picking bouquets of *muguets*—lilies of the valley—in the forests surrounding her village. Paulette had an entrancing way of tilting her head when she paid attention, and she would do this when listening to Fabrice, as though trying to figure him out.

He felt accepted by her, as though she understood him. His parents called him "moody," implying that his seesaw emotions were troubling and wrong. But Paulette seemed undaunted when he was miserable one moment and euphoric the next.

"You are an intelligent, passionate young man," she said with an endearing shrug. "That is the way of it. *C'est normal.*"

Also, though his parents had discouraged his fervent love of words, Paulette assured him his writings were playing a part in history, in the rescue of La Belle France. Fabrice thrilled at her comments, and while he printed pamphlet after pamphlet, virtually asleep on his feet, he would imagine what it would be like to take her into his arms, to be able to claim her, to make a home together.

Sometimes Fabrice would go by the doctor's office, hoping to catch a glimpse of her, even though he was supposed to keep his distance from Dr. Duhamel except when absolutely necessary.

One night they shared a flacon of wine with Claude and the Belgian in the back room of the printshop. When the others left, Fabrice found his courage. He leaned in toward Paulette.

She shook her head, pulling back. "You are very young, *mon petit garçon.*"

"I'm not *that* young," he whispered in return. Perhaps it was the fervor in his voice, his absolute conviction. Perhaps it was the wine. But whatever the reason, she reached one graceful hand to him and ran her long finger across his smooth cheek where the whiskers did not yet grow. The pad of her finger left a trail of tingling heat on his skin.

She dropped her hand and blew out a long breath.

"It is because of this war," Paulette said. She gave him a shaky smile, but her sky blue eyes were filled with sorrow.

"*What* is because of this war?" Fabrice asked in a quiet voice, searching her face.

"That you are having these feelings. We are a generation out of place, Fabrice. Our childhoods have been robbed, ripped from our hands as surely as the Germans rob us of our food and art, our happiness, our very souls."

"But if I've been robbed of my childhood, then I am already a man. You could love a man, could you not?"

She gave a humorless laugh. "My dear, dear Fabrice. You are so brave, so capable . . . but you are still very young, and naive. Let's not get off track. Sit back, relax, and let us plan the victory dinner we shall make when we win this wretched war. What will be our aperitif?"

One day Fabrice was summoned to the doctor's office.

Paulette ushered him into an exam room as though he were a patient. The doctor asked him to take off his shirt and placed the cold end of a stethoscope against his chest, as though examining him.

"There is a submarine base in Saint-Nazaire," Dr. Duhamel said in a low voice. "The British forces want to attack it, but they need photographs. *Cough.*"

Fabrice coughed.

"The only people allowed to come near are children on field trips, who are shown the base as a way to impress them with the strength of the Nazi fleet. Garçon, you are doing an exemplary job with the informational pamphlets. But there are not many who could manage this assignment." He paused, gazed out the window for a moment, then turned back. "You are young enough to be in school. Are you good with a camera?"

This was his chance. Fabrice's heart pounded; it embarrassed him that the doctor would be able to hear it through his stethoscope. This was his chance to prove to Paulette that he was more than a boy.

"I will go," said Fabrice. "I will take photos."

"This is a very dangerous mission," warned the doctor. His tone had a resigned sort of hope to it. The physician had been a healer of bodies for decades, but was now called on to help heal his country, and seemed unsure that he was up to the task.

"I understand."

"I would not ask this of you, but this intelligence is essential for the Allies."

"I am not afraid. I want to do it."

Just then Paulette came to the door to tell the doctor he had a phone call.

Fabrice held Paulette's gaze and repeated, "I will go."

CHAPTER TWENTY-EIGHT

PRESENT DAY
CHÂTEAU CLEMENT

Cady

The château grounds looked different in the morning sunshine. The phantoms of the night had vanished, replaced by glistening trees and buildings freshly washed by the rain. Still, the beautiful morning did little to improve the estate's ramshackle appearance, much less the broken windows and graffiti.

As Lucy sniffed at the grass, Cady looked around.

Who would paint graffiti out here in the otherwise bucolic French countryside? Cady was accustomed to seeing "tagging" on the streets of Oakland, but she was disappointed to find it in this pastoral setting. She preferred to think of Château Clement as a place out of time, as in a fairy tale, but apparently it was as depressingly real as anywhere else.

The tag read JTC, in a stylized graffiti script Cady recognized from her days running the streets of Oakland. She had never been a tagger, but had known plenty who were. Jonquilla had tried her hand at it for a while, before she lost interest in anything but pursuing the next high. The last time Cady had seen her childhood friend, Jon was panhandling on a street corner in downtown Berkeley. Neither of them spoke. Cady gave Jon her last five-dollar bill and walked away.

Gravel crunched underfoot as Cady led Lucy across the courtyard to peek into the same window as last night. But now, in the daylight, she didn't hear band organ music, much less see what she'd thought—for an instant—she had seen last night. There seemed to be another structure within, as though the outer building were a shell built around a smaller interior construction. There were some covered items, what looked like old tractor parts, random pieces of lumber, an old tire. Panels here and there, like a very large three-part folding screen. Maybe she had imagined that one of the tarp-covered lumps was a carousel figure. Had she wanted to see it that badly?

It was still hard to make out much through the grime of the windowpane, but there were several large panels that appeared to be blackened with soot.

Jean-Paul had told her the carousel had been destroyed by fire.

She tried the doors, but they were locked.

Cady knew she shouldn't snoop, but other than holding a gun on her, Fabrice hadn't seemed overly concerned about her nosiness last night. She had started to go around the side of the building in search of another door when she heard the sound of breaking glass.

"What was that?" Cady asked Lucy, who sat waiting patiently, wagging her tail.

They hurried around to the back of the building.

A teenage boy was throwing rocks at a high window of a barnlike structure. He was tall and skinny, dressed in jeans and an oversized hoodie. He would have fit in well on the streets of Oakland.

"Hey!" Cady yelled in English, before realizing she wasn't sure of the equivalent in French. The kinds of informal utterances that were so important to actual communication were rarely taught in language class. At least she knew how to demand: "What are you doing here?"

She yelled: "*Qu'est-ce que tu faites ici*?"

The boy whirled around in her direction, slapped one hand on the opposite bicep and raised his arm into a fist, then ran.

"Little pissant vandal!" Cady yelled, again in English. She figured that her words, like his rude gesture, would need no translation. "Come back here and clean this up!"

The dog just stood there, wagging her tail.

Cady looked at her askance. “A lot of help you are.”

Lucy’s only response was to wag her tail with more enthusiasm.

“I’m going to assume you’re not exactly of the guard dog variety.”

Lucy sat very erect and licked her chops.

“Let me explain something to you, Lucy. Just because you’re big doesn’t mean you don’t need to show your teeth every once in a while. For instance, when some little idiot is vandalizing your master’s property.”

Lucy wagged her tail some more.

Cady continued her explorations, peeking into other windows. The first building seemed locked up tight, but the door on another outbuilding stood ajar, and within was a very old black car that looked like something out of a movie about World War II. Next she found a small square stone building, two stories high, its original purpose unknowable. It was unlocked, so she and Lucy walked in and climbed the stairs, Lucy sniffing the old wood, checking for mice. From the arched windows of the second floor—with two broken panes—Cady could see that the garden had once been laid out in a formal fashion, with a greenhouse-looking building at one end, a sunken garden surrounded by statuary, and a small pond at the end. A waterwheel still turned in the lazy current.

Cady took Lucy out to explore the remnants of the garden, finding shallow pools and fountains that no longer spewed. Statuary—an enormous pelican, a ball atop an elongated pyramid, an obelisk—was studded with orange and pale green lichen. Stone benches and trees were fuzzy with moss.

A soggy newspaper sat by the front gates. She picked it up, then gathered a few wildflowers in Olivia's honor—it was the sort of thing her friend was forever doing: slowing down and appreciating nature.

Shaggy hedges along the walkways had probably once been manicured into topiary. Cady wondered what shapes they might have taken then—geometrical or whimsical? Animals, or maybe spirals? Who were Yves and Josephine Clement, and what had their château been like in its heyday? Did they have a fleet of gardeners, or might Josephine have come out and snipped the trees into shapes, while Yves snapped his photos?

Cady remembered watching such a tree, in California.

Not the tree so much as the artist who tended to it: an old man. Impossibly old, it had seemed to Cady at the time. He was small but seemed uncomfortable with his body, as though accustomed to being a larger man. Or taller, at least. He used to stand before that tree, sometimes for hours, as if he were praying to an idol.

Some days he would do nothing at all besides simply studying and assessing. Most times he took his clippers from his pocket and snipped, sprigs so small that Cady could hardly see them as he flicked them aside.

From his labors emerged a Chinese-style dragon, like the ones in the Chinatown parades: flared nostrils and ears and all, wrapping around the trunk of the stunted tree.

Cady used to spend long stretches, sometimes hours, hiding behind the hedge, watching that old man as he sculpted the tree, conjuring his dragon.

One day the old man stopped coming. Soon the dragon grew ragged. Long, haphazard shoots sprang from its back, sprouted from its claws. The man returned and clipped it into submission again, but eventually he stopped coming altogether. The tree stood, still, but not the man.

When the shoots emerged again, there was no one to stop them. Eventually the tree came to look like any other, betraying no trace of the fierce dragon lurking within.

CHAPTER TWENTY-NINE

PRESENT DAY
CHÂTEAU CLEMENT

Cady

Cady brought the flowers into the kitchen, filled an old Perrier bottle with tap water, and placed the bouquet on the table in front of the fireplace. She filled Lucy's water bowl and petted the mellow dog while deciding what to do next.

Peeking into windows was one thing, but breaking into buildings was a step too far. Cady had left her miscreant days behind her. What she needed to do was to persuade Fabrice to speak with her about his family's history in general, and about the carousel in particular. He must know something.

Fabrice had responded well to the idea of her walking the dog and taking over the cooking. And if she was going to stay here, she wanted to dust and vacuum her room and clean the bathroom. All the living quarters seemed to be in need of a good scrubbing.

Cady roamed the château's ground floor in pursuit of cleaning supplies. She found the original estate kitchen, a massive room with scarred marble and wooden counters long enough for an assembly line of chefs, a wall of intricate cabinets, and an iron oven. Cady imagined the cooks tending bubbling cauldrons atop the stove, kitchen staff bustling about while chopping and slicing and peeling, farmers delivering baskets filled with local fruits and seasonal vegetables, hunters carrying in deer and rabbits hanging from rods, the day's catch.

A smaller room next to the large kitchen must have been a pantry. It was lined with shelves, on which still sat a few Mason jars full of canned fruits and vegetables as well as jam jars caked in grime and spiderwebs.

Cady peeked into half a dozen windowless chambers reminiscent of nun's cells, wondering if they had been servants' quarters, or offices, or storage rooms, or some combination of all three. She could practically see the flickering forms of spirits as she meandered along: an efficient head housekeeper, a dignified butler, an arrogant chef, a handful of scurrying housemaids.

At long last she yanked open a stuck wooden door and discovered a storage closet with cleaning supplies. They, too, were covered in dust, but trusting that soap didn't have an expiration date, she took an armful to her bedroom. She flung open the windows to allow the cool, fresh, early-spring air to chase away the staleness, and then she got to work.

An hour later, Cady noted with satisfaction that the bedroom looked and smelled much more inviting.

Her stomach growled. Last night Jean-Paul had mentioned that Fabrice had someone bringing him groceries, but if she was going to be doing the cooking, she wanted to do the shopping as well. Also, her phone still wasn't working, and she needed to call the rental agency to figure out what to do with the car. Surely her phone would work in town, or maybe she could find an Internet café.

The village of Saint-Véran was only a few miles away. She could walk there, if necessary.

Cady was gathering her things—her camera bag, her cell phone, her jacket, her money—when she heard the *scrape-thump* of Fabrice's crutch. She went out into the hall and peered down the stairs.

Fabrice was standing at the bottom step.

"I made you a list," he said, holding up a piece of paper.

"A list of what?"

"Things I need from the store. I want roast chicken tonight."

"Oh, good," said Cady, coming down the stairs to join him. "You must have read my mind."

He didn't respond.

"I mean, I was just thinking about food." The note included a hand-drawn map of the village, including the location of the *boulangerie* and a grocery store.

Fabrice grunted. "You can use my car. The keys are on a nail by the door, and the shopping bags, too."

"Does that old car run?" Cady asked. "The one in the shack out back?"

"What, the Deux Chevaux? Of course not. Take the Citroën. The French are great engineers. We invented cars, you know."

"Is that so? I seem to remember something about an American named Henry Ford. . . ."

He waved her off dismissively. "Ford was a latecomer to the scene. He invented the assembly line, is all. The internal combustion engine is the heart of the automobile, and that was invented by Lenoir."

"Huh. Well, learn something new every day."

Fabrice looked curious. "What car do you drive in the United States?"

"A Toyota."

He snorted and mumbled, "Japanese. It figures."

"Oh, by the way," Cady said, "there was a kid out in the courtyard earlier, throwing rocks at the windows."

Fabrice grunted.

"He did one of these," she said, copying the arm gesture in as discreet a fashion as she could, minus the bravado.

"Ah yes, the *bras d'honneur*."

"The 'arm of honor'?"

"It's meant sarcastically. It is a very rude gesture."

"Yeah, I got that. Do you know who he is?"

"*C'est un enfant à problème*," he said. Meaning, essentially, that he was a *jeune voyou*. A bad kid.

"I thought I might track him down, get him to come back and clean up his mess."

Fabrice's expression was unreadable. "Go buy the groceries, please. The boy is no concern of yours."

The trip into town was an easy drive down a straight highway. Tall rows of sycamore-like trees lining the road created a regal route, though a lethal one should a driver veer out of the lane.

To her left were extensive fields of lavender, and to her right were acres of olive trees. A few stone farmhouses, fallow fields, and vineyards dotted the low hills. The appearance of a walled cemetery announced the entrance to the village, its narrow and twisting streets flanked by stucco town houses.

Fabrice's map was easy to follow. He had even drawn tiny cars to indicate where to park.

The town, though small, had cell phone reception, and Cady immediately called the car rental company, which, after a few minutes of debating, agreed to send a tow truck from Avignon. Next she called the landlady of the room she had reserved in Saint-Véran and apologized for having to cancel her reservation. The woman was so surprised to hear that Cady was staying at Château Clement that she didn't even argue. Finally, Cady sent Olivia the rather histrionic text she had written the night before, along with a P.S. about how lovely the area was now that she was no longer stranded and the sun was shining.

Business completed, Cady paused to regroup and poke around the village. Her stomach growled again. That settled it: first stop, the *boulangerie*.

The store was crowded with locals purchasing their day's supply of baked goods, but Cady didn't mind the long line. She inhaled the aroma of fresh bread, her mouth watering at the sight of arched croissants and square *pain au chocolat*, flaky layers glistening with butter; tiny quiches studded with ham and herbs; long baguettes with their characteristic slash marks; the slightly sweet loaves of puffy brioche. When it was her turn, she asked for two baguettes and a round *boule de campagne*.

Then she ordered a *pan bagnat*, or bathed bread. It was a sandwich filled with typical Provençal ingredients: tomatoes, bell peppers, black olives, anchovies, and tuna—a *salade niçoise* between slices of crusty bread.

Cady was so hungry she couldn't resist taking a small bite while driving. Eating behind the wheel was considered a no-no in France, though, so she looked for a park, like those where she had often eaten lunch in Paris. Remembering the cemetery, she pulled in.

A gray-haired man dressed in a black overcoat, a white felt scarf wrapped around his neck, was tending to one of the markers. The graves were raised above the ground, with marble slabs covering the tombs. Many headstones held little oval photos of lost loved ones. Most were adorned with flowers, both fresh and plastic. Some had framed photographs sitting atop the slabs; others had military honors, or religious icons. A huge monument in the very center of the cemetery was emblazoned CLEMENT and listed dozens of family members. Clearly Fabrice's family had lived in this area, and had been important, for a very long time.

It seemed disrespectful to eat in the cemetery, so Cady sat in the car and finished her sandwich, washing it down with a bottle of Perrier. The *pan bagnat* was luscious, just as good as the Parisian sandwiches she had savored.

Meal over, Cady consulted her map and drove to the grocery store, which was even more fun than the *boulangerie*. Cady meandered up and down each aisle, lingering over the unfamiliar packets of pâté and *saucissons*, potato chips boasting the flavor of goat cheese, brightly colored packages of children's cookies, long whole vanilla beans in plastic tubes.

Her curiosity temporarily sated, Cady settled down to the business at hand: tonight's meal. Fabrice's list, written in a spidery, old-fashioned hand, included a whole chicken, potatoes, green beans, lettuce, preserved chestnuts, chocolate mousse, pistachio gelato, and a bottle of absinthe.

She added a few other staples to her cart and, unable to resist, tossed in a bag of goat-cheese-flavored chips and a "Yes" candy bar because the name appealed to her.

The unsmiling cashier was a blond woman in her thirties, who ignored Cady as she rang up the groceries but paused at the pistachio gelato.

"You are buying for Monsieur Fabrice Clement?" she asked.

"How did you know?"

"It is his usual Tuesday order. He called and said someone would be in to pick it up today."

"Is that right?" *He told me he didn't have a phone,* Cady thought. "Yes, I'm staying with him for a little while."

"You're *staying* with Monsieur Clement? At Château Clement?"

"Yes."

"You are American?"

Cady nodded. “From California. My name’s Cady Drake.”

“I’m Annick Boyer. *Enchantée*. How is Monsieur Clement?”

“Recovering from a hurt ankle, but otherwise okay. Do you know him, then?”

She laughed. “Of course. Everyone knows who he is. But he almost never comes into town, and does not allow people to visit him.”

“He has his groceries delivered, I take it?”

“Yes, Johnny used to deliver to him, but there was a problem.” She shook her head. “*C’est dommage*. I’m sorry to give up on him, but I’m afraid he’s a bad kid.”

“I saw a teenage boy on the grounds this morning—dark hair, tall, thin . . . ?”

She nodded. “Probably Johnny. Causing trouble?”

“I wanted to speak with him about something,” said Cady. “Do you know where I could find him?”

“His family lives on rue Champs. But I wouldn’t go over there, if I were you. It’s a difficult situation; the mother died, the father’s not around much—works a lot and drinks too much. It is not very nice.”

Cady nodded. “Okay, thank you. Is there somewhere in town where I could check my e-mail?”

“At the Hound Dog Café, around the corner. The owner, Hubert, is an Elvis Presley fan.”

“Thanks. Hey, is there a museum in town, or some other source of local information?”

“How do you mean?”

“I would like to find information about the history of Saint-Véran. I’m interested in the old carousel that used to stand on the Château Clement property.”

“The carousel! My grandmother said *her* mother remembered riding the château’s carousel during holidays.”

“Really?”

She nodded, warming to the theme. “The château was famous for opening its gates to the entire village for feast days, La Fête du Muguet, the fourteenth of July, that sort of thing.”

Cady knew the fourteenth of July was Bastille Day, but had never heard of the other holiday.

“Why did it stop?”

She pushed out her chin and tilted her head in a “who knows?” gesture. “World War I came along, the Clement family lost their money, and the lady of the manor died. There were rumors about her.”

“What kind of rumors?”

“In a village, there is always gossip, no? I really don’t remember. It was all long before my time. I’m sorry, I should help the next customer.”

Only then did Cady realize a woman was waiting behind her, a basket of groceries on her arm.

"Oh, sorry."

"*Je vous souhaite une bonne journée.*" The cashier wished her a good day.

Cady returned the sentiment, packed her items in the canvas tote bags Fabrice had given her, and headed back to the car.

Since she hadn't brought her computer along, she decided she would check out the café and send Olivia a proper e-mail on her next trip to town. Navigating her phone's tiny keyboard to compose a long message required more patience than Cady could muster.

It was a quick trip back to the château, where Cady parked the Citroën behind the main building. She carried the bags in through the side door, where Lucy greeted her, wagging her tail lazily. There was no sign of Fabrice, so Cady busied herself putting away the groceries and then snooped through the château a little more, nearly getting lost in the dizzying maze of flights and corridors, Lucy's nails clicking on the wooden floors as she trailed Cady from room to room. Besides empty chambers she found a nursery complete with a few dusty wooden toys, a sunroom with mostly broken panes, a pool table with ruined felt, a bundle of lace and shattered silk that might once have been a fine gown, and more carved rococo fireplaces and lintels.

When she stumbled upon a library that appeared to be in use—a manual typewriter and stacks of papers crowded the desk—Cady decided she had trespassed enough. She could only imagine Fabrice's reaction if she were to barge in on him in his private study.

So she returned to the kitchen, rolled up her sleeves, and got to work. The kitchen wasn't as bad as much of the château; still, the stove hadn't been scrubbed well in a good long while. Finally satisfied, she began to prep the chicken and vegetables for roasting, then cleaned the fireplace of ashes and brought in several armfuls of firewood from the woodshed to build up the fire.

How had Fabrice managed by himself for so long? Had Bad Boy Johnny been helping him? And what had happened between the two of them?

And what rumors had the woman at the grocery store been referring to with regard to Josephine Clement? What had this old château witnessed, over the years?

Finally the popping sound of tires on gravel interrupted her musings and heralded the arrival of the tow truck from Avignon.

CHAPTER THIRTY

PRESENT DAY
CHÂTEAU CLEMENT

Cady

Cady put the chicken and vegetables in the oven to roast so that they would be ready at six and would have time to rest before she and Fabrice sat down to dinner at six thirty.

At six twenty-five, she called Fabrice to the table. He appeared in the doorway, looking surprised. “Dinner? At this hour?”

“What’s wrong with the hour?” she asked.

His expression suggested she must be an alien life-form. “I don’t eat dinner until eight thirty or nine.”

“Oh. Well, then, today will be a new experience.”

He glared at her. She returned the stare, unblinking.

“Fine, we’ll eat,” he grumbled. Opening a drawer, he took out a flashlight and handed it to her. “Go down to the wine cellar and bring up a Sancerre from the Haut-Goujon.”

“A Sancerre?” Cady repeated, unfamiliar with the many varieties of French wine. In her world, wine was red or it was white.

“*Oui*. From the Haut-Goujon.”

“Haut-Goujon. Got it,” she replied, making a mental note. Sancerre, Haut-Goujon. “And where might I find the wine cellar?”

Fabrice showed her a small door off the hall. “Down those stairs, to the left. I can’t remember if it’s the second or third door. You will see—it is a room with many bottles of wine.”

“Very funny,” Cady said. She took a deep breath and started slowly down the stairs, her flashlight piercing the darkness below. She glanced back at the doorway. Fabrice stood there, backlit by the lamp in the hallway.

Cady shivered. She felt as if the damp stone walls were closing in on her, and she batted spiderwebs away from her face as she descended.

At the bottom of the stairs, she swung her flashlight beam around the cellar, noting a series of groin vaults and broad stone arches that led in many directions. Some of the arches opened onto cramped windowless rooms, but others were larger.

Okay, this is most definitely where the killer lurks at night.

Either that, or . . . could this have been the dungeon at one time, where the seigneur of the area locked up recalcitrant peasants? Did French châteaux even have dungeons? She wished she knew more about French history.

Olivia had been right about one thing, at least: France was not what Cady had expected.

After running into a few dead ends, she located the wine cellar. It was a dark, low-ceilinged space, reminiscent of a cave, and she had to crouch to enter through the stone archway. The cave smelled of wine and must, and contained half a dozen huge oak barrels as well as numerous wooden racks filled with dusty bottles.

"Sancerre, Haut-Goujon," she repeated, checking label after label, but without luck. "Come out, come out, wherever you are, my dear Sancerre."

After many minutes of searching the wine racks, pulling out first one bottle and then another, wiping off the dust and reading the label, she gave up. The chill and gloom of the place were getting to her, so she grabbed three bottles at random and hurried upstairs to the warmth and brightness of the kitchen.

"I said the *Sancerre*," Fabrice groused when she set the bottles on the table.

"This was the best I could do before the killer found me."

"What?"

"I tried, but it's a little confusing down there, not to mention cold and dark. You'll have to draw me a map next time if you want a particular bottle. For now, let's eat."

"Red wine with chicken," Fabrice complained, uncorking the bottle and pouring a deep red liquid into two goblets. "It is an abomination."

"So don't drink it," Cady replied, setting the baguette and a small plate of butter on the table, then taking her seat.

Fabrice gave a little half smile. "*Bon appétit.*"

That said, he tucked into his food.

Lucy kept a vigil close by, alert and expectant, and throughout their meal Fabrice fed the dog so much of the chicken that Cady finally said: "Maybe next time I should make Lucy her own bird."

Fabrice chuckled and slipped another chunk of succulent thigh meat to the canine.

"So, you never asked me what brought me all the way from California," Cady said.

He didn't reply.

"I have this wooden rabbit. It's a carousel figure, and I—"

"Don't tell me you're one of those people obsessed with that carousel."

"Who else is obsessed with it?"

"Every once in a while, a stranger comes along, asks to buy it, to look at it." He waved his hand, as though smelling something noxious.

"People are interested in history," said Cady. "That's what brought me to France. I was in

Paris taking photographs of carousels for a book."

He helped himself to more potatoes.

"Good dinner?" Cady asked, pouring him more wine.

He shrugged.

"So . . . the carousel's still here? In the outbuilding?"

He remained quiet for so long that Cady assumed he wasn't going to answer. But finally he said, "It's not even recognizable anymore. The place caught fire a long time ago, and then things got lost."

"Could I see it?"

"Why would you want to?"

"Well, as I started to tell you, I have a carousel figure in the shape of a rabbit. I call him Gus because I always thought he was carved by Gustave Bayol. But it turns out he wasn't. Anyway," Cady added hastily, seeing his attention drift to the dog again, "he fell over and I found a box in his belly, with a photograph that I believe was taken by your great-grandfather. And in the background is the carousel."

Fabrice let out a long sigh and washed down the last of his chicken with wine.

"I could get the box from my room. Maybe you would recognize the woman in the photograph."

"I don't have time for such nonsense." He got up, tossed his napkin on the table, and limped out of the kitchen.

Cady remained at the table for a long time, wondering if she should follow him or if he was coming back. Finally she got up, cleared the table, and washed the dishes.

The dog arched her back like a cat, stretching so hard that Cady heard her spine crack.

"I guess it's you and me, Lucy," Cady said softly, grabbing her flashlight. "Let's go stir up the ghosts outside, shall we?"

That night in bed she worked her way through more of *Le Château*.

Before she fell asleep, Cady made up her mind: She wasn't going to leave Provence until she got a good look at the Clement carousel. Whatever remained of it.

And if there was any possible way, she was going to figure out who her mystery woman in the photograph was.

She glanced at the note for the hundredth time: *Souviens-toi de moi*.

Remember me.

CHAPTER THIRTY-ONE

1900
AVIGNON

Maëlle

Their carriage finally turns into the gravel drive that leads to the magnificent Château Clement. The drive is long and straight, providing the newcomers the opportunity to take in the grandeur of the estate: Golden stone walls gleam in the late-afternoon sun; the chalky blue shutters line up in an elegant symmetrical march across the impressive façade. It is easy to imagine royalty in full regalia standing on the curved twin staircases that lead to the huge front entrance.

Maëlle's mouth falls open as she takes it all in. She can hardly believe she'll be permitted within those hallowed halls.

"Don't be too impressed," says Léon, leaning his head to hers. There are several of them in the carriage—the lucky ones who don't have to ride the steam traction engine with the disassembled carousel—and her thigh and shoulder burn where they are pressed tightly against his. "Rich people are just people; there are idiots and geniuses, just like the rest of us."

"But they are idiots and geniuses with great mansions, *un*like the rest of us," Maëlle responds.

He chuckles, and she preens with pleasure. Every smile she earns makes her happy, every grin makes her proud. And his egalitarian words speak to her heart: it is the sort of thing that her father—considered a radical thinker in their village—used to say: that no one person is better or worse than another.

The carriage swings to the right, coming to a halt at the back of the house. Tightly clipped hedges and Italian cypress trees lead to a formal garden featuring a series of descending ponds and a formal orangerie. Even from this distance Maëlle spies the bright orange fruits through the ample windows of the glass-paned building. Her mouth waters at the memory of an orange she once shared with her brother at Christmastime; it was tart and sweet with the bright freshness of a summer dawn.

Maëlle feels suddenly famished; will the family feed them? Will they be housed and fed with the servants? Until this moment she hasn't wondered about such prosaic concerns; all she could think of was seeing the château and witnessing the beloved carousel fully assembled at last.

And carving. Léon is the chief apprentice, of course, and master of this project. But Monsieur

Bayol had been very clear: The Clement family should be made happy. If they have any other jobs they would like to be done, the Bayol carvers must be at their disposal.

Maëlle has several carvings in her bag: the rose she showed to Monsieur Bayol six months ago, when she first arrived on his doorstep in Angers, and some small wooden toys she has been working on to give as a gift to Madame Clement. They are beautiful creations, tiny replicas of the carousel animals, cows and horses and rabbits with sweet faces and movable legs. Bayol mentioned that the Clements are anxious for children; Maëlle feels sure her toys would have pride of place in the nursery of the most elegant home.

Deep down, Maëlle wonders whether she is being too forward. But surely now is not the time for false humility.

A manservant has come out to meet the carriage, directing those within to step down, and sending the carriage on to the stables. By the time they descend, several others have emerged from the building, including a tall, dark-haired woman in the most beautiful dress Maëlle has ever seen.

There must be six yards of Belgian lace in her dress, and her well-coiffed hair is studded with pearls and flowers.

"I know it breaks with tradition," the woman says as she comes over to the group, "but I simply had to meet the talented group of artists bringing me my carousel! I am Madame Josephine Clement, and this is my dear husband, Monsieur Yves Clement, and we are so very happy to have you here!"

Every word Madame Clement says is breathless, as though she cannot contain her excitement. Maëlle watches in wonder. She had assumed the lady of the manor would be distant and haughty, but Madame Clement is like a child at Christmas.

Maëlle glances up at Léon, and finds his eyes lingering on Madame Clement. A serpent of jealousy wriggles deep in her gut. She looks down at her drab, dusty dress and traveling coat, then tucks an errant lock of hair under her hat.

Several of the maids are attractive as well. Maëlle has never been the type to be jealous of other women. After all, she didn't want what they had; she wanted the life men had. But now . . . Her mouth goes dry as Madame Clement is formally introduced to Léon. Does their greeting linger a fraction of a second too long? Monsieur Clement is clearly much older than his lovely young wife. He is fair complexioned and regal-looking, though he stands an inch or two shorter than Josephine.

Finally it is Maëlle's turn to be introduced.

"Maëlle Tanguy?" repeats Madame Clement. Her voice is deep and soft, sweet cream over raspberries. "That sounds like a Breton name."

"It is, yes, madame. I am Breton."

"Why, I am from Quimper myself!" Josephine says, a huge smile lighting up her face. "*Eus pelec'h emaoc'h*?"

She asks in Breton: "Where are you from?"

It brings tears to Maëlle's eyes to hear the language of her parents. She realizes, with a deep pang, how long it has been since she has lain in bed with Erwann, trading dreams and fears and plans in a mixture of Breton and French, as they always spoke together.

"I am from a town called Concarneau," Maëlle responds. "It is a fishing village on the coast, not far from Quimper, actually."

"Ah! This is wonderful!" says Madame Clement, clapping her hands beneath her chin. "I am so happy you are here! We shall have many days to speak of our homeland. But for now, I am sure you are exhausted from your travels. Please allow my housekeeper, Madame Boucher, to show you to your rooms, while Monsieur Derridan takes the men to their quarters."

Maëlle feels a vague sort of panic at the base of her throat as she watches the men leave. Léon does not turn around to say good-bye. She is alone.

Madame Boucher is an ample woman in a dress made of fine dark silk, which seems to strain against her enormous bosom. The keys on a huge ring hanging off her belt clank as she marches along officiously. Maëlle, carrying her own bag, trots to keep up.

Madame Clement is nothing like what Maëlle had expected of a wealthy benefactress, but Château Clement itself displays more grandeur than she could have imagined. Crystal chandeliers and a massive, sweeping staircase. The balustrades and passageways, the hewn stone and painted panels. The arches and doorways and paneling made of oak and mahogany, beautiful and gleaming with polish but unadorned.

Maëlle chases the housekeeper along a hall, around a corner, and down a half staircase into a set of public rooms lined with more leather-bound books than Maëlle has ever seen in one place. Then they proceed up a longer staircase to a narrow hallway lined with several doors. Madame Boucher is unsmiling as she opens the door to a bedroom with a beamed, sloping ceiling and a window that looks out over the stables. There is an enormous bed made up in luscious white linens, a small writing desk, and a tall armoire. A thick wool rug warms the stone floor.

"I hope this is adequate for your needs," the housekeeper says.

"It is beautiful," Maëlle replies.

"There is a washroom down the hall. We have running water here, so you won't need a chamber pot. The stones become chilly in the evening; I shall have the maid set the fire when you retire.

Please let me know if there's anything else you require." Madame Boucher does not make eye contact, and Maëlle can't help but feel as though she is being treated better than is proper, that she is an underling, an impostor. Never in her wildest dreams had she expected to be housed in a luxurious guest room. The servants' wing would have been more than adequate.

"Madame—" Maëlle is about to say as much, but when the housekeeper pauses in the doorway and meets her eyes, she simply says, "Thank you."

"Oh, one more thing. Are you familiar with electric lights?"

"They have installed some electric lightposts in Angers. But . . . not in a home."

"I thought not. You move this switch, thusly, and the lamp is lit, just that quickly. You see?" She demonstrates, moving a toggle attached to the wall. The overhead lamp comes on immediately. It is bright, almost glaring, even though it is still light outside.

After Madame Boucher bustles off down the hall, Maëlle puts her clothes away in the armoire, fragrant from cedar and small sachets of lavender hanging on the rod.

She knows she should go outside with her checklist to be sure that every box transferred from the train to the steam traction engine has arrived safely at the château. But she hesitates, sitting on the edge of the bed. Exhaustion overwhelms her. She lies back, closing her eyes for a moment and breathing deeply. The mattress is so soft it feels as if she is floating on a cloud; it reminds her of a painting of napping cherubs she saw in the cathedral in Angers. Scents of rosemary and wild thyme waft in on the breeze through the open window, and the coverlet smells subtly of soap.

It is far too good for her, but she will relish it.

She will close her eyes for just a few moments, and then she'll get to work.

Her last thought before falling into a deep slumber was to wonder where Léon would be sleeping tonight, which pillow would be lucky enough to cradle his handsome head.

But when she dreams, it is not of Léon's kisses. Instead, she has a vision of the carousel come to vibrant life, whirling around to the tune of the band organ, delighting all who see it.

CHAPTER THIRTY-TWO

PRESENT DAY
CHÂTEAU CLEMENT

Cady

The next morning, Cady dressed in jeans, a thick sweater, and boots, slung her Nikon around her neck, and headed downstairs.

Fabrice was shuffling around the kitchen, keeping one hand on the counter to steady himself.

"*Bonjour*," said Cady to Fabrice.

"*Bonjour*," he said, seeming vaguely surprised to see her. His voice was croaky, as though he was unaccustomed to speaking.

The dog got up from her bed near the now-cold fireplace, stretched languidly, then came over to Cady with her tail wagging. Cady caressed Lucy's back and scratched her ears. At least *somebody* was happy to see her.

"Want me to make breakfast?" Cady offered, setting her camera on the counter. "I got a good feel for this kitchen last night. With a little tutoring, I could probably even master your espresso machine."

Fabrice did not answer, much less pause in his actions.

Coffee people. Cady understood. Those addicted to caffeine often had these morning rituals, putting one foot in front of the other till they reached the kitchen, then measuring out the grounds and tamping them down, pouring the boiling water over them, inhaling the delicious aroma, and readying themselves for the first restorative sip.

Then again, Fabrice often responded with a grunt. Perhaps it was simply his way.

Cady got herself a small plate and cut a piece of bread.

"Who is 'Anon'?"

"What?"

"I've been reading *Le Château*—and before you stop me, I'm just asking whether 'Anon' was translated properly. In English 'anon' means something's going to happen soon, but it's archaic English, rarely used."

"You should always read a book in its original language."

"You mean it wasn't translated properly?"

He picked up her camera and studied it, playing with the dials and knobs, looking through the lens. Finally, he said: "That translation was suspect, yes. But in this case, Anon is a name. There is no translation."

"Who does it refer to?"

"What are you taking pictures of?" Fabrice asked, ignoring her question.

"I thought I'd take some of the château grounds, if that's all right with you. The old buildings, the olive trees, and—"

"When are you going shopping?" Fabrice demanded.

"I just went yesterday."

"We need more bread. And we'll need dinner tonight."

"I got some pasta yesterday, and a few other things I could throw together for dinner. . . ." At the look on Fabrice's face, she cleared her throat and said, "Never mind. I'll run into town and pick up a few things. Happy to do it." Cady wanted to take her computer to the Internet café anyway. On top of which, a daily trip to the *boulangerie* didn't sound like the worst idea in the world.

"What kind of sauce for the pasta?" Fabrice asked.

"I was thinking a simple marinara, but I'm flexible. Do you have a favorite?"

"Alfredo."

"Okay then, Alfredo it is. I'll make a big salad, and garlic bread. Of course."

"What's 'garlic bread'?"

"What's *garlic bread?*" she repeated, unsure if she had understood him correctly. How did anyone not know garlic bread? "It's . . . bread, with garlic. And butter. Lots of butter. In fact, that might be the most important part. You warm it in the oven and . . .” She sighed and sought the proper word. In English, she said, “Ambrosia.”

He fixed her with those questioning hawk eyes. “*Que-ce que c’est* ‘ambrosia’?”

“I don’t know the word in French. In English *ambrosia* means the food of the gods.”

“Ah.” He nodded and said, “*Ambroisie.*”

“*Ambroisie.* Good to know. But seriously, you’ve never had garlic bread?”

He shook his head.

“And here I thought you Frenchies were more accomplished than Americans in all things food-related.”

Once again Fabrice grunted in reply, setting a tiny cup of espresso in front of her, with a square of chocolate on the plate.

“But this, right here,” she said, holding up the sweet morsel, “makes up for a lot.”

Fabrice scowled at her over the rim of his espresso cup. “I thought you said I wouldn’t even know you were here. This morning I know you are here.”

Embarrassment washed over her. Cady hadn’t realized she was being chatty; it was rare for her.

“I . . .” She tried to think of something to say.

He gave her another dismissive wave of his hand. “Ignore me, I’m a mean old man. This is why I’ve lived alone all these years.”

Cady managed a smile.

He handed her some euros. "Here, for the groceries. For yesterday, and today."

"Thank you, but I'm happy to pay for them. It's a contribution to the household. You're kind to let me stay here."

"I'm not kind."

"But you let me stay here."

He looked at her again, doing that strange tilt of the head, as though trying to figure something out, or preparing to say something. It was there and gone so quickly that Cady wondered if she imagined it. But she had seen it once before: the first time they had met, outside, when he was holding a shotgun on her and Jean-Paul.

"Take the money, Cady," Fabrice said. He left the cash on the counter, grabbed his crutch, and shuffled out to the hall. Lucy got up slowly, stretched again, then turned to follow him.

"Lucy, come here, pup." Cady called Lucy back, picked up the leash and camera, put on her coat and hat, and took the dog outside for her walk.

Dewdrops sparkled in the slanting morning sun; longer shafts of grass held several in a row, like a string of beads. The dewdrops twinkled and winked, casting their light first this way, then that, now violet, now blue, now green, as through a prism.

Cady's photographer mind immediately strategized how to capture them from the best angle:

on her belly in the mud, using a telephoto lens. Her Argus camera would be best. But she knew from experience that it was impossible. It was like taking photos of sunsets: Even the prettiest photo could not capture the true multidimensional magic of the ever-changing light.

Dewdrops refracting the clear light of morning, Cady decided, were a lesson in enjoying the temporal, the ephemeral.

Lucy spied a jackrabbit and nearly yanked Cady's arm out of its socket attempting to give chase, but otherwise she trotted along calmly, looking up at Cady with bright eyes, as though to telegraph how happy she was to be sharing this beautiful morning. The dog seemed to embody the Zen notion of living for the moment, reveling in the here and now: the scents in the bushes, the wetness of the grass under her paws, the simple pleasure of taking a walk with a friend.

Not many foster homes kept animals, so the only other pet Cady knew well was the nearly feral tabby Maxine had rescued, named Daisy. It was an ugly, cranky thing of uncertain heritage who spat at anyone who approached. Nonetheless, Daisy had pride of place on a chifforobe in the shop. About a year after Cady began working at the store, she arrived one morning to find Maxine crying, bent over a too-still mound of orange-and-gray fur. Daisy had passed away during the night.

Cady remembered observing Maxine's grief and thinking, *This is what it's like to love something that is unlovable.*

Cady walked Lucy farther around the property, trying to take a page out of the dog's book and focus on her senses. The air was fresh and cold, and carried the soft scents of early spring: budding fruit trees, bulbs pushing their way up through newly warmed soil, the rich aroma of lavender and rosemary bushes warmed by the sun and touched by dew. The outbuildings were still enshrouded in the morning mist, and everything was lit by the silver light of early morning.

She snapped some photos, crouching to angle her camera this way and that, trying to capture the odd juxtaposition of the graffiti against the historic buildings. The mist lent an aura of otherworldliness to the scene.

There didn't appear to be any new graffiti decorating the outbuildings, so maybe the "bad kid" had found something else to do.

What was this kid's story?

Lucy did her business behind a bush and Cady contemplated whether she was expected to pick it up—but this being France, and the countryside, she let it go. Parisians loved their dogs, but seemed content to leave their droppings where they fell, apparently too chic to scoop up doggy doo-doo.

Back in the château there was still no sign of Fabrice, so Cady took Lucy off the leash, filled the dog's water bowl, and headed to her bedroom. As she had with her apartment in the Latin Quarter, she was developing her daily routine, making Château Clement feel more like home.

Maybe all those years spent bouncing from one situation to the next had been good for something, after all.

CHAPTER THIRTY-THREE

1944
FRANCE

Fabrice

His cover story was that he was going to visit his grandparents in the countryside outside of Nantes. He was to take the train to Nantes, where he was to find the *boulangerie* on the rue Morgan and ask if they might have a particular rye boule "that my grandmother loves." The contact would then give him a ride to the outskirts of Saint-Nazaire, and give him enough information to blend in with the arrival of the student group on their field trip.

If Fabrice had tried to pass into Vichy, he would have needed a special permit, almost impossible to get. But German-occupied France allowed some movement, and it was easy enough to get on the train. If it weren't for the presence of the Nazis, he could almost imagine there was no war going on as he watched the countryside fly by. Though he missed Paulette already, it felt good to get out of the city, leaving behind claustrophobic curfews, hiding in doorways to avoid the police patrols, fearing betrayal at every turn.

On the train Fabrice could imagine something different for himself: that he was older, dashing, brave. He envisioned joining the Free French Forces, earning a chest of medals like his father had from the First World War. He daydreamed about the moment he would stride back into the doctor's office—to Paulette—after accomplishing his mission.

He would no longer be a boy, but a triumphant soldier of the Résistance.

The shopkeepers in the *boulangerie* were hushed and wary, and the man who drove Fabrice the rest of the way was a coarse farmer who smelled of sweat and spoke little other than to relay instructions. There was no buoyant sense of camaraderie here, just fear and grim desperation. The farmer's truck was old and uncomfortable, squeaking and lurching as though about to break down. He dropped Fabrice a mile from the base and told him to hike through the woods to the northeast and then to wait for the school bus to arrive.

The Nazi guards standing at the base entrance were almost as young as he. Fabrice hesitated when he saw them, but when a teacher yelled at him to get in line, he melted into a school group that had arrived for their visit.

The farmer had warned him that the head

teacher was a Nazi sympathizer, but since there would be several different classes mingling together a new face was unlikely to be noticed. Fabrice prayed none of the students would notice that he was out of place.

Once they were through the gates, Fabrice relaxed. The Nazis were proud of their base, and of their submarines. They encouraged the students to ask questions, and within the large group it was easy enough to snap photos. He committed to memory the layout so he could draw a map afterward, and when the class was climbing back aboard the bus he slipped into the woods to await the farmer with his truck to take him to Nantes.

He felt triumphant. The whole endeavor had gone so smoothly Fabrice decided he would volunteer for more such missions, would embrace *clandestinité*, severing ties with his family and going all in for the remainder of the war.

Brutal reality came crashing down upon his fantasy when, on the return trip, the train screamed to a stop outside of Le Mans. Soldiers clambered onto the train, their boots treading heavily on the floor in ominous thunder. Along with most of the men on the train, Fabrice was searched. He had sewn the rolls of film into the lining of his hat, which lay safe and uninspected on the seat while they went through his satchel and frisked him, shouting questions at him. He repeated the story of visiting his good Catholic grandparents who lived in a farmhouse outside of Nantes, tearing up in fear when another man in the same train car was struck repeatedly by a soldier, then hauled off the train. The soldiers, disgusted by his tears, derided him and left.

The rest of the train ride was spent in stunned relief and humiliation, liquid fear still running through his veins.

But back in Paris, Fabrice realized that surely he was old enough now for Paulette. He felt a hundred years old, in fact.

When he showed up at the doctor's office with the film, Paulette jumped up and ran across the reception room to embrace him.

"I'm so glad! Oh, Fabrice, I was so scared for you!"

It was all worth it. For this. Holding her in his arms. It was all worth it.

But they were not alone. The doctor came out and ushered Fabrice into the examination room. "You didn't tell anyone where you went? Not even my secretary?"

"No, of course not. But surely she knows?"

"She knew you were going somewhere, but not the location or reason."

"But—"

"My point is not to trust anyone. Not *anyone.*"

Fabrice nodded and pulled the film out of his hatband, handing it to the doctor, who nodded and smiled.

"Excellent," he said.

"Also, I drew a map, and wrote down all the numbers and other pertinent information. Everything I could remember."

"You are a hero, Garçon."

"I am but a Frenchman," Fabrice responded, feeling noble and patriotic, wishing Paulette could be there to hear their exchange.

CHAPTER THIRTY-FOUR

PRESENT DAY
PROVENCE

Cady

Cady stood in line at the *boulangerie* behind a white-haired woman who couldn't decide what she wanted for a large gathering of family visiting from Lyon. Once again, enveloped by the delectable aroma of fresh bread, and enthralled by the variety of tempting goods in the display cases, Cady didn't mind waiting.

"What did I tell you?" a man's voice said from behind her. "There is only one *boulangerie* in town. It was just a matter of time before our paths crossed again. *Bonjour*, Cady."

"*Bonjour*, Jean-Paul," Cady replied. They exchanged kisses on the cheek. "I've been meaning to call you."

"Do you like the place you're renting?" Jean-Paul asked.

"Actually, I've had a change of address. I'm staying with your cousin."

"At Château Clement." It wasn't so much a question as a statement.

"Yes."

"Fabrice asked you to stay with him?"

"I wouldn't put it that way, exactly, no. We made an arrangement: I have someplace to stay in exchange for walking his dog and cooking. And now I'm grocery shopping. I'm sort of an all-around Girl Friday."

He looked nonplussed.

"He needs help, Jean-Paul, you know that," Cady said in a quiet voice. "He's a cranky old man but he's on his own and shouldn't be. He needs someone."

"I realize that. It is why I came from Paris in the first place."

"But it's been a couple of days."

"One full day."

"Still."

"I was picking up bread before going over there right now. We take our time; this is how we do it in our family. He has to get used to the idea of permitting me to help."

"After you left that night I tried to go, too, but my tires were slashed, and it was raining. Fabrice allowed me to spend the night, and—"

"What do you mean, your tires were slashed?"

"Just what I said. I don't know the word *slashed* in French; do you know it in English? Like . . . cut?"

"Who would do something like that?"

"At first I thought I might be caught up in a movie plot. Like a newcomer's tires are slashed so she has to stay at the creepy old château."

"I don't understand."

"You know, to be murdered . . . Sorry, I was making a joke, but I don't think my humor translates across languages. My guess is a kid named Johnny, who apparently had a falling-out with Fabrice and has been vandalizing the place."

He took a deep breath. "I'll have a talk with his father."

"No! No, please don't. I have no proof, none, zero. It wouldn't be fair to get the boy in trouble for something he may not have done. And anyway, he's going to make it up to me—to Fabrice, I mean."

"How's he going to do that?"

"I'll deal with it is my point."

The old woman at the head of the line finally shuffled off with a massive bag full of baguettes, boules, and croissants, so Cady stepped up to the register and ordered a *pain au chocolat*, two baguettes, and a large brioche.

"My cousin likes *pain de mie*."

Jean-Paul had moved up behind her as though they were together, placing one arm atop the glass case as he ordered the *pain de mie*. He stood close enough for Cady to inhale his scent: a slightly citrus musk. Talk about ambrosia.

"Also," Jean-Paul said to Cady, "you aren't allowed to leave town without trying the escargot. It is our custom."

"Thanks, but I'm not sure I'm up for snails. Where I come from we step on snails; we don't eat them."

He scoffed. "You really must try true escargots before you leave France, but the escargot I am speaking of now is a pastry. You'll thank me."

Jean-Paul spoke rapidly in French and the baker's wife handed Cady a coiled roll filled with pistachio and chocolate.

Jean-Paul insisted on paying for everything. "What is happening with your car?"

"The rental company had it towed to Avignon. I don't have Internet access at the château, and my phone is having trouble receiving messages, so I was on my way over to the Hound Dog Café to check my e-mail." She patted the computer bag slung over her shoulder.

"I'll go with you."

"I hear he's an Elvis fan."

"You could say that."

To Cady's eyes the Hound Dog Café was more tavern than café. A well-stocked bar ran along one side, and a pool table crowded the opposite corner. The walls were studded with posters of Elvis Presley, from the early movies featuring him as a slim, handsome young man, to the jump-suited version not long before his death.

Hubert, a paunchy, middle-aged man with long sideburns, looked a little like Elvis Presley in his Vegas years. He stood behind the bar drying glasses with a towel and greeted Jean-Paul by name when he entered. Two old men sat hunched over beers at the bar; a small mixed group of middle-aged men and women had pushed two tables together and were chatting; a young couple giggled and leaned toward each other over their table.

Cady ordered a coffee, Jean-Paul asked for a Fernet-Branca, and they took a seat by the window.

She tried the pastry. The layers were rich with butter, tender inside with a satisfying crunch at the edges. The filling of pistachio and chocolate was scrumptious. She glanced up to find Jean-Paul's eyes on her.

"Good?" he asked.

"Mmmmmm," was all she could manage. She brushed a few flakes off her lips. And then: "You're right, I thank you."

He smiled.

"I wanted to ask you something," Cady said. "You mentioned your mother has copies of the old photos taken by Yves Clement. Do you think she would share them with me?"

"I'll ask her, if you would like. Why don't I bring them to the château—it would be interesting to see what Fabrice would make of them."

"He's a fascinating man."

One corner of his mouth kicked up. "I suppose that's one way to put it."

"I was thinking, he must have been writing in Paris during the bohemian heyday, right after World War II. Imagine the people he might have known."

"According to what I've heard, he thinks that was the last time Paris was interesting. Fabrice doesn't have much time for Paris, much less my 'fancy education.' "

"Well, I envy you. I never went to college."

"No?"

She shook her head. "I barely made it out of high school, really. I wasn't what you'd call a natural student."

"You seem to have done well for yourself."

"I read," Cady said, then stopped herself. She had almost confessed to him. "Slowly, but I read a lot."

He nodded. "Didn't the writer Ray Bradbury say something about that? That he was 'library-educated'?"

"I hadn't heard that, but I like it." She sipped her coffee and for a moment let silence fall over them. Finally, Cady added: "As I mentioned in Paris, I'm reading your cousin's *Le Château* right now."

"Yes, I'm impressed. That's not an easy read."

"Well, I'm making my way through the English

translation. And I confess, I have no idea what's going on. But he describes bits and pieces of the château, so it's fun to track those down and see what he's talking about. The man at the bookstore told me it was a roman à clef. Did you know that?"

Jean-Paul nodded.

"It would be much more intriguing if I had any idea what was going on. Do you know whether the carousel was completely destroyed in the fire?"

"Some say there were parts that remained, relatively unscathed. But it's all conjecture; I think Fabrice is the only one who knows for sure."

"Well, I'm working on him. In the novel, he refers to an 'apprentice' staying at the château, and working there for a period of time, but he's referred to only as 'Anon' or 'Anonymous.' I wish I had the key that went along with the novel."

Jean-Paul's sherry-colored eyes lingered on her for a long moment, and she thought she saw sadness in them. He had a quick wit and an easy smile, but she wondered: Had his fiancée really run off with his business partner?

"How long are you planning to stay?" Jean-Paul asked.

"I don't have a plan, exactly," Cady said, her stomach fluttering as the words came out. "I'm sort of playing it by ear."

"No one's waiting for you back in the States?"

"No," she replied. "How about you? You don't need to get back to Paris?"

He gave a ghost of a smile, and a barely-there shake of his head. "You heard what Fabrice said. My wedding was canceled at the last minute."

"I'm sorry."

"Thank you. But it was for the best. And Fabrice got one thing wrong: I left her, not the other way around."

"Why?"

He gazed into his glass. "She deserves someone better."

"Someone like your business partner?"

He gave a humorless chuckle. "*Ex*-business partner. But yes. He is probably a better man than I."

Cady had no idea how to respond. Their gazes met again, and held.

"So, Cady, what I still can't figure out is what you're doing here."

"I could ask you the same thing."

He chuckled. "Perhaps. But Saint-Véran is my native village, and I am spending time with relatives, trying to look after my cousin and the château I will one day inherit. Whereas you . . ."

"I'm butting in? Are you telling me to leave?"

"Not at all. I'm just trying to . . . what is the phrase? 'Figure you out.' "

She let out a quick laugh. "Well, let me know

what you come up with. I could use a clue myself. As you know, I was trying to track down the provenance of my carousel figure, which led me here. But now that I'm at the château, I have come to realize that at this point . . ." She took a deep breath, let it out slowly. "The idea of spending a few nights at a mysterious château—one featured in a novel, no less—is pretty exciting. I guess I'm just . . . playing it by ear."

"As you said. So . . . no plans."

"No plans. And you? What do you intend to do with the château once you inherit it? Move in, have those kids you were talking about, become a country gentleman?"

"Not exactly, no. I would like to bring in a structural engineer to assess how much work—and money—it will take to renovate the château, bring it up to modern standards. And then"—he shrugged—"there are a couple of chains that run châteaux as small hotels, wedding venues, that sort of thing."

"It seems a shame to let the château leave the family."

"You Americans are very romantic about history, are you not? Perhaps that is the result of having less of it than we. Remember, I did not grow up at the château, and have no sentimental attachment to it. When Fabrice's father, Marc-Antoine, didn't return after the First World War, it was not properly maintained and became a ruin, really."

"Why didn't Fabrice's father return?"

"He married a Parisian, and you know how they are."

"I don't, actually, but I know what Fabrice would say about that."

"Ironically, of all the extended Clement family, Fabrice is by far the most Parisian. He was born and raised there, after all."

Again Jean-Paul held her gaze. His manner wasn't flirtatious—at least she didn't think it was. But there was something . . .

She cleared her throat. "About those plans . . . Is there sufficient demand for a hotel in this small village?"

"I think so." He nodded. "Saint-Véran is close enough to Avignon to take advantage of the tourists. At least that is what I'm banking on."

"Still, after all these generations . . ."

"There's virtue in returning it to its former glory and opening the doors to the public—if it's still salvageable, that is."

"You think it's that far gone? Some of the floors are slanting, and there are cracks in the walls, and a few leaks, but still . . . it seems solid."

"I can't know for sure until I have it properly inspected. My cousin hasn't allowed it, and the situation is . . . It can be awkward. Not only is Fabrice not the friendliest guy in the first place, but I don't want him thinking I'm anxious for his demise."

She nodded. "I can understand that."

Jean-Paul's eyes shifted to something behind her. "Excuse me, please, one moment. I see someone I must speak to."

"Of course. I wanted to check my e-mail anyway."

She logged on to her e-mail and was thrilled to find a message from Olivia:

> **You are too much, my friend. I leave you alone in a foreign country for a few days, and already you're living with an old man and his dog? In a CHÂTEAU???**

Olivia continued with a funny story about their latest adventures in home renovation, during which Sebastian had stepped in a bucket of water while attempting to strip the wallpaper off the walls of their old Victorian and uncover the original plaster.

> **They say couples learn a lot about each other during a home renovation. I have learned that Sebastian has many sterling qualities but being a handyman is not among them. I fear for the future, as**

ladders will soon be involved. The over-under for our next trip to the E.R. ($$$!) is three days. Care to make a wager?

Olivia's chatty tone and good humor brought a smile to Cady's face. She liked to think of herself as a loner, but the truth was she wouldn't have made it without Maxine, and then Olivia. Even Jonquilla, now that she thought about it. Each had been an echo of her character, in a way—a big part of how she came to know who she was. What would life be without a single friend?

Did Fabrice have anyone? After eighty-something years on this planet, how could he walk so alone? With family nearby, no less.

Cady was writing a short missive to Olivia when Jean-Paul appeared, holding by the scruff of his collar the teenager she had seen throwing rocks.

"Cady, I would like to introduce you to Johnny," Jean-Paul said in French. "He has something to say to you."

"*Désolé*," Johnny said in a sullen tone.

"Thank you," Cady replied. "You should apologize to Fabrice as well."

He shrugged and avoided eye contact, looking around the bar.

"I'm not sure what the minimum wage is in France, or even how much it would cost to repair the damage you've done," Cady said, channeling the words Maxine had used on her after she'd stolen several items from her shop. "Luckily I had insurance on my rental car that will pay for the tires, but you owe Fabrice several hours of your time. Come to the château tomorrow after school and you can start to make it up to him."

"Yeah, sure," he said. "Can I go now?"

Jean-Paul released him and the teenager slouched out the door.

"He won't show up, you realize," said Jean-Paul, taking a seat.

"You never know," said Cady. "It worked on me, back in the day."

"I have a feeling there's more to that story."

She smiled. "I'm a woman of mystery."

"Another coffee?"

"No, thank you. I have to go grocery shopping. Pasta's on the menu tonight."

"I like pasta."

"Oh, I . . . it's not really my place to be asking people to dinner."

"It's not really your place to be living with my cousin, either, but you're doing it."

"It *is* still his château, after all."

"I realize that," Jean-Paul said stiffly. "I'm just frustrated that I am unable to get him to open up to *me.* It's a little—what is the word?—*galling* to have tried for so long, and then you come along with your whiskey, and just like that . . ."

"Well, then . . . Monsieur Mirassou, would you honor us with your presence at dinner this evening?"

Jean-Paul relaxed and smiled. "I accept with pleasure. However, if I may be so bold, it is not even noon. I see you have your camera with you. Why don't we take a trip to Avignon? There's a historic carousel in the Place de l'Horloge that you could photograph for your collection."

"Why would you want to take me to Avignon?"

"Do you not wish to pick up a new rental car?"

"I do, but . . . Are you trying to get rid of me?"

"It is not exactly that," Jean-Paul said as they stood and gathered their things. "I simply want to be sure you are able to make a fast getaway, just in case."

CHAPTER THIRTY-FIVE

1900
CHÂTEAU CLEMENT

Maëlle

The sounds of hammering and the whining of hand-cranked drills fill the courtyard as Bayol's crew gets to work, assembling the numbered pieces like a jigsaw puzzle. Five men work to put the carousel together, while the others busy themselves with the construction of the salon façade, the entrance of which will be flanked by two special horse statues evocative of the carousel figures within the structure. Panels with intricately painted scenes line the walls, their gilded frames following liquid Art Nouveau lines.

The engineer tinkers with the steam engine, and joins the rods and cranks. The front rod moves up and down, the rear rod swivels on its hinge as the ride rotates on its track under the platform floor. It is essential that everything work smoothly, without a hitch, before they return to Angers.

The crew eats together in the servants' dining

room off the large kitchen on the ground floor. It is only when they are seated that Maëlle realizes perhaps the rumors are true, that the Clement family is not as wealthy as they first appear. Léon tells Maëlle that half the servants' chambers are empty; he points out where the rugs are threadbare, corners of the gardens untended. He mentions, with scorn in his voice, that Madame Clement has worn the same dress twice since they arrived two weeks ago.

"I wear the same dress every single day," Maëlle says with wonder. What must it be like to don a different gown each morning, changing again for dinner? "Their closets must be enormous."

Léon laughs, a full-throated sound that she has not heard in too long. Maëlle tries not to smile, not to show how much it means to her. Is it her imagination, or has he been less attentive than before? When she asks him about it, he declares it is because he is in charge of the work crew; he must be even more discreet.

But for a man in charge, he disappears frequently during work hours. The other men keep his secrets; they won't tell Maëlle where Léon goes, using vague terms like "taking a break" or "he had to run into town for supplies." As if Maëlle doesn't know, much better than Léon, what supplies they may or may not need. When he disappears, the result is chaos on the job site. Romain is a talented carpenter but he does not understand how the mechanism—the cranks, gears, and shafts—must interact with his woodwork. Guy is a gifted engineer, focusing exclusively on the engine, the rods, and the tracks. The others are too young to take the initiative, so they wait for guidance.

In Léon's absence, Maëlle steps in to read the blueprints and coordinate their efforts. Soon the men begin to look to her for direction.

When she throws herself into her work she can forget that Léon looked too long at the attractive scullery maid this morning. When she feels the wood beneath her hands and watches how the disparate pieces come together, the art of the carousel sings to her like a siren.

Madame and Monsieur Clement stop by the job site to inspect the progress. It is only then that Léon appears, giving them the tour as the man in charge. Maëlle notices how he lingers by Madame Clement's side, attending to her every remark. He makes her laugh; she throws her head back, showing delicate white teeth; her long neck—there is a small heart-shaped mole that seems more enhancement than flaw—is adorned with a glittering gold cross.

Just looking at Josephine's ecru lace dress makes Maëlle feel insignificant and small, like an ant. She has never been one to lust after wealth, but now she wonders: What would it be like to wear such a thing? Beside Josephine's bright vivacity, Yves Clement looks inconsequential; he is graying, and his slight frame is almost gaunt. He says little, seemingly content to allow his wife to shine. Maëlle can't help but imagine a man like Léon in his place, standing tall, wearing a beautiful brocade vest and brandishing a silver-headed cane.

Maëlle averts her gaze, praying that no one could sense what she is feeling.

She looks up to find Josephine's eyes on hers. It is probably her imagination . . . but it seems like Josephine is reading her mind.

CHAPTER THIRTY-SIX

PRESENT DAY
AVIGNON

Cady

All the way from Paris to Avignon," Cady said as they gazed at the cobbled ruin of the Pont d'Avignon, "I had that stupid song stuck in my head: *'Sur le pont d'Avignon, l'on y danse, l'on y danse.'* "

"Hard to imagine much dancing happening here now, isn't it?" Jean-Paul responded. He had been the consummate tour guide, explaining that in the Middle Ages Avignon had flourished because of its location on the Rhône River, and had once been the seat of the Pope. "The current metropolis spills out far beyond the original city gates, of course, but most of the medieval ramparts remain."

Within the massive stone walls encircling Avignon was a labyrinth of cobbled streets and lantern-lit passageways. Jugglers and musicians entertained tourists in the Place de l'Horloge, a long square that stretched out in front of the Hôtel de Ville, or city hall. Vendors sold handmade jewelry and beautiful scarves, imported handicrafts from Kenya, and leather goods from Italy. Crowded cafés vied for space on the terraced square, and musicians and a juggler entertained visitors.

"Busy place," Cady said. "And it's not even tourist season."

"In the summer, Avignon's population is said to double with visitors. It is not Paris, but it is a popular destination, for foreigners and French alike."

Holding pride of place at the top of the Place de l'Horloge was the rococo Belle Époque Carousel. The running-board panels along the crown were lined with lightbulbs, inspiring Cady to imagine how it appeared at night, lighting up this stone plaza. Two levels of prancing horses and tilting carriages made their endless circles to a carnivalesque *oompah-pah*, and several children, red-cheeked with excitement, waved to their parents as they whirled by.

Cady snapped numerous photographs, but the Avignon merry-go-round wasn't distinctive enough to merit a special mention in a book focusing on Parisian carousels.

Just then several small papers skittered by in the wind. Cady was reminded of cleaning up after her last Prospective Parents fair at the Tilden Park carousel in Berkeley. The discount name tags hadn't stuck well to fabric, and at the end of a long afternoon the weary social workers had given Cady the task of chasing down the fluttering stickers: Connor and Maria and Kristin and Tyrone. Prospective parents, blowing away in the wind.

"Are you all right?" Jean-Paul asked.

Cady realized she had been staring at the carousel through the lens of her camera, as though frozen.

"Yes, sorry. I'm done here. What's next?"

"The Palais des Papes."

"Lead on, Jeeves," Cady said grandly. "I shall reward your efforts with a handsome tip at the end of the day."

"Will you, now?"

"I'll feed you pasta, at least."

"I accept. *Après-vous, madamoiselle.*"

A short, narrow street led from the plaza to the fortress-like Palais des Papes, or Papal Palace. The tall, brooding Gothic structure loomed against the afternoon sky, grim and threatening.

"This would be your palace, then?"

"Pardon?"

" 'Jean-Paul' sounds like a pope's name. So this would be your palace."

He looked confused.

"Sorry. It wasn't very funny anyway," Cady said. "So, the architecture here seems so different from Paris."

"Yes, the medieval center of town has more in common with the south of France, and Spain. Avignon didn't technically become part of France until the late eighteenth century, after the Revolution. Until then, it was a papal property. The cathedral is worth a visit," said Jean-Paul, checking his watch, "but I don't know if we have time to go in today."

"That's all right," Cady said, eyeing the line of visitors waiting to purchase tickets to tour the palace. "It's a beautiful day, and I'm enjoying my walking tour."

"The Librairie Roumanille is down that way," he said, pointing toward a stone passageway. "It is said to be one of the oldest bookstores in all of France."

"That I have to see," she said.

They walked down the rue Saint-Agricol, taking in gorgeous painted doors and small statues of saints set into shadowy niches on the sides of ancient stone town houses. They paused to peer in the windows of an antiques store displaying several wooden carvings, making Cady wonder again how Gus had ended up at a flea market in San Francisco, where Maxine had found him.

"It is time for lunch," Jean-Paul announced as they left the bookstore.

"But we're having pasta for dinner."

"And?"

"I wasn't planning on having a big lunch. Maybe just grab a quick sandwich."

He shook his head. "We eat dinner late in this part of France. You need a good lunch."

"Fabrice said something about that last night, when I served dinner at six thirty."

"Here it can be very hot and . . . what is the word? *Maggy?* Very humid in the summertime. So people take advantage of the cool of the evening to sit outside and enjoy their meal. It doesn't cool down until well after eight. Let's stop here: La Cour du Louvre is a wonderful restaurant."

Cady might have passed right by the small passageway had Jean-Paul not pointed it out. It led to a courtyard strung with fairy lights, the restaurant's decor bohemian but elegant. Jean-Paul asked if she would let him order for her, and, feeling adventurous, she agreed.

Cady sat back in her chair and noted, with some surprise, that she was extraordinarily relaxed. Partly it was the simple fact that Jean-Paul preferred to speak English. As much as Cady enjoyed exploring the world opened up by a new language, and knew her fluency was improving, speaking French with Fabrice had been draining. Cady feared that she missed at least twenty percent of what he said—maybe more—and virtually all of the nuance. She had to concentrate at all times, imagining where one word stopped and another began, but taking care not to get so caught up in the mechanics of syntax and grammar that she lost the flow of the conversation.

It was exhausting.

So it was a welcome respite to be able to speak her own language, and Jean-Paul rarely failed to understand. But there was more to it than just the ease of communication. There was something comforting about Jean-Paul, an ease with which he operated in the world. She envied him his self-confidence.

"Do you know this wine?" he asked, holding up a bottle with a fancy label.

"No," said Cady. "I've been to Napa and know a little bit about California wines, but French wine is a complete mystery to me. I am, I fear, an uncouth savage."

Jean-Paul laughed. "Then we must do something about that, *ma chère sauvage*. This is Châteauneuf-du-Pape."

"Again with the popes?"

"It is the name of a village, not far from Avignon. I believe a pope had a castle there, yes." He poured the ruby red wine into her glass.

"Well, I do love the name. *Châteauneuf-du-Pape*." She repeated it: sha-toe-nuff-du-pop. "I could say that all day. Châteauneuf-du-POP!"

He raised an eyebrow.

"Sorry."

"Don't be. You are charming. I've just never really thought about the name before."

Me, charming? That was a first. But then everything about this trip was a first.

"Try it," Jean-Paul urged.

She brought the glass to her lips, but paused when she noted his eyes tracking her movements. "You always watch me when I eat and drink. Is it like the walking thing? Do I drink like an American or something?"

He gave her a slow, sexy smile. "It is nothing like that. You seem to enjoy the flavors so much . . . and what is more sensual than a beautiful woman eating and drinking?"

"I'm hardly a beautiful woman, Jean-Paul. What is it you want from me?"

"I beg your pardon?"

"The first time we met, you offered to buy my rabbit from me. And then you took a day to escort me around Paris, and now all around Avignon. Why?"

"As I said, you are—"

"A beautiful woman. Right. Sell it somewhere else."

"I'm sorry, Cady, but I don't understand how I have offended you."

Cady took a deep breath and tried to rein in her temper. Was she just being paranoid? Probably. The French were famous for being sensualists; maybe that's all there was to it. She took a deep quaff of the wine, which was full-bodied and delicious. This time Jean-Paul made a point of looking away as she drank, which struck her as funny somehow.

"I'm sorry, Jean-Paul," Cady said. "I'm just . . . not good with people."

"If anyone deserves to be angry, it is I. You have moved in with my cousin, and I imagine you are supporting his belief that he should fight against my attempt to sell the château. Isn't that correct?"

"You're saying I'm interfering?"

"I'm saying that this is family business, and it's complicated. I don't mean to be unkind, but you don't understand all the players, or the history—not to mention that you will be long gone while the rest of us suffer the consequences."

"There's— I'm—," she stammered as the waiter set two steaming copper pots on the table. "I know sometimes I push too hard. But I think Fabrice—"

"Cady," Jean-Paul interrupted, "could we make a pact, just for the present time, to enjoy our food? One should never argue over a meal."

"Of course," Cady said, holding up her wine. "To détente."

"*À détente*," he said, clinking her glass.

After a leisurely lunch of monkfish and potato *dauphinoise*, followed by pungent local cheeses and crusty bread, accompanied by the delicious and delicate wine, Jean-Paul insisted they share a citron tart with Italian meringue.

"I can't believe I ate all that," she said as they left.

"Yes, you put up a good fight, but you were seduced by our local cuisine. It has been known to happen to many an American tourist. What you need is a long walk, which is fortunate, because the car is parked quite some distance away."

As they strolled in the early spring sunshine, Jean-Paul pointed out various local landmarks and features of Avignon's medieval architecture.

"You know, if you ever get tired of being a fancy Parisian architect, you would make an excellent tour guide."

"Thank you. That is good to know."

"Or . . . I forgot. You plan to become a wealthy developer of historic properties."

"So our détente is over already," he said with a sad smile. "Do you have something against making money?"

"No. And of course, the château will be yours to do with as you will. It's just so *historic;* it seems a shame to have some hotel chain turn it into some plastic version of itself."

"Best Western does a wonderful job."

"Best Western?" In Cady's mind any motel chain was synonymous with cheap lodgings. She thought back to motels she had stayed in over the years—the funky carpets, the dubious sheets,

the moldy showers. “You’re kidding me, right?”

“I’m completely serious. They’ve been acquiring old properties, renovating them, updating when necessary—you may have noticed that the bathrooms in old buildings can be appalling, for example. And they run them as luxury hotels. They’re very beautiful.”

“If you say so,” she said skeptically. “You bought me that fantastically sumptuous lunch, so at this point I’ll pretty much agree with anything you say.”

“Aha, so I have found the way to make you cooperative.”

“I’m always cooperative.”

He chuckled. Back in the car, he negotiated heavy traffic and a string of roundabouts to get out of the city, then announced: “I am taking you on a quick detour.”

“I still need to do the shopping and make dinner.”

“It will be quick.

“You see?” he said, pulling up in front of an eighteenth-century stone building called Le Najeti Hôtel la Magnaneraie in Villeneuve-lès-Avignon, just five minutes outside of Avignon proper. “It is a beautiful hotel, run by Best Western.”

As Jean-Paul rolled past slowly, Cady caught a glimpse of the ornate lobby.

“Wow. I have to say, you were right. This place

is . . . well, it's gorgeous. I really had no idea. So they're interested in turning Château Clement into a hotel?"

"I've only had a preliminary discussion with some of their people. It is a possibility." Jean-Paul glanced over at her. "I know it sounds romantic to renovate a château, Cady, but not only do I lack sufficient time and money—something like that has to be a labor of love. I would have to move back to Saint-Véran full-time. . . ." He shook his head.

"Was your fiancée interested in updating the château?"

"She . . ." He trailed off, seemingly searching for words. "She decided she did not like the idea of small-village life."

"I think it's charming," Cady said with a sigh. "And I think renovating the château would be enchanting."

"*I* think you are a romantic," Jean-Paul said. "Fabrice learned the hard way how difficult it is to bring a place like Château Clement back to its former glory."

"Yes, he mentioned that. Fabrice has no children, has never been married?"

"I believe he was married, briefly, a long time ago. When he lived in Paris. But from what I understand, it lasted only a few years. He's been in love with someone else, a different woman, all his life."

"But he's so . . ."

"Old?"

"I was going to say *grumpy.* Hard to imagine him being head over heels in love."

"He's not the first man who's been a fool for love."

"I've got news for you: It goes both ways. So who is—or was—she?"

"I guess you have not gotten to that part in *Le Château.*"

"It's in the book?"

"You have to look for it. If my memory is correct, I believe he just refers to her as '*la minette.*' "

"I thought that was a sauce for oysters."

"That's *mignonette.*"

"Language is hard."

"It is."

"Hold on—Fabrice wrote the book a very long time ago. You're saying he's *still* suffering from unrequited love?"

"As far as I can tell, he has been in love with *la minette* since he was a teenager. They met during the Second World War, fighting with the Résistance in Paris."

"Really? Fabrice was part of the Résistance?"

"He doesn't like to talk about it, of course. He was very young at the time."

"And what happened to 'Minette'?"

"According to Fabrice's book, she was consumed by the dragon of Fontaine-de-Vaucluse."

"That doesn't sound good."

"It's one of the parts of the book that is very hard to understand. As I recall, the story is a lyrical, stand-alone chapter toward the middle of the book. A little on the pretentious side, if you ask me, but that was the style he was writing in."

"So I've been learning. What else can you tell me?"

"In the book *la minette* is from the town of Fontaine-de-Vaucluse. When she disappears in Paris, the main character—who I assume is actually Fabrice—goes to search for her there. It's not far from Saint-Véran and Château Clement, which was what brought him to the family château for the first time."

"But he never found her?"

He shrugged. "It's not clear in the book. It's possible he found her and she rejected him, or perhaps she really had been killed, though not by a dragon, of course."

"Did you ever ask him?"

"As I believe I've mentioned before, Fabrice and I are not close."

"Why?"

"He doesn't like me."

"He doesn't like anybody," Cady pointed out.

"True, but he *really* doesn't like me."

"Why not?"

He gave her a look. "You're very direct."

"Sorry. No guiles."

There was a long pause as they drove past acres of vineyards and olive orchards. Cady rolled down her window and inhaled deeply of wild thyme and rosemary.

"In the summer there are fields here of sunflowers, strawberries, and cherries," Jean-Paul said. "And soon that whole hill, there, will be covered with almond blossoms."

"It's a lovely region," Cady said. "So different from Paris. I suppose that's why people speak so fondly of Provence."

Jean-Paul nodded. After another long silence, he said, "As I told you, there's a long-standing rift in the family. Yves and Josephine Clement lived at Château Clement from the turn of the twentieth century until after World War I. They had one son, Marc-Antoine."

"Marc-Antoine was Fabrice's father, right?"

He nodded. "Yves inherited the estate from his own father, which meant Yves's two brothers—not to mention his three sisters—did not."

"It doesn't seem fair that they wouldn't get anything."

"It is not fair, of course. But it is necessary. Otherwise a large estate would be divided up among the children, and then their children. . . ."

"Until there's no estate left."

"Exactly. The right of primogeniture, under which the firstborn inherits the family property, isn't fair, but it makes a certain amount of sense to property holders—not just the aristocracy, but wealthy farmers as well."

"So that's what caused the rift? They were jealous of Yves? It wasn't his fault he was the firstborn."

"It's a little more complicated than that."

"The woman at the grocery store said something about rumors concerning Josephine . . .?"

He swore under his breath and shook his head. "That is the problem with living in a small town."

"She didn't tell me what the rumors *were,*" Cady added. "Just that there were some."

"That's in the past, long gone."

"Probably easy to say that, since you're the next in line to inherit the château."

"Actually it goes first to my mother, but she doesn't want it. I'll share any proceeds with the family. There's no one else in my generation who wants to take it on, anyway. It's part of a bygone way of life, in some ways more burden than gift."

"So, what were the rumors?"

"You are very curious about my family. I thought you were looking for a carousel."

"I am. I just . . . I never knew my family, and I find convoluted intergenerational stories fascinating."

"From my perspective, they're less fascinating than tedious. But how is it that you never knew your family?"

“I’m an orphan,” Cady said. The punch to her gut was still there, and she supposed it always would be. But she forced herself to say the unvarnished truth: no softening, no beating around the bush. She was an orphan with no family. Still, she didn’t look at Jean-Paul at that moment, preferring to be spared the sympathy or morbid curiosity she so often saw in people’s eyes when she told them about her upbringing.

“You were raised in an orphanage?”

“That sounds like something out of a Charles Dickens novel. Do they still have orphanages in France? In the States it’s the foster system, usually.”

“You grew up in a foster home?”

“A series of foster homes. I was a bit of a handful. When I got older I was moved to a group home, until I met a woman who let me live with her my last few years of high school.”

“You never knew your parents?”

She shook her head, focusing on the passing landscape and concentrating on keeping the emotion out of her voice. “There was some kind of legal issue—one of my bio parents refused to sign the paperwork, or couldn’t be found, or something. In any event, when I was a baby I wasn’t adoptable. And the older kids get, the harder it is to find adoptive parents. I never got that lucky.”

“So you are a woman without a history,” he

said. Cady still hadn't looked over at him, but his voice was soft, kind. Too kind.

"I have a history," she said, her tone defensive. "I just don't happen to know what it is."

"Even families that know one another may not truly know their own history," Jean-Paul said tactfully. "If you wish to know the truth, the rumor in my family is that Marc-Antoine, the only child of Yves and Josephine and heir to Château Clement, was not, in fact, Yves's natural child."

"You mean he was adopted?"

He shook his head. "Marc-Antoine was rumored to be illegitimate, the child of Josephine's extra-marital affair."

"But if Yves was not Marc-Antoine's biological father, then one of Yves's brothers, or one of their sons, should have inherited the estate, not Marc-Antoine, right?"

"Exactly right. My grandfather's grandfather, Thierry, was Yves's brother. He insisted that Château Clement should have gone to him, and therefore to his eldest son, and then to Gerald, and then to *his* eldest, Louise, who is my mother—Gerald had only girls. My grandfather Gerald is still alive, and he continues to insist that Fabrice has never had a legitimate claim to the château."

"Ironic, then, that you're inheriting it anyway."

"Isn't it, though?" He gave her a sideways

glance. “Generations of bad blood in the family, and all for nothing. On the other hand, I suppose my grandfather, and his father, would have loved to preside over the château these past decades. Though with the world wars and the economic changes, I’m not sure they would have done anything more with it than Fabrice has. Probably would have bankrupted themselves trying. All things considered, it worked out for the best.”

“And you’ve been trying to stay out of the drama?”

He nodded and blew out a long breath. “It’s not easy. Every family gathering, every holiday, every event . . . It may have been beautiful at one time, but ever since I’ve known it, Château Clement has been a broken-down old place, and a source of contention. What is the phrase in English? An ‘albatross’ around the family’s neck?”

“How is it that you speak English so well?”

“I was at Cambridge, England, for a year. And English is the default language for international contracts. It was necessary that I become reasonably fluent.”

“Still, it’s impressive.”

“Hey, your French sounded very good when you were asking the waiter for the monkfish recipe at lunch.”

She sat back in her seat and patted her stomach. “Speaking of lunch, I can’t believe you convinced me to eat that meringue. Though I'll be dreaming of it tonight."

His eyes slid over to her, and lingered. "Perhaps you need a *sieste*."

"I thought that was a Spanish thing."

"Close enough. In some ways this region has more in common with Spain than with the rest of France. We're only a few hours from the border."

"Get out of here!"

"Wait—what? Where?"

She laughed. "I think I just found an expression you don't know. It means, 'I don't believe you.' We're only a few hours from Spain?"

"Maybe four to the border. About four and a half to Barcelona."

"Europe amazes me. It takes six hours to get from Los Angeles to San Francisco—and that's all still within a single state—but here you could drive from France to Barcelona in less than that."

"Perhaps you should stay longer and explore."

"You're right. I probably should."

Jean-Paul sat up straighter. "It looks as if you will—we seem to have forgotten to go by the car rental office."

CHAPTER THIRTY-SEVEN

1944
PARIS

Fabrice

"This is disgusting," Paulette said, reading one of Fabrice's pamphlets, in which he summarized reports from Vichy-controlled France, where Marshal Philippe Pétain—chief of state of Vichy France—blamed moral corruption for France's defeat. He called on women to return to the domestic sphere and have babies, and officially banned them from wearing trousers. Women were not allowed to hold a job or have a bank account without the permission of male relatives.

"And now, from what I hear from my relatives in Provence, the Italians have withdrawn and the Germans are rounding up the Jews," Paulette said. "Just as they did here."

"I heard about that, too," said Fabrice. "I wrote about it last night."

It was just the two of them in the printshop. It was heaven. Fabrice was doing all the work while she read through his pamphlets, but he didn't mind. He would do anything to keep her here with him, always.

They were supposed to use only their noms de guerre and not to mention anything personal, but Fabrice spoke to Paulette honestly, sharing with her about his life, his father's experience in a German hospital, his carpentry shop. He even mentioned the Château Clement.

"Château Clement?" she said, putting down the tract she was reading. "You are related to the Clements of Château Clement?"

He nodded, unsure whether it was a good thing or a bad one. His father had been ashamed of his aristocratic roots, preferring to create what he referred to as his happy-but-humble family home as a carpenter.

"But I am from a village called Fontaine-de-Vaucluse," Paulette exclaimed. "That is not more than a few miles from Château Clement!"

"I've never been to Provence."

"Never?"

He shook his head. "My father is estranged from his family."

"Why?"

It was odd, but until this moment Fabrice had never really wondered why, had never inquired as to the details of the family drama. It was not a secret so much as simple knowledge, something he had grown up with, like the scent of freshly cut wood. The Clement family rift had seemed as natural and expected as the incessant sawdust on the tile floor of the workroom, mounding in the corners until his mother would become angry and finally sweep it up herself, giving the sawdust to the man who kept rabbits, or to the icehouses to keep the ice frozen during the sweaty summers. Or now, during the war, to the neighborhood bakers and butchers as a filler for breads and sausages.

"So you mean to tell me you're the heir to a grand château, and you've never mentioned that in all your attempts at seducing me?" she said, a teasing smile playing on her lips.

Fabrice could feel himself blush. He had never thought of himself as an heir, but of course he was; he was the eldest son of Marc-Antoine, himself an only child. Fabrice had a sudden flash of the future: he and Paulette, returning to Château Clement after the war, mending the rift in the family, becoming admired, invitations to their sumptuous dinners highly sought after.

His daydreams made him blush even more intensely.

Paulette pretended to straighten the stacks of papers coming off the printing press, to give him a moment to pull himself together. Fabrice wondered how he knew this, but he did know. This was how she was. He knew her. He loved her.

"Paulette," he said, taking her hand in his, "I am old enough to feel what I am feeling. I know I'm younger than you, but my mother is older than my father by two years. It is not unknown."

She gave a breathless sort of laugh and pulled her hand away, fiddling with the printing press. "It is not only that, Fabrice."

"Please, Paulette," he said, sensing he must make his case, that he might not have another chance. "I've never felt anything like this before. I can't think, I can't eat, I can't do anything unless it's for you. I will love you forever, Paulette. I would never leave you. I would never hurt you."

He leaned in, hesitated for a moment, then kissed her.

She kissed him back. It was everything he had fantasized about, and more. It was sunshine and gold, it was a Shakespearean sonnet. It was an end to this war, it was the defeat of the Nazis. It was manhood. It was exquisite.

CHAPTER THIRTY-EIGHT

PRESENT DAY
CHÂTEAU CLEMENT

Cady

Jean-Paul dropped Cady where she had parked the Citroën, saying he needed to stop by his mother's house and would meet Cady later, at the château. She went grocery shopping and as she was driving back to Château Clement, she realized that his car was right behind her. When Jean-Paul pulled up alongside Cady in front of the château, Fabrice was outside with Lucy, and frowned at the sight of them together.

"Why did you bring *him* with you?" Fabrice demanded. "And where have you been all day? My invitation for you to stay has been revoked."

Cady hoped she misunderstood, but this was an easy one: *Mon invitation est révoquée.*

"Fabrice." Jean-Paul stepped in. "Be reasonable. Cady—"

"What do you have to say about it? Her being American is a lot more interesting than your being Parisian. At least she brings whiskey."

"I brought bread," said Jean-Paul, holding up the bag from the *boulangerie*.

"Well, that's something," Fabrice said grudgingly.

Another car turned into the long gravel drive.

"Who's that, now?" Fabrice demanded.

"I believe that would be Dr. Miller," said Jean-Paul.

A fifty-something bespectacled man pulled up and got out of the driver's seat. "*Salut*, *Fabrice*! *Ça va*?"

"Go away," Fabrice said. "I didn't call you."

The doctor greeted Jean-Paul and Cady politely, then faced Fabrice.

"Annick Boyer, from the grocery store? She tells me you've been laid up for a while. And Jean-Paul mentioned it as well, as did his mother. So you see, people worry about you."

"I'm fine," groused Fabrice.

As Cady watched the old man, thinking of what Jean-Paul had told her about an unrequited love, she wondered about his cantankerous ways. Was it simply the grumpiness that at times accompanied old age? Or was there something more going on? At the moment, Fabrice seemed truly overwhelmed, standing with three people in front of him. Perhaps he had a social phobia; these sorts of things weren't often diagnosed in his generation. Maybe that was why the two of them got along so well.

"Well," said Dr. Miller in an upbeat tone. "Since I came all the way out here, and you are clearly using a crutch, why don't you let me examine you?"

"Please, Fabrice," said Jean-Paul. "Let the doctor take a look."

"Fine," said Fabrice, limping over to a stone bench. Jean-Paul moved to help him, but he waved him off, saying, "I'm no invalid."

Dr. Miller did not seem put off by Fabrice's attitude. He knelt in the gravel and examined his ankle and lower leg. After a few minutes, he stood.

"We would need to take a radiograph to be sure, but it does not appear to be a break, only a bad sprain. That is good news. But for a man your age, it will take some time to heal."

"I do just fine."

"I have to tell you, Fabrice, I don't feel good about you being out here all by yourself. The risk of re-injury or a complicating fall is great. There are rehabilitation centers—"

"Don't waste your breath," said Fabrice. "I'm staying here."

"But—"

"I'm not alone. The little girl's here. She cooks."

The doctor looked at Cady.

Cady raised her hand. "*C'est moi*, I do believe."

Fabrice had called her *petite fille*, which meant "little girl"—but also meant "granddaughter."

Cady had never had a grumpy grandfather or a goofy uncle. She had read about such characters and had watched them in movies for years. Now she had Fabrice, at least for the time being.

"I'll take good care of him," she said.

"I'll be around for a while as well. He won't be alone," Jean-Paul said to the doctor, stepping forward.

Again Cady bristled. After the day they'd spent together, she should have felt closer to Jean-Paul, and she did . . . except that she still hated the idea of turning the château into a chain hotel, no matter how well done, or how much economic sense it made. Château Clement was like a treasure trove of family history; how could he even consider letting that go?

Dr. Miller left them with basic instructions: Keep the ankle elevated as much as possible and apply cold packs.

As the good doctor's little car disappeared down the drive, Jean-Paul turned to Fabrice and said, "Thank you for not greeting us with the shotgun this time."

Fabrice shrugged and scratched under Lucy's chin.

"So," Cady said, "am I now allowed to stay here again? It's up to you, of course, but I'd like to know one way or the other."

When Fabrice didn't answer, she held up the heavy grocery bags and added, "Because if I go now you will never know the wonders of American garlic bread, which is an experience not to be missed. I have all the ingredients right here, ready to go. Yes or no?"

He looked at her for a long minute, heaved himself off the bench, and limped into the house.

"*Comme tu veux*," he called over his shoulder.

"I'll take that as a yes," Cady said as she and Jean-Paul followed.

"And that, gentlemen, is why garlic bread is universally beloved by my people," said Cady as Fabrice and Jean-Paul served themselves third helpings of the wonderfully flavorful concoction. It had turned out particularly well tonight, probably because the bread itself was so good. "And here I thought the French were the ultimate gourmets."

"I have no idea what she's talking about; do you, Fabrice?" Jean-Paul teased.

"No idea," Fabrice said, slipping a crust of the buttery bread to Lucy, who was trying to hide beneath the table but was so tall that when she stood, the table hovered and tilted, forcing them all to dive for their glasses.

That Fabrice deigned to answer at all made Cady smile. "You two probably haven't ever had really good mac-n-cheese either, have you?" She didn't know how to say the term in French, so she said it in English.

"Mac and . . . *quoi*?" Fabrice said.

"It's pasta with a cheese sauce. Baked in the oven, and sprinkled with bread crumbs or, if you're feeling wild, with potato chips. It's incredibly good. Not as good as garlic bread, I'll grant you, but still very good. I'll make it for you," she promised, then wondered if she would be here long enough to try out all her recipes. She already felt . . . what was it? At home? Was that possible?

Perhaps the garlic bread had worked its magic on Fabrice, or perhaps he was just tired, but tonight he seemed to be in a halfway good mood and enjoying the conversation. Cady wondered if, despite his protestations to the contrary, he might be lonely. How could he not be, out here in this huge château, all alone except for Lucy? But then perhaps he wasn't as alone as she'd thought; he had people like the doctor and the teenager who delivered his groceries, and everyone in town seemed to know him.

"Fabrice," she said, "when you were in Paris after the war, in the late forties and early fifties, is it true you knew Albert Camus and James Baldwin?"

The men launched into a discussion of authors and artists she'd never heard of, tossing around terms like "phenomenological—in the Heideggerian sense" and the "theory of pure surface." She regretted her lack of formal education now more than ever. Yes, she read voraciously, and was observant. But how did one make up for a pure lack of education? How long would it take to catch up?

On the other hand, did anyone *really* need to be able to toss around terms like "Heideggerian"?

Cady set about opening the wine, filling their glasses with a generous splash of the ruby red liquid, feeling like a servant at a literary salon in the Latin Quarter.

"To the power of American garlic bread to bring people together," said Jean-Paul, holding up his glass. "*Salut.*"

Even Fabrice joined in the toast.

Cady decided to get over herself; to listen and learn. She brought out her journal and started taking notes as Fabrice and Jean-Paul continued to talk of the Parisian post–World War II literary scene.

"What are you writing down?" Fabrice asked.

"I don't know a lot about that time period. Actually, I don't know much about literature in general. I'm taking notes of authors I'd like to look up."

Fabrice nodded, as though approving of her actions.

"You know, Fabrice," said Jean-Paul, "Cady will have to leave soon, probably in the next day or two. Why don't I come stay with you for a little while?"

Cady opened her mouth to contradict him, but swallowed her words. She already felt so comfortable here and had imagined staying for longer than "a day or two," but she was reminded once again that Fabrice was not *her* cousin. It bothered her that Jean-Paul seemed to be pushing for something diametrically opposed to what Fabrice had always wanted, but this was not her family's château, or her ancestral village, or really any of her business. Jean-Paul had been kind, but he couldn't have made that distinction any more clear.

Staring at the fire, she absently stroked Lucy's espresso brown coat. Most of the dog's fur was wiry, but her head and ears were pure velvet. Lucy's breath was steady as she slept, counting off the seconds, the moments. Once, Cady had been sent to "mindfulness class" and learned that Buddhists occasionally rang a bell, at which point everyone was supposed to stop what they were doing and concentrate on nothing more than breathing: in and out, in and out. The whisper of the air traveling through one's throat and into one's lungs, a reminder that all we have is the here and now, what's in front of us. No past, no future, just this moment.

But, Cady remembered thinking in class, as she sat uncomfortable and cross-legged on the floor, *what if this moment, the one right this second, sucked?*

"Cady?" Jean-Paul interrupted her thoughts.

"Sorry. What?"

"Everything okay?" he asked.

"Of course. Sure."

"Cady"—Fabrice waved a scrap of paper in her general direction—"go get us another bottle of that Bordeaux. I drew you the damned map you asked for."

"I'll get it," said Jean-Paul, getting to his feet.

"No, really," said Cady, taking the note and grabbing the flashlight from the counter. "I like going. It's a mysterious French wine cellar. Can't get enough of it. We don't have anything like it where I'm from."

Lucy lifted her anvil-size head.

"Especially with my trusty canine companion for protection. C'mon, Lucy."

She left the men talking about Paris in its bohemian heyday. Jean-Paul, of course, had gone to the Sorbonne and to Cambridge. He was educated, erudite, at home with great literature and great ideas. Meanwhile Cady could barely make it through Fabrice's novel, and even then didn't understand most of what she was reading. She had realized with a start last night that Fabrice had been younger than she was now when he wrote it. She yearned for a copy of *The Lion, the Witch and the Wardrobe*. Or maybe Harry Potter. Something she had read before, repeatedly; a book with a story line told in a straightforward fashion. Fantasy was one thing; this "new novel" business was something else entirely.

Down in the cellar, lost in her thoughts and with only the beam of the flashlight to guide her, she turned into the wrong room and walked straight into a pile of boxes.

Out of one spilled some very old film cartridges. Exposed, but undeveloped, film cartridges.

CHAPTER THIRTY-NINE

PRESENT DAY
CHÂTEAU CLEMENT

Cady

"I thought maybe I'd have to send a search party."

"Look what *I* found." She set the bottle of Bordeaux on the table and beside it the box of film cartridges.

Fabrice gave her a side-eyed glance. "A box of garbage? Plenty more where that came from."

"It's not garbage, Fabrice," Cady said, unable to contain her excitement. "These are photographs waiting to be developed—and look at the handwritten notes! I think these must have belonged to your grandfather."

"That reminds me," said Jean-Paul. "I brought Yves Clement's photographs from my mother's house as well." He leaned over and extracted a thick manila envelope from his leather courier bag. "These are copies; the originals are in the archive. Do you remember, Fabrice? I tried to show these to you a few years ago—"

"*Ça me fait chier ça*," said Fabrice. Cady wasn't sure of the expression, but she caught the general gist: He didn't care to see them.

"But they were taken by your grandfather, of this very estate," Cady urged. "Okay if I look through them?"

He shrugged.

Cady took the photos out of the envelope and studied them. As Jean-Paul had told her, most were of the people who used to work the estate, primarily in the fields. They fed right into her imagination of the ghosts roaming the grounds of the château, though unfortunately there weren't many interior shots. Yves Clement appeared to have been a nature lover: There were dozens of photographs of birds—quail and grouse—horses, goats, and hunting dogs.

"And these are of Josephine Clement," said Jean-Paul, handing her half a dozen photographs of a lovely young woman with a delicate face, her dark hair piled in a huge halo in the Gibson-girl style. A distinctive mole on her neck looked almost like a heart. "She was very young when she married Yves: only eighteen, and he was nearly forty. But by all accounts they appeared happy together."

"At first," grumbled Fabrice.

"What happened later?" Cady asked. As soon as she spoke, she remembered the rumor that Josephine had been unfaithful.

The men exchanged a quick glance, but neither spoke.

"Where'd you get these pictures, anyway?" Fabrice asked.

"My mother had them."

"Stole them, more like."

Jean-Paul's jaw tightened. "After Yves's death, when Marc-Antoine remained in Paris rather than returning to claim the château, it was left to ruin. Some family members came in and took things, yes. Mostly mementos."

Fabrice stared into the fire.

"I've told you before, Fabrice. I would be happy to arrange for some of the items to be brought back, if you like, or at least arrange some visits so you could see them." Jean-Paul seemed to be choosing his words carefully. "But if family hadn't come in, it all would have been lost. You know the place was thoroughly ransacked during—and after—the war."

"I came here then. I know exactly the condition it was left in. What I'm unclear on is the extent to which my so-called family took part in the destruction."

"Anyway," Cady said after a long, uncomfortable pause, "these photographs are great, right? Not just in subject matter—Yves was a talented photographer. Look at his use of shadows. They're so . . . evocative."

"I've always thought so," said Jean-Paul, digging through the tall stack. "And these will be of particular interest to you—they're of the carousel."

Cady accepted the photos with reverence and starting flipping through them. Most showed the actual construction of the carousel, men fitting together the different parts of the mechanism. Carousels were driven by steam engine back then, and Bayol was famous for using bellows in some of his animals to create sounds. Unfortunately, there weren't many close-ups, and the faces of the workers were hard to make out: The shots were mostly of groups of people laboring at their tasks. The photographs most interesting to Cady were those of workers doing touch-up painting and applying protective varnish, since these showed the fanciful animal figures: horses, chickens, cats, dogs, pigs, and rabbits—as well as one rocking carriage and a spinning tub.

The photographs were all black-and-white images, so the typically garish, whimsical colors were lost. But the images did give a sense of the carousel.

"As I understand it," said Jean-Paul, "the carousel didn't come alone, but with a kind of decorative salon that housed it. It wasn't strong enough to stand up against the elements, however—especially our Provençal winds—so it was brought in pieces and assembled within an outer building. Right, Fabrice?"

Fabrice grunted and took a drink, then nodded.

"And it's still there?" Cady asked.

"What remains of it," said Fabrice.

"As I told you, I have a carousel rabbit figure that might have been part of the set. A photo that was hidden within the figure bears the Château Clement stamp. Also," Cady said, hardly able to contain her excitement as she flipped to a photograph of a woman working alongside the men, "I think I have a photograph of *this* woman. I'll be right back."

Cady literally ran up the stairs, down the grand hall, through the book-lined room, up the steps to the red hallway, and into her room to grab the box that had been hidden in Gus's belly, along with her photos of Gus, and the love note she had been using as a bookmark. Then she ran back.

Fabrice looked amused and annoyed at the same time. "What's got into you?"

"Look at this," Cady said, panting. She placed the box in front of Fabrice.

"Go on, open it up."

Fabrice lifted the lid and peered inside. He picked up the photograph first, gazed at it a long time, and let out a "Huh." Then he stroked the braid of hair and read the little love note. He put everything back in and shut the lid.

"Where'd you find this?"

"It was hidden in the belly of my rabbit." As she spoke, she slid a couple of her eight-by-ten prints in front of him. "This is Gus."

Fabrice let out a breathless exclamation and sat up slightly. He gazed at the photos as though enthralled. She handed him more.

He nodded. "You see these *muguet* flowers here? I remember those."

Cady had looked up the word *muguet* after Madame Martin used it in Paris. In English, it meant "lily of the valley." Little white bell flowers along a slender stalk.

"So it made its way to America," Fabrice said, his voice filled with a kind of wonder.

"You know it?"

"This rabbit used to be here."

"With the carousel?"

"It was inside the house, here, actually."

"Do you know who carved it?"

"Whoever carved the carousel, I assume."

"And you saw it here, at the château?"

He nodded. "After the war, my father and I came back to stay for a while. There was still some heavy furniture, that sort of thing, that hadn't been looted. Some guy came in and bought a bunch of it, said he knew a market for European antiques. We needed the money."

"This is amazing," Cady said. "I've had him for years. I've always loved him, and wondered where he came from. I'm sorry he's not in good shape—I was going to restore him, but I wasn't sure how that would affect the value."

"You know how to restore things like this?"

"I'm no expert, but yes, I used to work in an antiques store, and I did a fair amount of restoration."

"Huh."

Fabrice gazed into the fire again, sliding back into his uncommunicative mode. Still, this was by far the most interest he had shown in anything since she'd met him.

"Do you think I could see the carous—," she began.

"Enough already," interrupted Fabrice. "Where's that whiskey?"

Cady went to get the bottle from the cupboard over the refrigerator.

"Fabrice," Jean-Paul said, "how would you feel if I moved in here for a while, just until you feel better?"

"I've got more than enough help with the girl here." He gestured in Cady's direction.

Jean-Paul glanced at Cady. "Cady has other things to do. She's a photographer, on assignment. She'll be on her way soon. I'm family."

"She can take all the pictures she wants around here. And anyway, she's American. I like Americans more than family. What's family ever done for me?"

"It left you this château, for one thing,"

answered Jean-Paul. "And we would have been a part of your life if you'd have let us."

"This château that you adore? You don't fool me, Jean-Paul. You just want to dismantle it, sell it for parts, and run back to your precious Paris."

"I want to *salvage* it. If I can. There's a difference. If you would just allow me to bring in some people to inspect it—"

Fabrice waved him off angrily.

Cady did her best to pretend she wasn't listening as she cleared the table and cleaned up the kitchen. Part of her thrilled to Fabrice's words, to think she was preferred. Part of her clearly didn't understand the family dynamics, and it felt awkward after Jean-Paul had gone out of his way to show her around Avignon. She felt torn about the fate of the château; like Fabrice, she wanted to see it stay in private hands, loved and taken care of. But she understood Jean-Paul's point as well; a building like this was meant for a different time, a different way of life. Who had the resources for the renovation necessary to maintain such a residence?

She remembered having a fantasy, a very, very long time ago. Of living in a huge old home and filling the rooms with unwanted children. It was a nice dream, but as an adult she'd realized it wasn't much of a recipe for making a living.

"You should leave, Jean-Paul," said Fabrice, raising his voice. "Go tell your grandfather you'll get this place, quite literally, over my dead body."

"Fabrice, please—"

"Go!"

"I apologize. I seem to have ruined what was otherwise a lovely evening." Jean-Paul stood, the muscle in his jaw working. "Cady, thank you so much for a delicious dinner. You can keep those photos for now, if you like. Fabrice, I enjoyed speaking about your days in Paris. I look forward to hearing more soon."

He held out his hand. Fabrice looked at it, sighed, and shook hands with Jean-Paul as though it pained him.

"Cady," he said with a nod to her. No kisses this time.

She followed him out the door to the hall.

"Jean-Paul," she called.

He hesitated for a moment before turning around.

"I'm sorry about this. You know how cranky he is."

"I do. I've known him my whole life, Cady, as has my mother, and her father before her."

"I didn't mean . . . I don't mean to barge in where I'm not wanted."

"He wants you more than me, or anyone else in the family, apparently."

"Well . . . thank you for today," Cady said, coming to stand near him. "I really enjoyed the tour of Avignon."

"Thank you for dinner. And for opening my eyes to the wonders of garlic bread."

They remained for a moment in the narrow corridor, standing by the chalky-blue wooden door, enveloped by the scent of old stone and the damp, musty air. It could have been another time, another place, two servants lingering by the help's entrance, trying to unravel the whims of the irascible master.

Jean-Paul's tongue played with the inside of his cheek for a moment as he studied her face. He lifted one hand, very slowly, and grasped a lock of her hair, caressing it between thumb and forefinger.

"Silk," he said, almost to himself. "I wondered what it felt like."

"It's the French shampoo," Cady said, wincing at the inanity of her words. "Probably."

Jean-Paul let out a soft chuckle and dropped his hand. "Anyway, good luck with him. You have my number if either of you needs anything. I'll be in touch."

He turned up his collar and ducked out the door into a fierce, frigid wind.

Cady shut the door behind him and returned to the kitchen, where Fabrice remained by the hearth, brooding, gazing at the dying flames.

She sat in the chair Jean-Paul had vacated.

Ten minutes of silence passed, interrupted only by Lucy's muffled snoring and the hiss of the fire, the wind and rain hitting the windowpanes, every second counted down by the ticking of the clock with no hands.

Finally, Cady said, "I would give anything for a family. Even one that annoyed me."

Fabrice's seafoam green eyes, foggy with age, fixed on her. Despite their senescence, they seemed able to see beyond the surface. Once again Cady was reminded of the way Maxine had looked at her: as though she *knew.*

"You are alone?" Fabrice asked.

Cady didn't usually think of her situation in such blunt terms. But yes, she walked through this world alone.

She nodded and stared at the fire, opening her eyes wide to fight the tears that gathered. She felt as vulnerable as the little girl who had ridden round and round on the Tilden Park carousel, yearning for parents, dreaming of belonging.

"Well, Cady, I'll tell you a secret," said Fabrice in a voice as sad as the moaning winds rattling the windowpanes. "In the end we are all alone. Each one of us."

CHAPTER FORTY

1900
CHÂTEAU CLEMENT

Maëlle

Maëlle slips in through a side door, heading to her room. Though it has been many days since they arrived, Maëlle still feels like an intruder in the halls of the great château. She hurries down the corridors as quietly as she can, hoping not to be noticed.

"Maëlle," comes Madame Clement's voice.

"*Oui*, madame?" she says, turning toward her. "May I do something for you?"

"Guess what I have? *Chouchenn*!" she says, holding aloft a bottle of Breton-style mead.

"Pardon?"

"Come, have a drink with me?"

"Madame, I—"

"Please, call me Josephine," she says with a laugh. "I think I can't be more than a year or two older than you. And we are all Bretons here, are we not?"

Maëlle feels at a loss for words. Her father

always used to preach to her, as Léon does, that no person was better than another, no matter how wealthy or influential. *We are all created equal,* he declared, reciting slogans from the French Revolution. Maëlle had turned the argument to her favor, using the same logic on him when insisting that she be allowed to carve: If no one person is better than another, then why can't a woman have ambitions just like a man?

But now, facing Madame Clement's—*Josephine*'s—fashionable, lace-covered dress, her pearl earrings and finely coiffed hair, Maëlle feels unsure. Lesser. Naive in the ways of the world.

Josephine's manner is easygoing, friendly. But Maëlle still finds it hard to meet her eyes, to chat as though she were with a friend. Is it typical for the lady of the manor to ask an artisan to join her for a drink?

"Y-your husband is not here?" Maëlle stammers.

"He goes to bed very early and gets up before dawn. We have opposite schedules; I'm afraid I'm a night owl. When we were first married I tried to wake at the same time as he, but I found myself sleeping away the afternoons! So now I appreciate having the evenings to my thoughts, while he awakens early to work in his darkroom."

"I'm sorry, I feel very ignorant. But what is a 'darkroom'?"

"You're not ignorant at all. It has to do with the art of photography. The film must be developed in the dark, and then special chemical baths are used to make the pictures appear. It's quite an intricate process."

"Oh," says Maëlle. She can't think of anything else to say.

They are still standing, awkwardly, in the wide paneled hallway that leads to the room of books, and on to the stairway to Maëlle's room. She yearns for the white linen softness of that bed after a very long day of labor.

On the other hand, her days are spent exclusively in the company of men, and the idea of feminine conversation appeals. And in any case, Monsieur Bayol's words come back to her: She must keep the clients happy. Who is Maëlle Tanguy to refuse a drink with a lady like Josephine Clement?

"So, won't you join me?" Josephine repeats. "I'm sure it seems . . . forward, perhaps, or strange. But I am surrounded every day by men—as are you! In Quimper I had many friends, but not here. And I would love to hear more about your work, and how you learned to carve. You fascinate me: a woman artist!"

"Thank you," Maëlle says, blushing. "Yes, of course, I would be honored to join you for a drink."

"Wonderful! Follow me." Josephine leads the

way down the corridor to a small sitting room, its heavy wooden furniture brightened by a cheery fire. They take seats at a small table near the hearth, and Josephine pours a bit of the mead into two aperitif glasses from a set perched atop a nearby shelf.

"*Yec-hed mat*!" she says, holding up her glass and uttering a traditional Breton toast.

An hour, then two, pass as they sip the *chouchenn* and reminisce about their homeland: They speak of the stiff white lace caps traditionally worn by women in Breton, called *coiffes*, and the striped shirts, called *marinières*, of the navy and fishermen—the stripes make them easier to see in the waves in case they fall overboard. They speak of the fishing boats going out to sea in the mornings, the ruggedness of their rocky coastline. The blush-colored stone and sands of the pink granite coast.

"You miss it, then?" asks Maëlle. "Even living here, in such a grand home?"

Josephine looks around the room at the rich paneling and the long brocade drapes, the fine wood furniture. "I'm very lucky, I know. And Yves is very good to me. Although . . . it is true that things are harder these days than before. The lands aren't producing as they once did. . . ."

Maëlle thinks about what Léon said, about the signs of things slipping.

Josephine waves it off. "But never mind that. We are still lucky, are we not? And Provence is beautiful; the vegetation is stark, but I've grown used to it. And the winds carry the most amazing scents, have you noticed?"

"I do! I notice it every morning when I open my window. Herbs, and lavender."

Josephine nods. "And I don't miss wearing the *coiffe Bretagne*! My mother was very traditional, and she insisted that I wear it. I hear fewer people are donning it these days."

Maëlle smiles. Her mother used to make a fuss as well, but Maëlle didn't listen. She preferred to wear a Parisian-style hat or nothing at all. Not that she had many choices.

"But I do miss my family, and my friends," says Josephine. "I spend hours every evening writing letters, and I await their return missives with eager anticipation. Still, it is not the same as sitting and talking with friends."

"No, of course not."

"There is a . . ." Again she glances around her fine parlor, as though taking it all in. "There is a 'loneliness of kind' here. I miss having a woman to talk to, a friend who understands."

Maëlle nods, pleased to think *she* might be considered a kindred spirit to someone as fine as Josephine Clement.

"Also," Josephine goes on, "I miss our wild Breton coast. The Mediterranean is calm and warm, very peaceful, like a very large bathtub! But it is not the same. I always liked the crashing of the waves upon the rocks. My mother told me it was not decent to react so strongly to such passion."

"Mine said the same!" says Maëlle, amazed and pleased to have so much in common with a woman who owns a château.

"So, tell me about how you came to carve with Monsieur Bayol," Josephine says. "Ever since he told us about you in his missive, I have been so intrigued. A woman carver!"

Maëlle finds herself opening up to Josephine, describing how she learned to carve from her father, and how she and Erwann shared long talks back in their humble home in Concarneau. She tells her how Erwann had encouraged her to go, and how sad and alone—yet excited—she felt while watching him recede as the train jolted away from the station. Maëlle tells of getting lost in the streets of Angers on her way to find Bayol's factory, and how everyone had laughed at her when she made known her intentions of becoming an apprentice. Of her warm little room off Madame Bayol's kitchen—and how much nicer her accommodations were here in Château Clement.

"That bedroom makes me feel like . . . *Marie-Antoinette*!" Maëlle declares, giggling. For the first time since Léon cut her out, Maëlle does not think of him, but only of her art, and her new friend.

Josephine lets out a peal of laughter that sounds like church bells, and pours more mead into their tiny glasses. The room is warmed by the fire, and their spirits buoyed by the company, their talk, and the *chouchenn.*

Two women. New friends banishing the loneliness of kind.

CHAPTER FORTY-ONE

PRESENT DAY
CHÂTEAU CLEMENT

Cady

The next morning Cady walked into the kitchen to find a tall stack of books sitting on the counter.

"What's all this?" Cady asked, picking one up. The pages were yellow and foxed with age; the cover was green linen. Inside was an inscription: *To my friend and colleague, Fabrice Clement. Simone de Beauvoir.*

"Simone de Beauvoir?" Cady asked. "*The* Simone de Beauvoir?"

"You said you wanted to read more," said Fabrice. "These are by some of the people we were talking about last night."

"They're incredible. But . . . they're in French."

"You speak French."

"Not perfectly."

He waved a hand. "Well enough. Make a little effort. You should always read books in their native language, if you possibly can."

Again she wondered whether the English version of *Le Château* might be missing—or had mistranslated—some critical points. The first time she had tried to discuss the book with Fabrice, he'd threatened to throw her out; the second time he avoided the subject. She wondered if he'd be more amenable now. Maybe tonight, after he enjoyed his aperitif.

"You know," Cady said, studying the fat volumes, "these books might be worth real money, Fabrice. A lot of these are signed first editions."

"What do I care, at this point? I guess Jean-Paul will sell them all off, soon enough, when he sells this place."

"And what do you think about that?"

There was a long pause as the espresso machine hissed and spit. When Fabrice finally set a tiny cup of coffee in front of Cady and answered her, his tone was muted. "It doesn't matter."

"Doesn't it?"

"This place defeated me, and it would do the same to him," he said, growing agitated. "At least maybe he's smart enough to get out from under it right away, make a life for himself back in Paris."

She decided to change the subject. "I wanted to ask you: Would you mind if I developed the film cartridges I found? They've been exposed, but not developed."

He gave her a blank look.

"In other words," she tried again, "there might be photos that are salvageable."

"After all this time?"

"Maybe, maybe not. Old film is resilient; they found some from Shackleton's expedition to the Antarctic in a block of ice, and developed them one hundred years later."

"Do whatever you want. What do I care?" He went back to reading his newspaper.

"You're not curious? There could be photos of your family."

"Some things are better left as they are." He made a dismissive gesture. "Take them if you want, but I don't want to see them."

"So it's okay with you if I have them developed?"

He shrugged. "Build a fire with them, for all I care."

The question was where and how to develop them. What Cady wouldn't give for access to her old darkroom. France was more old-fashioned than the United States, and Avignon was a fairly large city, so there might still be film-developing services available. But could she trust such precious film to a commercial lab? She longed to do it herself. Just the thought of the chemical smells made her nostalgic for long afternoons spent in darkness, listening to audiobooks as she dipped sheets of specially treated paper into their chemical baths, one after another, watching an image appear where once there was nothing.

Those solitary afternoons had been a salve to her soul: first as a teenager, when she was just learning, and later as an adult, when photography became her living.

"When are you going shopping?" Fabrice asked.

"This may come as a surprise to you, Fabrice, but half the day doesn't have to be taken up by shopping. A person could buy enough for several days and not go to the store every day."

He looked at her.

She smiled. "But I had planned to go this morning."

"I want fish for dinner," he said, handing her a list.

"Fish it is. Oh, hey, guess who I ran into in town yesterday?"

"I give up."

"Johnny."

"Johnny Clement?"

"He's a Clement? The teenager who was here, throwing rocks?"

"The town's full of Clements."

"So I'm learning. Anyway, he's coming over to work after school."

"Work where?"

"Here. He's going to clean up the mess he made."

Fabrice snorted. "I'll believe that when I see it."

"He's clearly going down a bad path," she said to Fabrice. "You need to reach out to him."

"Why me? He vandalized my place."

"I know that. But I have a little experience with this sort of thing. I was a bad kid myself. As were you, unless I miss my guess."

He glared at her.

"Kids need a lifeline. He might be a lost cause, but it's worth a try. Sometimes it takes just a little help. Look, I'm an outsider. I don't have any authority here. But maybe if you talk to his father, tell him he'll be coming here to work it off . . ."

"Hand me the damned phone."

"Remember how you told me you didn't have a phone that first night?" she teased as she grabbed the old-fashioned landline. It had a cord long enough to cross the kitchen.

"Didn't want to be bothered. Besides, there was no one to call."

Cady smiled as she watched him look up the number, running his gnarled finger down a long list of handwritten names and numbers in a battered old address book.

She imagined the "C" section of his address book was full indeed.

Cady was perusing the limited fish selection at the grocery store when the cashier, Annick, waved her over.

"If you are looking for fish you should buy direct from the trout farm. It is a business that has been run by the same family for generations. There's a lovely *fromagerie* on the way there as well."

Cady bought the rest of her groceries and followed Annick's directions down a winding mountain road along the river. She arrived at a clutch of stone buildings, one of which was clearly a large private home, with picture-perfect lace curtains in the windows and a fat cat lazing on the porch in a shaft of April sunshine.

Inside the shop, a plump, red-faced woman greeted her with "*Ah oui*, you are the American staying at the château?"

Word had spread.

"How is Fabrice doing?" asked the woman. "I hear he hurt his ankle."

"He's doing better, thank you. I'll need two trouts for our dinner."

"The fish here is very special, you know," the woman said as she used a large net to scoop a wriggling trout out of the tank, laid it on the table, and knocked it out in one smooth move. Cady grimaced and focused on the view of the emerald green river through the window. It was fun to think about buying fish at the source, but Cady was most definitely a city girl, more comfortable with buying meat under plastic at the market.

"The river Sorgue comes out of the belly of the mountain in Fontaine-de-Vaucluse. Not a small spring, mind you, but an entire river, flowing just like that, out of the rock. This is why it is always very cold, even during the hottest summers. No one knows where it comes from; no one has been able to reach the bottom."

Cady remembered Jean-Paul mentioning the town; Fabrice's "Minette" was from there, and supposedly it had been home to a dragon, once upon a time.

"I'll take a pack of smoked trout as well," Cady said on impulse, as the woman handed her a bag along with a small piece of paper with a recipe for *truit Provençal*, made with classic herbes de Provence.

Next, a "quick stop" at the *fromagerie* turned into a forty-minute tasting odyssey, as the cheese-maker introduced her to the local *fromages*. A goat cheese called Banon was small, round, and pungent, wrapped in chestnut leaves and tied with raffia. Another, Brousse du Rove, was considered *petit lait*, and came in tall little tubes covered in woven wicker.

She splurged, buying two of each, in addition to a wedge of Roquefort, a small round of Camembert, and a jar of onion compote.

Back home in Oakland, Cady hadn't been one to give in to impulse. But she was in France, after all.

• • •

Cady carted the groceries into the kitchen and found Fabrice in his favorite chair in front of the fire. Despite railing at the doctor's advice yesterday, he had been following directions, putting his ankle up and icing it frequently throughout the day.

"How's your ankle?"

"A little better, maybe," he said, watching her unpack. "Where'd you get all that?"

"From an amazing *fromagerie* on the way back from the fishery."

He glared at her. "Only idiots buy at *fromageries*."

"I never claimed *not* to be an idiot."

"Speaking of idiots, Johnny will come after lunch."

"Why is he so mad at you?" Cady asked.

"He didn't bring me what I wanted. So I fired him."

"And then the grocery store fired him." Cady unpacked the brown paper bag from the trout farm.

Fabrice eyed the packages as they came out of the bag. "The trout woman talked you into buying too much."

"She didn't talk me into anything; I bought just as much as I wanted to buy. And anyway, I'm paying for the groceries today, so don't worry about it."

"*Mais ça coûte les yeux de la tête.*" Which literally meant that it cost the eyes from the head.

She took a deep breath, gesturing at him with a knife she had picked up to wash. "Look, old man, this is my first and probably only time I'll ever be in France, and I was at a Provençal *trout* farm in the *mountains.* So if I want to buy myself some smoked fish, then it's nobody's business but mine."

He raised his eyebrows as if to say *Sheesh,* and turned his attention back to his newspaper.

"Could I ask you something?" Cady asked.

"Seems like that's about all you do."

"You're forever reading the paper. Why are you so interested in the world if you won't take part in it?"

"The paper gets delivered. I didn't ask for it, but as long as it shows up, I might as well read it."

She smiled. "Today the fish woman told me about the town called Fontaine-de-Vaucluse. You mention it in *Le Château* as well."

"It's a famous place. Pétrarque lived there. He wrote some of his most famous verses while there."

"He was a poet, right?"

"You don't know Pétrarque? He is credited with inventing romanticism."

"I didn't realize there was ever a time without romance."

Fabrice snorted in an almost-laugh that delighted Cady. "I meant in literature. It was in Fontaine-de-Vaucluse that he wrote his most famous lines, for his beloved Laura: 'The waters speak of love, and the breeze, the oars, the little birds, the fish, the flowers, and the grass all together beg me to love forever.' "

"And did he?"

"Did he what?"

"Love forever?"

"Yes. Yes, he did," Fabrice said in a somber tone. "*Now* what are you smiling about?"

"You," said Cady, heating water for coffee. "You act like a cranky old grump, but you're such a romantic underneath it all."

He snorted. "You remind me of . . . someone I knew when I was a teenager."

"This was during the war?"

He nodded.

"Jean-Paul mentioned that you worked with the Résistance."

He inclined his head, just barely, a far-off look in his eye.

"I saw some plaques in Paris; I wasn't sure what they were about, but Madame Martin told me they were in memory of guerrilla fighters with the Résistance."

He nodded. "I fought in combat only at the very end. A terrible clarity occurs when a person has nothing left to live for."

"You had nothing left to live for?"

"My family had been taken away by the Gestapo." His tone was matter-of-fact, but his mouth twisted slightly as he stared at the non-existent fire in the hearth.

Cady tried to think of some response adequate to the situation, but words failed her. Then she remembered the people who felt compelled to say something about Maxine's death, and decided to hold her tongue, to sit silently and share the moment, however uncomfortable.

"I would like to go back to Fontaine-de-Vaucluse," Fabrice said suddenly. "I would like to see it one more time, before I die."

"Would you like me to take you?"

He got up and started to walk out of the room, but at the doorway he turned and said: "Yes. In a day or two, when my ankle is better, we'll go to Fontaine-de-Vaucluse. And . . . if you still want, I'll show you that damned carousel."

"Really? Now?"

"Your little friend Johnny is due any minute. You deal with him, and take this dog out, and then make dinner, and if I still feel like it, we'll look at it after a whiskey."

CHAPTER FORTY-TWO

1944
PARIS

Fabrice

A blue scarf hung in the window of Dr. Duhamel's office.

Fabrice spotted it at the last moment and ducked into the entrance of the apartment building next door, pretending to search the buttons for a name, as though he were visiting a friend.

His heart hammered in his chest. This was like being searched on the train, but worse. Fabrice had come to think of the doctor's office as not so much his sanctuary as his escape from the boredom and grueling sameness of living under Nazi occupation: It was the source of glamour and intrigue and romance.

Slowly, very carefully, trying to regulate his breathing, he peeked out from the doorway. He prayed that he'd gotten it wrong, that perhaps his eyes were fooled by a trick of the golden evening light glinting off the window.

He was not wrong. The maid Carine had hung

her blue scarf in the window. It was the prearranged signal of a mousetrap. The Gestapo would descend upon the headquarters of a cell, then remain within, quietly waiting for others to appear: couriers, messengers, anyone related in any way to the others in the cell.

What now? The instructions were clear: If you saw the signal, you were to melt back into the non-shadow world. And wait.

But he had to find Paulette.

He ran to Claude Frenet's home. They had grown closer through their shared goals, but nonetheless they remained more colleagues than friends. Still, for want of someone else to share with, Fabrice had confided in Claude his love for Paulette.

Claude's mother tearfully informed Fabrice that Claude had disappeared; she hadn't seen or heard from him since the night before. Now Fabrice was pierced by another fear: Would Claude betray Paulette? And the rest of them? Had he already? For all Fabrice knew, Claude might have been an infiltrator all along; he might have been the one to turn the cell in, to reveal the work of the doctor and his wife.

And Paulette? Had she been taken? Fabrice didn't even know her last name. The reality chafed him, the fear stabbed. He should have insisted, should have forced her to tell him. He should have foreseen the possibility of something like this.

Frantic, Fabrice searched Paris for her: from cafés to bookstores to the neighborhood he had followed her to once, where he thought she lived, near the Moulin Rouge. Nazis flirting with Parisian women outside the nightclubs made him sick, but he smiled and waggled his eyebrows at them to avoid suspicion. People said the prostitutes were guilty of *collaboration horizontale*, essentially collaborating on their backs. But what choice did they have? Fabrice was doubly disgusted by the bankers and businesspeople becoming wealthy under the German occupation. And the ones who moved, cowlike and docile, into the new Nazi reality.

Fabrice spotted a red beret on short, honey-colored hair. In a spasm of relief he grabbed the woman's arm and spun her around, but it was not Paulette.

The German officer with her berated him, but Fabrice hardly registered the words. He wandered off and headed to the only other possible rendezvous point he could think of: the printshop.

The shop had been ransacked, the door left ajar, the precious machinery destroyed. Fabrice stood in front of the broken printing press, defeated, then heard a footstep behind him.

He turned to find Claude pointing a gun at him.

"*You?*" Fabrice demanded. "You're the traitor?"

"No," Claude insisted, shaking his head vehemently. "It wasn't me. I barely escaped with my life. I can't go home, I—"

Claude had let the pistol droop in his hand. Fabrice knew that he was afraid of guns, and in a calculated move, he leapt on his former comrade. The gun fell from Claude's hand and skittered along the ink-stained wooden planks, and Fabrice dove for it. The men grappled, rolling on the floor, and though Fabrice was younger and smaller, he was the better fighter, more willing to be vicious.

He stood and loomed over Claude, pointing the gun at his head.

"It wasn't me!" Claude yelled. "It was *her!*"

"Who?" Fabrice demanded.

"Michelle." Paulette's nom de guerre. "Your girlfriend, the one you love so much."

It was falling off a cliff. It was drowning. It was being lined up against a wall and shot, the bullet tearing into his gut.

"Wh-what are you talking about?" Fabrice stammered.

"*She* was the collaborator. They got to her family, in her village in Provence, and threatened them. She betrayed us."

"I don't believe you."

"Ask the doctor, or the maid—Carine was one of the first to suspect."

"I can't. Everyone's gone."

"Think about it, Fabrice. How did the Gestapo know about Pierre and Françoise, or Monsieur R., or any of the others who went off on missions and never returned?"

Fabrice tried to think. Everything hurt. The scrapes and bruises from grappling with Claude were nothing compared to the pounding in his head, the sick sensation behind his eyes, the belief that his heart was actually shattering into shards that were crowding his chest and tumbling, bleeding and broken, into his gut. He fought the compulsion to vomit.

"Remember when you went to take the photos outside of Nantes?" Claude continued. "The doctor told her you had been sent to Brest. He had his suspicions about her even then."

Fabrice remembered: Paulette had seemed shocked to see him when he walked into the office after returning from his trip to Saint-Nazaire. At the time he thought she was overwhelmed with relief, full of emotion upon his return. That was the first time he had held her in his arms. Could it be possible that she had intended to send him to his death?

Fabrice lowered the gun, but continued to hold his onetime friend by the collar. His emotions and thoughts were at war; he had lived so long under the threat of betrayal, suspecting one day the woman at the *boulangerie*, the next the boy who swept the floor at the printshop, the day after that the old woman on the corner who sat in her window and peeked out at the world through shredded silk curtains.

"We have to *run,* Fabrice," said Claude. "Run and hide. I heard her call you by your real name; they might already know where you live. We are not safe; our *families* are not safe."

"What do you mean, our families?" Fabrice asked, his voice barely above a whisper. He felt drained of energy, and finally released Claude, sliding down the wall to sit on the dirty floor beside him. "My parents know nothing about my actions."

Claude let out a harsh laugh. "You think the Gestapo cares that our families are innocent? They are not known for their discretion. It might already be too late. You should go to them—or better yet, ask a neighbor to check, just in case there are soldiers there waiting for you already."

Claude grabbed a pipe overhead and hauled himself to his feet, wincing and holding his arm over his chest. Dully, Fabrice wondered whether his punches, fueled by fury and fear for Paulette, had broken a rib.

Claude was only a year older than Fabrice, but his eyes belonged to a much older man. They were still just teenagers, but they had both changed since the war began, and even more since working with the Résistance; they had become hard, distrustful, wary.

"Well, *I* am going to run," said Claude, with sudden fervor. "It has been more than three years; this war cannot last forever. The Free French are working with the Allies; they will liberate us eventually. Of this, I am sure. Until then, I will live in the shadows. As should you."

Fabrice watched as his friend limped toward the back door, opened it a few inches, and peered out to check that the alley was safe before slipping through. The metal door clanged as it swung shut.

Should Fabrice believe Claude's version of events? If Claude himself was the informant, wouldn't it make sense to cast blame elsewhere? Still, there was something about his words that resonated. And no matter whether it was Claude or Paulette or someone else who had betrayed the cell, Fabrice had to run and hide. But first he had to be sure his family was safe.

His parents were innocent of anything but repairing statues, but it did not take much. Only a whisper of association, and they could be disappeared as swiftly and surely as the next person.

He saw their faces in his mind: his mother's patient, gentle smile; his father's serious, dark gaze; his little sister's chubby red cheeks. There were moments when he despised them, felt they were holding him back . . . but they were his family. They were all he had, and he loved them. Surely he had not put them in danger? They had nothing to do with any of his actions. If he had to, he would turn himself in to the Gestapo, confess to everything, to keep them safe.

Tears stung his eyes as he sprang to his feet, flung open the door, and ran down rue Saint-Séverin and across boulevard Saint-Michel, the streets he had run through as a child, toward the apartment he had shared with his family his entire life. His father's woodworking shop was on the first floor of a building on the Impasse Hautefeuille, not far from Place Saint-André-des-Arts. A small sign, CHARPENTERIE CLEMENT, was the only indication.

The OUVERT placard hung in the window, but the door was locked.

Fabrice banged on it and yelled, fighting panic. The door was never locked during business hours; Marc-Antoine did not believe in turning anyone away, especially now. The family needed every job that came in, in order to pay the rent, to find food, to survive.

Guilt washed over him. Fabrice was supposed to have been here working beside his father, planing planks and carving details, using rotten-stone and pumice to bring the wood to a high polish. He was supposed to have been here.

He banged on the door again. "*Maman*! *Papa*! *Capucine*!"

Still nothing. He was about to use his key when he saw the silk curtains rustle in the window on the corner. Fabrice ran into the apartment foyer and up a winding stairway to the second floor. He banged on the door of the old woman but heard no answer. He tried the knob; it was unlocked, so he burst in.

The old woman was sitting in an upholstered chair by the window. The apartment was humbly furnished, and Fabrice remembered a time when his mother had sent him with a hunk of bread and a pot of soup when the old woman suffered from pneumonia. But for the life of him he could not remember her name.

"Did you see anything?" he demanded. "Have you seen my family?"

She shrank back from Fabrice's ire.

"*Madame, excusez-moi.* But did . . ." He was afraid to even say the words. "Did anyone come? Did the . . . did soldiers come?"

Finally, she answered in a flat voice: "*Ce matin.*"

This morning.

"But what did they . . . where did they go?" he stammered. "What do I do?"

She pulled her black shawl tighter and shook her head, sadness in every move.

"What do I do?" Fabrice shouted, wanting to hit her, wanting to hurt her. Wanting to ask why she did not intervene to help the kind neighbor lady who had sent her bread and soup when she was ill.

Fabrice returned to Charpenterie Clement,

hesitated a moment, then slipped his key into the rusty lock and turned the latch. He pushed the door in carefully.

"*Allo*? *Maman*? *Papa*?"

He knew it was dangerous; the Nazis often left a young soldier behind to round up the strays, anyone coming to look for their loved ones. But in this moment Fabrice almost hoped for arrest, to be reunited with his family, even under these circumstances. He was desperate to know what had happened to them, where they had been taken. Would they be sent to a work camp? Or perhaps they would be released—some people were released, after all, and Marc-Antoine had skills that might be useful to the occupying forces. Capucine was nothing but a sticky cherub, barely five years old; surely she would not be seen as any kind of threat. Or . . . would his parents be tortured for information? Information about *him?* They knew nothing; he had never told them about any of his activities. Which meant they would have no tidbits to offer the Gestapo to trade for their lives.

These thoughts whirled around in Fabrice's head, incessant, excruciating.

The workshop was empty; boot marks marred the film of wood dust on the broad-planked floor. One shelf had been knocked over, the tools and squares and knives scattered in the doorway.

Upstairs, in their apartment, a pot of cabbage

soup still sat on the stove, but the fire was off, the broth gone cold. He ducked into his parents' bedroom, and then the one he shared with his baby sister. The beds were neatly made, but the closet doors stood open, the contents ransacked. Surrounding the small desk by the window, papers and books had been tossed on the carpet like oversized confetti.

The Nazis came for people, but they always checked for valuables. It was the way of it.

Fabrice stumbled back down the stairs, his mind a blank.

The Madonna stood atop the workbench, her hand repaired, her blue velvet robes mended, fruitlessly praying for them all.

Fabrice knocked her to the ground, cursing her name.

CHAPTER FORTY-THREE

PRESENT DAY
CHÂTEAU CLEMENT

Cady

Johnny showed up with a black eye.

"Where'd you get that?" Cady asked.

He shrugged. "A fight."

"I should see the other guy, huh?"

"What?" he asked with a sneer.

"It's something we say in English if someone was hurt in a fight, like the other guy had it worse. Never mind. Some things don't translate."

Something about the way Johnny held himself, his defensiveness, made Cady wonder if there was something else going on.

It's none of my business, she reminded herself. She had already butted in far more than was expected, or probably socially acceptable, given that she was an interloper in a small village, a foreigner who would be leaving soon.

She put the teenager to work covering up the graffiti tags with paint she'd found in the shed by the old car. Then she had him take the measurements of the windows he had broken and sweep up the glass. He didn't speak much, mostly grunting his replies, not unlike a certain grumpy recluse.

"So, why have you been over here vandalizing Fabrice's things?"

"He's a jerk."

"A lot of people are jerks. But you know, when someone makes you mad, there are other ways to deal with it, rather than lashing out."

"Whatever."

"Why did you slash my tires?"

"I thought Fabrice got a new car," he said, dumping glass shards into a plastic trash bin. He shrugged again. "My mistake."

While Johnny worked, Cady brought her cameras out and started snapping photos of the old buildings, the shadow of a cypress on the gravel drive. She loved the slanted spring light of mid-April. It was chilly in the shadows, warm in the sunshine—she wanted somehow to capture that feeling on film.

She noticed Johnny sneaking glances at her while she twisted this way and that to get just the right angle.

"Want to try?" she asked, holding out her Leica camera.

"Nah. I have a phone."

"Taking pictures with a phone is really

different. And this way I get to develop my own photos."

He rolled his eyes. "You sound like the tile guy. He's always going on about old-fashioned photography."

"Really? The tile guy? Here in town?"

"Yeah, there's a tileworks on the outside of town. There's an old Italian man there, named Guido."

Just as she had with the dimensions of the new glass for the windows, Cady jotted down the information in her journal.

"What do you keep writing down?"

"Everything. Things I need to remember, like phone numbers and names. And other things, too: ideas, or recipes, or just . . . anything. Since I've come to France, there are lists of French words and phrases I need to look up."

He turned his attention back to scraping the glazing from the window frame.

Cady tried again to peek into the outbuilding that held the carousel, but as before, she couldn't see much more than amorphous black shapes.

She thought about what Fabrice had said about showing her the carousel, and what she'd promised: to take him to Fontaine-de-Vaucluse when his ankle was better. She hadn't been entirely sure she'd still be in France, much less Provence, in "a day or two." Jean-Paul would probably be happy to see her gone. The charge to change her flight reservation was not insignificant, and she had assumed she would be back in Paris in time to make her plane. But now . . . ?

Oakland seemed less and less real to her lately. The wind-tossed scents of lavender and thyme—the aroma of Provence—seemed to be seeping into her, holding on, making her feel almost as if she belonged in this foreign country, in this small village, in this decrepit château.

She wasn't going anywhere, at least not for the moment. If she could get access to the antique carousel, she would change her ticket in a heartbeat and damn the expense.

CHAPTER FORTY-FOUR

1900
CHÂTEAU CLEMENT

Maëlle

Maëlle had thought staying at Château Clement would allow her more time with Léon, out from under Monsieur Maréchal's direction and Madame Bayol's astute gaze. But since they arrived, Léon rarely pays attention to her. It makes her think back with longing to his annoying teasing on the train.

They had taken one walk together, down through the gardens, along the intricate topiary, which she thought lovely but he deemed a "dreadful attempt to harness the wilds of nature." She argued that in one sense any sort of gardening was an attempt to harness the wilds of nature, but weren't some gardens lovely? He had snorted in disgust.

"I think Château Clement is the loveliest place I've ever seen," she said, her chin rising in defiance. "And the Clements are so kind and genteel—they're not at all the spoiled rich people you thought they'd be. Admit it."

"I'll admit no such thing. I'll tell you a secret, though: The only reason you were allowed on this trip is that you are half price."

"What are you talking about?"

"Bayol wanted you out of the factory—you're too much of a 'distraction,' he said. Little girls don't belong in such an arena. So he wrote to the Clements and told them they could have you for as long as they wanted you, for half what they would pay for even the lowliest assistant in the shop."

Maëlle's mouth fell open, but she didn't know how to respond. She studied the intricate shapes of the topiary, feeling a deep-down but strangely detached sense of devastation. Simultaneously, she tried to talk herself out of it: *It was nothing personal.* Everyone had implied that the Clements had money trouble; it only made sense they would seek a bargain. And everyone knew that women were thought to be worth less than a man. Everyone knew that.

Léon was staring at her, but when she did not react with anger or tears, he let out an exasperated sound and stormed off, his boots clicking on the hewn stone of the walkway.

Since then he had disappeared increasingly frequently, or when he did appear he was drunk. More than once Maëlle had to hide his intemperate state from their patrons. She set up a pallet in the back of the building so he could sleep it off without returning to his rooms and alerting the household staff to his inebriated presence.

In the meantime, the carousel is developing before her eyes, little by little, pieces coming together, the joints filled and sanded, primed and painted, gilded and sealed.

She hears the men snickering, talking about how Léon is keeping warm these days. Humiliation stings, but it hardens something deep down inside her. Have they always known? Is that why they whisper in front of her, or is it simply that she is a woman and therefore not privy to their jokes?

Finally, Maëlle decides she's had enough. If she is mistress of this project, then so be it. But if so, she will take a page out of Monsieur Maréchal's book, and yell.

"Where is he?" she demands of Romain as he brings in a stack of new lumber on his shoulder.

"Who, mademoiselle?"

"You know very well who. This carousel is supposed to have nine men working on it. I realize that as a woman I am worth at least two men, but since Léon Morice is being paid for his labor I would like to know where he is."

The men hoot at her tone, and the assertion of her worth.

"Is he in town, at the café?" she persists.

Guy, with whom she had traded interesting conversations over the past ten days, steps forward.

"I saw him out in the vineyard this morning, Maëlle. He . . ." Guy drops his voice. "He wasn't alone."

"Thank you, Guy. Everyone carry on." Maëlle hopes her voice sounds as steady and stern as Monsieur Maréchal's always did in the factory, though she fears it shakes slightly. "We should have that mechanism running within the next few days, and if the painting of the salon remains on schedule we'll book tickets back to Angers within the week."

Then she unties her apron, tosses it on the sawhorse, and leaves the building. She heads down the drive, through the vineyard, to the edge of the surrounding woods, where she hears a twig snap.

"Léon?" she calls out, venturing into the forest.

She happens upon Yves Clement, with his ever-present camera.

"Mademoiselle! How nice to meet you out here. Are you a nature lover like me, then?"

"No. I mean yes, monsieur."

He crooks his head and smiles. "You're not sure?"

"It's not that . . . Yes, I am a nature lover, and your woods are so lovely. All of the grounds, in fact."

"But you are not enjoying nature at the moment?"

"No, monsieur. At the moment I'm looking

for my—" She hesitates, then says, "My master, Léon Morice. Have you happened to see him?"

"No, I'm sorry to say. Though as it happens, I've been searching for my lovely wife this morning," he says. "I wanted to show her a bird's nest I found. Would you like to see it?"

"No, no. I'm sorry, monsieur," says Maëlle. She felt a wave of heat sweep over her, leaving nausea in its wake. "I-I really must get back to the carousel. Another time, perhaps."

He nods, then lifts his camera to his eye and focuses on a leaf hanging listlessly upon a loose branch. "Tell you what: If I find your master, I'll send him back to the carousel building. And if you find my wife, you'll send her back to me, *hmm?*"

"*Oui*, *monsieur*, of course."

Maëlle hurries away, choking back tears and disgust, engulfed by a ravenous sense of betrayal. *They are together. They must be.* This is why Josephine was asking all those questions about Léon the other night. Of course.

Josephine and Léon. Maëlle can't get the image out of her mind: Léon leaning down to kiss that heart-shaped mole on Josephine's long, pale neck. And why wouldn't he fall in love with her? Josephine is pretty and wealthy and sweet, and always smells like roses. And Léon is dashing and handsome, a vital young man next to that corpse—a very genteel corpse, but still—that

Josephine calls husband. It would be like night and day, to be kissed by a man like Léon after knowing only Yves's touch.

She can hardly even blame her friend. Except that . . . Josephine had become her trusted confidante. Almost a sister. Or so she'd thought.

Maëlle lurches back toward the carousel building, unseeing, until she falls against an old oak and closes her eyes in despair. Last night she had dreamt that Leon and the other men had boarded the train back to Angers without her; she had awoken with her heart pounding, as she called out and chased the train, but to no avail. It was as though happiness, which not long ago had seemed within her grasp, was pulling farther and farther away no matter how fast she ran.

For now, all she can think to do is to carve. Maëlle returns to the job site and inspects the carousel figures for nicks and scratches sustained when they were mounted onto the mechanism. They are now speared through by their metal rods, which are then inserted through the floor and ceiling and attached to the cranks that will make them prance.

As always, Maëlle hears the laughter of children in her mind as she works. But the Clements *have* no children. They have been married for years, without being so blessed.

Who will ride this beautiful carousel, then?

CHAPTER FORTY-FIVE

PRESENT DAY
CHÂTEAU CLEMENT

Cady

All evening, Cady felt like the proverbial kid waiting for Christmas morning. She had never actually *had* that idyllic experience, but she was sure that if she had, it would have felt like this. She could hardly enjoy her meal, so excited was she to lay eyes on the carousel that Gustave Bayol had carved for Fabrice's grandparents.

Afraid to spook Fabrice, she was careful not to mention it as they savored their trout Provençal.

"Did you enjoy it?" she asked, as Fabrice used a piece of bread to sop up the remaining sauce on his plate.

"*C'est pas mauvais*," he said with an inclination of his head.

"From you that's high praise indeed," she said. "Fabrice, would you tell me more about your work with the Résistance during the war? I'm so interested in that period of time."

He looked into the depths of his white wine, which glimmered golden in the firelight.

"I was just a kid, fooling around."

"A screwup?"

"A screwup. It was like I was playing a game. Little did I realize . . ." He trailed off. When he declined to say anything more, Cady cleared the table, scraping the fish bones into the trash.

"You should take the trash out so it doesn't stink," said Fabrice, standing and grabbing his crutch. "And if you still want, I'll show you that carousel."

Cady slung her Leica around her neck.

They went together to the garbage cans, and finally over to the building that housed whatever remained of the carousel. Fabrice struggled with the rusty padlock for a few minutes, and then asked Cady to step in and help.

The large, barnlike door creaked as it opened. Inside, the pitch-black was interrupted only by the weak light of the moon struggling through a few high, dusty windows. There was a stench of old soot and rodents.

"There's no electricity out here," Fabrice said, as he and Cady cast their flashlight beams around the interior.

At first Cady saw nothing more than the hulking dark blobs she'd noted through the window. But then she realized that under and behind other junk—tarps and random pieces of lumber, a broken chair, an old wheelbarrow—were the remains of an antique carousel, damaged, dismantled, its parts scattered about the building.

And sitting toward the rear of the building was the main mechanism, the running floor and overhead crown marred by several gaping, charred holes—but essentially intact.

Only two carousel figures, a cat and a pig, still remained affixed to the floor, poles running through them. One was an outside stander—a figure that did not move—and the other an inner row jumper. Several other animals were scattered about the dusty building, their seams splitting, joints loosening. She also spotted something that must have been a spinning tub, and another piece that might have been a rocking carriage.

Overhead, the flashlight illuminated a once-grand rounding board—the "crown" of the carousel—with alternating painted panels and carved shields. The center room, which traditionally housed part of the mechanism of the carousel and sometimes the band organ, was also covered in panels—some painted, others mirrored. All appeared to be nearly black with soot and dirt, any color lost to the elements and the night. The salon show front had been dismantled and the parts appeared to be leaning against opposite walls.

Cady approached an intact portion of the carousel, reached out, and ran her hand over the pig. His sweet face tilted to look up at her, tongue sticking out, big floppy ears inviting a child's touch. During the day, in good condition, it would have been charming; now, in the dark, encrusted with dirt and soot, it seemed almost nightmarish, as though it might come alive and give chase.

She found the telltale brass shield on its saddle blanket: Bayol's factory had made these figures.

Cady had taken hundreds of photographs of carousels, and had seen plenty of the individual figures being repaired and worked on, but never had she seen a carousel dismantled and disassembled, charred and left to deteriorate like worthless junk. It hurt her heart.

She lifted the Leica that hung around her neck and started snapping. She disliked using a flash, preferring natural light, but in case this was her one chance to take photos of this gravely wounded carousel, she wasn't going to pass it up.

"I'm telling you," said Fabrice, shaking his head. "I had someone look at it a long time ago. It's been looted, besides the fire damage, and there was water damage after that. It would cost more than it's worth to have it restored. And there's no way to get back all the original figures."

"Nonetheless, these are worth something," Cady said, her voice low and reverent, as though they were in a church. This was history beneath her fingers. Sooty, grubby history.

"Maybe they used to be, but look at them now. Just trash."

"No, Fabrice, they're not. They just need a little—or a lot—of cleaning, and some basic repair. They're worth the effort. They were carved by the House of Bayol, in Angers."

"So?"

"Bayol is said to be France's most famous carousel maker. He was a sculptor, an artist."

"Why should that matter to me?"

"Because they're valuable."

"Like I said about the signed books I have, I don't care. I have what I need. I won't be around much longer, anyway. Your boyfriend can cash these in, I guess, if that's what he wants."

"My boyfriend?"

"Jean-Paul."

"He isn't my boyfriend."

"Not what it looks like to me. Anyway"—he turned around, casting the beam of his flashlight on the figures, but not entering beyond the threshold—"this just seems sad to me. It was all built for my father, Marc-Antoine."

"He was the only child of Yves and Josephine, right?"

He nodded. "Sounds like you know my family history pretty well."

"Just trying to keep the characters straight."

"The way I heard it was that they had this thing built before my father was even born. I guess they wanted to fill it with kids, but it didn't happen that way. And Yves spent a fortune on it, not realizing he would need the money later to maintain the château through an economic downturn and then World War I."

"But Marc-Antoine must have loved it. And the village children used to come here for festivals."

"You've been here, what, less than a week? This town loves to talk." His beam rested on the old rocking carriage, a rose carved over its opening. "You really think you could do something with this old thing?"

"It's a job for a conservator. There are professionals who could—"

"I don't want any so-called professionals. If you want to clean this thing up, you can do it. Just you."

"I would need help, though. What about Johnny? It would be a perfect project for someone like him. And Jean-Paul, of course, if he would agree to help."

He snorted, but said: "Fine. You, the kid, and Jean-Paul. But I don't want any more strangers around; if you want to call in 'experts,' then wait until I die. After that, you could probably talk Jean-Paul into letting you do whatever you want. But until then, no outsiders on my property."

"Fabrice, you know Jean-Paul cares about

you, right? And yes, he's worried about what will happen to the château, but it's really not his fault that he's next in line to inherit. Or that his grandfather is a jerk."

He shrugged. "It's just that . . . this carousel seems like a metaphor. Everything beautiful and innocent is ruined."

She photographed the pig, the cat, and the carriage from several angles, wondering what the harsh light of the flash would uncover when she developed the film. Often the camera revealed things that her naked eye did not notice.

"How did it catch on fire, do you know?"

Fabrice remained quiet for so long she thought he wouldn't answer. But finally he said: "My father said his mother—my grandmother, Josephine—used to ride this machine at night. A lot of the people in the village thought Josephine had been unfaithful. . . ."

Cady snapped a few photos of the spinning tub.

"There was a problem with the steam engine, when the wrong kind of kerosene was used. Josephine's body was found here, after the fire was put out."

"I'm so sorry," Cady said, snapping photos of the rounding board overhead. "What a tragic accident."

"Some said my grandfather went crazy with jealousy and lit the thing on fire while she was out here. They thought he killed her on purpose."

Cady froze. Slowly, she lowered her camera and looked at Fabrice. His face was sketched with strange, strong shadows and planes from the flashlight beams.

"Did your father believe that?"

"All I know is that this is what a dream looks like after it's turned into a nightmare."

CHAPTER FORTY-SIX

PRESENT DAY
CHÂTEAU CLEMENT

Cady

Cady was wide-awake at six, anxious for the light of day.

She was excited to tell Jean-Paul that Fabrice had shown her the carousel, but her cell phone didn't get reception, and she didn't feel like she could chat freely on the telephone in the kitchen. Also, she was expecting Johnny to arrive early today for work. She would have to catch up with Jean-Paul later.

At the crack of dawn she dressed warmly and brought her camera bag outdoors. She propped open the large doors of the building and assessed the remnants of the dream in the clarity of early morning, white light slanting in through the high, dust-caked windows.

As usual, the daylight was better for her photography, but harder on the imagination. The haunted romance of the carousel had dissipated with the night; in its place was a complete and total mess.

Cady felt a flicker of self-doubt. Maybe Fabrice was right; was there even anything to salvage under all this grime?

She laid out her cameras, settled in behind the first lens, and started clicking.

When Johnny arrived, Fabrice directed them to a storage closet where they found fans, masks, and gloves left over from his earlier repair efforts. They brought their supplies to the outbuilding, opened the windows, and positioned fans to create a cross-breeze.

Johnny leaned against the outside of the building, brought a pack of Marlboros out of his pocket, and lit up.

Cady gave him an exasperated look. "We just set up these fans to save our lungs, and now you're going to smoke?"

He shrugged and gestured toward the interior with his head. "It's just a bunch of junk."

"That's what it looks like at first, I know. But a lot of junk only needs a second chance. Put out that cigarette while we're inside, please."

Grudgingly he did so, then followed her into the building.

"Check this out," Cady said, leading him across the floor of the carousel to one of the interior panels. She used a rag to wipe off a corner. "There's a whole painting under all that soot. See it peeking through?"

He squatted on the other side of the painting. "What do you want me to do, wash it off?"

"No, unfortunately it's not quite so simple. If you use soap and water it can actually get under the oil paint and cause it to flake off, or leave a foggy residue, called a 'bloom.' " It had been a while since Cady had cleaned old oil paintings with Maxine. She didn't want to do anything drastic, such as removing the varnish and risk removing original paint along with it. At first, at least, she wanted only to remove the soot to reveal the underlying painting. "We'll need a special solvent. I don't suppose there's an art supply store in Saint-Véran?"

He looked confused.

"That's a joke. I'm joking. Surely they'll have something in Avignon. Is there an art school there?"

"There's a university, and the Académie des Arts d'Avignon."

"Perfect. Where there are students, there are supplies."

"Or you could ask the florist, in Saint-Véran," Johnny suggested. "Her daughter does painting restorations for big museums; she trained at the Louvre."

"And she lives here in the village?"

He nodded. "She split from her husband and has a young daughter, so they moved back in with her mom."

"And her mom's the florist? What's her name?"

"La Toinon—she's a Clement too, but her married name is Goselin. So, how do you know how to do this kind of thing?"

"I learned it when I was about your age, actually. Help me bring these carousel figures over near the light of the windows. Very gently."

He did as he was told, and they started moving the menagerie. In total there were two rabbits, three dogs, a cat, and a pig. "I was a bad kid, like you. If you think Saint-Véran is bad, you should try being a delinquent on the streets of Oakland."

He stared at her.

"Anyway, one day—actually, many days—I stole something from a shop owned by a woman named Maxine. She sold antiques, and a lot of plain old junk. For some reason she decided to put me to work instead of turning me over to the police."

She paused, hoping he was taking in the significance of her words. It was hard to tell. Johnny had the flat affect of a lot of troubled teens, the result of covering up emotions for so many years for fear of being vulnerable. Unfortunately, it was hard to distinguish this kind of self-defense from a basic lack of understanding or lack of intelligence.

"So, anyway," Cady continued, while handing Johnny a broom and dustpan, "Maxine taught me how to clean and repair antiques, and I worked for her for a long time. She also taught me how to read."

Johnny said something in French that Cady assumed meant something along the lines of "No way!"

"It's true. I had been moved around a lot in school, and I'd managed to slip by without ever learning to read. I was your age. Can you imagine? All I knew before meeting Maxine was how to stay alive, and how to fight."

"You fight?"

"Not anymore. Learned to use my words instead. But if Maxine hadn't helped me, I imagine I'd be in jail right now."

He looked around the soot-filled mess of the building. "Maybe it wouldn't be so bad, compared to this."

She laughed. "Oh yes, it would. This carousel has real potential, Johnny. It's a part of French history, and your family's history. Trust me. You'll see. So, which university are you planning to attend? Are you thinking Avignon, or farther afield?"

"What?"

"You're, what, fifteen? Doesn't that mean university is coming up in a few years?"

The expression on his face suggested she had said something insane.

"Isn't university free in France? Or at least subsidized? That's a pretty sweet deal."

"Well, yeah, if you get in. But I'm not, like, a good student."

"Why not?"

He shrugged.

"Maxine always told me that it wasn't a crime to need help, only to fail to ask for help when you need it."

"You make her sound like some kind of saint."

She smiled as she thought of a "Saint Maxine," realizing that for the first time since Maxine died, she didn't have to fight the image of her dear friend and mentor falling, lying on the floor, the last breath leaving her body. The sensation of Maxine disappearing, abandoning Cady, right in front of her.

Instead, the first image that came to mind was one of Maxine sitting behind her cash register, flipping through a magazine; then Cady thought of Maxine wearing her big apron as she stood behind the worktable, tilting her head back to look through the bottom lenses of her bifocals as she studied a project. She thought of the moment Maxine had asked Cady to come live with her.

"I think maybe she *was* a saint, come to think of it," Cady said. "She saved me, anyway. 'Saint Maxine.' Has a nice ring to it."

Johnny said nothing, merely fixed Cady with a cautious look, as though he was just figuring out she was totally insane.

That's exactly what Cady had thought of

Maxine when the old woman made it clear that she was going to make Cady her next project. Cady might be in Provence for only a few more days, but sometimes that was enough time to throw someone like Johnny a lifeline, to change his perspective.

It struck Cady that here she was willing to reach out and connect, whereas in Oakland she shrank from it. Olivia used to try to get her involved in the Big Sisters program or tutoring high school students, but Cady always had some excuse for not doing so, always thinking that "someday" in the future she would become a foster mother and make her mark. Or . . . have her own baby. Just as with Maxine, Cady realized she hadn't thought about the miscarriage for . . . days?

Maybe Olivia was right—maybe there truly was such a thing as a geographical cure. For whatever reason, it felt easier to open her heart and mind and to move forward in this foreign place.

"Enough about Saint Maxine," Cady said, realizing that Johnny had finished sweeping up the area where the carousel figures had been. "For now, let's clean those windows so we can see better in here, and then line those panels up against that wall. Then we can clean them assembly line–style, once we have the right solvents. And let's put any other carved figures we find in this area," she said, gesturing to the alcove on the other side of the room. “That way we can see what we have.”

“So this thing used to be a carousel that, like, worked?”

“It was, yes. But there were many more figures than these; I’m not sure how many, but we can count the holes in the floor and figure it out.”

They worked companionably for a while; then Johnny asked, “How do you speak French so well?”

“I took classes. And I used to do the school photography for a French-American school near where I live in the States, so I met some French people there, and they helped me practice. But it all started out with a rabbit named Gus.”

He stared at her.

“Gus is a carousel figure. I used to think he might have been from this group here, but now . . .” She shrugged.

“I speak a little English,” he said. His accent was atrocious, so it came out more like “*Ah spick a leetle Unglish.*”

“That’s great!” Cady replied. “It’s much more relaxing for me to speak English. Want to practice?”

“A leetle.” Then he switched back to French. “But not now. I can’t clean and speak English at the same time.”

She chuckled. “You know, Johnny, you need to apologize to Fabrice.”

"He needs to apologize to *me*."

"Okay, maybe there needs to be a generalized détente between the two of you."

He shrugged.

"I know he's a grumpy old man, but he's done a lot in his life and he's seen a lot. You could learn from him. He's a famous author. And did you know he worked with the Résistance during World War II?"

He nodded. "Everyone says he was a hero."

"They do?"

"Yeah. He arrested a traitor here, when he came back to Château Clement after the war. A Nazi *collaborateur*."

"Really? What happened?"

"I don't know the details. That's just what people say."

They worked together for another couple of hours and made some headway. The air quality was already improving, and with a little organization it was easier to see what they had to work with. Once they got everything off of the carousel floor, Cady studied the holes for the poles and bolts and figured the carousel had originally had twenty-four animal figures, and maybe two spinning tubs as well as the carriage. They found three chickens, a horse, and another rabbit, which brought their total to twelve. If her calculations were correct, only half the original figures remained, and several of them were badly damaged. If they couldn't find the others, was it even worth trying to save the Clement carousel?

"Enough for today," Cady announced. "I'll need to go to Avignon for the specialty cleaning supplies. Now that Fabrice has finally let me in here, I don't want to screw anything up. Want to come with me, maybe visit the university?"

"Um . . . no, I have to go."

"Okay. See you tomorrow?"

He grunted his assent and slouched off.

Cady lingered, feeling itchy and in need of a shower. The place was a shambles. Even with the fresh air, it still carried the stench of soot and mold, the funky smell of a long-vacant building.

Could Cady help Josephine and Yves Clement fulfill their dreams by restoring the carousel, so it could again be ridden by delighted children? Was she even capable of taking on such a job, with only the dubious assistance of a recalcitrant teen and (if she could talk him into it) a disillusioned Parisian architect—a man who already seemed put off by her level of involvement in his family business?

It was ridiculous.

But when she closed her eyes, Cady could hear the tinny notes of the band organ, feel the whirling of the carousel, and see the lady of the manor, Josephine Clement, riding her custom carousel for eternity.

• • •

While Cady stood under the surprisingly strong and hot spray of the shower, an idea occurred to her: Could she add a chapter to the carousel book that would feature photos of a lost carousel at a virtually abandoned château?

She hadn't been able to see the photos she had taken yet, of course, but she knew from experience that they were good. The contrast of the sweet faces of the figures with their dilapidated state; the once-bright colors of the painted carvings declining into decrepitude. As Fabrice had said, a dream that had devolved into a nightmare.

She would do her best to transform that nightmare into something enchanting and lovable again, of course, but in the meantime a photo-essay documenting every step along the way could be fascinating. Wouldn't it be?

Cady wanted to run the idea past Olivia, and ask her to approach the editor at Addison Avenue Books. Cady knew she should write the publisher directly, and she would if the editor was open to her idea, but Olivia was so much better with people than Cady was. Olivia could make the pitch, and if they were interested, Cady would send a detailed proposal. She could just imagine the village rallying around the idea; it would be the perfect vehicle for them to show Fabrice their support.

Or . . . was she getting ahead of herself, as she was prone to do?

One thing that gave her pause was how Fabrice might react to such an idea. Of course she wouldn't do anything without his explicit permission, but he was so protective of his privacy. She hoped that simply asking him wouldn't set him off.

Most likely it was a moot point, anyway. Cady wasn't good at anticipating what might be of interest to other people; probably she was the only one who would be fascinated by a decrepit carousel.

She would run it by Olivia first.

CHAPTER FORTY-SEVEN

1945
PROVENCE

Fabrice

After the Allies and the Free French Forces arrived to expel the Nazis from Paris once and for all, the *collaborateurs horizontales* had their heads shaven and were forced to parade seminaked through the streets of Paris, admitting their sins.

It was a macabre spectacle. Fabrice remembered seeing these women before, feeling sympathy for their plight and their attempts at survival. Now, at the sight of their pale, blank countenances, their shorn heads, he felt nothing but shame and rage. He searched their faces fruitlessly for the one he wanted. For Paulette.

Had she truly betrayed their cell? The doctor and his wife, the maid, everyone who had worked together? They had all disappeared. Had Paulette been the one to take his family from him? Even little Capucine?

Unceasing doubts and fears spun around in his

head, a tornado of thoughts he could not control.

While the war still raged he had tried to go to Provence to search for Paulette, but he couldn't pass into Vichy France without special documents. Now that the occupiers were gone, he traveled to the town she had talked about: Fontaine-de-Vaucluse. He asked for Paulette in the *boulangerie* and the grocery, their shelves still bare from wartime shortages that had outlasted the fighting. But of course that must not have been her real name. She must have lied to him about it; perhaps she had lied about the town as well. She had known of his connection to Château Clement, and so she had lied about it to get him to talk.

Still, he tried going door-to-door. After the euphoria of liberation, grim realities had set in. People had the hollow eyes, the dull mien of survivors. The Germans had been expelled, but the farms had lain fallow or were studded with bombs, and supplies were stolen long ago. Ports, train tracks, and roads had been destroyed, leaving the transportation system in shambles. Meat was still rationed; hunger and disease were rampant. Armistice was followed by a summer drought and a bitterly cold winter, as though the seasons themselves were conspiring against the survival of the French people.

In Fontaine-de-Vaucluse, many people had been accused of being sympathizers. Several storefronts had been graffitied, their owners accused of collaborating with the enemy. Now was the time for repercussions, for revenge.

Fabrice followed the Chemin de la Fontaine, along the banks of the river Sorgue.

Huge dragonflies peppered the skies, shimmering iridescent greens and blues. He remembered his mother telling him that dragonflies were born of water, that this was why they were magical creatures. He never thought to wonder how she knew such things, but now he did. Now, he had a thousand questions for her. His father had carved her a wooden dragonfly; she asked Fabrice to hang it on a string for her, so it was suspended over their bed. Was it still there?

Fabrice had taken nothing from the house on that awful day of discovery. He had simply fled, then survived as best he could. He hid in the catacombs under the streets of Paris; he fell into another cell of the Résistance. He stole. He killed. He survived.

With every step, every breath, their faces haunted him: his mother, his father, his sister. And Paulette.

Fabrice passed a monument to Pétrarque, the poet who had once penned poetry to his chaste love, Laura. Fabrice thought with bitterness of all the verses he had written to Paulette over the past year, none of which he had shown to her, thank goodness. At the time he hadn't thought they were good enough; his words were inadequate to express the depths of his feelings, the complexity of his emotions with regard to her. But now he was happy to be spared that humiliation, at the very least.

A young woman was selling handmade items at a stand—small tablecloths and napkins. Fabrice couldn't help but wonder who would buy such things at a time when all were desperate for food, but perhaps setting a pretty table could take the edge off. He remembered how Paulette would recite her favorite recipes to pass the time while they worked or hid in passageways from Nazis.

The woman was pretty and young, with flushed cheeks and a sweet smile. He stopped to ask her if she knew a woman named Paulette, and described her as best he could.

She shook her head. "*Désolée, monsieur*. I'm sorry, I really don't know. She doesn't sound familiar."

He nodded, then lingered to look at her items out of politeness. He noticed a dragonfly motif on several items, and a few necklaces.

"*Pourquoi les libellules*?" Why the dragonflies? he asked.

"Most people sell the cicada; it is our Provençal symbol. But I prefer the dragonfly: They are descendants of the dragon that once lived here."

“What dragon?” Fabrice asked, amused.

Her chocolate brown eyes still held a spark of interest, of youth, of hope. Fabrice had celebrated his sixteenth birthday a few weeks ago, but he felt as ancient and hard as the stone cobbles beneath his worn-out leather soles.

“You have not heard the legend of Coulobres?” she asked, her eyes wide. “He was an enormous winged dragon who lived within the font where the river comes out of the mountain. He used to attack the people of Fontaine-de-Vaucluse until he was finally driven into the Alps and killed by Saint-Véran, Bishop of Cavaillon.”

Fabrice released a slight chuckle at the thought of dragons living within springs. He knew too well that monsters were human. There was no need to invent any when the humans were ghastly enough.

“They say there are ancient coins in that spring; the Romans used to throw them in to appease the dragon. No one knows how far down it goes.”

“It’s this way?” he asked, gesturing toward the winding path that led up the limestone escarpments.

She nodded; her shy smile held an invitation. “Not far.”

A lifetime ago Fabrice would have been thrilled to have a pretty woman look at him as though he were worthy of interest. Now he felt toxic, polluted. He felt sure he would destroy anything beautiful in his path.

He pulled a few coins from his pocket and bought a dragonfly necklace fashioned from tin and wire, then proceeded up the mountain.

CHAPTER FORTY-EIGHT

PRESENT DAY
CHÂTEAU CLEMENT

Cady

As she drove into town, Cady spotted the florist shop on the main road. An old stone house sat behind a tall cobbled wall, and was connected to the florist shop by way of a greenhouse pass-through. The shop doors were open.

Cady pulled into the small lot. Before getting out, she noticed her phone was getting service, so she sent a quick text to Olivia, outlining her idea of photographing the decrepit Château Clement carousel. California was nine hours behind, but Olivia was a night owl. After pressing SEND, Cady decided that her second thoughts were probably correct: Chances were good that no one would share her fascination for the *saloperie* of a once-beautiful carousel.

It was just as well. At least she wouldn't have to broach the idea with Fabrice.

Cady got out of the car and walked toward the florist shop. Standing behind the main counter, arranging flowers, was a woman of delicate stature, probably in her late sixties. With her big eyes and upswept salt-and-pepper hair, she looked like an aging Sophia Loren.

"*Bonjour*," she said with a cool nod.

"*Bonjour*," Cady responded in kind. The air was heavy with the floral aroma of roses and carnations, lavender and daisies. What would it be like to work in such perfume every day? Did a person stop smelling it after a while? Was it like a beautiful view, treasured at first but then forgotten? Or was it fully re-appreciated every morning, upon first stepping in amongst the flowers?

"*Est-ce que vous êtes Madame Goselin*?" Cady asked the woman if she was Madame Goselin.

"*Oui. Et vous*?"

"I'm Cady Drake," she continued in French. "I'm staying for a while with Fabrice Clement, at Château Clement."

The florist gasped and dropped everything, literally, roses tumbling from her hands as she came around the end of the counter. "I heard there was an American staying with him! Is he all right?"

"Yes, he—"

"His health?"

"He hurt his ankle, but Dr. Miller says he just needs to stay off of it for a little while."

"I heard he went out there to examine him. Please call me Toinon." She took Cady by both hands, squeezed lightly, and kissed her on both cheeks. Cady wouldn't have imagined it possible for the air to smell even better, but a subtle perfume, beyond the aroma of flowers, enveloped her now.

"Thank God you're there with him," Toinon continued. "Please, come, have an aperitif."

Before Cady could answer, Toinon closed the shop doors, flipped the sign to CLOSED, took Cady by the hand, and led her through the attached greenhouse. The glassed-in room was charming, but packed with so many tchotchkes and plants, antiques and pieces of garden furniture that they had to wind their way along a narrow pathway through the tumble.

"Excuse the state of this place," Toinon said. "My husband passed away last year, and running the shop by myself, I simply lose track of things. My daughter is here with me now, however, so I hope all that will change."

"I'm sorry to hear about your husband," Cady said.

"It was . . . a shock." Toinon stepped into a bright, airy kitchen with a big farmhouse table at one end of the room.

"I lost someone I cared for not long ago as well," said Cady.

Toinon turned around and took Cady's hands in hers again. She had tears in her eyes. "I'm so sorry. Who?"

“My . . . a friend, but she was almost like my mother.”

Toinon simply nodded and held Cady’s gaze. Cady could feel her own eyes well with tears at the evident sympathy in Toinon’s expression. The older woman simply held her hands in silence for a long moment.

Finally, she said, “*Bien*, come into the salon and we will share a glass.”

They passed through the large kitchen, and then into a minuscule office with a messy desk in front of a window and wall-to-wall bookcases, with a comfortable-looking love seat upholstered in sage green brocade.

On the couch was the most adorable child Cady had ever seen. No more than four years old, she had chestnut brown hair cut in a bob, bright brown eyes, and pink cheeks—one of which was stained with a liberal smear of chocolate. In her lap she held an illustrated book, almost half her size. She was dressed in an old-fashioned-looking cream-colored dress with an ashes-of-roses sash, complete with crinolines, but her feet were bare, their soles dirty.

“This is my granddaughter, Jacinthe. Jacinthe, please say hello to the lady.”

With some reluctance, the girl scooted off the couch, butt first, and stood in front of Cady, lifting her face and scrunching her lips, as though waiting for a kiss. Cady leaned down toward her, and Jacinthe gave her a sticky, chocolate-scented kiss on each cheek, intoning, "*Bonjour, madame*."

"*Bonjour, Jacinthe*," said Cady. "*Enchantée*."

"*En-chan-tée*," Jacinthe echoed, then crawled back onto the sofa to read her book.

The next room, which Toinon called "the salon," was a living room with a massive stone fireplace at one end, similar to the one in Fabrice's kitchen. A spiral stairway punctuated the middle of the space, and beyond that was a worktable, crowded with a palette and various jars and brushes. The faint smell of turpentine reached them, carried by a cool spring breeze from an open window.

"Please. Make yourself comfortable, and I will tell my daughter, Élodie, that you are here."

Toinon slipped through a door on the other side of the room, leaving Cady free to explore. The huge rough-hewn wooden mantel held pictures of what she presumed were family members, and souvenirs of a lifetime: a soccer trophy, a lumpy handmade ceramic puppy, an African wood carving, a few postcards propped against the wall.

She wandered around the room, pausing to check out the painting on the easel closest to the worktable. It depicted an ornate flower arrangement in a glass vase, the muted colors popping against a nearly black background. As she looked closer, she thought she saw leaves strewn around the vase, but they were so dark it was hard to be sure.

"Here we are," said Toinon, returning with her daughter and introducing the two young women.

Élodie had a pretty, mature face, accented with the pink cheeks and lips of her daughter. Petite and birdlike like Toinon, Élodie wore a pristine white skirt and a pale yellow sweater with pearl buttons.

Cady calculated the odds that when a stranger dropped by she would be dressed as though she had stepped out of a catalog. Pretty close to nil.

After exchanging hellos, Élodie disappeared into the small office while Toinon perched on a chair and gestured to Cady to take a seat on the couch in the seating area.

"So, please, tell us the news of Fabrice. When his father was still with him he used to come to town for groceries, but in the last many years he's become more and more reclusive."

"As I said, he's doing well." Cady almost felt as though she was betraying him, simply by speaking about him. He was so intensely private. Perhaps one reason he had allowed her to stay with him was that she was wholly unconnected to the village and the villagers.

Élodie returned with a tray that held a trio of bottles, three glasses, a bowl of mixed nuts, and a container of ice with silver tongs.

"What would you like?" Toinon asked after Élodie placed the tray on the large ottoman. "Pastis, Armagnac, or Génépy?"

"I . . . don't know any of them. Could you choose for me?"

Cady was pleased with her openness to the idea of trying something new, but then realized they both stared at her for a moment too long.

"Of course," said Toinon. "Here, perhaps you would like to try Génépy. It is made from flowers of the Rhône-Alpes."

"Thank you," said Cady. The fairy-tale nature of the place made her feel like she was in a movie, but of course she was always brought back to earth. She felt large and awkward, almost hulking, around such delicate, beautiful artists. "I was hoping I could ask you, Élodie, about what you might use to clean soot off of oil paintings?"

"It is best if you bring in your painting," said Élodie. "I would be happy to take care of it for you."

"It's not that easy, actually. I want to clean very large panels. . . ." Belatedly, Cady wondered if her work was supposed to be a secret. But if the checkout woman at the grocery knew about the Clement carousel, surely these women did as well. "They are part of the Clement carousel."

Toinon and Élodie exchanged a glance.

"But . . . ," Toinon said, "I thought it was destroyed long ago."

"It's been severely damaged, and many of the pieces are missing. But part of it is still there. Fabrice is allowing me to clean it up, and we'll see if there's anything left to salvage."

"Would you like me to come examine it?" asked Élodie.

Cady hesitated. Putting this into words in English was hard enough, but in French even more so. "Monsieur Clement, as I'm sure you know, is very private. He asked me to keep other people away, for the moment. I hope he will become more open with time, but for now it's just me, and Johnny Clement."

Toinon's eyebrows rose. "Johnny?"

"He's doing some cleanup work for Fabrice."

"Of course," Élodie said as she stood. She was soft-spoken but confident. "In the meantime, do you know anything about this sort of restoration?"

Cady nodded. "A bit. I used to work on antiques in California."

"Good, so you know the basics. First, check for loose paint. If things are intact, and it's just soot damage, this will help." She gathered supplies as she talked, explaining the different processes. She placed lint-free rags, soft brushes, cotton balls and swabs, and most important of all, a jar of special solvent, into a bag.

"Work carefully, just fifteen square centimeters at a time." She sketched out a square that looked about six inches in dimension, then turned to the oil painting of flowers on the easel. “You see? There are flowers and leaves here, placed carefully by the artist for a reason. The pink camellia means ‘I am longing for you,’ the purple hyacinth means ‘I’m sorry.’ The little white lilies of the valley mean a return of happiness. It was all part of a language, and if we can’t see them, they’re lost.”

Deep, delicate colors emerged from the dark background as she carefully cleaned her little square.

“It is slow, you see? You cannot rush, or you run the risk of rubbing too hard, pushing dirt farther into the varnish, or sometimes lifting varnish off altogether.”

She filled several more jars with different solvents, labeling them in a careful, French-style script.

“I wish I could come help you with it,” Élodie said when she handed Cady the bag. “It would be my honor to do so.”

“Thank you so much, Élodie. I will be sure to tell Fabrice; perhaps he’ll change his mind with time.”

“This is not healthy,” Toinon said with a shake of her head. “He needs family, and he is lucky to have them.”

“I agree,” said Cady. “I can’t imagine why he wants to be alone. But I don’t feel I can invite anyone, as I am his guest.”

“We understand. But please, if you can, perhaps you can convince him to change his mind.”

“I hope so.” The clock chimed five. “But now I really should be going. I have to shop for dinner, and I’ve already taken so much of your time. Thank you.”

As they passed through the little study again, Cady received two more chocolate-scented kisses from young Jacinthe. They continued through the vanilla-scented farmhouse kitchen.

“Before you go, I must show you this,” said Toinon. She led Cady on a narrow path around the edge of the crammed greenhouse.

There, nearly hidden by boxes and bags, was a carved wooden horse with a delicate, upturned face. Unless she missed her guess, it was a Bayol creation.

“Is this from the Château Clement?” Cady asked.

Toinon nodded. “I inherited it from my mother. I’m not sure how she came to have it. But . . . I know family members have taken things from the château through the years. It was abandoned for a very long time.”

Cady inspected the figure and found the telltale Bayol plaque affixed to its saddle; most of the original paint seemed intact.

“Do you think other family members might have parts of the carousel?”

“They might. I will ask. And if Fabrice truly

allows you to restore the carousel, of course I would like to bring this one back, to take its original place."

Cady bade *au revoir* to Toinon, watching as the fairy-tale cottage receded in her rearview mirror. *Fabrice must be insane not to want to be part of it all.* What wouldn't Cady give to have such familiarity, the sense of belonging to a world like that?

Now she just had to figure out how to get any other pilfered animals back without causing more upset among the Clement clan. She had the distinct impression that not all the relations were going to be as open and helpful as Toinon and Élodie.

CHAPTER FORTY-NINE

1900
CHÂTEAU CLEMENT

Maëlle

Maëlle and Josephine had quickly fallen into the habit of sharing a glass in the evenings. After they finished the *chouchenn*, Maëlle tasted cognac for the first time, and tried some local bitters and sherries. They shared confidences, Josephine telling Maëlle that the local Provençal people didn't trust her or like her much—they thought Bretons were sneaky and secretive, and drank too much. Also, she feared Château Clement's finances were in worse condition than her husband would admit—he had the soul of an artist, not a businessman, and his brother Thierry was putting pressure on him to give up the château entirely.

Maëlle told Josephine that she had turned down two marriage proposals from men in her village, and that her mother had cried at night both times. And after her mother got sick, she vowed to accept the next proposal, but her mother's condition worsened rapidly and she died too quickly for Maëlle to fulfill her promise. And Maëlle gave Josephine the little wooden animals she had made; Josephine had cooed in delight, and declared she would give them pride of place on the mantel in the nursery.

But now . . . Maëlle manages to avoid her patroness for two days. Finally, Josephine comes out to the carousel building.

The clanking and sawing stops immediately as the men stand respectfully. Maëlle does the same, putting down her paints—but swearing under her breath.

"Oh, it is lovely!" Josephine says breathlessly. "I didn't want to see it until it was finished, but I simply could not wait any longer. It is astounding!"

Josephine pauses, then says, "Maëlle, could I speak to you a moment?"

"Of course, madame."

"Outside?" Josephine leads the way to the courtyard, where a warm, strong summer breeze caresses their cheeks. She turns to Maëlle, searching her face. "Is everything all right, Maëlle?"

"Of course. Why wouldn't it be?"

"I thought . . . We had such a nice time in the evenings, but I haven't seen you lately."

"I've been busy, and very tired at the end of the day, that's all."

"I understand that Léon Morice has not been

showing up to work consistently," Josephine says. "Is that true?"

"Who told you that?"

"One of my 'informants,' " she replies with a little laugh. "Believe me, Maëlle, there aren't many secrets kept on an estate like this one. Gossip is rampant. So don't try to deny it. I know he has abandoned you."

Maëlle meets Josephine's eyes, wanting desperately to confide in her friend. But then she reminds herself: Josephine probably knows all this, since she herself has been with him.

"Oh dear, you have such a bleak expression in your eyes!" exclaims Josephine. "But of course you do. You are trying to do everything now, aren't you? You're running things here, a whole crew of men. You really are the most astonishing young woman."

"Thank you, but I have to get back to work."

"I—of course," Josephine says. "I'm sorry to have kept you. Silly me, with nothing to do but flutter about, whilst you must do the job of two men. I understand now. Just know that I have enjoyed our talks, and would love to see you this evening, even for a short time, if you aren't too tired."

Maëlle nods, fighting tears.

The next evening, Josephine calls out to Maëlle as she enters the house after work.

“Maëlle, it has been so long. Won’t you join me for a chat?”

“I’m sorry, I have been very busy, madame. *Bonne continuation*,” Maëlle murmurs as she walks swiftly past, avoiding Josephine’s eyes.

“ ‘*Madame*’?” Josephine says. “You’re calling me *madame* now? Now I *know* there’s something wrong.”

Maëlle shakes her head, wanting only to be back in the privacy of her bedroom.

“What is it, Maëlle? Please tell me. Are we not friends?”

Maëlle bursts into tears.

“Oh, oh dear,” Josephine says, putting her arm around Maëlle and rushing her into the parlor, then closing the door. She escorts her to the chair she had become accustomed to sitting in during their evening chats, hands her a handkerchief, and perches on the seat across from her.

“My dear, dear Maëlle. I know we’ve known each other only a very short time. But I feel so close to you already. As women, as Bretons. As kindred souls. Please, tell me?”

“Do you . . . do you love your husband, Josephine?”

“But of course! He is the kindest man I have ever known. Even in the family they say that Yves got all the sweet, and his brother, Thierry, the sour.” She smiles, slightly chagrined. “Then again, Thierry has three children already, and was married the year after Yves and I. So perhaps there is a reason he is blessed, and we are not."

"I . . ." Maëlle blew her nose in the handkerchief, then squared her shoulders and blurted out: "Are you having an affair with Léon Morice?"

Josephine rears back as though Maëlle had thrown a punch.

"What? I am most certainly *not* having an affair—I would never, and least of all with that scoundrel."

"You don't . . . You don't like Léon?"

"Well, he's a beautiful man, and I do love beautiful things," Josephine says with a smile and a nod. "But it is clear he has a wandering eye. And here he has left you to run this entire project, a young woman like you! I know you are very capable, remarkably so. But it doesn't seem fair to put all this on your shoulders."

Maëlle remains silent in her misery.

"I'm sure this is why you're crying, sweet Maëlle. You're overtired. We're working you too hard. Why don't you take a day or two off—all of the men could use a rest day, I'm sure."

"It's not that. I love the work," says Maëlle. "It's just that I'm . . . I think I'm with child."

CHAPTER FIFTY

PRESENT DAY
CHÂTEAU CLEMENT

Cady

The following afternoon, after doing her daily grocery shopping, Cady stopped in at the Hound Dog Café.

"*Bonjour*," she said, raising her voice to be heard over "Heartbreak Hotel," which was blaring in the background.

"*Bonjour*, *Americaine*!" Hubert called out.

Cady noticed yet another silent old man hunched over the bar and decided that Fabrice was looking better all the time. He might be grumpy, but at least he didn't drink the hours away, glowering at strangers over his beer.

"*Un café allongé, s'il vous plait*," Cady said in Hubert's general direction as she moved toward her usual table in the corner near the window. Her order was for a coffee with a dash of extra water in it. In France *café* meant espresso, which was sometimes too strong for her. But she had made the mistake of ordering an *Americano* in

Paris, and didn't enjoy the overly watered-down taste. Goldilocks-like, she had found the *allongé* to be just right.

She opened her e-mail and was happy to find a new message from Olivia. She treasured this connection with an old friend, someone who knew her as something other than "the American girl staying with Fabrice Clement." France had offered Cady the chance to explore a different part of herself, but it was grounding to have someone who knew where she was from. She hadn't realized how cut off she had been feeling, how adrift.

Cady barely noticed when Hubert placed the cup of coffee in front of her.

> **Hello, my dear friend,**
> **Well! You don't do things halfway, do you? Little did I know, when I was forcing you to go to Europe, that you would ingratiate yourself into a situation at a château out in the country, of all places. Maybe Sebastian and I should come visit you there?**
>
> **So, I talked to Marjorie at Addison Avenue Books, and she talked with her people.**
>
> **They didn't exactly go for your idea. They don't like the idea of**

your derelict carousel forming a chapter in the book.

Instead, they're interested in the possibility of making it into a different book entirely! Apparently a lot of people like abandoned things (see? It's not just you), and they think that with the photos, it could be really interesting. They want to see some examples. One thing: They want you to include the old man and his dog. Classic.

You'll still talk to me when you're a bestselling author, right?

The e-mail went on with some chatty details about the local farmers market and a show she had seen at Oakland's famous Paramount Theatre, making Cady feel like she had been chatting over coffee with her best friend. *Only* friend, really. It made her smile, but it also made her miss Olivia with a visceral yearning.

It wasn't just the ease of the language that Cady longed for, but the feeling of being understood without speaking.

Cady read through the e-mail message twice, and the part about the book three times. She sat back in her chair and gazed out at the alley beyond the window. Two elementary-age children walked past on either side of their mother, talking excitedly while she smiled and nodded, Madonna-like, exuding eternal patience. A hunched-over old woman held on to the arm of a middle-aged man who had two baguettes tucked under his other arm. An orange tabby perched on a windowsill across the way; Cady watched while the feline focused on the same passersby she did, its wide, intelligent green eyes taking in . . . what?

A book. An entire book about the dilapidated Château Clement and the process of restoring its damaged carousel. Could she pull it off?

One worry immediately gnawed at her, deep down. She was only now earning Fabrice's trust. Was it possible that he would cooperate, or—more likely—would he see it as the ultimate invasion of his privacy? He was so prickly. . . . How could she even approach the idea with him?

"You're the American?" came the raspy voice of an old man standing next to her table.

Cady had become so accustomed to strangers in Saint-Véran being nice to her that she wasn't on guard. But this man was agitated, swaying slightly on his feet. Her Oakland defensive stance came out.

"And who are *you?*" As she asked the question, she realized he was the man who had been sitting at the bar, hunched over his beer.

"Where do you get off, putting ideas in my boy's head?"

Cady wasn't catching every slurred word, but she assumed that was essentially what he was saying. It dawned on her that he must be speaking about her new assistant.

"You're Johnny's father?"

"Yes, I am. And I would thank you to leave him alone. He's idiotic enough without your American ideas in his head."

"Could I ask what ideas you're talking about?"

"He told me you think he ought to go to *university.*" He said this last with a snide, prissy emphasis.

"He seems intelligent, and sensitive," Cady said. "University isn't for everyone, but if he wants to—"

"This is none of your business. Who are you, anyway? You think you can come to our town and start meddling in other people's business?"

He called her a name: *salope*. She had learned this one by occasionally filling in at the French-American school during recess. Literally, it meant "slut," but it was often used to mean "bitch." Which was probably typical in English as well.

Cady's first thought was to return the favor, calling up a couple of choice words in French—a *connard* or a *crétin*; also learned on the playground at school, sorry to say—but she thought better of it. Instead she adopted a flat affect and listened to his bluster until he wore himself out. It was like sharing the bus with someone who was off his meds; he wasn't seeing *her,* but reacting to something in his own head.

After a few minutes the man stumbled increasingly over his words, and there was more time between insults, as though he was running out of steam.

"*Andres*," came a new voice. Jean-Paul rushed into the café, planted himself between Cady and her attacker, and went off on the man. Unfortunately, this gave Johnny's father renewed energy.

They argued loudly until Jean-Paul finally grabbed the older man by his upper arm and hustled him out the door. Andres cast a few more choice words—and the same *bras d'honneur* obscene gesture his son had used the other day—in the general direction of the bar, then reeled down the street.

"Nice to run into you again," Cady said after Jean-Paul came back into the café and ordered a beer. "What a coincidence."

"Hubert called me."

"Why?" She glanced over at the café owner behind the bar, pouring a beer from a tap.

"Because you were being assaulted. Didn't you notice?"

"It was just words."

"Bad words."

"I've heard worse. Besides, in French swearing

sounds so elegant. I think I learned a few new words." She patted her journal. "I should write them down."

He shook his head and chuckled.

Hubert brought Jean-Paul his beer and apologized to Cady, adding, "*Andres boit comme un trou.*"

Andres drinks like a trout.

"Why do you keep serving him?" Jean-Paul demanded of Hubert.

The bartender lifted his well-padded shoulders and put his hands palms up as if to say *What can I do?* "*C'est le vent qui lui rend fou*," he replied.

"It's not the wind that's driven him mad," Jean-Paul responded, "but the drink."

Hubert shuffled back behind the bar.

"*Putain*," Jean-Paul swore in French, running his hand through his hair. Cady's eyes lingered for a moment on the path of his fingers, which left little indentations in his thick brown hair. "*J'en ai vraiment marre de tout ça.*"

By which he meant, basically, that he was tired of all this.

"What are you so tired of?" Cady asked.

"Small-town minds, small-town gossip."

"It does seem to be quite the efficient communications system. So, you're speaking French to me now?"

He shook his head and smiled. "I felt like swearing, and you said it was more elegant in

French. Besides, I don't know that many good swear words in English."

"I could teach you a few choice phrases."

"I'm sure you could. I imagine you know quite a number from your days running the streets of Oakland."

"I do indeed," she said with a smile. Their gazes met and held for a few seconds too long.

"Believe me, it's not about you—Andres drinks too much, and his wife passed away suddenly last year. I have the feeling he finds teenagers challenging, to put it kindly."

"Also, he's not fond of Americans."

"That too, apparently." His eyes settled on her. "You're okay?"

"Of course I'm okay. People don't like me; I'm used to it."

"Why do you keep saying that?"

"Because it's true. It's always been that way. Anyway, I appreciate the whole knight-in-shining-armor thing, but it's not necessary. I can take care of myself."

"I know. So you've told me. But I think it's more than that; I think you don't like asking for help."

"I don't know about that—I asked Fabrice for help, and now I'm staying at his château."

"I think that was more about you offering help than asking for it."

"So." Cady cleared her throat and looked away

from those sherry-colored eyes. "What was Hubert saying about the wind making Andres crazy?"

"Haven't you noticed how windy it is here? Provence claims thirty-two different winds, coming from all directions. Each of them has a different name and a distinct character. But the mistral is master of them all—in fact, in the Provençal language *mistral* means 'masterly.' "

"I didn't know there was a Provençal language."

He nodded. "It's mostly died out at this point, but a few of the old people still know it. They say the mistral can blow the tail off a donkey or the horns off a bull."

Cady smiled and finished her coffee.

"When the mistral howls," Jean-Paul continued, "pets misbehave, and people complain that the roar of the wind gives them headaches and robs them of sleep. Also, supposedly it drives people mad: *c'est le vent qui rend fou.*"

"I have noticed the wind," she said. "I just never thought of giving a wind a name, much less a character. So the mistral is the bane of the Provençal existence?"

"Funny you should ask. There's a story my grandmother used to tell me about it."

"Well, don't hold back. I'm here to soak up the local culture, after all."

"Seems people got so sick of the mistral that

they found out where it originated, way up in the mountains, and a group of brave young men made a very strong door of thick wood, reinforced with iron beams. They took this up to the crevice in the rocks where the mistral originates, hammered it into the mountain rock, and managed to shut the wind in."

"That sounds like quite the door," said Cady.

"Never underestimate a determined Provençal man."

"I'll keep that in mind."

Cady licked some coffee from her lip and noticed Jean-Paul's eyes following the movement of her tongue. He cleared his throat and continued with his story.

"At first, everyone rejoiced at the stillness of the air. But after a while the humidity led to marshy conditions, and mildew destroyed all the crops. Insects multiplied, and everyone was miserable. So the young men went back up to the mountain to let the wind back out. There's something about negotiating with the mistral, making certain demands of it before agreeing to let it out, and the wind reneging on the deal, but I forget the details. The point is that now it blows away the clouds, which is what gives the area so much sunshine, dries out the grape leaves so they don't mildew, and cleans out the marshes."

She gave him a grudging nod. "Okay, that's a pretty good story."

“The old people draw it out with a lot of details and some shouting back and forth between the wind and the men,” he said. “Add a glass or two of wine, it can go on all night.”

“I’ll bet it can,” Cady said, and they shared a laugh.

“Anyway, I’m glad to see you.”

“Me, too. I have two very exciting things to tell you. First, Fabrice gave me permission to develop the film I found in the basement. Any suggestions?”

“I have a friend who’s an amateur photographer, with his own darkroom.”

“Would this be a tile man named Guido?”

“I see you’re really figuring out this town. You don’t need me at all.”

“I wouldn’t go that far. And now, for the *big* news: Fabrice showed me the carousel!”

Jean-Paul blinked. “He did?”

“I thought you’d be excited.”

“I am. Of course. That’s great news. Is anything still there? Is it intact?”

“It’s in terrible condition, and it looks like several of the animals are missing. But I spoke with Toinon and Élodie, and they gave me some supplies and advice about restoration.”

“Toinon and Élodie, too? You really are making yourself at home here in our fair town. So Fabrice is going to let you restore it?”

“I’m no professional, obviously, but he says

he won't let me call anyone else in. For now I'm it. I can at least clean things up a bit—Johnny showed up to work, and he's been helping as well. I wanted to ask you something else, too: It turns out Toinon has one of the animals from the carousel. I never thought to ask before, but does anyone else in your family have one, or do you know of anyone who might? Fabrice seems sure that family members looted things from the château."

"It's possible there are one or two floating about. But they might just as easily have been sold off decades ago."

Cady nodded. "It seems a shame to have them scattered. I would love to bring all the pieces back together again, to bring the carousel back to its former glory."

"Sounds like you're planning to stay a while longer."

"I canceled my return ticket. If Fabrice is okay with me staying, it seems like an opportunity I can't pass up. How often does a person stumble on an antique carousel in need of restoration?"

Jean-Paul held her gaze for a long moment. He smiled, but there was sadness in his eyes, like a haze hanging over a summer afternoon.

"So," Cady asked. "How about you? How long are you planning to stay in Saint-Véran?"

"I seesaw back and forth between staying forever, and hightailing it back to Paris. I suppose

I would always split my time between Paris and Saint-Véran, if I possibly could. Each appeals to me, in its own way."

"I thought you were tired of small-town gossip."

"I am. But I love the people here, and the slower pace of life. Not to mention the Provençal climate. And the truth is, in a small town a person can make a difference. Maybe if I stayed and became a part of village life, I could help change the tone of things." He shrugged and looked away, a muscle working in his jaw.

Cady wondered whether this was what Jean-Paul had referred to, when he spoke of being at a crossroads in his life. It occurred to her to wonder how long ago his marriage plans had fallen apart, and she was about to ask when he changed the subject.

"My grandfather Gerald would like to speak with you."

"Toinon mentioned him; she said he knew a lot about the history of the château."

"He does, yes. As you might recall, his grandfather Thierry believed that Gerald's father, Pierre, was the rightful heir to Château Clement, rather than Fabrice's father, Marc-Antoine. Gerald is what you say in English, a 'piece of work'? And, like Andres, he is wondering why an American is now living at the château with Fabrice."

"I'm happy to speak with him, though I don't know that I can tell him anything he doesn't already know. But I'd love to ask *him* a few questions."

"Do you have time now?"

She checked her watch. "Fabrice might be expecting me; I should call him and let him know I'll be late."

"He won't answer. He usually pretends he doesn't have a phone."

"Yes, I'm familiar with that gambit."

She dialed his number anyway, but as Jean-Paul had predicted, the phone rang and rang. Cady imagined the jangly sound echoing down the halls of the château, while a lonely old man sat by the fire and stroked his dog, ignoring the outside world, pretending he was safe, alone in his imagined cocoon.

CHAPTER FIFTY-ONE

PRESENT DAY
CHÂTEAU CLEMENT

Cady

As they walked toward Jean-Paul's childhood home, right outside of town, a huge dragonfly zoomed by, its iridescent skin flashing blue and green.

"It seems early for dragonflies," Cady said. "What are they called in French?"

"*Libellules*," Jean-Paul replied. "The cicada is the symbol of Provence, but a lot of people in this area are partial to the dragonfly. Did you know it begins life as a water nymph, before developing wings and flying?"

"That sounds like a metaphor," she said, watching the insect hover and dart this way and that.

"Doesn't it?" They passed through a little gate and walked down a brick path toward a huge stone farmhouse adjacent to a farmer's field. "In the summer this field is full of sunflowers."

"It's beautiful."

"It is," he said, his tone matter-of-fact.

"Do you see it?"

"What do you mean?"

"When you grow up surrounded by all of this beauty, do you relish it, or do you just take it for granted?"

Jean-Paul paused and looked back out over the little valley. "I loved running around the village as a kid, that much is true. But the house has always been a mixed bag for me. My father passed away a few years ago, but before that he was . . . troubled. And my grandfather lives here now with my mother, which can also be challenging."

Inside, the home looked lived-in and rustic but well appointed; there were lace curtains in the windows, a huge fireplace in the living room, and a table set up for *apéro*.

"Cady, this is my mother, Louise Mirassou," Jean-Paul said as he introduced an older, birdlike woman whose salt-and-pepper hair was styled in a practical bob. A scar under her right eye looked white against her subtly rouged cheek.

"It is such a pleasure!" Louise smiled broadly and left Cady in a faint cloud of perfume as they traded kisses. "I have heard so much about you, from my son and now everyone in the village, it seems."

"And this is my grandfather, Gerald Clement."

Gerald was not the imposing figure Cady had expected; he seemed shrunken, small. He shared a family resemblance with Louise and Jean-Paul, but unlike them he had an imperious expression, and when he spoke, his voice had a commanding edge.

They traded pleasantries. Gerald and Cady were directed to sit at the table while Louise and Jean-Paul poured glasses of wine and brought out a few small plates.

Cady tried to ignore the fact that Gerald was staring at her, without speaking, across the table.

At long last Jean-Paul and Louise joined them and they toasted to each other's health.

"I don't understand why Fabrice allows you to stay at the château when he won't allow anyone else, including Jean-Paul," Gerald said, shoving a cracker into his mouth. "What are you doing out there? What are you after?"

"I help him with the dog, and the groceries, and I cook." Cady wasn't about to volunteer information about the carousel, much less the film cartridges she had found.

Gerald harrumphed and sat back in his seat.

"It's hardly Cady's fault if Fabrice likes her, Grandfather," said Jean-Paul. "At least he's letting someone help him."

"He should have been carted off to a nursing home a long time ago," said Gerald.

"He wishes to stay in his home for the last days of his life," Louise said. "We can hardly blame him for that."

"We can blame him for keeping a château that is not rightfully his," Gerald replied.

Louise patted his arm and made a soothing murmur. She was like her son, Cady thought: a peacemaker.

Gerald turned back to Cady. "You've been asking questions about the carousel."

"Yes. What can you tell me about it?"

"If he's planning on using that infernal carousel to save his château—"

"I don't believe he's planning on doing any such thing," interrupted Cady. "But then again, I'm certainly not his spokesperson. If you'd like to know his plans, might I suggest you speak to him directly?"

"It's not that easy, as I believe you know."

"I was wondering, would you happen to know the whereabouts of any of the missing pieces of the carousel?" Cady asked. "I know Toinon has one, and thought perhaps others in the family might possess some of the other figures."

He fixed her with an intimidating look. Sitting here now, Cady thought, he seemed ridiculous, a pigeon with his feathers ruffled. But she wondered what Gerald had been like as a father to young Louise, ranting about the château he—and then she—should have inherited, or simply fixing her with that glare if she dared forget to make up her bed or talked back. This was the part about having family that Cady did not miss.

"Now you listen to me, young lady," Gerald said. "That carousel is none of your concern, and neither is Fabrice, or any of the Clement family, for that matter. I think it's high past time that you left our little town."

"Grandfather—," Jean-Paul began, but Cady waved him off, holding the old man's gaze.

"I'll leave when it suits me. By the way, can you tell me anything about an apprentice carousel carver who might have stayed at the château?"

"You mean Fabrice's grandfather?"

She stared at him but did not respond.

"That's what happened, you know. His grandmother, Josephine—my own father knew her, as did his father. Too well. She had an affair with an apprentice named Léon Morice while he was there to install the carousel. Haven't you noticed that Fabrice looks like none of us? The Clement family resemblance is strong. Josephine ruled that château as though she belonged as well. Another foreigner."

"Where was she from?"

"Bretagne."

"Isn't that . . . part of France?" Cady's gaze flickered over to Jean-Paul, who nodded.

"It is like a different world there, with different ways," said Gerald. "In any case, she was so proud of herself, marrying a Clement, becoming lady of the manor. She held herself above the Provençal people. For years she and Yves had no children, and then a handsome apprentice arrives on the scene, and voilà. Nine months later, a baby is born."

"I heard they used to have celebrations, and invite the whole village to ride the carousel," said Cady.

"Of course, they wanted to lord their wealth and good fortune over the whole village. There was a huge celebration to announce Josephine's condition, and the arrival of the carousel. My own father remembered riding it as a boy."

"Really? Did he tell you which animal he rode?"

He looked taken aback at her question, but then answered, "It was a, uh, pig. With its tongue sticking out."

"You remember that after all these years?" asked Louise.

Cady imagined she would remember riding the sea creature in Tilden Park for as long as she lived.

"What about the music? Did he say anything about that? Or the steam engine? What about bellows?" Cady continued. "Did he mention if any of the animals made lowing sounds?"

Gerald seemed nonplussed to have his rant against Fabrice's legitimacy derailed. "Why are you so obsessed with that carousel?" he demanded.

She shrugged. "It's my thing."

"Cady's a photographer," said Jean-Paul. "She came to Paris to photograph historic carousels for a book."

"Then she ought to go back to Paris."

"Papa—," said Louise.

"Grandfather—," said Jean-Paul at the same time.

"It's fine," Cady assured Louise and Jean-Paul. She smiled and popped a couple of almonds in her mouth, holding Gerald's gaze. "Honestly. I think Monsieur Clement and I understand each other. But I'm not ready to go back to Paris yet, as I want to clean up the carousel a little, see what's there and whether it's salvageable. Unless Fabrice asks me to leave beforehand, that's my plan."

"Thank you for the wine, *Maman*," Jean-Paul said, standing and pushing in his chair. "I think we've subjected Cady to enough of a trial for today. Cady, ready to go?"

"Oh, sure," she said, standing and trading kisses with Louise. "It was so nice to meet you. And Monsieur Clement." After a brief hesitation she leaned over to give him the double kisses as well. "I wish you a good day."

Jean-Paul ushered her out a side door. The late-afternoon air was chilly, but the sun was warm and welcome on her skin.

"That went well," said Cady.

Jean-Paul glanced down at her, an amused look

on his face. “It was pretty cheeky of you, asking him about the missing carousel animals.”

“You think he has some of them?”

“Very possibly. Or at least he knows where they are. He seemed to remember the pig pretty well. I’ll find out.”

“Thanks. Anyway, I figured it was worth a try. As I said, I’m used to people not liking me, and since he was already inclined that way, I figured it couldn’t hurt.”

“Why do you think people don’t like you?”

“They don’t.”

“Fabrice does. *I* do.”

She smiled. “That makes me wonder, sometimes. Jean-Paul, why did you offer to buy my rabbit, sight unseen? And then every time the carousel came up in conversation, it seemed like it bothered you.”

He blew out a long breath. “I’ve tried to approach Fabrice about the possibility of saving the château, from several angles over the years, including the idea of using a restored carousel as a tourist attraction. I came back to Saint-Véran, thinking I would try one more time to talk to him about the possibilities, but you saw how he greeted me. And then he let you in, not only to the house but apparently into his heart. I’m happy for him, but it’s also been a little . . .”

“Galling?” she suggested.

Jean-Paul nodded, leading the way around the house to the ground floor, where a picturesque stone veranda sat under a pergola. A vine twisted its limbs around the posts, bare of leaves but covered in small green buds, promising greenery and flowers to come.

He opened a set of French doors and waved her in.

"This used to be a storage area and wine cellar, but I made this entrance and converted it into an apartment for when I come to visit."

Inside, golden gray stone walls formed a backdrop to simple furniture: a kitchenette with a small table in a dining alcove, a bedroom area with a bath beyond. There were fine built-ins and niches with artifacts on display, and a few bright oil paintings livened up the muted walls.

"It's lovely," said Cady as she took it all in.

"It's not easy to shoehorn things like plumbing and electrical into old stone walls," Jean-Paul said as he showed her around the small unit. "But the historic character makes it worth it."

"So this is how you know so much about restoration?"

"I do a lot of historic redesign with my architecture firm. And I love old buildings—the history, the romance, the craftsmanship. Which is how I know exactly what I would be getting into with the family château." He shook his head. "I've gone over it and over it in my head, and it just doesn't make any sense to try to take it on. Not alone, anyway."

"Aren't there any other family members interested in taking part?"

"No, they're all busy with their lives, and it's a massive undertaking."

She noticed a roll of blueprints alongside a sheaf of papers with familiar-looking handwriting and drawings.

"Are these by Fabrice?" she asked, picking up the stack. "They look like the maps he draws for me, of the village and the wine cellar."

"Yes, they are. When he came back to live at the château with his father in the seventies, Fabrice intended to renovate it. Apparently he and his father repaired some of the woodwork and redid a few of the rooms, but their grand plans fell by the wayside eventually."

"And the blueprints are of the château?"

He nodded. "My ex-fiancée and I did some work on them."

"This was back before she decided small-town life wasn't to her liking?"

"Exactly."

"So, it would take a whole fleet of help to get the château into shape?"

"Or at the very least"—Jean-Paul fixed Cady with a look she had come to know, a look with a sort of puzzled, intrigued, yet ever-so-slightly-annoyed smile—"a really committed partner."

"I can't get over the way you look at me."

"How do I look at you?"

"As though you don't *want* to like me."

After a momentary pause, he said, "You're leaving soon."

"So you keep reminding me. I told you, I canceled my ticket back."

"You mean you're never leaving?"

"Of course I am. But it's open-ended at the moment."

They fell silent. They were standing in the middle of the apartment, facing each other, each caught up in thought. Cady reached out and placed her hand on his chest. He looked down at it, a carefully neutral expression on his face.

"Oh yes," Cady said in a quiet voice as she let her hand drop. "I remember you told me you weren't good enough for your ex-fiancée. I'm pretty sure my ex felt I wasn't good enough for him, too. But the truth was, I was way too good for him. Of course, I didn't know that at the time. That's part of the knowledge that came with growing up."

"Are you suggesting I haven't grown up?"

She laughed. "Not at all. You look grown-up, and you have a *very* grown-up-sounding job at the 'firm' in Paris."

"Where I'm not working at the moment, as I play around in Saint-Véran."

"Is that how you see yourself?"

He gave a wry chuckle and shook his head.

"To tell you the truth," he said, "I don't know *what* I'm doing. I seem to be at something of a crossroads in my life. The only thing that makes sense to me lately . . . is you."

They gazed at each other for a long moment.

"What *you* need," Cady said finally, "is to spend a little time fixing up an old carousel."

CHAPTER FIFTY-TWO

1900
CHÂTEAU CLEMENT

Maëlle

"You do not think me wicked?"

Josephine takes a moment to respond, as though choosing her words carefully. "To be perfectly honest, I might have, a few years ago. But now . . . it is easy to see that women are afforded a different lot in life than men. We all have passions, do we not? Why is it that the men are allowed to express theirs, whereas we are expected always to be such paragons?"

Maëlle shakes her head and keens into her handkerchief. "I th-thought he *loved* me."

"Of course you did," says Josephine, rubbing Maëlle's back.

"I've never before . . ." She hiccups. "I mean, I've hardly even kissed a boy before."

"Not even the two men who offered you marriage?"

"Not even them—just quick pecks. Nothing like with Léon . . ." She can still feel the sensation of his mouth on hers. "He talked of taking me to Paris, of showing me the world. He said we would sculpt together, traveling from château to château to work under the patronage of wealthy art lovers. But now . . . what do I do, Josephine?"

Josephine gives her a sad smile. "Could you go back to your family, in Bretagne?"

"How could I? I ran off to the city, and now I come back unmarried, with a baby? My mother's not alive; we would simply be a burden on my father."

"If he loves you, he won't see it as a burden."

"My brother is sick as well; I have been sending half my wages home."

Josephine makes a *tsk*ing sound. "And your wages are a scandal. For a talented, intelligent woman like you?" She frowns and shakes her head.

"And . . . how could I work? The world is not kind to an unwed mother—or to the child that comes of such."

They sit in silence for a long moment, each lost in her own thoughts, gazing into the fire that pops and hisses in the hearth.

"Let's look at this another way," Josephine says after a moment. "What would you have done if you hadn't found yourself in the position you're in now?"

"How do you mean?"

"Pretend you'd never met that *crétin* Léon

Morice. Would you go back to Bayol's workshop in Angers when you're done with the carousel?"

"I did learn a great deal there, it's true," Maëlle begins, not wanting to be ungrateful. "But it's difficult. I am the only woman, as you can imagine. And I feel . . . Well, Monsieur Bayol and the others call me 'little girl.' It has been a revelation to be here at Château Clement, to be in charge. It is the one blessing that came of Léon's irresponsibility."

"What is in your heart of hearts? If you had been born a man, for instance. What would you most want, in this whole wide world?"

Maëlle gives a shy smile.

"If I were a man? Promise you won't laugh? I had a fantasy that you might ask me to stay on at Château Clement, to carve your lintels."

"My lintels?"

"Your doorways, and window frames. Fireplace mantels and columns . . . they're beautiful wood, but so . . . plain. Rather severe, even. Can't you imagine them covered in the leaves and berries of the woods that surround the château?" Maëlle blows quietly into the handkerchief again, but she is no longer crying. "And the birds that your husband loves so well?"

"Whenever you speak of carving, your whole face lights up," says Josephine.

"Ever since I was very young, I've been happiest with wood under my fingers, cradled in the palms of my hands. I feel as though the very spirit of the wood calls to me, asking me to release its figures. I love the sharpness of the knives, the pointiness of the awls and veiners, the way the planers smooth things out. I even love sanding—and *no* one likes to sand." She shakes her head. "It makes no sense."

"I beg your pardon, but it makes a great deal of sense." Josephine's voice gentles. "But here is what I find interesting: I think most women, when asked what they dream of, would mention a kind husband, and having children. Making a family."

"I know it sounds . . . unnatural." Maëlle hesitates. "But all I've ever wanted to do was carve. I helped raise my younger sisters, and I love them, but I don't feel the same urges some women do. I never wanted this. To be a mother."

"Like I do," says Josephine. "Personally, I grow weary of people telling me what is 'natural' for a woman. Are we not humans with varied emotions, just as men are?"

Maëlle begins to cry again, whimpering into her already damp handkerchief. "How can the fates be so cruel? How is it that I should find myself in this condition, while you . . ."

"Remain childless." Josephine's voice is flat, but she grabs the iron poker and stabs at the fire with vigor, sending up a spray of orange sparks. "The fates are cruel, indeed. But it occurs to me,

Maëlle, that the fates are a little like the winds that sweep over these lands."

"How so?"

"There is a local story about negotiating with the wind known as the *mistral*. It seems impossible at first glance, but . . . perhaps the fates can be negotiated with."

CHAPTER FIFTY-THREE

PRESENT DAY
CHÂTEAU CLEMENT

Cady

The next morning Cady got to work on the carousel bright and early, excited to try out some of the products Élodie had given her.

Johnny showed up, as sullen as ever, but right on time. And then Jean-Paul appeared, wearing torn jeans and a sweatshirt over a stained white T-shirt.

"Guido's expecting us after lunch," Jean-Paul said. "He's not sure he'll have much time to spend with us, but he says you are most welcome to use his darkroom."

"That's great," said Cady, her eyes traveling over his outfit. "I notice you're wearing work clothes."

"I assumed fixing a broken-down old carousel might be dusty work." Jean-Paul looked around the building. "This is . . ." He trailed off with a shake of his head.

"*C'est un saloperie*," Johnny said, referring to the building as a pigsty, essentially.

It did look like a chaotic muddle. But now more than ever Cady was able to envision what it *could* be. Last time she and Johnny had started to organize the figures according to level of need. The old poles were still scattered about, some still attached to the platform while others lay like kindling on the floor. The scenery panels, rounding boards, and mirrors from the original structure were black with soot, but appeared largely intact. She had no idea how to fix the motor or reconnect all the cranks and pistons to make it whirl around again, but that would be a later step.

First things first: to reclaim the art.

Johnny insisted on broadcasting the playlist on his phone—including songs by Johnny Hallyday and Johnny Cash, both of whom he claimed to be named after—so they listened to a mix of American favorites and Europop while the three of them got to work.

Cady showed Johnny how to clean off the ornately framed mirrors, taking care to avoid any broken glass, while Jean-Paul rolled up his sleeves and started tinkering with the engine and the sweep mechanisms; he had researched carousels the night before, trying to understand how the basic machinery worked.

Cady found an old ladder and climbed up to check out the rounding boards, where flat decorative panels took turns with three-dimensional shields boasting jesters' faces. Using cotton balls soaked in the specialty cleanser Élodie had given her, Cady carefully wiped soot and grime from the painted sections.

Inch by inch, she uncovered delicately detailed landscapes and wild animals, tigers and lions as well as mythological creatures: a unicorn and a hippogriff. Thanks to the cleaning solution, the process was straightforward enough for Johnny to handle it, with the instruction to proceed slowly and gently. Cady was eager to move on to her true love: the carousel figures themselves.

She climbed down from the ladder to check out Johnny's progress with the mirrors, then went over to see what Jean-Paul was up to: He was on his back and had crawled under the platform with a flashlight.

"What are you looking for?"

"Just wanted to see how it works," came his muffled reply. "We could probably reinstall those poles without too much effort, as long as all these pistons are still working. But of course the poles will wait until you've got the pieces in good shape."

"Do you suppose there's any way to track down all the missing figures?"

He crawled out from under the carousel floor. Cobwebs stuck to his hair, and dirt and soot smeared his sweatshirt. He looked . . . adorable.

"It would take a lot of detective work," he said,

jumping to his feet and putting his hands on his hips. "And even if you tracked them down, if they wound up in the hands of collectors they would cost a fortune. How would we come up with the money to pay for them?"

"Good question."

"As I told you, I'll make sure there are no others left in family hands. But beyond that, would they have to be originals?"

"What do you mean?"

"I've seen carousel pieces, here and there, over the years," he said. "Junky pieces you could pick up cheap, redo, and add to the menagerie."

Cady thought back on the wood carvings she had noticed in the antiques shop display in Avignon, and the carousel horse she had admired in Maxine's window so long ago. Jean-Paul was right—there were random carousel animals to be found, especially those in need of restoration. But did she have the time? How long could she impose on Fabrice? His ankle was improving, and knowing him, she realized he might ask her to leave again if she displeased him in some way. And besides all that, she had a life in California she should be getting back to. Didn't she?

"Think about it," said Jean-Paul, warming to the theme. "You could adopt figures and add them to your set."

Over the years, Cady had photographed carousels that contained a menagerie of animals, carved by different artists. The children didn't mind; in fact, they loved the variety. Who said Château Clement's carousel animals had to be a matched set?

She thought back to Maxine adopting broken, misshapen, unwanted items, cleaning them up and loving them and finding them a home.

Making them whole again.

After a pleasant lunch with Fabrice—Jean-Paul and Cady held up most of the conversation, but Johnny and Fabrice put in a comment here and there—Johnny left for the day, and Jean-Paul and Cady headed to Guido's place.

"His family from Italy came after the war," explained Jean-Paul as they drove. "A lot of Italians, and Spaniards, immigrated into France following World War II."

"I thought France took a while to recover after the war."

He nodded. "It did. But Italy and Spain were hit even harder."

Given the small-town feeling of Saint-Véran, Cady had expected to find a very small shop. But Le Bricolage de Valenti turned out to be an impressively large store, providing not only tile but other floor coverings and installation supplies to the entire region.

Guido greeted Jean-Paul with enthusiastic kisses on the cheeks, and was charming to Cady.

He apologized for being too busy with customers to show them to the darkroom, but assured Cady that she should help herself and that she would find everything she needed.

Guido wasn't exaggerating; his darkroom was well supplied. Most darkrooms were extremely orderly. So much of the work was done in the dark, or near-dark, that it was essential to have all the items close at hand and in their right place. Dozens of neatly labeled bottles and jars lined the shelves: DEVELOPER, STOP BATH, FIXER.

"I've never done this before," Jean-Paul said. "Put me to work?"

Cady smiled. "This is more a one-person job. But you can keep me company."

She showed him how to uncoil the rolls of film, using only the sense of touch in the absolute dark, loading them onto reels to produce negatives. These needed to dry for a while before she and Jean-Paul could examine them on the light table to see whether there were any photos that were salvageable, and worth printing.

In the meantime, they went back to the Bricolage and perused Guido's floor-covering selection, amusing themselves by finding old-fashioned-looking ceramics and stone that would look good in this room or that of Château Clement. Guido kept a portfolio of historic homes he had helped to supply in renovation. Cady watched as Jean-Paul flipped through the laminated pages, pointing to a hallway here, a set of bay windows there, speaking of which elements might work in his family's château.

"I thought you said you weren't planning on renovating it," Cady teased.

He gave her an enigmatic smile and a subtle shrug.

Guido joined them. "I keep telling him, he has to work on that place himself, with his own hands." He held his own meaty hands up as examples. "*That's* what will bring a place like the château back from the brink."

Jean-Paul kept his eyes on the book, a thoughtful look on his face.

When they returned to the darkroom to study the negatives, a surprising number of the images seemed to have come out.

"Now comes the fun part," Cady said. "Hit that light switch, will you?"

The red light came on. Using the enlarger, she projected the images onto photographic paper.

The pans were all laid out in order, their appropriate chemical baths within. Cady showed Jean-Paul how to use tongs to gently dip the first page in the developer, and watched the magic of the photograph appearing.

The first several images were of workers in the fields. The edges had been compromised, but the imperfections added to the sense of history.

"This reminds me of playing with lemon juice

when we were kids, and calling it 'invisible ink,' " said Jean-Paul, as he brought another print out of the bath.

"It really is astonishing. It still takes my breath away. In early photography they figured out how to make the images appear, but not how to keep them fixed. So photos would appear only briefly before fading away. Imagine how frustrating."

She hung the photos up on the wire overhead, where they dripped into a shallow pan.

"Memories from a hundred years ago, or more," Jean-Paul said, perusing them. "*Merci beaucoup, Yves Clement.*"

"Check out this one," Cady said. She held a print of a handsome, dark-haired man leaning back against a carousel cat.

"That must have been the apprentice named Léon Morice," said Jean-Paul. "He was identified in some of the other photos we have, though this is the only close-up I've seen."

"I thought it was a young Fabrice, at first," said Cady.

"Fabrice was blond—that's one thing that saved him in World War II."

"I don't mean in coloring, but in facial structure."

Jean-Paul studied the photo over her shoulder. "I don't see it."

"It's not the way he looks now, of course," she said, trying to ignore the electric feeling of

Jean-Paul pressing, just barely, against her back. "But the photo on his book jacket looks a lot like this. I've got the book at the château; I'll show you when we go back."

The next several photos showed half a dozen workers laboring over the carousel, including a woman who looked like a chubbier version of the woman in the photo Cady had found in Gus-the-rabbit.

"I wish there could be a way to figure out who she was. It's driving me crazy."

Jean-Paul shook his head. "There was no listing of a woman working for Bayol. I checked. She might have been a servant of some kind, or a maid at the estate who pitched in."

"Maybe," Cady said, still wondering as she moved on to the next picture, which was taken from a different film cartridge.

"Oh, look, do you suppose this is Marc-Antoine as a teenager?"

"That's Josephine, for sure, so it probably is. These must have been photos from much later."

They were smiling, and the first few looked like they were fooling around; the last two were more formal portraits of mother and son.

"These are great," said Jean-Paul. "Up until now we only had earlier portraits of Josephine, and none of Marc-Antoine past the baby stage."

"Maybe these will interest Fabrice; they're his father, after all." Cady slipped the next piece of paper into the chemical bath. "Jean-Paul, check this out. It looks like a fire in the carousel building."

Three sequential photos seemed to have been taken from an upper-floor window of the château, looking down over the building. The first showed just a subtle glow, but in the next two the fire had grown.

"But why would Yves have stopped to take photographs?" Cady asked. "Wouldn't he have run to help his wife?"

"Maybe he didn't realize she was there," he said. "Yves was an artist; he probably thought it was beautiful. And it is, in a dark sort of way."

"If he was taking these photos, does that prove that he wasn't the one to set the fire?"

"Does it matter, at this point?"

"I suppose not. When did the fire occur?"

"I'm not sure of the exact date, but it was after Marc-Antoine had gone to fight in the First World War."

"So these photos of Marc-Antoine must have been taken soon before he left. He looks like such a baby, doesn't he?"

Jean-Paul stood near her. The red light made them both glow; the quiet, enclosed room felt a thousand miles away from the rest of the world.

"So, have we gone through all the negatives?" asked Jean-Paul.

"I think that's about it. Darn it. I was hoping to

find something more about the mystery woman. Why was her picture inside my rabbit?"

"You are such a curious woman," he said. "What is it they say in English? 'Curiosity killed the cat'?"

"Does that mean you're going to kill me for diving into your family secrets?"

He laughed. "Not at all. But I can't vouch for my grandfather."

They gathered their things, went into the store to thank Guido for his help, and then Jean-Paul drove Cady back to the château. She asked him to come in so she could show him Fabrice's author photo.

Fabrice wasn't in the kitchen or his sitting room, so they went straight to Cady's chamber off the red hallway. Along the way, Jean-Paul checked out the empty rooms, the ruined plaster, the water stains. Cady remembered he had said he hadn't been allowed past the kitchen in years; she hoped he wasn't becoming even more discouraged about the state of the manor.

"I've noticed that there's a strong family resemblance with many of you Clements," Cady said. "The shape of your eyes, the bridge of the nose, the cheekbones. But not Fabrice—or even Marc-Antoine, now that I think about it. Check this out."

She handed him her copy of *The Château*, turning it over to display the author photo. Then she put the photo of Léon Morice next to it.

He nodded slowly. "So you think my grandfather is right? Josephine had an affair with Léon Morice?"

"He was very handsome."

Jean-Paul smiled. "And would that be enough reason to go outside her marriage?"

"No, of course not. And clearly, I'm in no position to judge her. It's just that . . . her husband was so much older than she, and they had tried for years to have children, but couldn't. And then a handsome apprentice comes along and . . . ?"

"And stays in the house for months, carving."

"Sounds like a romantic setup."

"Yes, it does."

Cady stood by the doorway, running her hands over the swoops of the wood carvings: the flowers and berries, a little wren. The wood had a velvety finish, not a varnish but similar to what Maxine always called a "French polish," accomplished through a many-layered buffing process. It was slick and inviting under her fingertips.

Jean-Paul's hand settled over hers. She tilted her face up to his.

"This is probably a bad idea," he whispered.

"I know."

You're a terrible judge of character, Drake, she told herself. Nonetheless, she wrapped her arms around his neck and pulled his lips down to hers. The kiss was the gentlest she had ever experienced, the brushing of a butterfly wing, the softness of the dawn.

But then it deepened. The kiss caught fire, and swept them both along with it.

Cady had forgotten this sensation: the wildness, the wantonness, the yearning. How long since she had felt such reckless ardor? The stolen moments of that long ago one-night stand, fueled by alcohol, didn't count. This was liquid, uninhibited passion, desire coursing through her veins. This was the feeling of Jean-Paul's chest under her palms, his whiskers tickling her cheek, his mouth moving down to nibble her neck.

She wanted this. She wanted Jean-Paul. She wanted *more.*

CHAPTER FIFTY-FOUR

PRESENT DAY
CHÂTEAU CLEMENT

Cady

Afterward, Jean-Paul had to leave for a commitment with his mother. They had spoken little as they picked up their discarded clothing and dressed, both apparently avoiding discussion of what had just happened, not to mention the future.

Her body felt deliciously sated, but her mind was frenetic. Unable to shake her restlessness, Cady went back outside to the carousel.

She had to run a cord from the nearby garage to power a work lamp, but she liked the feeling of being with the carousel at night, alone. The shadows somehow seemed part of it. She could practically hear the *tinks* and *clanks* of the workers she had seen in the photographs earlier in the day; again, she wondered about the lone woman in the group, working alongside the men.

Souviens-toi de moi.

And Cady envisioned Josephine, riding her

custom carousel alone at night. Round and round.

"Paulette was sitting right there, on that horse," said Fabrice, appearing in the doorway, looking a bit like a ghost himself.

"Oh! You startled me."

"Sorry," Fabrice replied, though he didn't look particularly sorry. His eyes never left the carousel horse.

"I thought you said you never found her."

"I didn't find her—she found me. The war was over, but it was a . . . difficult time for everyone. We were overjoyed at first, of course. But the repercussions were cruel."

"The country was devastated."

He nodded. "Rationing went on for years afterward. But it was more than that. It's . . . it's a terrible thing to be invaded. I suppose it's only natural, only human, that alliances are formed, betrayals made, revenge taken."

Cady remained silent, running her hands over the curves and divots of the horse's mane.

"It turned out she had given me her real name, after all: Paulette Olivier," Fabrice continued. "But she wasn't from Fontaine-de-Vaucluse per se; she was from a little farm in the countryside."

"You found her?"

"More than that. I killed her."

CHAPTER FIFTY-FIVE

1945
CHÂTEAU CLEMENT

Fabrice

Fabrice had been staying in the château, derelict as it was, for several days. His many cousins in town, to whom he had introduced himself for the first time, didn't have much after the war. Still, they had offered him a warm bed to sleep in, and a place at their tables, but Fabrice declined their offers. He had heard too many stories from his father about their vicious rumors against his grandparents.

They appeared to be generous, but if there was one thing Fabrice had learned from the war, it was the wretched sting of betrayal.

Besides, he preferred the desolation of his father's once-beautiful childhood home. It suited his own bleak interior. The remnants of old leather-bound books and Turkish rugs under-foot—marred by rodent droppings and mold—seemed to embody the faded aspirations of his soul. The useless ticking of the massive grandfather clock, missing its hands, reflected the crooked, rancid beating of his heart.

The château had been looted, anything of value that was portable having long since been stolen. Still, many papers and photos remained. Fabrice spent untold hours looking through old wooden toys in what had been his father's boyhood room; reading his grandfather Yves's journals; and examining stacks of his grandmother Josephine's correspondence, bound together with tattered blue silk ribbon.

And of course, there was the carousel.

His father had told him about joyous festivals when the children from the village were invited to ride the carousel. That was before the rumors and innuendo had finally estranged the family from the villagers, before things fell apart.

A few of the carousel figures were still intact, as was most of the actual mechanism, though all were covered in soot and grime. Still, the ruins drew him out in the evenings; he liked to smoke there in the dark, when the silvery light of the moon filtering through the dirty windows lent everything an air of ghostly nostalgia. He could practically hear the raucous music, could see his father as a boy, whirling round and round with the other village children. His former friends.

And one night, this was where he stumbled upon Paulette.

Her hair had been shorn, like that of a prostitute; her dress was fashioned out of a burlap sack. Her cheeks were wet with tears, but she cried silently. She sat on a once-whimsical carousel horse, unmindful of the soot. A gun in her lap.

"It was you?" Fabrice finally managed.

She nodded.

"They took my family."

"I know. . . . Fabrice, I'll never be able to tell you how sorry I am. I'll never be able to explain—"

"They took my family!" he raged, running toward her.

She held up the gun with both hands, training it on him. He paused, coming to a stop right in front of her, trying not to heave, to vomit. Wanting to kill her; wanting to kill himself.

"Listen to me! Please, Fabrice, just *listen.*" The tears kept flowing, but her voice was steady. "I had no choice. They threatened my family. My mother, my brother and sisters . . . The Gestapo threatened such terrible things. . . ." Finally, she started sobbing aloud. "I'm so sorry, Fabrice, I am *so* sorry."

"*Stop saying that!* It doesn't *matter* how sorry you are. It doesn't matter, don't you understand?" He glanced down at the gun, still trained on him. "Go ahead and shoot. It seems fitting that I would be murdered by the woman I loved."

"It isn't for you," Paulette said, her voice now quiet, calm. "It's for me."

She lifted the gun and placed the muzzle to her temple.

He lunged, grabbing her hand. A shot rang out.

CHAPTER FIFTY-SIX

PRESENT DAY
CHÂTEAU CLEMENT

Cady

"Fabrice?"

The old man had stopped speaking, staring at the carousel figure for so long that Cady started to worry. But he seemed to be telling his own story, in his own time.

"There were terrible retaliations for the French who cooperated with the Germans. We called them *collaborateurs*. But when you live with your occupiers, like we did . . . Well, there are many sides to every story."

"So what happened, when Paulette came?"

"She was sitting on that horse, the one you're cleaning. Just sitting there, but with a gun in her hand. She had heard that I was looking for her; she said she knew I would come out to the carousel eventually."

"Why?"

"We used to talk about my family's château back in Paris. Before she betrayed us all, before she gave my name to the Gestapo. She was the reason my family was taken."

Cady let that sink in for a moment.

"My mother and sister did not survive. My father did; he never blamed me for what happened, though of course he had cause. I found him after the war. One thing you can say about the Germans: They kept excellent records.

"After I made money off my writing, my father and I came back to the château and lived here together until his death at the age of eighty-two. We worked together to renovate it, for a while. Sometimes when he and I carved together, he would say it was God's cruel joke, to allow him to live so long, after taking the lives of his wife and child. But I knew the truth: God did not take their lives; *I* did."

"Fabrice, it wasn't your fault. It was war. The Nazis committed atrocities. . . . It wasn't your fault."

"It was," he said, his voice matter-of-fact as he gazed into the shadows. "It *was* my fault. My father begged me to keep out of it, to work with him in his woodshop, to survive."

"And you did survive."

He nodded grimly.

"So did I," Cady said, thinking of the last time she had seen Jonquilla—or Maxine, for that matter. She thought of the baby she had mis-carried, and the wretched, desperate urge to continue, even while leaving others behind. “So what happened with Paulette? She threatened to shoot you?”

“No, she tried to shoot herself. I wrestled the gun from her, but my cousins, Pierre and his brothers, were coming out to meet me at the château. The gun went off, but neither of us was hurt. They heard the shot and found us, and took her to be arrested.”

“And hailed you as a hero.”

“She was put on trial as a traitor, which, of course, she was. . . .” He trailed off, clearing his throat. He stroked the head of the horse, running his fingers along its wavy, beribboned tail. “Eventually she managed to kill herself while in prison. Can you imagine the pain of being called a hero for leading to the death of the woman you love?”

“If Pierre and the others hadn’t found you, would you have let Paulette go?”

Fabrice did not answer. He just turned and walked out into the black night.

The next day Jean-Paul arrived early and found Cady sitting on a low stone wall in the courtyard, perusing *The Château* and trying to compare a few passages to the French version of the novel, which she had found in the book room.

Their eyes met as he walked toward her. He looked delicious, and all she could think of was the feeling of lying in his arms yesterday. The scent of him surrounding her; the enchanting warmth of his bare chest under her palms; the way his whiskers tickled and scratched.

From the heat in his gaze, she could tell he was remembering the same thing.

"I wish I could have stayed last night."

"Me, too."

"No renovation this morning?"

"Of course. I was just looking through the book, trying to find a few answers. Or insights, at least. What do you think this poem means? Can you tell if it's translated properly?"

He read:

> Round and round on the carousel. Will I
>   ever catch up?
> The apprentice Anon
> Round and round, chasing
> like a fairy tale
> The horses run and run but never arrive
> The carousel carver bows down
> And within the healed wound,
> the figure keeps the secret
> Anon

"It seems basically correct," said Jean-Paul. "But I wouldn't have translated *panser* here as a healed wound—*panser les plaies* can mean to heal or lick one's wounds, but I think in this instance the word could mean something like this part, here, of an animal." He patted his flat stomach.

"The torso? As in belly? As in the belly of my rabbit?"

"It could be," he said. "You found something there, after all. That would mean that Fabrice knew about the box as well—or maybe he'd heard the story, at least. But what secret did the box reveal?"

"I'm trying to figure that out. I wish I knew who 'Anon' was."

Cady went on to tell Jean-Paul what Fabrice had said the night before, about Paulette's betrayal and his finding her sitting on the carousel horse. "So this is one of the reasons he's been tormented all these years. He feels guilty because he was fooled by her, and she betrayed his family."

"I don't think that's exactly on point," said Jean-Paul. "In fact, I think he feels guilty because he still loves her. To this day, he still cares."

"But . . . she led to the death of his mother and sister."

"That's where the guilt comes in. But love is not always sensible. In fact, it almost never is, is it? I know you're reading his first book, but the theme runs through all of his novels: an unrequited love that leads to disaster. Much like the poetry Pétrarque wrote while at Fontaine-de-Vaucluse." He held his hand out for the book. "Look at the dedication of *Le Château*. It's a quote from Pétrarque, about his Laura:

> I see, think, burn, weep; and the one who undoes me
> is ever before me thanks to my sweet pain:
> a war, my condition, filled with ire and pain;
> and only thinking of her do I have some peace

"I can't believe it," said Cady. "How could you love someone who had betrayed you like that?"

"Love is pain, I think was his point."

"You can say that again," Johnny said, joining them right at that moment. "So, what are you doing sitting around? Don't we have a carousel to save?"

CHAPTER FIFTY-SEVEN

PRESENT DAY
CHÂTEAU CLEMENT

Cady

Cady's favorite part of the day was watching Johnny speak to the owner of the art supply store in Avignon about the carousel, passion in his words. She had taken him with her for supplies, and it seemed that he had caught the fever.

Once a person understands the value of reclaiming trash, Cady thought to herself, *it's tough to go back.*

They also stopped by the university briefly, "just to look." It was obviously not up to Cady to decide whether Johnny pursued a higher degree, but she wanted him to understand that it was a possibility.

As they were driving back to Château Clement, Cady's phone beeped.

"Could you check and see if that's Jean-Paul?"

"It's someone named Olivia," Johnny, said scanning the text. In heavily accented English, he read: " 'When can they see some examples for ze book about ze derelict château and carousel, with photos of ze owner and dog.' What is 'de-re-lict'?"

"Run-down, old."

"Aaah," he replied, reverting to French. "But you're serious? You want to do a book about Fabrice's creepy old place?"

"I don't know. I'm thinking about it. I'd like to. But . . ." Her voice trailed off. How was she even going to approach Fabrice with the idea? He could simply say no, of course, and that would be that. Still, even asking him would have to be handled very, very delicately or he would fly off the handle.

"Why do you care so much? You're not even from here. My dad says you're obsessed with my family."

"Well . . ."—she had a sudden vision of wrapping her arms around Jean-Paul's well-muscled torso last night—"maybe *some* members of your family."

"Why? Family's a pain in the ass, people always asking where you're going, knowing someone everywhere you go."

"That's why you should consider going to university. Seriously. I never had the chance to go, myself, but it sounds like a lot more fun than hanging around Saint-Véran your whole life. It's a great little village for families and old people like me, but someone like you should experience more before you settle down."

He seemed to be weighing her words.

"You should speak to Jean-Paul about it. He went to Paris for school and stayed."

"That's because his dad used to beat his mom and everything."

"He did?"

"Yeah. He was a drinker, too, like my dad. But at least my dad didn't hit my mom. He just hits me, every once in a while, when I drive him really crazy."

"Is he the one who gave you that black eye?"

He shrugged. "I asked for it."

"Johnny," Cady began, realizing that if everyone thought she was meddling before, this was even worse, "your father shouldn't hit you. If you need—"

"Seriously," he said, cutting her off, "it's fine. We're fine. We understand each other. And it's been hard for him, since my mom died and everything."

"I'm sure it has."

"But . . . maybe you're right. Going to university could be cool, maybe."

"Maybe. Talk to Jean-Paul."

"I don't know if I could even get in."

"There's no way to know until you try."

He nodded and looked out the window.

"So, what happened to Jean-Paul's father?"

"He got cancer and died pretty fast after that. I got the feeling no one really minded. I heard he beat Jean-Paul up really bad one time, when Jean-Paul tried to defend his mom. Not too long after that was when Jean-Paul went to live in Paris; my mom said he stayed with some relatives there so he wouldn't have to come back home on vacations."

"Was this Madame Martin?"

"Maybe. I forget the names."

They had arrived at Château Clement. The tires crunched on the gravel as Cady pulled down the drive and around the back.

"Would you like to stay for dinner?" she asked. "I went shopping earlier."

"Nah," Johnny said. Fabrice had opened the back door and was standing on the threshold, Lucy beside him. "I think Fabrice has seen enough of me lately. But thanks."

"Anytime. At least wish Fabrice a good night before you go, will you?"

They got out of the car, called a *salut* to Fabrice, and Johnny helped Cady to unload the supplies into the carousel building.

Then he bade Cady good night and went over to speak to Fabrice. Cady lingered, lining up the supplies just so and giving the two a moment alone. It pleased her that they didn't just exchange a quick word but conversed for several minutes. Maybe Johnny really did just need a little friendship, a little guidance. And Fabrice, too, for that matter. Could she have actually accomplished some good with her stay in Saint-Véran?

But Johnny gave her an odd look when he left—part guilty, part embarrassed—and then quickly shifted his gaze away and loped down the drive.

Cady read bleakness in Fabrice's eyes before he turned his back to her and limped toward the château.

"Fabrice, is everything okay?" Cady called out.

He ducked into the servants' entrance.

Cady trailed him inside. He continued down the narrow corridor without looking back, the rhythmic tapping of his cane on the old stones seemingly counting down to . . . what?

When he reached the kitchen threshold, he paused.

"Fabrice?" Cady tried again. "Johnny's been doing really well lately, but if he—"

"Johnny's not the problem."

"Then . . . ?"

Fabrice turned toward her, very slowly and deliberately.

"Cady, are you taking your photographs of Château Clement—and of *me*—to make a book?"

"No, no, of course not. I mean, I suggested to my publisher that your carousel might make a nice addition to the book, and I . . ."

A curtain came down over his features.

"But, Fabrice, I would never—"

"I thought you were different, Cady. Get your things and get out of here. I'm serious this time."

"Fabrice, please listen to me. I wouldn't have done anything, and certainly would not have *published* anything, without your permission. Of course not. I just—"

"I'm so sick of people, I could just spit," Fabrice said, studying the old stones as if seeking clarity in their unyielding hardness. "You would think I'd learn. This is what comes of having people around. Lucy and I were just fine, and then you come along, and you act a little like her and . . ." He looked at her with the saddest eyes in the world. "And then you betray me, just as she did."

"Who, Paulette?"

"I'd like you to leave, Cady. Please be gone by morning."

"But . . . we haven't gone to Fontaine-de-Vaucluse. And the carousel—"

"*Please,* Cady, leave this old man in peace." He shuffled into the kitchen and closed the door behind him.

Cady packed her things and walked the couple of miles into town, trailing her small suitcase behind her, her photography bag weighing heavily on her shoulder. She made her way to Jean-Paul's apartment.

“Cady! What a lovely surprise,” he said, but then his eyes flickered down to the bags she was holding. “Everything okay?”

“Fabrice kicked me out,” she said, her voice shaking.

“Oh, Cady, I’m so sorry. Come in and let me make you something. Coffee? Apéritif?” He picked up her bags and ushered her inside.

Her arms ached from lugging the bags all the way into town—stepping behind the stout plane trees for protection when cars came speeding past along the highway—but the weariness she felt was not due to that as much as to her emotions. How could everything have gone so wrong so fast? She felt as if she was back in foster care, when she would start to feel relaxed in a new situation, letting her “real” self shine, starting to care for the people she was with, and then she was abruptly yanked out, left completely unmoored.

She took a seat at his little kitchen table, and he moved aside a thick roll of blueprints and a pad of graph paper.

“You’ll join my mother and grandfather and me for dinner, and spend the night, and we’ll figure out what happens next. We can go talk to Fabrice together, if you like.”

“It was just a stupid misunderstanding, but he wouldn’t even let me explain.”

He blew out a long breath. “Listen, Cady,

he's been remarkably open to you so far. But I think you must know that Fabrice hasn't allowed people into his life for a very, very long time."

"I know. I just felt like we had a . . . connection."

"I think you did. Or you *do.*" He set a small glass of Campari in front of her and added a splash of mineral water. "Give him a day or two to cool down, and see what he says then. Do you want to tell me what set him off?"

"Well, Johnny—"

He rolled his eyes. "What's Johnny done now?"

"No, nothing like that. Johnny read a text I received, about the idea to do a book about Château Clement, with photographs."

"You mean the carousel?"

"It started with the carousel, but then the publisher liked the idea of me hanging out in a decrepit château with an old man and his dog, and they thought it could make a really cool book."

Jean-Paul remained leaning against the counter. His typically open expression seemed suddenly guarded. "You're planning to do some sort of exposé on Fabrice?"

"No, of course not. I would certainly never have done anything without his permission. It was a fantasy, really—I just love taking photographs, and of course the idea of them being published was enticing, but I would never do that. Not without permission. I know I have a few boundary issues, but not like that."

After a beat he nodded. "Good. Glad to hear it. So Fabrice wouldn't let you explain all of that?"

She shook her head and took a long pull on her drink. "It was almost as if he was waiting for me to betray him. The way Paulette did. He said I remind him of her."

There were footsteps overhead, and the muffled sound of voices. Jean-Paul glanced at his watch. "I should go help my mother prepare dinner. Will you eat with us?"

"Thank you, I would like that. Could I just wash up . . . ?"

"Of course," he said. He went into the bathroom, flipped the light on, and handed her a towel. "Take a shower, whatever you like. There's no rush; dinner will be an hour at least."

"Thank you."

"You're welcome. Cady," Jean-Paul said. She turned back to him. "You're telling me the whole truth? Nothing else happened?"

She gave a humorless laugh, and refrained from slamming the bathroom door between them.

Cady allowed herself a quick, frustrated cry in the shower. She still blamed it on hormones—*it had* better *be hormones,* she thought. If this was what came of aging, she was going to be seriously pissed off. But again, she'd been staying in Saint-Véran only a short period of time. It seemed like forever in some ways, but in reality, her time in the Provençal countryside was barely a blip on the screen of her life, much less in the life of a town old enough to remember dragons.

She dressed and headed for the side kitchen door of the main house, where Jean-Paul had brought her in before.

Cady raised her palm to knock but hesitated at the sound of raised voices.

"*Elle est une intruse,*" said a voice she thought belonged to Johnny's father, Andres. "She's an interloper, probably wants to make a fortune on that carousel."

"She was *helping,*" came Jean-Paul's ever-patient voice. "In addition to taking care of Fabrice, she's finally gotten him to allow her to unearth the carousel—and yes, it will be worth a lot of money if we can fix it up. It could help with raising funds to properly restore the château. And she might even have discovered some photos from Yves Clement that shed light on our family history."

"My point is, she's *not* family," said Gerald. "She should go spend her energy on her own family and leave ours alone."

"Jean-Paul tells me she's an orphan," said Louise. "She doesn't *have* any family."

"That's her problem, not ours."

"It might be one reason she doesn't understand how family works," said Louise gently.

"Cady told me herself that she has some problems recognizing boundaries," said Jean-Paul. "Sometimes she can seem . . . pushy, or forward. But that's probably the reason she's gotten so far with Fabrice."

"Family is family," said Gerald.

"And she's *not* family," said Andres.

This was what they thought of her. Cady couldn't listen anymore.

After she lost her baby and apartment and then Maxine passed away, Cady had found herself stunned at how quickly things could change. And now she felt that way again. Just yesterday she had been restoring antique French carousel figures, listening while Fabrice confided his darkest stories, making love with Jean-Paul, feeling like a part of things. But the truth was this: She wasn't wanted here. She didn't belong.

Cady returned to Jean-Paul's apartment and penned a brief note thanking him and saying good-bye. On the kitchen table, as before, sat the rolled-up blueprints and hand-drawn sketches of Château Clement. But alongside them was a formal letter from an auction house, pertaining to the approximate value of "one Bayol carousel, circa 1900."

Fabrice had repeatedly accused Jean-Paul of wanting to cash in by "selling the place off for parts." Had he been right all along? Had Jean-Paul been helping with the carousel restoration only because it would be worth a lot of money?

Or was she becoming like Fabrice, seeing disloyalty around every corner, allowing one betrayal to taint everything else?

None of it mattered anymore, anyway. The time had come for her to leave. After a moment of internal debate, she decided to leave her exposed film cartridges with the photos she had taken of Lucy, Fabrice, and the carousel during her stay at Château Clement. Let the family do with them what they would. That way, at least, Fabrice wouldn't worry that she had shared them with anyone.

Then she grabbed her bags and slipped out into the early evening.

She was dry-eyed now, beyond tears. But the problem with a small town was that even though she'd been here only a short time, people recognized her. What she wouldn't give to be back in Paris this instant, walking those streets, reveling in her anonymity.

Anonymity.

Olivia used to say that, historically speaking, "Anonymous" was a woman. Anon.

What if . . .

What if the "apprentice" who stayed at the château wasn't Léon Morice at all, but a woman?

The woman. The one in the photograph—the secret kept in the rabbit's belly.

She dropped her bag and took the envelope of historic photos she had developed out of her satchel. In the photos where she was working on the carousel, the woman had looked a little chubby to Cady. But now Cady saw it: The woman wasn't chubby.

She was pregnant.

CHAPTER FIFTY-EIGHT

1901
CHÂTEAU CLEMENT

Josephine and Maëlle

The camera feels awkward in her hands, and she has to squint to see through the tiny hole. How did Yves manage to keep the lens so steady? Was it the result of practice, or was it his resolute way of doing everything he did?

"You stand right there," Josephine tells the mother of her baby. "With the carousel behind you."

"Here? Like this? At least let me take off my apron."

For many months, Maëlle has worn increasingly looser clothing to accommodate her swelling belly as she carves the lintels, mantels, newel posts, and doorways throughout the château. Josephine, for her part, has gained weight and, in the end, resorted to placing a small pillow under her skirts. Yves is ignorant of the ways of women, and so over the moon at the thought of Josephine having his child that he does not notice the obvious details. Some of the more astute housemaids have their suspicions, and Josephine can only pray that they hold their tongues. But no one else pays attention to the quiet carver who fills the halls of the château with the scent of freshly sawn wood and the *scrip-scrape tink-tink* of her work, her passion, her joy.

The truth gnaws at Josephine; she cringes at the thought of deceiving her dear husband. She would have confessed a thousand times already, but Yves is such an upstanding man that if he discovered the truth, he would step aside and allow his brother to take over the château. It would break his heart. Their infant son, Marc-Antoine, named for Yves's father, has already brought them such joy that she prays her husband will understand, in the long run.

"No, no," Josephine tells Maëlle. "Stay exactly as you are, right this moment. This is how I will always remember you; this is how your son should know you. You are an artist, a sculptor."

"He will never know me," Maëlle says, in the saddest voice Josephine has ever heard.

She lowers the camera. "He will, Maëlle. When he is old enough to understand, he will know of the apprentice who came to stay at Château Clement. I will make sure of it. I will tell him to look inside the rabbit on his eighteenth birthday. He will know he was loved by the Aspiring Apprentice from Angers."

Maëlle nods.

Her son will grow up a Clement. He will never want for anything, or know the acid rejection of being an illegitimate child.

Josephine has been writing letters, securing commissions for Maëlle all over France. Soon she will move on to the next château; a family who lives outside of Nice had already offered her a commission. She will be able to sculpt. Even though she is a woman. Even though she must remain anonymous.

Maëlle has carved a single, stand-alone carousel figure. She has created him, from start to finish, all by herself. He is a rabbit with a sweet expression, every inch of him fashioned with whispers of love and hope and encouragement. She allows herself to dream that her tender endearments will infuse the very wood of the figure, reaching out across the years to comfort and console her son and future generations.

Maëlle lifts her chin, and Josephine snaps the picture.

CHAPTER FIFTY-NINE

PRESENT DAY
PROVENCE AND PARIS

Cady

There was no taxi service in town, but Hubert knew a man who drove people to the train station for a set fee, so Cady got a ride into Avignon. She had planned on catching the next train to Paris, but then reconsidered and asked him to drop her at a decent hotel near the Gare d'Avignon, which turned out to be a beautiful Best Western.

There was one more thing she wanted to do before she left Provence.

Cady had intended to rent a car the next morning, but wound up staying in her hotel room for two full days. She snuck out to a corner grocery to buy a bottle of wine, a bag of chips, and a package of Petit Écolier cookies, and tried to re-create the debauched retreat that had helped soothe her wounds in Oakland, but was disappointed to discover that there was no French version of *Hoarders* showing on the television. She didn't have the heart to watch anything, anyway. But neither was she ready to face the outside world.

Cady looked again and again at the photograph and the note that had brought her to Château Clement: *Je t'aime toujours, et encore. Souviens-toi de moi.*

I love you always, and still. Remember me.

As she lay on her bed, becoming far too well acquainted with her hotel room ceiling, she reviewed her recent actions in her head.

And realized something.

What had she done in Saint-Veran that was so awful? She'd helped an old man, however briefly, and befriended a troubled teenager. She had even made a few inroads with some of the villagers, enough to think that, with time, she could have built some relationships. At least she had made an effort.

Cady had always been an awkward kid, unlikable. But . . . was she really all that bad? She might be gruff or abrupt, she might have a few boundary issues, but she wasn't *malicious.* She had never deliberately set out to hurt another person.

And after all, who said a bad seed couldn't sometimes grow into a decent tree?

The next morning Cady rented a car and drove to Fontaine-de-Vaucluse. She wanted to see the home of the dragon for herself.

The village was located in a dead-end valley, closed in by an enormous limestone cliff. Parking was plentiful and a lot of the shops and restaurants weren't yet open for the season; clearly this once-sleepy town had become a tourist destination, but it was probably overrun with visitors in the height of the summer. She thought about Fabrice's suspicions regarding his family's motives concerning Château Clement; did they really want a similar fate for their sweet little village of Saint-Véran?

It's none of your business, Drake, she told herself. Not anymore. It never had been, actually, but at this point . . . it was depressing to realize that Cady's sojourn in Provence would be relegated to a tiny footnote in her life. Before long the complex interwoven web of stories, of Fabrice and Paulette, Marc-Antoine, Yves and Josephine, Johnny, Léon, and the anonymous woman who worked on the carousel—and of Jean-Paul—would recede in her memory, as surely as the tide on a moonless night.

Still. Olivia had been right. Coming to France hadn't been running away, but running *to* something. And Cady would carry it with her the rest of her life.

She walked past the crude stony bulk of the tenth-century Church of Saint Véran, complete with a rough-hewn statue of the dragon at its entrance. A man at a crepe stand directed Cady to walk up a trail called the Chemin de Gouffre, beside the river Sorgue, to find the source of the water—and the supposedly fathomless home of the mythical beast. She passed bistros and ice cream vendors, most still shuttered, awaiting tourist season. Sun filtered through the leaves, dappling the scene with a kaleidoscope of light and shadow.

The air still held a cool April crispness, and church bells chimed eleven as she climbed. Mallards quacked and warblers flitted through the overhanging plane trees. Despite her misery, Cady felt a kind of peace manifest in the calming murmur of the Sorgue and the stillness of the giant ferns along its banks. The waters were crystal clear, a beautiful bright green over waving weeds and a brilliant turquoise when pooling in eddies over white sands. As she progressed up the hill, huge white streams poured over boulders down toward the valley.

Higher up, the river disappeared under rock and brush, but Cady kept going, determined to find the famed well from which the Sorgue sprang.

Finally she arrived at the mouth of a cave in a dramatic granite escarpment, at the base of which was a swirling green pool. The font, the source.

The home of the dragon.

"Unfathomable," Cady said aloud.

"But beautiful," replied a man's voice.

She turned around to see Jean-Paul.

"What—what are you doing here?" she demanded. "How did you know where I was?"

"The man who drove you to Avignon is a Clement cousin. He told me the hotel he dropped you at, and the woman at the front desk let me know when you were leaving and told me you asked for directions to Fontaine-de-Vaucluse."

"Let me guess—she's yet another Clement cousin?"

He shook his head. "But I can be convincing when I put my mind to it."

"You're quite the detective."

He inclined his head, just slightly. "Somehow I knew you wouldn't just run away. Not like that."

Their eyes held for a long moment. Cady searched for a response, but finally looked back to the pool without speaking.

"I have something in the car for you," said Jean-Paul.

"What is it?"

"Someone named Olivia Gray sent you a large, heavy package from the U.S. There's a rabbit drawn next to the address."

Her heart sank. *Thanks a lot, Olivia.*

"It must be my rabbit. My friend knew I was working on the Clement carousel." She blew out a frustrated breath. "Okay, I'll get it from you and take it back with me. But . . . you tracked me down to Fontaine-de-Vaucluse just to give me my package?"

"Not exactly, no," he replied. "Fabrice is here. He couldn't make the climb with his ankle, but he's sitting on a bench by the Sorgue. Waiting."

"Waiting for what?"

"For you." Jean-Paul put his hand out to her. "Trust me?"

She shook her head. "I saw the carousel estimate on your table, Jean-Paul. You kept telling me you weren't interested in selling the château for parts, but you were planning on cashing in on the carousel?"

He blew out an exasperated breath. "I told you that I've been trying to come at the château restoration from several different angles. Yes, the carousel could offer us a special kind of attraction; it might give a bank the confidence to give us a loan. And it turns out that Fabrice has some money set aside that he'd like to put toward restoration, and my mother and even my grandfather have agreed to go in on it with me. We're still talking . . . but it just might happen. And you've been part of that. I can't believe that you ran away just because of this, without talking to me about it. Especially not after what happened between us."

"It wasn't that."

"Then what?"

"I overheard you and your family talking. I know I'm . . ." She shook her head, trailing off, looking down into the dragon's cauldron. Even after her revelation in the hotel room, it came to her, almost like a mantra: "I know I try too hard. I'm too much. People don't want me."

"Cady, I wish you would believe this: You're *not* too much. You're a little . . . different, but different doesn't have to mean bad. We French enjoy a more rarefied taste in many things."

She managed a smile. "But your family's right when they say that Château Clement isn't my home, and the Clements aren't my family."

"That doesn't always have to be the case."

"What does that mean?"

"It means that sometimes these things can change." He held his hand out to her again. "Please take my hand, Cady, and let me bring you to Fabrice. In a very rare move, he has an apology he would like to offer you. It's only fair to let him give it to you in person, and if you still want to leave, then I will give you your rabbit, and you can go."

They descended the hill and found that Fabrice had moved from the bench to a nearby café, where outdoor heaters kept the terrace warm. Just the sight of his tousled gray hair and hawk eyes filled her with a sense of nostalgia, as if he really were a long-lost grandfather.

He hoisted himself to his one good foot as she approached. On the table was a bottle of Châteauneuf-du-Pape and three glasses.

“I ordered oysters,” Fabrice said before she could even sit down.

“I . . . to tell you the truth, I’ve never had oysters.”

He raised his eyebrows. “Never? This is a scandal. You are in France, so you must try them now, fresh from the Mediterranean. You will love them, as I loved your garlic bread. And Jean-Paul insisted that Châteauneuf-du-Pape is your favorite wine, though red doesn’t usually go with oysters.”

“Fabrice, didn’t you want to apologize to Cady?” Jean-Paul suggested, his voice gentle.

Fabrice nodded, but looked away. When he spoke, his voice was low and gruff. “Cady, it’s possible I overreacted. I’m sorry.”

“I hadn’t agreed to do the book project, Fabrice,” Cady said. “I did pitch the idea, but I wouldn’t have gone through with it unless you granted me permission. And I was pretty sure I would never get your permission. I just got so excited. . . . I liked the idea of including photos of the château, and restoring the old carousel, but I wasn’t going to expose you.”

“I think I knew that. Afterward, when I thought about it. And then Jean-Paul told me you left your film rolls at his place. I just . . .” His voice trailed off with a shrug. “I guess I always expected another betrayal. Jean-Paul here tells me I need to change my way of thinking.”

As Jean-Paul poured the wine, Cady decided she was sick to her soul of secrets.

"There's something else," she said carefully. "I think Gerald's side of the family is right. At least, partly."

She told Fabrice and Jean-Paul what she suspected about the woman in the photographs.

"You're saying she's Fabrice's grandmother?" Jean-Paul asked. "The woman you found in the photograph in your rabbit?"

She nodded but glanced at Fabrice. "I don't know . . . I mean, I know there were rumors about your father's legitimacy as heir, and I hate to add to them."

"I'm so old now, it doesn't matter anymore. But the truth is, my father knew Yves was not his natural father."

"He did?" asked Jean-Paul.

Fabrice nodded. "After the war, when I was reunited with my father, he told me part of the story, and then I found letters at the château that helped me put together the rest. My father spent two years in a German hospital during World War I, and when he was released he had a stack of mail waiting for him. There were letters from his father, Yves, about Josephine, and what she was going through toward the end of her life. Word had reached my father before then that his mother had died in an accident, but it wasn't until he read the letters that he understood the rumors, the gossip about her. . . . It was Yves's brother, Thierry, who was the most vicious. But Thierry's son Pierre—Jean-Paul's great-grandfather—was almost as bad. And he passed the attitude on to his son, Gerald."

Cady glanced at Jean-Paul, who inclined his head. "I never knew Pierre, but my grandfather has always been a mean old man, even when I was a kid. I sometimes wonder if that was why my mother gravitated toward my father; his temper seemed familiar to her."

"They tormented Josephine and Yves for years. The night of the accident, Josephine asked Yves to help her start the steam engine of the carousel. They'd lost almost everything by then, and no longer had more than a single housemaid, so there was no one else to help her. But Yves refused, so evidently she tried to do it herself, but used the wrong kerosene—she didn't understand there were different kinds.

"Yves had invested far too much money into commissioning the carousel, which his brother harassed him for mercilessly. So he hated the contraption by then. And on that night his mind had been poisoned by his brother's innuendo against Josephine as well; so he suspected she was meeting a lover. After the accident, he was distraught, and essentially drank himself to death within the year."

"So gossip destroyed them both," said Jean-Paul.

Fabrice nodded. "Josephine had been lying all along, but not in the way her husband thought. She missed her friend Maëlle, and their time together. She was lonely, and anguished not to be able to confide in her husband about their son."

"And this Maëlle woman was the apprentice who stayed at the château," Cady began, "and it was she who had a baby—your father, Marc-Antoine?"

"Yes. Yves had never suspected; it was only after Josephine died that he found letters to her from Maëlle, and put it all together."

"And you've known this all along?" Jean-Paul asked Fabrice.

"I've known for quite a while, yes. But I swore I would go to my grave vexing Gerald, at the very least. I just kept hoping he'd die before me. Those people killed my grandmother Josephine and destroyed Yves's happiness, just as surely as they killed my Paulette."

"But it all happened a very long time ago, Fabrice," said Cady. "It's not the same village anymore; there are some very kind people, people who care about you."

"I suppose. The whole story is written down in the novel I've been working on. Another roman à clef, but this one has an actual key this time—and it's a relatively straightforward narrative of my life."

"Wouldn't that be called a memoir?" Cady asked.

"Well, well, look at Mademoiselle Literature over here," he said, casting her a sidelong glance. "Whatever you want to call it, it lays out the whole story, as far as I know it."

"So you always knew that the artisan, Maëlle, was your natural grandmother?" Jean-Paul asked.

"Among the letters awaiting my father was one from his mother, telling him about Maëlle, and about the special rabbit she had carved for him. He had run off to the war without telling his parents of his plans, so she wasn't able to fulfill her promise to Maëlle, which was to tell him about his birth mother on his eighteenth birthday."

"Why didn't you ever look inside the rabbit?" Cady asked.

Fabrice chuckled. "We had no idea there was actually something hidden *inside* the rabbit—we thought her reference to a secret within the rabbit was figurative, not literal. Rabbits are the symbol of fertility, and all that. When we sold off some furnishings and such after the war, the dealer took the rabbit from the nursery by accident. My father hadn't meant to sell it, but we did need the money at that point."

"Do you know what ever happened to Maëlle?" Jean-Paul asked.

"No." He shook his head. "My father searched for a while, but she was working as an itinerant carver, and he never found her. He tracked her down to a château in Nice where the family had her carve a niche for their chapel, and the owners there said she had gone on to another position near Bordeaux. Much later, in Josephine's desk, I found a few letters from Maëlle postmarked San Francisco, but that was the last we heard of her."

"She came to the U.S.?" Cady asked.

Fabrice nodded. "She sent a beautiful colored postcard to Josephine, displaying the buildings from the Panama-Pacific International Exposition in 1915. She said she had found meaningful work, and more opportunity, in the 'New World.' "

After everything that she had gone through to track down where Gus came from, Cady was amazed to think she might have walked some of the same streets as his carver, Maëlle, back in California.

"And do you know for sure who Marc-Antoine's biological father was?" asked Jean-Paul.

"Josephine mentioned only that Maëlle was 'friendless,' " said Fabrice, "which was a euphemism for being an unwed mother at the time."

"Fabrice," Cady said, "you really do look a lot like Léon Morice, the head apprentice working on the carousel."

"The one everyone assumed Josephine had an affair with?"

"Exactly."

He shrugged. "I suppose that makes sense. It

doesn't particularly matter to me, to tell you the truth. Not after all this time."

"In the end, I suppose official provenance doesn't matter, does it?" Jean-Paul said, holding Cady's gaze. "Maybe family is just what you make of it."

"Sounds like a T-shirt slogan," said Cady, taking a sip of wine, "but I like it."

"You'll be pleased to hear that I let Toinon's girl, Élodie, come out to take a look at your progress on the carousel," said Fabrice. "She said you've done an excellent job so far. Toinon yelled at me for letting you go. Louise came and gave me an earful as well. And Johnny—you've got a true fan in that boy."

There was a long pause.

"Tell her the best part," Jean-Paul urged.

"Arthur, the village mechanic, checked out the steam engine. He thinks he can get the mechanism running again."

"Are you serious?"

"I've decided that for the Fête du Muguet, we're going to have the carousel ready to ride."

"But you have only half the animals," Cady said.

"The mechanism can still run without some of the figures. And Jean-Paul thinks he can shake a few more out of the family clutches."

Jean-Paul nodded. "One or two, at least. Apparently my grandfather has the pig with its tongue sticking out, the one he mentioned the other day."

"And I'd love to reunite my carved rabbit with the rest of the carousel figures Maëlle helped to work on," Cady offered on impulse. "It seems only right that Gus should stay at Château Clement, where he came from."

"Once we get the thing actually functioning, I guess we'll have to invite people around to see it," said Fabrice in a cantankerous tone that no longer fooled Cady. "Johnny went and blabbed to the kids in the village, and now they're all excited. Hard to believe they'd want to leave their video games for an afternoon, but it seems so."

"What are you saying?"

"I guess you were right about Johnny; he's a decent kid."

"No, I mean what are you saying about . . . me?"

"I'm saying we need your help to finish everything up in time. The fête is only a couple of weeks from now." Fabrice's voice gentled. "Come back to the château, Cady. I told you a while ago that you should ignore me—I'm just a mean old man. The fact is, you can stay as long as you like. Stay forever, as far as I'm concerned. And you'll have unlimited free rides on the carousel."

Cady looked out over the river Sorgue, at a loss for words. She had experienced these emotions once before: when Maxine had asked her to come and stay. It was the offer of belonging, of family. Not of blood, but of kindred souls.

A dragonfly flew by their table, glinting green, yellow, and blue in the golden light of late afternoon. It skittered along the waters of the Sorgue, then disappeared in the direction of the source.

Three pairs of eyes watched, wondering at the many-winged descendant of the great dragon that had once terrorized the countryside.

And at long last a huge platter of oysters arrived.

"That makes twenty-one animals, with Gus," Cady said, checking her notebook as she and Jean-Paul meandered down rue de Rivoli after leaving an antiques sale in Le Village Saint-Paul, a famous *brocantes* district of Paris. "Just three more figures to go, and we'll have a full carousel."

"What do you suppose Bayol would think of us adding non-Bayol horses to his menagerie?"

"Don't forget the hippogriff," she said with a smile. "I think he'd like it, actually. At the very least, I imagine he'd be glad that we're bringing his *manège* back from the brink. And I think Maëlle would as well."

"I think you're right."

They walked several blocks in companionable silence. Cady enjoyed threading through the crowds of locals and tourists as they continued down the busy boulevard; after the sleepiness of Saint-Véran, the overflowing brasseries and incessant traffic were invigorating. Still, she thought, it would be nice to get back to the peace and quiet of the countryside.

She glanced up at Jean-Paul. She had found him attractive when first they met, but now she couldn't stop looking at him. She was falling, hard, and the fluttering in the pit of her belly threatened to develop into full-blown panic.

"Remember to breathe," Olivia had responded when Cady had called and told her what was going on. *"Stay in the moment, keep your heart open to possibility, and have fun! What's the worst that could happen? You've always got a spot on my couch. . . . But seriously, a French lover and restoring a lost carousel sound like a lot more fun. Maybe Sebastian and I will come for the Fête du Muguet!"*

So Cady tried not to get too far ahead of herself. In this moment, in the here and now, she was strolling down a Parisian boulevard hand in hand with a kindhearted, talented, handsome man. She was on the hunt for three last carousel figures to complete a precious Bayol carousel once lost to history. She had been instrumental in helping an old man reunite with at least some of his family, and she had found a semblance of a home, of connection—however temporary—in the charming village of Saint-Véran.

Cady Anne Drake had accomplished something. It was hard to say what the future would bring, but she was determined to remain open to however it might unfold.

Dusk was falling by the time they reached the plaza in front of the historic Hôtel de Ville. The merry-go-round there, called the Carrousel La Belle Epoque, was lit up like a Christmas tree. The two-storied *manège* was a classic example of the Parisian carousel: horses and carriages, joined by more-modern sportscars, all painted in garish reds, blues, and yellows; ceilings and running boards dotted with exquisite oil paintings, mirrors, and carvings. Cady had photographed it when she had first arrived in Paris, what seemed a lifetime ago.

It looked different to her now, after she had spent so much time with Bayol's farmyard animals. Its frothy exuberance formed a strong contrast to the restrained, simple but sweet elegance of the Château Clement carousel.

A small girl with a pageboy haircut and a bright red coat stood nearby with a stooped gray-haired man who leaned on his walker. The girl was crying angry tears, her arms crossed tightly over her chest.

Cady caught the old man's eye.

"My granddaughter is afraid to ride the carousel

by herself, but I'm afraid I can't manage it," said the man.

"*Quel dommage. Comment tu t'appelles*?" Cady asked the girl, who scowled at her in sullen silence.

"This is Agnes," the man replied.

Cady smiled. "You know what, Agnes? I haven't been on a carousel for a *very* long time. Not since I was about your age. Would you like me to go with you?"

After a moment's hesitation, Agnes gave a grudging nod.

Jean-Paul bought them two small paper tickets. When the tinny notes wound down and the machine came to rest, Cady took Agnes by the hand and they climbed aboard. After some deliberation, they chose side-by-side horses.

Cady helped Agnes onto one steed and threw her own leg over the other, then gripped the pole, feeling a little thrill of impatience.

A few moments later, the carousel started up with a jerk. The horses galloped up and down, and music filled the air. As they gained speed, the Hôtel de Ville, the cafés that ringed the plaza, the cars and pedestrians crowding the surrounding boulevards, all meshed into a blurry kaleidoscope of light and color.

Each time her horse whirled by, Agnes waved to her grandfather. He smiled and held up his hand in return, every time.

Cady joined in, waving to the girl's grandfather, to Jean-Paul, to the tourists and the locals and to all of Paris.

In her mind's eye, at least, they waved back.

AUTHOR'S NOTE

Who amongst us hasn't thought of carousels with nostalgia?

Years ago, when I was working as a social worker, one of my colleagues was a young woman who had been raised in foster care. She was one of the strongest people I've ever met, wise far beyond her years, and yet she struggled to fit in and contribute to the world. She told me about attending "prospective parents" fairs, one of which was held at a park with a merry-go-round. That bittersweet image haunted me . . . and inspired the character who would later become Cady.

Years later, while visiting Paris, I saw a sweet-faced carousel cow for sale at an antiques fair in the Marais. The vendor explained that the figure was made by the famous French carousel carver Gustave Bayol. Bayol was already a well-known sculptor when he established one of the earliest French carousel factories in Angers; even after he sold the factory to his foremen, the House of Bayol continued for decades to create exquisite hand-carved carousels. Recently, I had the opportunity to interview a professional antique carousel restorer, Lise Liepman, in her studio not far from my home in California. Lise has worked on several Bayol figures over the course of her career and described what it felt like to work on such sweet-faced masterpieces.

Thus the ideas for *The Lost Carousel of Provence* started to come together. I make annual visits to stay with friends and relatives outside of Avignon, and have visited many of the châteaux—in varying states of repair—that dot the French countryside. While driving by one such dilapidated old mansion, my local companion told me it was inhabited by a reclusive old man. I wondered . . . what if Cady was somehow drawn into such a situation by the search for a Bayol carousel figure? When I read that Bayol had made custom carousels for a number of wealthy château owners, I knew I had my story. That was when Maëlle, the Aspiring Apprentice of Angers, began to whisper to me about her own quest.

Château Clement is based on an actual building, but is a wholly fictional locale—as is the Provençal village of Saint-Véran. And while I use the actual names for the characters of Gustave Bayol and his apprentice Léon Morice, their stories are entirely works of my imagination.

QUESTIONS FOR DISCUSSION

1. Imagine you have just arrived in a foreign city (Paris, Rome, Moscow, Beijing—you name it!) where you do not speak the language, or have memorized only a few words or phrases. How would you cope? Do you think being a cultural and linguistic "outsider" would give you unique insights?
2. How do you interpret the novel's epigraph by Pablo Neruda, which reads: "My soul is an empty carousel at sunset"?
3. Do you have any childhood memories of riding on carousels? What is the first thing you remember about it?
4. Why do you think so many people feel a sense of profound nostalgia when thinking about carousels?
5. Originally built to train warriors to fight, carousels later became a festive recreation for adults, and we now associate them with the innocence of children. What do you think these changing functions reveal about how society has changed over time?

6. Cady's personality was profoundly affected by her lack of important human connections as a child. Do you think her uniqueness works as a strength or a weakness for her?
7. Would you characterize Maxine as a mother figure for Cady? Or as a loving friend? Do you feel there's a difference between maternal love and the love of a friend?
8. What role does Olivia play in Cady's life? Was Olivia right to try to talk Cady into doing something because Olivia thought it was in Cady's best interests? Is it ever acceptable to push someone we care about to do something they are hesitant to do?
9. Cady mentions that photographing carousels brings her a kind of "painful joy." What do you think she meant by that? Is it a feeling that you've experienced in your own life?
10. In what ways is Saint-Véran like any American small town? In what ways is it different and uniquely French?
11. Have you ever toured a scary—or just run-down—old mansion? What was it that made the greatest impression on you? If you could live in a large old house like Fabrice's, would you? Why or why not?
12. Cady feels as though she "fits" better in France than in the United States. Have you ever wound up someplace new or foreign where you felt more at ease, more "yourself"?

13. How does Cady's lack of family history tie into her search for Gus-the-rabbit's provenance?
14. William Tammeus wrote: "You don't really understand human nature unless you know why a child on a merry-go-round will wave at his parents every time around and why his parents will always wave back." What do you think this suggests about the meaning of being a child? Or of being a parent?
15. Fabrice feels a lifelong sense of guilt for something he did as a brave but unthinking teenager. His circumstances were extreme, but have you ever done something similar? (Or maybe you still do!) Is rushing into something, feeling as if one is in a play and not understanding the possible repercussions, something to be restricted to childhood, or does it have a place in the adult world as well?
16. Jean-Paul is at a turning point in his own life. Do you think he is more open to helping Cady because of that? Are there times in your life when you've been more or less open to allowing someone new—and rather unorthodox—into your life? Is that a positive, or a negative, mind-set?
17. Is Jean-Paul wise to consider selling Château Clement to a hotel chain, or should he indulge in the dream of trying to update

the mansion and run a small hotel himself? What do you think he will choose to do with his inheritance? What would you *like* him to do?

18. Maëlle makes a series of life choices—as you read, did you characterize her choices as brave or as foolish? As selfless or as selfish? Given her circumstances and the time in which she was living, were other options available to her? What do you think gave her the courage to do what she did?
19. Maëlle feels as though she is happiest—and most truly herself—when she is able to coax a form out of a chunk of wood. Have you ever felt that way about a work or craft, or anything that you create? Is it important for everyone to have this kind of passion in life?
20. There are many historical precedents to this story, but do you feel it is far-fetched to think two women, Josephine and Maëlle, would hatch the plan they did and carry it out? Under what circumstances is it acceptable to engage in an act of deception of this magnitude? Did the good they accomplish justify the deceit?
21. What is the significance of Cady's riding the carousel at the end of the book?

Books are produced in the United States using U.S.-based materials

Books are printed using a revolutionary new process called THINKtech™ that lowers energy usage by 70% and increases overall quality

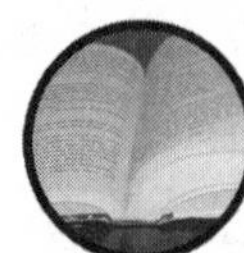

Books are durable and flexible because of Smyth-sewing

Paper is sourced using environmentally responsible foresting methods and the paper is acid-free

Center Point Large Print
600 Brooks Road / PO Box 1
Thorndike, ME 04986-0001 USA

(207) 568-3717

US & Canada:
1 800 929-9108
www.centerpointlargeprint.com